The Winter Sea

Di Morrissey is one of Australia's most successful authors. She trained as a journalist, working in the media around the world. Her fascination with different countries – their landscape, their cultural, political and environmental issues – forms the inspiration for her novels. She is a tireless activist for many causes and also established The Golden Land Education Foundation in Myanmar. Di lives in the Manning Valley, in New South Wales.

The Winter Sea

Di Morrissey

PAN BOOKS

First published 2013 by Pan Macmillan Australia Pty Ltd

First published in the UK in paperback 2015 by Pan Books
an imprint of Pan Macmillan
20 New Wharf Road, London N1 9RR
Associated companies throughout the world
www.panmacmillan.com

ISBN 978-1-4472-8323-2

1 3 5 7 9 8 6 4 2

A CIP catalogue record for this book is available from the British Library.

Printed and bound by CPI Group (UK) Ltd, Croydon, CR0 4YY

For GianCarlo Manara

*Through your friendship and your films, you were the
first to open my eyes to the magic of Italy!*

Acknowledgements

For my darling partner Boris. With love and thanks for all you do for me.

Love and thanks to my wonderful children, Gabrielle and Nick, and my beautiful grandchildren, Sonoma, Everton, Bodhi and little one on the way! (Love you Mimi.)

Liz Adams, my very good friend, who happens to be the gold standard of editors!

Ian Robertson, lawyer extraordinaire! Thanks for all you do on my behalf.

To the Pan Macmillan family: Ross Gibb, Roxarne Burns, Samantha Sainsbury, Jace Armstrong, Katie Crawford, the entire sales and marketing team, Tracey Cheetham and all in publicity, Hayley Crandell, Rowena Lennox and Danielle Walker. Thank you for being such a great team.

To the Puglisi fishing dynasty: Lee, Josie and Mick. Thank you for sharing family anecdotes, facts and stories.

To all who fish, may we continue to sustainably enjoy, protect and preserve our beautiful seas and all the creatures.

I

The Aeolian Islands, off the coast of Italy, 1906

THE OCEAN UNFURLED IN a glassy curve as the boy leaned over the side of the boat, seeking his reflection in the mirrored surface of the wave's underbelly. For an instant Giuseppe d'Aquino thought he saw the face of an old man staring directly at him. It was somehow familiar with its popping pale blue eyes, fat lips and bulging cheeks; the expression was questioning, with a slight air of disappointment.

With a sudden surge, the foaming wave doubled in size and slammed against the wooden *barca*, pushing the little fishing boat sideways. The face disappeared into the splintering water and a hand quickly grabbed the boy by the back of his shirt.

'Giuseppe! You must be careful.' His father's admonishment was nearly ripped away in the mounting wind as he pushed the boy under the small shelter in the bow of the boat. The covered space had just enough room to stow some food and water, as well as a lantern.

'Lie down. The rain is coming, but it will soon pass.'

Despite the sea swell and the pelting sheets of grey rain that blotted the sky, the small boat ploughed on. It rode to the crest of a wave before crashing down into a trough, then climbing another wall of water rising ahead of them.

The boy lay curled, his face buried in his arms, breathing in the salty fishy smell he knew so well. He imagined he could see through the hull of his father's boat, down through the churning ocean, down to the sea floor where the deep-ocean creatures lived. He knew about many of the fish that swam beneath them. His father had taught him about those that skimmed just below the surface, moving fast and furiously; and the fish that liked to cruise midway between the surface and the bottom, greedily eyeing the bouncing fishing lures; and those fish that lay in wait – camouflaged in crevices, weeds and sand – on the sea bed.

He heard his father curse as the small craft, after being momentarily airborne, slammed into a wave, its wooden hull shuddering. Giuseppe remembered the time when the men had returned to the dock swearing and shouting. The villagers had waited in fear on the seafront as news of an accident at sea, the loss of a man overboard, spread among them. Uncle Salvatore had drowned during a storm, swept overboard too swiftly for any rescue.

In spite of the dangers of the sea and the men of the village who had been lost to it, Giuseppe knew that the sea was his present and his future, as it had been for his father and his grandfather and his great-grandfather. The people of their island village lived with and for and by the sea. No one asked for, or expected, more than what had gone before and what had always been.

2

Lying in the bottom of the fishing boat, waiting for the scudding rain to clear and the sea to calm, Giuseppe felt grown up. He was ten years old and at last his father had brought him out to hunt the bluefin tuna. He lay still and quiet as the storm blew itself out and the clouds rolled away to reveal the twilight sky, studded with glowing evening stars. His father nodded towards him, and Giuseppe sat quietly as the other fishermen, his two older brothers and his Uncle Rocco, continued to row further out into the Mediterranean Sea. Their island, just one of the scattering of Aeolian Islands off Sicily, receded from sight as darkness fell.

Giuseppe could no longer see any of the other boats that had set out with them, but he could hear the men who manned them shout to each other across the water, their voices tinged with eagerness and excitement. No matter how many times they had already faced the challenge of catching one of the great kings of the sea, the thrill as well as the danger of the hunt was always there.

His father said to him, 'Now we must find our bait so that we can lure a *tonno*.'

Giuseppe knew that the bait his father was after were small silvery fish, which were attracted to the boat when the fishermen shone their lanterns on the surface of the ocean. He had no idea how his father knew where to find them, but he did, and the nets were quickly lowered over the side to catch the tiny fish.

'Careful, careful,' shouted his father as the fishermen began to raise their nets. But the men didn't need to be told. They knew that if the delicate fish were not netted gently, they would panic and try to escape through the net and quickly die in a shower of sparkling scales. So the small fish were carefully placed into specially made baskets that were tied to the side of the boat, just below the water line.

3

After the fish were settled, the men tried to grab a few hours sleep curled in the bottom of the boat. They'd need all their strength for the morning, when they would travel west in search of the powerful bluefin tuna. Uncomfortable as they were, they slept well, dreaming of the fight ahead.

Before daylight, Giuseppe's father woke them and they all shared a meagre breakfast of bread and cheese. As the first streaks of light glowed across the sky, they began to row.

'Keep your eyes peeled, my son,' Giuseppe's father said. 'Watch for sea birds. In the mornings the big *tonno* likes to laze in the water near the surface, so that he can bake in the sun after a night catching fish. The sea birds will see his fin and go to investigate. When we see those birds, we will investigate too.'

Giuseppe's eyes scanned the horizon until they hurt, but he could see nothing. Suddenly one of his brothers shouted, 'Look, over there,' and pointed to the north.

Giuseppe still could see nothing. The oarsmen began rowing hard in the direction his brother had pointed and at last Giuseppe saw several sea birds diving into the water.

'I can see the birds,' he cried excitedly.

'Quiet,' his father hissed. 'If there are *tonno* there, we don't want to startle them.'

As their little boat drew closer to the diving sea birds the men saw that there was indeed a school of tuna. A boat could take only one fish, which could weigh up to five hundred kilos. The fishermen needed to select a suitable catch and detach it quietly from the school before the rest of the tuna were startled and dived deep into the sea, beyond their reach.

As the men pulled the heavy wooden boat towards a huge fish, one of Giuseppe's brothers took up a position beside one of the baskets of bait fish. Everything now depended on his precision and accuracy. His task was to attract the tuna to the boat by throwing some of the little fish into the water. Judging just how many little fish were needed to make the tuna interested in coming close enough to the boat so that the harpooner could strike was a skill. There would be only one chance.

The little silvery fish flashed in the sunlight as they were released. When a tuna saw them darting free it rushed and grabbed them. A few more fish were thrown to the tuna, bringing it closer to the boat. Then Giuseppe's brother took one of the bait fish out of the basket and squeezed out its eyes before throwing it into the sea. As the sightless little fish hit the water, it was confused and, rather than swimming away, it began to swim in circles beside the boat. Quietly the rowers brought their oars into the boat. Full of confidence and lured by the bait, the tuna lunged towards the blinded fish, almost bumping the boat in its eagerness. Holding his breath in excitement, Giuseppe realised that this was the moment they could catch the *tonno*.

He watched as his eldest brother stood in the bow of the boat holding a harpoon, which they called a *traffena*. It was a fearsome weapon, somewhat like a farming fork except that it had seven prongs, each with a barb at the end. With the confidence and skill gained through years of practice, the young fisherman braced his legs and then hurled the harpoon at the tuna, aiming at the vulnerable spot at the back of its head where the spinal cord met the brain. Hitting anywhere else on the fish was useless, for the tuna was well protected and the harpoon would not be effective. Giuseppe's brother had told him this many times for he was proud of his ability as a harpooner; their father had trained him well.

The aim was true. Giuseppe found it hard not to shout with excitement. Although everyone else was elated, they remained tense and watchful as the fish still had to be landed.

The wounded tuna dived deep, desperately trying to escape its attackers, and the attached harpoon line raced through the water. Because the fishermen knew that a tuna could dive to great depths, the line attached to the *traffena*, made of the finest Italian hemp, was three hundred metres long. But this tuna did not dive very deep at all, perhaps only half that distance. Giuseppe's brother placed his hand on the line to judge how much weight would have to be applied in order to bring the fish to the surface and gradually he began to haul it towards the boat. He pulled slowly, working out how much fight was left in the big fish. Sometimes a tuna tested and tricked the man with the line, swimming slowly upwards, before spinning and turning to dive deeper, catching the fisherman unawares. They all knew there was no point in hurrying. Time was on their side and they didn't want to lose the catch now.

After a while, Giuseppe's brother spoke to his father. 'He is getting tired. It won't be long.'

But the great fish was not yet ready to give up. It made one last desperate lunge and, as it neared the fishing boat, Giuseppe glimpsed its flashing, distressed eyes.

'It is nearly finished,' said his brother. 'He is weakening.'

The sun was high now and as Giuseppe peered over the side of the boat, he could see the *tonno's* glittering silver-blue skin, small golden pectoral fins along its spine shining in the sunlight.

As they hauled the huge fish in closer to the boat, Uncle Carlo made a final *coppo* – death strike – spearing the fish with a second *traffena* to ensure that the magnificent fighter was truly dead. Only then was the tuna carefully brought to their boat and tied alongside.

Now it was time to celebrate. Giuseppe's father shouted across to another boat in the distance to tell them of their good fortune. Someone from that boat shouted back that they, too, had had good luck.

When they returned to the village with their catch there would be celebrations to acknowledge the prowess of the fishermen. Giuseppe was proud he had been part of the hunt. He longed for the day when he would be the one standing in the bow, *traffena* poised, ready to strike, pitting his skill against the sleek, powerful kings of the sea.

*

Giuseppe was a shy teenager, brown skinned, barefoot, with laughing eyes and a mischievous grin that showed his neat white teeth. On market day the village girls clustered around the stalls, flirting with him behind their mothers' backs. He was strong and looked older than his fifteen years. Older girls teased him and watched him as he sat on his father's boat mending nets, or moved nimbly around the dock where fish and shellfish were laid out for sale on wet wooden tables and in cane baskets. But his father kept a wary eye on him and warned Giuseppe about straying into the alleys and lanes tucked between the little stone houses where young women called cheekily to him from windows and doorways, some threatening to empty their chamber pots into the alley.

Giuseppe had felt very proud when he began to work with his father. Not only was he doing a man's job, he was contributing to the livelihood of his family. In a very poor region of Italy, their island was one of the poorest, not that Giuseppe was aware of how deprived his family was. Their small home sheltered them, and his mother and grandmother always had food on the table even if, at times, it was very simple fare. Everyone was expected to pull their weight.

Their island was dry and rocky. It was set among a group of active volcanic islands off the coast, which included Mt Stromboli. It had no natural water source so could not produce much food. The villagers relied on the treasures from the sea. They collected water from the roofs when it rained and stored it in barrels but there was not enough water to grow much in the way of crops. They grew tomatoes and eggplants in tubs and hand watered them. Fig and olive trees survived in the hills. Wheat could not be grown on the island, so it was infrequently imported from the mainland, and bread was baked only once a month. At the end of four weeks it was dry and hard. Giuseppe's grandmother was often heard to mutter, 'No water, but plenty of earthquakes. What was God thinking when he made this island?'

Like the other young boys on the island, Giuseppe had received very little schooling. The nuns had taught him his letters and his numbers, but since he had become a productive family member there was no more time for such luxuries. Still, he was pleased that he had received even this rudimentary schooling. His parents had not bothered sending his sisters to school at all. They thought it was better for them to stay at home to help their mother, and get married as soon as possible, then start their own families. Giuseppe had only two sisters, and he was quite fond of them. He sometimes thought of his other three sisters and one brother who had failed to survive childhood. All the families he knew had lost young children to disease or malnutrition and this seemed to Giuseppe to be the normal state of things.

One morning Giuseppe was helping his father salt some fish, ignoring the teasing calls of the village girls, when he noticed Alfonso the shepherd, who lived in the hills, leading his donkey cart onto the dock. On the cart sat his daughter, her eyes averted and her face screened by a curtain of curls.

Giuseppe was surprised to see the shepherd speaking with his father.

'Son, put those salted fish into Alfonso's cart,' his father directed. 'I need to discuss a matter of business.'

Giuseppe moved slowly, taking his time to settle the fish into the back of the cart, while trying to see the young girl's face. But the girl didn't speak to, or look at him. He walked to the donkey and fondled its ears as the two men talked seriously. Eventually his father went to his boat and took out an old anchor, which he then put in the back of Alfonso's cart with the fish.

'I am sure that I will be able to do something with the anchor. I understand your idea,' said Alfonso. Then, pushing his woollen hat back on his head, he spoke to the girl. She leaned down and lifted a cloth bag from beneath her feet and held it out for Giuseppe. For a moment he felt the touch of her fingers and caught a swift glimpse of her eyes, which reminded him of the blue-black waters of the sea before a storm. He clutched the soft bag, recognising the lanoline smell of freshly shorn wool, and tried to think of something to say to her. But before a word could come out, Alfonso had climbed onto the seat beside his daughter and the cart moved away, clanking over the cobblestones. As the donkey trotted away, Giuseppe watched the breeze lift the long dark curls that spilled over the shawl around the girl's shoulders.

'Take the wool to your mother,' directed his father. 'She is expecting it.'

It was many months before Giuseppe saw the girl again. Then it was winter and crystals of ice glittered on the stony ground as Giuseppe and his father climbed slowly up the rugged hill path leading to the small farm where Alfonso lived. One of Giuseppe's sisters was to be married and a wedding feast was planned, so his father had come to buy a small goat for the celebrations. The villagers could rarely afford to purchase meat, so buying a goat to eat was a special occasion.

Giuseppe was grateful for the thick sweater he wore, spun and knitted by his mother from the wool his father had bought from Alfonso. As they reached the shepherd's small home, they were greeted by Alfonso standing by a low stone wall. Giuseppe's father explained what he wanted and the three of them walked into a field where the goats and sheep grazed on winter stubble.

Alfonso turned towards his hut and called, 'Angelica, bring me a rope.'

Almost at once the young girl, who had so captivated Giuseppe with her curls, came hurrying out of the hut carrying a short rope, which she gave to her father. He selected one of the goats and tied the rope around its neck.

Giuseppe felt overwhelmed by her proximity but could think of nothing clever to say. He only asked, 'Are you sad that this goat is going to be killed?'

She shrugged. 'My father chose it for you. Do you care about the fish you catch and kill?'

Giuseppe answered, 'Sometimes, yes. The big fish are very beautiful. Strong fighters. Have you ever been on a boat?'

She shook her head. 'No. I like the hills. And the company of sheep, not fish.' She paused then added, 'The wool, it looks nice. Your mother is very clever.' She hurried away, her curls bouncing, feet flying.

Before Giuseppe and his father left, the two men went to the back of Alfonso's hut. Giuseppe followed them and, to his surprise, he saw that Alfonso had constructed a simple blacksmith's forge there. From the back of the forge, the shepherd brought out a small anchor to show Giuseppe's father.

'It is not finished. It still needs adjusting,' explained Alfonso. 'But the swivel head, designed to release if the anchor snags, works.' His normally dour expression creased into a smile. 'I followed your instructions.'

After his father had examined the anchor, Giuseppe looked at it. He could see how the release bar would stop the anchor from being lost on the sea floor or on the reefs. Giuseppe was proud of the way his father was always thinking of ideas to improve his equipment to make it more efficient and reliable.

'This is a great invention. You must come out on our boat to see it working,' suggested Giuseppe's father.

'We are not sea people,' said the shepherd.

Giuseppe glanced around the barren karsts rising from the steep hills and thought how desolate the wind-swept landscape looked; he guessed that Angelica and her father would feel as uncomfortable at sea as he did here.

Giuseppe and his father walked back home, leading the goat. When they came to the ridge that stood above the village Giuseppe looked down at the familiar sights of the little port below. He could see the narrow alley-ways and steep steps where houses, festooned with poles of washing, stood cheek by jowl, so close that one could almost reach across to rap on the window of the house opposite. He could see his own small house where his family lived in two rooms and where the ceiling was always hung with fishing nets. A broader cobbled street circled the village. It ran along the harbour front, where crab pots were piled high and men squatted to gossip as they mended their nets. Small fishing boats were tied to the iron bollards along the stone sea wall. At one end of the wall on the steps worn down by centuries of seamen's feet, young boys sat and fished. It was from these steps that each year the priest would bless the fishing fleet. Past the sea wall lay a pebbled beach, where upturned dinghies and small wooden boats were tied above the high-water mark. Near them a deep-water channel ran into the open sea beyond the arms of the cove. This small village was his home and as he walked with his father towards his family's house, he felt happy with his little world.

*

The wedding of Giuseppe's sister was an occasion for much festivity. The young girl was marrying a village boy, whom she had known all her life. Families on the island always intermarried. It was expected; the island was their world, where else was there to go? Giuseppe's father was pleased with the alliance, for his daughter's future husband came from another prominent fishing family. Everyone on the island believed that the only defence against poverty was family, so he had ensured that his daughter married into a hardworking and respected one.

The couple walked to the church in their best clothes. The priest stood among the incense and statues and blessed their marriage. Afterwards was the great feast. The goat had been slaughtered and was roasting on a spit over the coals, basted frequently with olive oil and rosemary. All the guests were waiting eagerly for it to be ready.

Giuseppe's mother, Emilia, and her daughters had spent days preparing food, which was amazingly inventive considering the small variety of ingredients available on the island. There was sardine pasta with raisins and pine nuts; pasta with eggplant; couscous and pasta with sword-fish, which was especially appreciated, for although the fishermen might catch swordfish, the fish was far too valu-able for the families on the island to eat and were always sold. The feast would end with cannoli, fried pastry stuffed with ricotta cheese and honeyed figs. Giuseppe's father had imported wine in a hog's head for the event since the island could not produce grapes in any quantity. Although the wedding was extravagant by the standards of the village, it was always the custom for the father of the bride to put on such a feast for it showed not just the standing of the family in the little port, but also the importance of its patriarch, and Giuseppe's father was determined to show that he was a noteworthy man.

*

One Sunday, several months after the wedding, Giuseppe's mother asked him to take some salted fish to Alfonso in the hills to exchange for some wool and some goats' cheese.

Giuseppe felt shy approaching the farm where Alfonso lived with his daughter. But when Alfonso saw him trudging up the hill he greeted Giuseppe cheerfully and led him into the kitchen, calling to his daughter to bring him some water.

The stone cottage was small, but dark and cool. A large fuel stove that provided heat in winter sat in one corner. Giuseppe had noticed a mud-brick oven outside the cottage where Alfonso cooked in summer. A wooden table and chairs sat in the middle of the room and a spinning wheel stood in a corner. But what really caught Giuseppe's attention was a shelf on one of the walls, stacked high with books. There looked to be about twenty and he stared at them in astonishment.

Alfonso caught his expression and reached for a book that had an illustration of a pirate glued onto its cover. 'Can you read, boy?'

Giuseppe nodded. 'I know my letters and I can read numbers.'

'That's not reading. Have you read a book?'

'No,' Giuseppe said quietly.

'Would you like to?' asked Alfonso.

Giuseppe wasn't sure. His parents respected those few people on the island who were fully literate, but the d'Aquinos thought that there was little need for their family to acquire the same skills. What use would they be for fishermen?

Slowly Giuseppe nodded.

Angelica, who had returned with the water, gave him an encouraging smile. 'My father thinks that everyone should read books,' she said.

'Can you read those books?' asked Giuseppe with a faint challenge in his voice.

'Of course. I have read all of them,' said Angelica.

Giuseppe was taken aback but Alfonso laughed.

'That is not quite true, Angelica, but if you like, Giuseppe, you may come here and read any of my books. I could help you.'

So once a week, on Sundays after church, Giuseppe made the journey into the hills to read with Alfonso.

'What do you want to read books for? We own no books, you will never be able to afford to buy books,' said one of his brothers.

Giuseppe shrugged. 'It might be useful one day.'

'You just want to hang around his daughter,' said another brother.

Giuseppe glared and stomped away. But the remark was partly true.

Angelica intrigued him. Giuseppe knew that she roamed with the sheep and goats and seemed as much a creature of the hills as they. Occasionally he came across her perched on an ancient stone wall watching the animals. He was self-conscious, afraid to speak to her for any length of time, aware that he might displease her father while she, who had seemed so shy the first time he met her at the dock, appeared at ease and chatted to him freely about his life on the fishing boats and in the village. Giuseppe realised that, although they were about the same age, her knowledge about most things, except fishing, made her seem much older than he was. He knew that his mother would never speak to his father with the same confidence and composure as she did with him.

Eventually one day he asked her, 'Why are you able to talk like this? You seem to know so much about everything.'

She gave a short laugh. 'I might live a quiet life away from the town, but I read books and I speak with my father. He is a clever man and tells me many stories.'

Giuseppe couldn't imagine having long conversations with his own father. His father made pronouncements and all the family agreed with him. Giuseppe said defensively, 'My father teaches me to fish. It takes many years to learn. You don't need books to learn how to read the wind and clouds, to understand what the colours of the sea mean, to watch the birds to see the movement of the schools of fish, or to notice the clues that show where the big fish are feeding.'

Angelica jumped down from the wall. 'That may be true, but my father can teach you many other things. I will come and listen to you read some time.'

And so, occasionally, Angelica would appear at her father's door and listen to Giuseppe as he read, trying not to stumble over the words.

Within a year Giuseppe's reading skills had vastly improved and Alfonso decided that it was time for him to borrow books rather than continuing to read aloud. Giuseppe's visits to the farm became less frequent, but he still found time to climb into the hills to talk to Alfonso. Alfonso had lived away from the island. He had travelled, and was better educated than almost anyone else in the village. Giuseppe had no idea why Alfonso had left the island but he knew that he had returned when Angelica's mother had died. Giuseppe loved to hear the stories of the time that the shepherd had spent in the north of Italy. Alfonso talked about Italy's history and politics, and the country's future, and Giuseppe concentrated as he listened to the shepherd.

15

Giuseppe tried to imagine the scenes of cities with streets crowded with people, shops filled with clothes and exotic food and furniture that was shining and new. Alfonso loved to speak of the theatres, music halls, opera houses and cinema houses showing silent films. He even tried to explain to Giuseppe about the motor cars he had seen, but Giuseppe found it hard to grasp such a concept. It was a world that Giuseppe could hardly believe, it was so far removed from the simple village where he'd been born and had always lived. Now Giuseppe even started to wonder about the authority of the elderly priest, who was considered to be the wisest and best educated man on the island, but whose horizons and experiences seemed severely limited when compared to those of Alfonso. Not that Giuseppe voiced these thoughts aloud. Nevertheless, talking with Alfonso, Giuseppe found himself increasingly curious about life beyond the confines of his village. If he couldn't visit the places Alfonso had been to, he could at least read about them, and dream.

'Giuseppe,' said Alfonso one day as the two sat at the shepherd's table, 'you know that Italy is quite a new country, only about fifty years old?' Alfonso often liked to raise subjects that he suspected Giuseppe knew little about and Giuseppe liked to listen and learn.

'But that can't be true,' replied Giuseppe. 'I know that it must be old because there are lots of ruins on our island. Some of them must be older than fifty years.'

Alfonso smiled. 'Of course they are. For centuries many different people have lived on this island – Greeks, Romans, Moors and Christians – and they all left a legacy of their time here through the buildings they made. No, what I am saying is that before 1861 Italy was made up of a lot of independent states – Sicily, Piedmont, Naples, Calabria and so on – but they became united as one country under Victor Emmanuel II.'

'But Father, you have told me that the country is not united,' said Angelica as she joined them at the table. 'You said that the people don't feel like Italians at all.'

'You are right. I have travelled throughout this land and I have found that it is full of divisions. People are loyal first to their village, then to their region and finally, if they think of it at all, they are loyal to Italy.'

'My father says that when he travelled to the north of Italy, the people there could barely understand him.'

'Why was that?' asked Giuseppe, who thought that it would be impossible not to understand the clear-speaking Alfonso. 'I never have any trouble understanding what you say.'

'Thank you, Giuseppe. No, what Angelica means is that our dialect here in the south is so different from the way they speak in the north that we are virtually speaking a different language.'

'So the north is really different from here?'

'Places like Turin have very modern ideas. There is even a factory there that makes Fiat motor cars. Some in the north look down on people from the south and think that they are ill-educated peasants.'

Giuseppe looked embarrassed because he knew that this was true of his family.

'Cheer up, Giuseppe, not all the people of the north are as advanced as the people of Turin. I worked for a while in Venice. It is a mighty sea port, but it struggles with modernity, just as we do in the south. Ten-year-old children work such long hours in the glass factories that they fall asleep beside the ovens. Venice is a very unhealthy city and many people there die from tuberculosis and malaria.'

'But the people in the north don't suffer the hardships that we do here. Tell us again about the earthquake in Messina,' said Angelica.

'I've told you that story many times over, though I suppose I can tell it once more – but only quickly. We have work to do and Giuseppe must get home before it is dark,' said Alfonso as he settled back into his chair.

'I was not in Messina when the earthquake occurred, Giuseppe, but I went there only a few weeks later and I saw the terrible destruction. Before the earthquake, Messina was a thriving port city, then disaster struck one morning in December 1908. In thirty seconds, one hundred thousand people perished and all the buildings in the city were destroyed. At first the government did not believe what had happened and they did very little to help, although the king visited the site. Now the government is supposed to be rebuilding the city, but everyone knows that such reconstruction just presents an opportunity for some people to make a lot of money through graft, fraud and embezzlement.'

'That is terrible,' said Giuseppe. 'Why don't the people do something?'

'When Sicily first became part of a united Italy, Sicilians were very excited. They thought that the government would help them rise out of poverty, but instead they were burdened with heavy taxes and conscripted into the army. Because of the mountainous terrain in Sicily and lack of government interest, policing was poor and violent gangs developed.'

'Mafiosi,' said Giuseppe, for everyone knew of these gang members' stranglehold on power in Sicily and on the nearby islands.

'Most Sicilians are very accepting of the natural disasters that occur in this region. They think that there is nothing that can be done about them. But they are very disillusioned by the government in Rome and don't like the unrestrained violence at home, so many of them emigrate.'

'They go to America, don't they, Father?'

'Yes, thousands of Sicilians leave every year, knowing that they will make a better life for themselves there.'

'A cousin of my brother-in-law's went and wrote back to say that he owns two suits,' said Giuseppe, looking down at his ill-fitting trousers that had already been worn by two of his brothers. 'I think he is lying as I don't see how that is possible.'

'It might be,' said Angelica. 'I would like to go and find out.' She looked at Giuseppe. 'What about you?'

'Me?' He shook his head. 'I will never have the chance.'

'Don't be so sure, Giuseppe,' said Alfonso. 'Life can be unpredictable.'

The Italian Front, 1917

The small army tents were barely discernible as they clung to the rocks that gave little protection against the sleeting rain. Inside their miserably cold dugouts and dripping canvas caves, the men hunched over damp cigarettes, dissecting the rumours and speculating about what could be happening on the front.

Italy had entered the Great War in May 1915, joining the Allies. Austria, to Italy's north-east, was convinced that if it attacked Italy along the Alps that divided the two countries, it would overthrow the Italian army. The Italians knew that if the Austrians were allowed to move down from their high vantage point in the mountains and spill out onto the plains below, the Italian army would not be able to contain them. So far eleven battles had been fought between the two armies, but although the Italians had contained the Austrians the enemy remained in the high mountains, an ever-present threat.

The weather closed in over the Julian Alps where the Isonzo River cut through the steep, rocky valley and swept southwards. Giuseppe d'Aquino huddled into his worn army great coat as the shower turned to a downpour. From the chill in the wind he knew snow was falling on the upper peaks. Although he was only twenty-one years old, after months of fighting he felt like a seasoned veteran. Around him were soldiers of many ages, drawn from the countryside, their faces and hands weathered from farming. Initially they were united in their efforts to attack the Austrians, but now they were increasingly discontented. The men felt abandoned in their alpine hellhole near the small town of Caporetto, pawns in a game that, for many, had sapped their respect and will to fight for their country.

He listened quietly, for perhaps the hundredth time, to the endless complaints of his fellow soldiers.

'General Cadorna, what does he know?' asked a corporal. 'He is forever getting rid of officers.'

'Everyone knows that if they do not immediately succeed in battle, then he fires them. We've had five battalion commanders in the last few months, not that the last three were any good,' responded his friend.

'Hah,' said the corporal. 'Would you want to lead men into battle if you knew that failure meant dismissal? Better to be cautious than sorry.'

'Well, if you don't fight properly, you don't win.'

Giuseppe had heard this argument before. The first time he was shocked. He had assumed that the educated officers would know what they were doing, but now as the fighting wore on it was clear that this was not the case. I've changed, he thought to himself. Once I would never have questioned a man so clearly superior to myself, but now I cannot accept that such people know everything.

'Of course, General Capello is different,' continued the corporal. Everyone nodded, for they all had great confidence in their area commander who always favoured offensive action. 'But I heard a rumour that he is ill and has been sent to Padua to recover.'

The other soldiers looked horrified by this information. They were to go into battle the next day.

'It might not be true,' said the corporal. 'Anyway, even if he is well, how can he fight properly with this equipment? It's rubbish.'

No one argued with this. Italy simply did not have the industrial capability to switch quickly to war-time production and so what weapons the soldiers had were inadequate.

'It's the fault of those socialists in Turin. I heard from my brother that they are deliberately sabotaging the factories because they don't want to be in this war. Well, what about us? We're in the thick of it and there's never enough ammunition,' said another soldier, whose speech clearly identified him as a northerner.

'And we don't have enough artillery,' said the corporal's friend.

'I have also heard,' said the corporal, who seemed to have an unlimited source of gossip, 'that those socialists have now been sent up here to help with the fighting.'

There was immediate outrage.

'What good will they be?'

'Are they being punished, or are we?'

'We won't be able to trust those socialists. They won't fight.'

Although all these complaints were very real and easily justified, Giuseppe knew that the biggest sense of injustice among the soldiers stemmed from the army command's total neglect of them. No one was interested in their welfare or morale. Between battles there was no attempt to provide the men with any leisure activities, let alone allow them home on furlough, so they had nothing to do but play cards and worry about their families.

Who would protect them and make sure that they had enough to eat?

As the men continued to complain, the unit sergeant rose to his feet. He was a small, wiry man, well respected by his men.

'Best you all get a good night's sleep now. We'll be attacking in the morning, but those Austrians won't worry us, will they?'

'No, Sergeant Tommasi,' said the men as they settled themselves into their cold, damp dugouts. As far as they were concerned, the Austrians were inferior soldiers. Giuseppe always felt safe near the sergeant, who was a good leader in battle and knew what to do to stop his men from being killed.

The enemy bombardment started early the next morning and lasted for two hours, but the Italians were used to enemy fire and they stayed safe in their dugouts. But then, everything changed. The bombardment was fiercer than anything they had experienced before and their meagre shelters were quickly destroyed. Suddenly, Giuseppe found that he couldn't breathe. He clutched at his throat.

'Mustard gas,' yelled Sergeant Tommasi to his men, and put his gas mask over his face.

Giuseppe felt paralysed, but the sergeant thrust a gas mask into his hands and did the same with many of the other men. But for some it was too late and they fell, writhing on the ground in agony, the poisonous gas damaging their lungs. Grabbing his rifle Giuseppe followed Tommasi. It was obvious that all their defences were broken; the enemy army came pouring towards them but they were ready to take them on. Then suddenly the Italians realised that these men charging towards them were not Austrian soldiers at all. They were wearing German uniforms!

Everyone believed the Germans were vastly superior fighters to the Austrians and now their belief was proved true. The Germans moved rapidly down towards the valley, opening up the Italian line. Italian morale plummeted. They could fight the Austrians, but against the Germans they felt powerless. By nightfall thousands of Italians had given themselves up as prisoners. Their war was over.

Tommasi, however, was prepared to take on the Germans. He and his unit fought hard all the next day, but it was clear that they were no match for the superior German tactics and equipment.

As darkness fell, the corporal finally said what they had all been thinking. 'Should we surrender to the Germans? We can't beat them.'

'Do you want to spend the rest of the war as a prisoner or do you want to go home?' Tommasi asked what remained of his unit. Many of the men were wounded. They were tired and demoralised.

'Home,' whispered Giuseppe. The other men silently nodded their heads in agreement.

'All right, then,' said Tommasi. 'Home it is.'

Led by Sergeant Tommasi, Giuseppe and the remains of the unit picked their way along a narrow path. At times Giuseppe struggled to keep up, for the soles of his boots had now given way and sharp stones jabbed his feet. He gave a cry of pain and stopped, leaning on his rifle. The other men sat at the side of the path, sheltered by tall trees, and watched Sergeant Tommasi pull off Giuseppe's boot to examine his bloodied foot. The combination of a rag, some dry grass and a tattered sock was the best repair Sergeant Tommasi could manage before he told them all to move forward.

Suddenly the corporal grabbed Giuseppe's rifle and flung it into the trees, and then did the same with his own.

'*Phhht!*' He pursed his lips. 'We don't need these anymore.'

He gestured to the other men to do the same. After their initial surprise, they quickly followed suit.

Ignoring the pain in his foot and with the aid of a stick, Giuseppe plodded down the valley road, joining an increasing flow of other soldiers who had also decided that war was no longer for them.

Civilians, fleeing the advancing enemy with their possessions in carts and barrows, competed for road space with the retreating soldiers. Italian reinforcements, sent forward in an attempt to retrieve the situation, found it impossible to get through. But the retreat remained leisurely and orderly, as though the troops had all the time in the world to reclaim their own piece of sanity and peace by the fireside of home. The men helped themselves to food and drink as they passed through deserted villages. When they passed an officer, Sergeant Tommasi insisted that the men salute, which they did. Some officers, though surprised, returned the salute, others shouted at them, ordering them to return to the battle. But the men just kept marching south. At one stage, a staff car drove towards them and the men drew to the side of the road to let it pass. They recognised the hated General Cadorna in the back seat and, unbidden, they drew themselves up to attention and saluted as the car went by.

Giuseppe marched on, listening to Tommasi insist that what they were doing was no disgrace. How much better would it be for their families that they should return to them, rather than be prisoners of the Germans?

'After all, it has been the simple soldiers who have been let down by the army command, not the other way around,' said Sergeant Tommasi.

And this is the same government that let down the people of Messina, thought Giuseppe to himself. It does not care for ordinary people at all. And what will happen to them now? Then he remembered what Alfonso had said about America. Maybe he should go there, too, away from this country with so little to offer. Perhaps he could talk Angelica into going with him. The idea put a spring into his step. He could not wait to get back to his island so that he could talk to them both.

*

But when Giuseppe eventually returned to the island, tragedy awaited him. His father had terrible news. In Giuseppe's absence, Angelica had died.

'How? What happened?' he asked, distraught.

His father shook his head. 'It was sudden. There was no treatment. It was God's will. Will you go and see Alfonso?'

Giuseppe walked the familiar track across the hillside and a fierce wind slowed his steps and echoed the cries in his heart. The stone cottage seemed to crouch low against the wind and for the first time he was not impatient to reach it. Alfonso saw him coming and stood waiting for him outside the hut, a lone figure silhouetted against the grey sky.

Alfonso remained still, waiting until Giuseppe reached him before moving, lifting his shoulders in a gesture of helpless bewilderment. The younger man ached as he saw the deep pain etched on Alfonso's face and swiftly embraced him.

'My daughter is gone. She was the light of my life,' said Alfonso, his voice choking in grief.

Giuseppe nodded mutely, too sad to speak.

'Angelica, my angel . . .' Tears formed in Alfonso's eyes. 'She was a wild, free bird. Few could have tamed her.' He paused. 'She called your name . . . at the end.' He couldn't speak further and turned away.

Together they walked to the cottage, the haven Giuseppe had often thought about often during the cold, harsh and dangerous times at the front. How he had longed for the wise companionship of Alfonso, the joy

25

of discovering a world through the pages of books, and, always, the presence of Angelica. And he had allowed himself to dream, to plan, to think that one day he would make a new and different life with her in America.

Giuseppe and Alfonso sat in their usual places. Giuseppe's eyes were inevitably drawn to the little window where, so often, he had glimpsed Angelica, curls bouncing as she ran, hurrying the goats and sheep down from the high ground to the cottage so that she could spend time with him.

Alfonso now seemed a man drained of energy and enthusiasm. It was as though his very essence had evaporated. He told Giuseppe that Angelica had cut her leg and it had become infected; no one knew how to stop the infection and in the end it had killed her.

Giuseppe knew that for Alfonso, no one could replace Angelica's company, with her keen intelligence and teasing sense of humour, but just the same, he offered to visit Alfonso regularly. To his surprise, Alfonso rejected his offer.

'No! You must make a new life for yourself. I have nothing more to give you.' Then the shepherd turned and walked away, back into his hut.

*

Even when the war came to an end, life on the island remained hard. Some of the fishermen who had served in the army returned to the sea. Others lay buried on the battlefields. Poverty on the island was worse than before, as some of the boats that had been requisitioned for the war effort were never returned. The islanders wondered what the whole point of the war had been. They had certainly got nothing from it.

But discontent was not confined to the island. It had spread throughout the country. In spite of the subsequent resounding victory at Vittorio Veneto, the humiliation of

Caporetto continued to bring shame on the men who'd been there. The crumbs given to Italy at the Versailles peace settlement were regarded as insulting. Half a million Italians dead, a ravaged countryside, a poor economy, high unemployment and inflation, and the disrespect of their allies were all there was to show for Italy's war efforts. Moreover, increasing disillusionment with the weak government had led to growing unrest across the country with strikes and clashes between different political factions. Politically motivated street fights, even murders, were becoming common events in the cities.

Giuseppe felt restless and wished Angelica was there to discuss these matters with him. Nor did he have Alfonso to talk to because, since her death, the shepherd had retreated from all society, drinking grappa and disappearing for long solitary walks in the hills, and refusing to speak to anyone.

One evening at the kitchen table, after his mother and grandmother had dished up potatoes roasted with garlic and olives and tomato passata made from the few tomatoes they had grown, Giuseppe put down his fork and said quietly, 'There is no future here for me. I want to leave. There is a big world beyond this island and I want to try my luck. I have been thinking about this for some time now.'

'You have listened to Alfonso too much,' said his father.

'No one is making a decent living here,' insisted Giuseppe.

'Our great-grandfather, our grandfather and our father have managed here on this island,' said his oldest brother as he dipped his spoon into his dish. 'Our family is strong. We will survive.' The other men around the table nodded their heads in furious agreement.

Then, to everyone's surprise, Giuseppe's grandmother, Celestina, spoke up for him. 'The people who have gone away from here are doing better than us,' she said. 'This island, it's drier than a stone. We can hardly grow our own vegetables. Soon we will be eating rocks. We buy water when our tanks run dry. Fancy buying water! What a way to live! We have nothing. One day I asked the butcher for some old bones for soup and he laughed at me and told me to go to the cemetery for them!' She shook her head. 'And as for that shrivelled prune of a milk man!' Celestina made a rude gesture with her hand and Giuseppe tried not to laugh. His father and brothers kept their heads down, as his mother joined the old woman in speaking her mind.

'Yes, he is watering down the goats' milk!' she agreed. 'Sometimes I think that things will never get better.'

'Will you go to America?' asked grandmother Celestina. She pursed her lips. 'That is where everyone goes.'

'But what would you do in America? You only know how to fish,' asked one of his brothers.

'Your brother-in-law's relatives work in factories in America. They make good money. Where would his family be without the money they send back home?' said Celestina before she added pointedly, 'We could do with some of that.'

'How can we afford to send Giuseppe to America?' demanded his father.

'You don't even have a pair of shoes,' scoffed one of his brothers.

'He has his old army boots,' said his mother. 'They can be repaired.'

Grandmother Celestina spoke again. 'We all need to put everything we have kept under the bed towards his fare. Giuseppe has broad shoulders. He will go to America and work hard and make good money. He will send back his money to repay us, and then he will come back and choose a wife.' She scraped the last of the potato onto Giuseppe's plate and they all turned to look at Giuseppe's father, who slowly nodded his head in agreement, and so the matter was decided.

2

It took many months before the d'Aquino family raised enough money to purchase Giuseppe's boat fare to America but in the meantime he was the centre of attention wherever he went in the village. He was envied, encouraged and sometimes made to feel that he was carrying the dreams and aspirations of all the other families in the little port as well as his own.

It seemed to him that in one way or another all the villagers had contributed to making his trip possible, whether by giving a small donation, or a gift of clothing or practical items, or by entrusting him with the addresses of relatives. Their contributions ensured they all had a vested interest in Giuseppe's journey. Everyone also anticipated that it wouldn't be too long before Giuseppe set himself up and started sending money back to his family from America – which would then be shared in various ways throughout the village.

Grandmother Celestina was proud of Giuseppe and boasted that he would make a big success of himself in America. Nonetheless, she fretted that she would not live long enough to see him return to the island and choose a wife.

Her friends were quick to tease her. 'He might choose an American wife,' they commented. Whereupon Celestina sniffed that he would always choose a village girl, as they were much better cooks than American girls.

Like most of the villagers, Giuseppe and his family had only a hazy idea of what America might be like. His brother-in-law told him of the letters he had received from his cousin, which described buildings as high as a hill, streets as wide as four *barcas*, shops and places to eat with an abundance of all kinds of food, including their own Sicilian dishes and even Neapolitan pizzas and a description of the busy factory in which he worked. Giuseppe was impressed, but hoped he would find work as a fisherman rather than working in a factory as he had no real idea what a factory was.

As his departure drew closer the weight of leaving felt heavy on his shoulders. He knew that he needed to make good, not just for himself, but for all the family and friends on his island who had given him whatever they could manage from their meagre savings to pay for his passage.

One day, Giuseppe was surprised when he was given a good second-hand suitcase by his father.

'Where did this come from?' he asked.

'Alfonso,' his father replied. 'He came into the village quietly yesterday afternoon and said that he had heard that you wanted to go to America. He said that he had no further use for his suitcase, so here it is.'

Giuseppe was grateful that he would no longer have to carry his clothes in a bundle. Later when he opened the case he found, tucked into an envelope, some money and a note wishing him all the best for his new life. Eventually he had just enough money to pay for a third-class ticket to America. It was arranged that someone from his brother-in-law's family, who lived in New Jersey, would meet him in New York.

'You stay with his family,' said his mother firmly. 'Until you make money, and come back home and choose your wife.'

As the day of his departure approached, Giuseppe imprinted the scenes of the island in his head and on heart. His old clothes were darned, cleaned and folded but before they were placed in his suitcase his father told him that he had something else to pack.

'I have made you this *traffena*,' he said. 'I hope that you will have the chance to hunt a great fish when you are in America.'

Giuseppe looked at the familiar, fearsome weapon with its seven prongs and sighed. 'Thank you, Father, it is wonderful.'

Celestina also had a gift for him. She took him aside and pressed a yellowed envelope into his hand. 'When you need to, sell this – but don't let them cheat you.'

Giuseppe was shocked when he unfolded the small square of paper and saw a gold ring set with a red stone. 'I can't take this!' The last time he had seen his grandmother wear this ring she had been dressed in her best black dress and her fine lace collar, celebrating her wedding anniversary. Since Grandfather Bruno died, she'd never worn it again.

'This ring belonged to my grandmother so it is very old. I hoped that I might be able to give it to your wife one day but it is more important for you now as you start your new life in America. Sell it when you need the money,' she insisted.

'Nonna, I don't know what to say. I hope I never have to sell it and I will bring it back for you to wear on my wedding day,' said Giuseppe.

She gave him a wistful look and said, 'I'll be waiting for that day.'

As the news soon spread around the village that Giuseppe was leaving the island on the inter-island ferry that day, emotions ran high. Some of his friends teased him. Some commiserated with him about how much he would miss his home and family. Others said they wished they had the same opportunity. Everyone agreed that leaving was a large and possibly irrevocable step in his life.

His mother could not stop crying as she walked with him to the harbour where all the villagers were lined up along the sea wall to watch him clamber into the little boat that would take him to Messina. From there he would take the ferry to the mainland and then a train to Naples. For many of the islanders, the idea of travelling to the mainland and then on to the large port of Naples to board a liner for America was an adventure in itself.

Giuseppe, his dark hair plastered in place, felt as uncomfortable as he looked, dressed in dark serge pants and a shirt with a tie. Along with a slightly too large jacket, his clothes had been gathered from boxes and cupboards where they had waited for special occasions. He was wearing shoes for the first time, rather than his mended army boots which were packed in his suitcase. The shoes had belonged to the baker's brother who'd been killed in the war. They were too small for the baker but now they were polished and threaded with new twine shoelaces and fitted Giuseppe well enough.

As his suitcase, labelled with 'G. d'Aquino' painted in white letters on it, was loaded onto the boat, his friends called out to him, wishing him luck and good fortune in America. Giuseppe farewelled his family and the islanders, wondering how long it would be before he saw them again.

'You work hard,' said his father as he hugged his son, a tear forming in the corner of his eye. 'And God go with you.'

The small wooden vessel moved out of the bay and Giuseppe watched the familiar shape of his rocky island home fade into the distance. He hoped that, from a hillside, Alfonso was watching as the boat carried him to a new adventure. He knew that he owed a debt to Alfonso and Angelica, for it had been they who had first sowed the idea that it was possible to make a new life in a different world where the horizon was not limited by poverty.

Hours later he arrived at Messina, where he had to wait until the next day for a ferry to take him to the mainland.

The trip to the Italian mainland in the overcrowded ferry did not take long and he made his way to the train station easily. He found, however, that there was not a train to Naples until the following morning, so he made himself comfortable on the platform and, after eating a couple of eggs, some cheese and some hard bread, which his mother had packed for him, he settled down for the night.

At about six o'clock in the morning the train pulled into the station and Giuseppe realised that he had not yet bought a ticket. He raced to the ticket office, where there was quite a long queue.

I should have bought the ticket last night, he thought to himself. Now I could miss the train.

He almost did, for the queue moved very slowly, but at last he had the ticket in his hand and he ran for the train. By the time he had stowed his bag and taken his seat on the packed train, it had started to move, belching black smoke from its engine.

Italian trains were in a parlous state after the war, and Giuseppe found the third-class carriage very dirty and crammed with people. He managed to squeeze onto the corner of a seat and he watched through a grimy window as the train chugged slowly through the countryside, passing towns and villages.

Night fell and he ate only a little more of his mother's food, deciding to save as much as he could because the trip was taking a lot longer than he had thought it would. For a while he was able to doze, but he awoke with a start to the clatter of complaining steel wheels as the wheezing engine pulled into a siding. Then the lights in the train went out.

At first the passengers ignored this unscheduled stop but after an hour or so some got down and walked along the track to the conductor's carriage demanding to know what was happening. Eventually the dim lights came on again. Through the window Giuseppe could see the swaying lanterns of the conductor and engine driver as they walked along the railway embankment, calling replies to questions from irate passengers.

The water jugs in the carriage were soon emptied and what little food people still had was shared or eaten surreptitiously in the dark. Giuseppe shared the last of his food with an elderly woman. Then those people who had wandered along the tracks boarded the train again as whispers circulated about the possibility of attacks by the bandits who roamed the countryside in this region.

It was daylight before there was a lurch and a grinding of wheels then, with a blast of steam and a mournful toot of its whistle, the train rolled forward. As it gathered momentum and turned back onto the main track, the *click-clack* of its wheels picked up speed, trying to make up for lost time.

But Giuseppe was worried that he might not get to his ship in time. He'd lost too much time on his journey.

As soon as he arrived in Naples, he asked for directions to the port. Twice he got lost and had to be redirected. When he finally arrived at the wharf he discovered that the *SS Providence* had sailed for New York earlier that morning. He stood staring at the empty pier, bewildered and disbelieving that the steamship that was to have taken him to his new life in America had left without him.

'No, no, no!' he cried.

He ran from one end of the port to the other, desperately hoping that there had been some mistake, that the ship was tied up somewhere else, waiting for him. But the whole place was deserted.

He slumped onto a crate and put his face in his hands. How was he going to explain what had happened to his family? He felt so foolish. He should have allowed more time to get to Naples, he told himself. There had been so many delays he hadn't foreseen.

Then his embarrassment was quickly replaced by fear. What was he going to do now? How long would he have to wait for the next ship? How much would it cost him to stay in Naples to wait for another boat? He might once have been a brave soldier, but now he felt like a little boy. He wished he could conjure up Alfonso or his father and ask them for advice. He thought of Angelica and wondered if she would be sympathetic or whether she would just laugh at him, sitting so dejectedly on the empty dockside. That thought galvanised Giuseppe into action. He stood up and headed for the shipping office, which he had seen at the entrance to the port, to find out if there was something he could do.

When he got there, he blurted out his story to the shipping clerk who seemed totally disinterested and shrugged his shoulders at the naive young man who was so obviously a peasant. But an older woman, overhearing the conversation, took pity on Giuseppe. She came forward, smiling. Giuseppe was grateful for her sympathy and poured out his story to her. But when she told him there was not another ship sailing to New York for two weeks, Giuseppe's face fell. He explained that he didn't have enough money to be able to afford to stay in Naples for two weeks as well as buying a boat ticket.

She understood his dilemma. 'You could buy a ticket on the *Ricconigi*. It's a cargo ship that takes some passengers and it's due to sail at noon tomorrow.'

'For America?' asked Giuseppe, his eyes lighting up.

'No. Australia. It's all I can suggest. Because it's a cargo ship, it will only cost you the same as the ticket to America.'

'Australia.' Giuseppe stared at her. He tried to recall what he'd heard about it. 'It is so far from here, the bottom of the world. I don't think that I know anyone who has been to Australia.'

The woman laughed. 'Many young men from the south of Italy have gone there, Sicilians, Calabrians. I am told that they work in the sugar cane fields. Hard work, but they make money.'

'I'm a fisherman,' said Giuseppe proudly.

'Then maybe you'll have the opportunity to fish in Australia,' said the woman. 'It's up to you, of course.'

Giuseppe thought for a moment, but it seemed he had few options and he couldn't disappoint his family by returning home. Maybe he would make enough money in Australia to travel on to America.

'I will go,' he said.

He paid for his passage and left his luggage with the kind woman at the ticket office.

With twenty-four hours before the ship sailed, Giuseppe set off to explore the historic city of Naples.

He was overwhelmed by the grandeur of the buildings, fountains, statues and ancient ruins and for the first time he became aware of the rich cultural heritage of his country. He realised how little he knew about its history other than what he'd learned from Alfonso. Later in the day he sat at a table in the Piazza Dante sipping a cold drink. He was shocked at the price of the food at the cafe, so he decided that he would wait until he was on the ship before he ate again.

He watched the people hurrying across the square and wondered what they all did and where they were going in such haste. Here everyone was on the move. Even when they were seated at tables they seemed to be busy, engaged in energetic conversations, so different from home where the men idled away the day, quietly chatting and smoking as they mended nets or contemplated the fishing conditions. Here in the city there was urgency in the air and music everywhere.

Tears came to Giuseppe's eyes as he listened to a man with a fine tenor voice on the other side of the square sing with all his heart, as passers-by dropped coins into the hat at his feet. But before the tenor had finished the song, a group of youths, wearing black shirts and shouting slogans, stormed around a corner, knocked him over and took his money.

Seeing Giuseppe frown, the waiter leaned across to Giuseppe and said, 'These are the thugs of Mussolini who are against the socialists and communists. The authorities let them get away with too much, even murder! These fascists assault anyone opposed to their own views. I do not think this is what we fought for.'

Giuseppe nodded, although he was hazy about politics.

'It is a disease, all this political unrest,' added the waiter. 'And we Italians will suffer because of it.'

'I am leaving Italy,' blurted out Giuseppe. 'I am sailing to Australia.'

The waiter wiped Giuseppe's table with a wet rag. 'Who do you know in Australia?' he asked.

'I don't know anyone there. I was on my way to America and I missed the boat. My train was late.'

The waiter shrugged. 'Maybe it is fate that you will now go to Australia. Good luck, eh? Ciao.'

'I hope so,' muttered Giuseppe as he left the table and hurried across the square, avoiding the chanting youths who were shaking their fists outside a small shop. The shopkeeper had fled, leaving them to help themselves to his fruit.

Giuseppe returned to the wharf that evening to sleep for the night while he waited for the *Ricconigi* to dock. As he walked across the pier, he saw another young man. He asked him if he was going to Australia, too.

'Yes, I am. I am here early because I know that if you're travelling on a cargo ship you want to board quickly to grab the best bunk. Six and more to a cabin gets pretty cosy.'

'You've travelled before?' asked Giuseppe.

The other man shook his head. 'My brother went out to Australia last year on a cargo ship and he warned me. He also told me to get to the meals early, too.' He winked. 'Stick with me, I know my way around a ship and I've never even been to sea!' He laughed and stuck out his hand. 'Antonio.'

'Giuseppe. Giuseppe d'Aquino.'

'You from Sicily?' asked Antonio, recognising Giuseppe's accent. 'Where are you headed?'

'I was planning to go to America but I missed the boat. Now I have decided to go to Australia. I don't know what I'll do when I arrive. I'm a fisherman.'

'I'm headed to Queensland to join my brother in the sugar cane fields. But I don't plan on staying there,' said Antonio. 'I've heard there are plenty of other opportunities. Even looking for gold!'

'I only know about fishing.'

Antonio shrugged. 'Well, you're on your own there.' He pulled out a cigarette and lit it. 'You want to eat a pizza? I know a cheap place,' he added.

Giuseppe was hungry and it seemed Antonio knew his way around Naples. 'Okay. But I don't have much to spend. Have you been in Naples long?'

'A few weeks. I stayed with a friend from my town. He showed me around.' He looked seriously at Giuseppe. 'Where I am taking you, you won't need much money, but be careful with what you've got. The pickpockets are good here.'

Giuseppe was about to say that he kept his money in his shoe, but felt a little foolish, so he patted his jacket and said, 'My grandmother sewed a special flap in the pocket for me.'

'Yeah. Men like us get marked as country boys and easy targets. Where's home?'

As they walked back along the harbour front, Giuseppe told Antonio about his island, fishing with his father and brothers, and what a struggle life had been for them all.

Antonio nodded. 'Yeah, lots of people think the same. It's no wonder people are leaving Italy by the thousands. There are only old people left in my village in Sardinia. Most of my friends have gone to America.'

The pizzeria was as Antonio had described: a hole in the wall with a wood-fired oven, a small cart to carry the ingredients and a couple of wooden tables and chairs. One man was expertly punching and flipping balls of dough, stretching them to a circle, smearing on tomato paste, a handful of cheese, some onion and olives and then sliding them on his wooden paddle into the mouth of the oven in front of the burning bits of wood. In a few moments the pizzas were cooked and after a toss of basil leaves on top, they were served to the customers.

Giuseppe handed over a few coins and bit into the thin crunchy crust. He closed his eyes in ecstasy. 'You are right. This is good, very good indeed.'

Antonio smiled. 'I can show you more of Naples if you like.'

When they had finished their pizzas, Antonio took him down a street where voluptuous girls in daring clothes leaned against doorways, and taunted and teased the two good-looking young men as they walked past.

'They charge too much. Sailors have spoiled them,' muttered Antonio, trying to sound very much a man of the world. 'You had a girl yet?'

Giuseppe shook his head. He knew what Antonio meant, but said, 'I'd rather save my money. Maybe the girls in Australia will be happy to go with a nice Sicilian boy, eh?'

Antonio gave a quick grin. 'Maybe you could come to Queensland with me. We could team up together.'

'Maybe,' said Giuseppe, glad he'd found a friend.

Antonio chuckled. 'We might get lucky at sea, eh? While the mammas are sick in their bunks!'

They made their way back to the wharf and settled down for the night. Sometime in the small hours of the morning, the *Ricconigi* docked. Giuseppe raced to the ticket office to retrieve his suitcase and as soon as they were allowed, he and Antonio hurried on board to find their cabins, which were down a dim passageway but close to each other.

'Take that top bunk, next to that porthole. Stash your gear under the bottom bunk and don't trust your cabin mates. Always keep your money on you,' Antonio advised Giuseppe.

But even the ebullient Antonio had fallen silent when they'd seen the tiny and dingy space the bunks occupied. The narrow cabin smelt stale. The thin coir mattresses were covered with grey bedding that looked as though it hadn't been washed for many journeys. The toilet and bathing facilities were rudimentary. Later they were told that if clothes needed to be washed, water had to be drawn from over the side of the vessel.

When they went to eat, another shock awaited them. What passed as the dining room was a narrow space off the galley where the food was prepared. Passengers helped themselves in the small serving area and then either sat on the few chairs that were lined against the wall or took their meals to any space they could find. The evil smells from the greasy galley encouraged many to take their food up into the fresh air on the deck, even though their meals got cold more quickly there.

The menu seldom varied. Breakfast was dry biscuits and weak coffee with sugar but no milk. The rest of the meals were variations of pasta, generally macaroni, teamed with boiled beans and chunks of meat. While regular meat initially seemed a luxury to many of the passengers, the grey glutinous mass soon lost its appeal, especially as it was always tough and sinewy.

'No wonder the ticket was so cheap,' muttered Antonio.

The first day was a blur as Giuseppe followed Antonio around the ship and the *Ricconigi* steamed from the Bay of Naples past the towering hulk of Mount Vesuvius, capped in cloud. They realised they were sailing on an insalubrious vessel where the human cargo was of less value than the commercial cargo in the ship's hull.

41

The sixty or so passengers divided themselves into two sittings for meals, the women and children eating first, since they made up the larger number. Many of the mothers with children were going to join husbands who'd gone ahead to Australia, sometimes years before. Dressed in dark and modest clothes, they sat on chairs in the shelter of the deck, gradually forming small groups to knit and crochet as they talked and watched their children play with whatever the youngsters could find to entertain themselves.

Giuseppe noticed a small group of Maltese on board. The Italians and the Maltese barely fraternised. The Maltese considered themselves superior to the southern Italians and kept to themselves, complaining bitterly to each other and to the crew about conditions on the ship.

The Italian men formed a loud and cheerful group sharing similar stories. They all had plans and hopes to succeed in Australia. Everyone seemed to have relatives or to know someone there and they entertained each other by relating tales they'd heard of this new country. Giuseppe tried to learn as much as he could from these stories, picking up clues about where might be the best place to find work. From what he heard, Australia seemed to be full of dangerous animals, spiders, snakes and especially sharks.

'*Squali*, yes, we have them also in Sicily – sometimes they swim with the tuna, but they are harmless,' said Giuseppe.

'You wouldn't get me trying to catch one,' said Antonio.

Other men told stories they had heard of people dying in the desert, being attacked by wild dogs and ferocious pigs, and Giuseppe realised how little he knew about Australia. It did not sound an inviting place at all, but at least no one had heard about any earthquakes happening there.

'What about the cities? Are they safe? I prefer to be in a town on the coast so I can fish.'

'Giuseppe the fisherman!' they laughed. 'You'll have to start as a deckhand. Maybe you should get off at Fremantle. They have fishing boats there.'

Giuseppe thought that this was the best idea he had heard since he boarded the ship.

'Maybe I will,' he said.

After they had been at sea for a few days, it occurred to Giuseppe that he should write a letter to his parents and tell them of his change in plan and explain that he was not on his way to America but was now going to Australia. He asked the purser for some paper to write his letter and went to find the small room that passed for a recreation area. Several older men had commandeered this space in the evenings where they noisily smoked and played briscola. In the mid morning, however, this room was generally empty as it was hot and stuffy and most of the passengers preferred to be up on deck.

Stepping into the room, Giuseppe was surprised to find a young woman looking through a shelf of books. He stopped in the doorway, catching his breath. She had her back to him, but what startled Giuseppe and brought a rush of emotion to his heart was the sight of the long auburn curls that tumbled down her back. Although her hair colour was different, the beauty of her curls reminded him of Angelica.

He coughed politely and she jumped in surprise, dropping a book.

Giuseppe hurried forward and picked it up.

'I'm sorry, I didn't mean to surprise you . . .' He handed her the book and was suddenly at a loss for words at the sight of her pale creamy skin sprinkled with freckles and her brilliant blue eyes that reminded him of the ocean on a summer morning. She smiled at him as she took her book from him and said something in English.

'I don't speak *Inglese*,' he said despairingly. 'Do you speak Italian?' She shook her head but smiled at him still.

Giuseppe looked at the title of her book, which was in English. He scanned the remaining books on the shelf, which were mostly in Italian, then selected one and held it up. 'I'll read this one.'

She nodded and looked pleased, or perhaps impressed. Then she pointed to a map of the world tacked onto the wall. 'Fremantle, Melbourne, Sydney?' she asked speaking slowly, pointing to each of the ports the *Ricconigi* would dock at in Australia. Her voice had a delightful lilt to it.

Giuseppe couldn't keep his eyes off her face, thinking he had never seen anyone so beautiful. She was an angel. She was like the madonnas he'd seen in Alfonso's art books. She was unlike any other girl he'd seen before. Her skin glowed as if she was lit from within. He immediately compared her with Angelica but while Angelica was of the earth, a wild free spirit of the hills, she had not excited in him the sensations that this girl did – the quickening of his breath, the shiver in his body, the racing of his pulse. This girl was the sky, the sea and soft breezes, and she stirred him in a way he'd never experienced.

She tilted her head, giving him a quizzical look, the corners of her mouth lifting again in a smile.

Giuseppe tried to refocus his attention on the map. He pointed to the girl and then back to Australia. 'Where are you going to get off?' he asked in Italian.

She understood. 'Sydney,' she said slowly and clearly. 'Sydney.' She pointed to the map.

Giuseppe quickly threw away the idea of getting off the *Ricconigi* in Fremantle.

He smiled back at her and said, 'Yes. I am going to Sydney also.' He tapped his chest. 'I am Giuseppe.'

'Bridget,' she said. And then added, 'Bridie. Bridie.'

'Bridie,' he said, savouring the word.

She gestured to the map on the wall and showed him an island in the North Sea. Then she tapped on her chest, and pointed at Ireland. Giuseppe understood and he was glad that Alfonso had let him study his atlas. He showed her the pinprick that was his island off the Italian coast. 'That is my home.'

She peered closely and made a gesture with her fingers to indicate that it was a little place.

Giuseppe nodded and laughed. 'Yes, small.' He lifted his arms like a weightlifter. 'But it's a tough, strong place.' He kissed the tips of his fingers. 'And a good place.'

Bridie said something more to Giuseppe, but he did not understand and their conversation faltered. Then Bridie pointed to the paper in Giuseppe's hands and made a gesture like writing with her hands.

He looked at the pen and paper he was holding. 'I am writing to my mother. *Mia mamma.*'

'Ahh, Mamma.' She nodded and smiled again. Giuseppe attempted to keep the conversation going but they struggled to understand one another. After a few more minutes Bridie nodded at him in a gesture of goodbye and taking her book, she left the little library room.

'*Arrivederci,*' Giuseppe called.

Giuseppe wrote his letter, guessing that his family would probably take it to the priest to be read. Giuseppe told them that he would write again when he arrived in Australia, and that they weren't to worry. When he returned the pen to the purser, knowing that the officer spoke English, Giuseppe politely asked him if knew anything about the Irish girl, Bridget.

'She's travelling on her own. Some of the Maltese women who can speak English keep her company and she plays with their children occasionally.'

Giuseppe was shocked. 'She seems very young to be travelling on her own. Italian girls wouldn't travel like that. It's a shame we can't talk.' He suddenly had an idea. 'Why don't you start some classes so we can learn English? She could help.'

At first the purser shook his head but when Giuseppe persisted, he finally said, 'I have some English phrase books and an English dictionary. I'll see what I can do.'

Giuseppe could not interest anyone else in learning English. Nevertheless, armed with the books the purser had lent him, he hung around the recreation room until he spied Bridie. He greeted her and showed her his English books. Her eyes lit up. She made a little pantomime of reading and writing.

Giuseppe nodded enthusiastically.

With a few hand motions towards a clock, they arranged to meet each morning and again after dinner in the little rec room. But this idea proved difficult to put into practice as Bridie ate at the first sitting with the other women, and after the second sitting the men wanted to play cards and drink in the room.

'Then I will eat early too!' said Giuseppe.

At first eyebrows were raised when Giuseppe joined the women to eat at the first sitting. For the first few days Giuseppe and Bridie were watched with open curiosity. But when the purser came in and chatted to them, translating between Italian and English, and handed them a grammar book he'd found, his actions placed the stamp of authority on their friendship, giving it legitimacy among the other passengers.

Giuseppe found himself smoothing his hair, straightening his shirt, washing his face and hands and ignoring the ribald teasing of his cabin mates before he joined Bridie at mealtimes. She was always neatly dressed, her hair tied back with a ribbon at the nape of her neck.

After a while no one took any further notice of them, even when Giuseppe suggested to Bridie that they eat their meals out on the deck.

The dictionary became their best friend. Passing it back and forth to look up words, Bridie and Giuseppe began to ask each other questions and answer them. Sometimes the purser sat with them and helped. Some of the Maltese passengers asked to join in because the young pair were such joyful company. They laughed a lot at each other's mistakes and Giuseppe was surprised at how at ease he felt. Bridie was always polite and very self-possessed, but Giuseppe soon realised that she came from a small village, too.

The *Ricconigi* didn't call into any ports as it sailed towards the Suez Canal; the days at sea seemed interminable. Some of the children became bored. Often the women would take to their bunks feeling ill, miserable and lonely. Matters were made worse when their vessel broke down in the canal and they spent days wallowing at anchor before they were under way again.

The men were restless and sometimes arguments broke out.

But Giuseppe was unconcerned. For him, each day started in the happy knowledge that here was another day to spend with Bridie. For now, despite the language difficulties, both were discovering how much they enjoyed each other's company and were slowly unravelling their childhood stories with the help of the dog-eared dictionary.

They took to walking around and around the deck for exercise and these times didn't always require conversation. Once when a cool breeze was blowing and Bridie shivered in her light muslin top, Giuseppe took off his jacket and draped it over her shoulders, letting his arm rest lightly there for a moment.

After they had finally passed through the Suez Canal, the weather deteriorated and became stormy. The bulky ship dived and rolled. Many passengers were sick and the crew member who acted as medic soon ran out of ideas and treatments.

Bridie and Giuseppe, however, revelled in the brisk breeze and rolling sea. They moved two deckchairs as far out of the wind as they could to wait out the storm, preferring the blustery conditions on deck to the sour-smelling cabins below. It was wet and windy, but strangely warm.

A passing sailor gave Giuseppe a grin, but motioned to the horizon. 'Watch the storm, it could get worse. Keep your lifejacket handy.'

'Can you swim?' Giuseppe asked Bridie, making a swimming motion with his arms.

She shook her head, looking alarmed.

He reached over and took her hand, smiling reassuringly, and pointed to a lifeboat tucked along the deck. He pretended to row and stood up and held his hand over his eyes as if peering out to sea, then gave a salute and a thumbs up.

Bridie laughed. At that moment a rain squall rushed in, soaking the deck. They both leapt back as a strong gust of wind hit them, almost knocking them off their feet. Giuseppe grabbed Bridie's arm as she slipped. But she appeared exhilarated as the wind whipped around them. In seconds her ribbon had loosened and she grabbed it to stop it from flying away, untying her hair in the process. Giuseppe felt his chest tighten at the sight of her damp ringlets blowing around her laughing face. He leaned forward and kissed her on the cheek. Then he pulled away, shocked by his impulsive move, hoping that she wouldn't be angry.

Bridie touched her cheek where he'd kissed her, smiled shyly and shook her head.

'I'm sorry, Giuseppe, but you don't understand. I'm happy to be your friend but that's all I can be. You see, I am going to Australia to marry a man I've known since childhood.' As Giuseppe tried to follow what she was saying she pulled out a chain from around her neck. On it hung a locket, which she opened. Inside was a picture of a young man. She pointed to him and then to her finger, miming putting on a ring.

'Ah. I understand,' he said quietly, barely glancing at the man's face, but looking deep into Bridie's eyes.

Then he added in halting English, 'You travel to him alone. Very brave.'

'I thought it would be an adventure! Ronan has a job in Sydney. He wrote and asked me to marry him, so I got a job as a nursemaid to an English family who were travelling to Italy. When they got to Naples I left them and bought a ticket on the *Ricconigi*. But I was so lonely by myself until I found a wonderful friend.' She smiled at him warmly.

Giuseppe, while not understanding all that she said, realised that she was spoken for, but said, 'We can still be friends, *si*?' He smiled gently, touched her hand and took a slight step back.

Bridie looked pleased, and nodded her head. Simultaneously they stepped out onto the windswept deck and continued their walk.

Giuseppe was determined to maintain their friendship. He tried to remain at ease with her and took on a more brotherly, protective attitude. However, in the dark, alone in his bunk as he listened to the snoring and coughs and rumblings of the men around him, he ached and longed for Bridie. As well as the physical yearning he was experiencing, he was saddened knowing that she would marry someone else.

When he mentioned Bridie's impending marriage to Antonio, his friend scoffed.

'Why would you want to marry her anyway, when there are lots of good Italian girls in Australia, just waiting for you? You are not experienced enough in the ways of the world, especially women, to make the right judgment yet.' To change the subject, Antonio asked, 'Have you decided what you will do when you get to Australia?'

'I will go to Sydney, but after that maybe I'll go cane cutting with you in Queensland.'

'Good idea. It's hard work, but you'll make money to be able to send home to your parents.'

Even with the knowledge that she belonged to another man, Giuseppe was blinded by Bridie. If he saw her in the distance he caught his breath, felt his heart race and a smile came to his face unbidden. He took joy in the time they had together on the ship, a time between decisions, a time just for them, with no one to intrude. Standing beside her at the ship's railing as they watched the ocean swell, the occasional bird circling overhead and the foaming white wake behind them marking their voyage from their homelands, he wished this journey would never end.

When the *Ricconigi* finally arrived in Bombay, everyone was relieved to be going ashore at long last. Giuseppe disliked the large black ravens that swooped around the ship and the dock, thinking they looked evil. Antonio wanted to leave the ship as soon as it docked, to explore the city, so Giuseppe decided to ask Bridie if she would like to come with them.

India shocked the three of them, especially its beggars.

'There is poverty at home in Italy,' said Antonio. 'But it is nothing like this.'

'When I look at some of those beggars, it makes me feel as though I have everything,' agreed Giuseppe.

None of them had any rupees to give to the people who swarmed around them, putting out their hands and crying, 'Baksheesh, baba,' but the three of them realised that however much they gave, they would never be able to satisfy all of those who asked.

'Come on,' said Antonio. 'Let's see if we can find something to eat that tastes like food.'

'I'll pay, if we can find somewhere that will take my English money,' said Bridie. 'You two can pay me back later if you like.'

They found a restaurant that was very cheap and tentatively decided to share a curry. They all found it hot but the two men had no trouble in eating it and they laughed at Bridie's brave attempt to do the same. The restaurant owner, seeing her difficulties, brought over another dish of rice and vegetables, which she enjoyed.

'That was delicious,' she said when she had finished. 'I had forgotten what food really tastes like after that rubbish we get on board.'

They spent the rest of the day wandering around the crowded city, taking in its sights, sounds and smells. Giuseppe almost had to pinch himself to believe that he was in such an exotic country. He knew that it would be very hard to explain to his family just what India had been like when next he wrote home.

All three of them regretted having to return to the *Ricconigi* late that afternoon, but they were due to sail for Colombo early the next morning.

'The one time when you want the ship not to work, it does. I was hoping that we could stay here a bit longer,' said Antonio. 'I suppose we have to make up for the time we lost at Suez.'

But they found Colombo to be a pleasant city, not as overwhelming as Bombay had been, although a lot hotter. After wandering along the sea front they decided to venture into the local markets. They were all amazed by the wares for sale: silks, spices, golden jewellery and all manner of carved objects. Giuseppe wanted to buy something to give to Bridie as a souvenir. One of the stalls sold carved elephants, which he thought would be perfect, but he had no rupees and he could hardly ask Bridie for a loan. As Antonio and Bridie wandered off ahead, Giuseppe stood looking at the variety of elephants the stall keeper had on offer. They ranged from one that was almost life sized to other smaller ones made from ivory or wood. Then he saw the purser coming towards him. He quickly spoke to him, and the purser nodded before handing over some coins.

'Pay me back in lira when you return to the boat,' he said.

When Giuseppe asked, in a mixture of English, Italian and hand gestures, he learned that the money the purser had lent him would pay only for a very small elephant. He picked up a wooden one.

'Sandalwood, sandalwood,' the vendor assured him.

Giuseppe paid the asking price and raced off to catch up with Bridie and Antonio.

'I buy for you,' he said, giving the little carved elephant to Bridie.

'Thank you very much, Giuseppe. I shall treasure this and when I look at it, I will always remember this day.'

Giuseppe was not entirely sure what Bridie had said, but he could see that she was pleased with the present.

Back on board, as the ship sailed south towards Australia, Giuseppe worked even harder at his English lessons. Sometimes Bridie read to him from the book she was reading, and he was able to grasp the gist of it, and he took pleasure in the sound of her voice.

They were both excited when the purser announced that there would be a Crossing of the Equator ceremony and they were looking forward to the special party. Until now the passengers had been ignored by the crew, regarded as a hindrance rather than paying passengers, so everyone was pleased about this big social event in which they would all participate.

King Neptune, scarcely recognisable as the purser in a green beard and once-gold robes, greeted them all. A shallow pool was rigged up on the deck and the men were tossed into it after being painted with some jelly-like substance. The children squealed with laughter at the sight of the adults being heave-hoed by the sea king. The women, gathered like a black-robed court, watched in amusement. At one end sat the captain in his white uniform looking faintly amused. He had rarely been seen on the voyage and the passengers regarded him in some awe.

When it was Giuseppe's turn to be thrown into the water, everyone cheered. He was well liked. The women admired his strong brown torso, his muscular arms and legs, and his open face that seemed to reflect his big, generous heart. The men also found him entertaining, warm and good company.

Afterwards, Giuseppe came over to Bridie and thrust a piece of paper towards her so she could see it. 'Look! From King Neptune!' He laughed.

She couldn't help smiling at his infectious delight. The certificate was ornate, edged in gold scrolls and featured a watercolour painting of King Neptune with his seaweed beard, a crown and a trident that was reminiscent of Giuseppe's *traffena*, but the paper was yellowed with age, as though it had been stored for some time. It announced he had successfully 'crossed the line' and had been welcomed by King Neptune to his court in the seas beyond the equator.

At that moment Mr Armellini, one of the Maltese passengers, approached Bridie and Giuseppe, holding a camera. 'Miss O'Grady, can I take a photograph of you and your friend?'

'Why yes, thank you, Mr Armellini,' said Bridie politely.

Giuseppe was thrilled to have his picture taken with Bridie. He grabbed his shirt and flung it on as Bridie rose from her seat to stand beside him. Giuseppe could feel Bridie's thin blouse through his damp shirt on his cool arm. Smiling broadly at the camera lens they were a contrasting couple: Bridie neat as a pin, and Giuseppe with wet tousled hair, a crumpled shirt and bare brown legs, holding his certificate. Both had big spontaneous smiles and the moment captured them very much at ease with each other.

'I would like a copy of the photograph, Mr Armellini,' said Giuseppe.

'I can arrange that,' he answered.

They each received a copy of the photograph several days later and it became Giuseppe's most prized possession.

Later that evening, after King Neptune retired to the deep, there was music and dancing. Several of the Italian men brought out their accordions and mandolins and everyone joined in singing the old favourites. Giuseppe recognised some of the songs he'd heard in Naples. When everyone started dancing, the purser, now back in his usual uniform, asked Bridie to dance. Then when they had finished dancing, it was quite natural for Giuseppe also to take her in his arms and join the other dancers. For those too brief moments, as he held Bridie close, he thought again how lovely she was.

*

There was great excitement on board the *Ricconigi* as it approached the coast of Western Australia. Some of the passengers were disembarking at Fremantle, the first port of call. The ship anchored some distance from the shore and a motor launch brought immigration officials out to it. All the passengers were summoned to the main deck to go through the immigration process. That was when Giuseppe heard some of the passengers whispering about a notorious dictation test.

'What does this mean?' Giuseppe asked Antonio.

'Something to do with speaking English, maybe,' said his friend, shrugging his shoulders.

Mr Armellini, standing next to them, shook his head. 'It's the Australian government's way of rejecting migrants they think are unsuitable.'

'But my English is still poor,' protested Giuseppe. 'I might fail.'

'The test might not even be in English.'

'You mean it will be in Italian,' said a relieved Antonio.

'It could be in any language,' said Mr Armellini. 'If they don't want you, they will make it impossible for you to pass.'

'But that is so unfair,' protested Giuseppe.

'Let's hope they like the look of us,' said Antonio. However his fears, and those of the other passengers, were put to rest when no one from the *Ricconigi* was told to sit the test.

When Giuseppe reached the head of the queue he greeted the official with a smile, but was quickly rebuffed.

'What part of Italy are you from?' the official asked brusquely.

'Sicily, signor. Sir,' he answered politely.

The official glared at him and, looking down at his paperwork, muttered, 'Another wog come to take the jobs of good Aussie workers. I reckon you lot aren't much better than the Abos.'

Giuseppe didn't understand all the immigration official's words, but he knew that he was not speaking words of welcome. He hoped that the rest of Australia was not going to be like this. Clutching the piece of paper he'd been handed by the officer, he joined Antonio, who was standing with Bridie.

'Are you coming ashore with us to explore our new country, Bridie? I have my landing permit,' said Giuseppe happily.

'Yes, please. I'd feel safer with two escorts,' she said with a laugh.

They found the streets around the port very flat, but there were some imposing and solid buildings. They took a tram along High Street, alighted and walked back towards the harbour looking in shop windows.

Giuseppe was startled at the prices of goods and it began to concern him that he had very little money. Unlike Bridie and Antonio, no relative or friend would be meeting him to help him find somewhere to stay and get work, as there would have been in New York. How was he going to live? He could see fishing boats in the harbour and he wondered if he should stay in Fremantle and try and get a job on one of them. But the thought of having to leave Bridie a second before he had to made him give up that idea.

It took the ship three days to reach Melbourne, where most of the Italians were disembarking. In all that time Giuseppe thought about how he would support himself until he got work. Eventually he came to a decision.

As they met for their regular morning walk around the deck before breakfast, Giuseppe turned to Bridie.

'Bridie, can I ask for your help when we go ashore in Melbourne?'

Seeing his serious face, Bridie nodded. 'Of course, Giuseppe.'

He reached into his pocket and took his grandmother's ring from its little yellow envelope and showed it to Bridie.

He explained that it had belonged to his nonna, and that although she had wanted to keep it until Giuseppe came back to the island to find a bride, she had decided that it would be of more use to him if she gave it to him straight away.

'I have very little money. I do not want to sell the ring, because it is all that my nonna had to give me, but I must. Will you help me to sell it, Bridie?' Giuseppe had looked up the words he needed and practised what he wanted to say to her.

Bridie took the little ring and looked at its worn band and little red stone.

'It's so sad that you have to sell something that your grandmother gave you. Are you sure that you really want to?'

'I have no choice. I asked Antonio to help me, but he said to ask you because he doesn't speak English, and you will get a better price.'

As soon as the ship tied up in Melbourne, the two of them set out to find a pawn shop. It wasn't very hard. There were quite a few around the dock area. But none of the pawn shop owners thought that the ring was worth very much at all.

'The band is badly worn and that stone is only a garnet. It's not worth more than its gold weight,' one of the pawn brokers explained.

'How much then?' asked Bridie.

'Two pounds.'

Bridie explained to Giuseppe that two pounds was not a great deal of money, but it would be enough to tide him over for a while, if he was careful.

'Then I must do it,' he said and tears immediately came to his eyes at the thought of selling the ring that had been so precious to his nonna. 'It is all she had to give me,' he said as he handed it over.

They walked slowly back to the ship saying very little, but both of them were impressed by the hustle and bustle around them. Trams rattled along the streets, competing for space with numerous motor cars. The shops were busy and full of exciting things to buy.

'It looks as though Australia is a wealthy country,' said Giuseppe as they climbed the gangplank. 'We will both do well here.'

'You are probably right. Giuseppe, will you excuse me, I need to go and lie down for a while,' said Bridie. 'I'm tired from all our walking.'

Giuseppe watched her turn and go towards her cabin.

I do not have her for much longer, he thought sadly to himself. I will miss her.

It was dawn as they approached Sydney. The two dark arms of the northern and southern headlands of the harbour emerged in the misty light. Giuseppe stood alone at the railing, wondering what lay beyond the embrace of the cliffs where a line of white foam marked the crashing waves.

As they sailed through the magnificent heads, he caught his breath. Not only was the harbour spectacularly beautiful, but he could see inlets and bays and rocky points where he knew lobsters and rock fish would hide.

He returned to the stuffy cabin that had been his home for so many weeks, grabbed his suitcase and headed back to the deck. The passageways were crowded, but he quickly found Antonio.

'We will keep in touch,' said Antonio. 'When it is the right time to head to the cane fields, I will let you know.'

'That sounds good,' said Giuseppe.

On their way to the upper deck they discovered a knot of irate Maltese confronting the purser and demanding to see the ship's captain.

'I think they are complaining about how badly they've been treated. More like cargo than paying passengers,' whispered Antonio. 'They want a refund! I don't think that will happen. Maybe they should take their story to the newspapers. Let's watch the ship dock.'

Already the railing was lined with people watching the steamer manoeuvre towards the sprawling dockyards of Woolloomooloo. The *Ricconigi* swung alongside the long wharf. Giuseppe saw crowds jammed onto the dock, fighting for space with motor cars and trucks and even a small train line.

He felt a tap on his shoulder and he turned around to see Bridie, dressed in a bright blue outfit with a small hat perched on her auburn ringlets. Her cheeks were pink with excitement. Giuseppe made room for her to squeeze against the rail.

There was a great long blast from the ship's horn and the rattle of the dropping anchor chain as fat ropes were swung down to the wharf to secure the vessel. People along the wharf could now recognise friends and family on the ship and there was much waving and shouting and dabbing at tears. To be heard above the melee Giuseppe leaned closer to Bridie's ear.

'You see Ronan? Your fiancé?' He used the word she'd taught him.

She shook her head. 'Not yet, but I am sure he will find me. Look, the gangplank is being lowered.'

Bridie turned and began edging through the crowd, and Giuseppe followed her through the press of passengers heading the same way. Ahead she stopped and turned back to Giuseppe and waved to him.

'I am coming!' he said. More and more people crowded towards the gangplank eager to disembark. Giuseppe tried to step around a woman and her children and their bags but the woman pushed in front of him and, surrounded by her excitable children, blocked his way.

When Giuseppe finally reached the top of the gangplank, he spotted Bridie's blue hat in the crowd below on the dock. He watched as a man waved to her and in a moment they were embracing. And then she was gone.

He pushed down the gangplank and through the knots of reunions, tears and laughter, past those still desperately looking for their relatives but Bridie was nowhere to be seen.

He couldn't believe that she'd just vanished, disappeared from his life without even a proper farewell. Feeling despondent, he went to the cavernous shed at the end of the wharf, where he saw Antonio talking to another Italian.

'I thought you'd got lost. Did you say goodbye to Bridie?' asked Antonio.

Giuseppe shrugged. 'No, I missed her. She's gone and I don't even know where to.'

Antonio placed a sympathetic hand on Giuseppe's arm. 'It is best this way. She has her life. She asked me to give this to you.' He handed Giuseppe a little envelope.

Giuseppe recognised it straight away and hurried to look inside. It was indeed Celestina's ring.

'Giuseppe, she gave me this note, too.'

Giuseppe opened it.

I saw how sad you were to part with this ring, so when I told you I was resting, I went back to the pawn shop, and bought it back for you. It is a thank you gift for all your kindness to me on the voyage. I would have been very lonely without your cheerful company. I hope that someday you will be able to give this ring to the girl you intend to marry. I think she will be a very lucky girl. All the best for your new life, Bridie.

Giuseppe didn't understand everything that Bridie had written, but he knew enough to be able to explain to Antonio what she had done.

'What a kind woman. She will make a wonderful wife, no doubt. But cheer up. This is Vincenzo, a distant cousin of mine.'

Giuseppe shook the young man's hand.

'Welcome to Australia,' said Vincenzo.

'Vincenzo's taking us to his uncle who imports Italian wine. He has an office in his warehouse not far from here. He wants us to come for a drink to celebrate our arrival! Come on, you never know who you might meet in our new country!'

Antonio linked his arm through Giuseppe's and the three young men sauntered along the waterfront.

3

CARRYING THEIR CASES, DRESSED in their best, Giuseppe and Antonio followed Vincenzo along the wharf to Vincenzo's uncle's office and warehouse. Although Giuseppe was still feeling despondent about not saying goodbye properly to Bridie, the enthusiasm of the others was infectious. And he was feeling strangely at home. The salty smell of the air, the bright blue sky and sunshine, and the activity around the harbour made him think that he might be able to find a job somewhere around here. He'd noticed men on the wharves doing the back-breaking work of loading and unloading cargo. He could see houses crowded together on the hill behind the wharves. The scene almost reminded him of his fishing village, although instead of the backdrop of wild exposed hillsides, here there were solid multi-storey buildings. But it wasn't the city that interested Giuseppe as much as the waterfront.

The minute they walked into Vincenzo's uncle's darkened storage shed, Giuseppe and Antonio began to sigh. They could hear mandolin music and smell the rich tomato aromas of pasta asciutta. After the terrible food on the *Ricconigi*, their mouths began to water.

They entered a large back room, lined with crates and large wooden barrels and shelves stacked with wine bottles. In the centre of the room a long table was spread with food. Along the table empty chianti bottles wreathed in raffia had candles sticking out of them, wax running down their sides in fat, greasy rivulets. An older man was playing a sentimental tune on a mandolin, which wrenched at their hearts. There were a lot of people sitting at the table enjoying the food and wine. A plump, jolly-looking man waved at them to take a seat and told them to help themselves. Vincenzo took Giuseppe and Antonio over to meet him.

'This is my uncle, Giovanni Bruscioli,' he said. 'Uncle, here are Giuseppe and Antonio, who have just arrived in Australia today.'

'Welcome, welcome,' responded Uncle Giovanni. 'Help yourself to whatever you want. Introduce yourselves to my friends. Maltese, Italian, they all know each other and you will soon know them, too.'

Giuseppe quickly did as he was instructed. The pasta was delicious. If he could eat like this every day in Australia, he would be very happy. Spearing a piece of macaroni, he asked: 'Who made this? It is as good as the food my nonna makes.'

'Signor Rizzo, a friend of my uncle's,' replied Vincenzo. 'He started a pasta factory not far from here in Stanley Street. It's very successful. And if you are lucky, our friend Sando, here, will make you a beautiful sauce to go with it – and serenade you as well!'

Sando, the mandolin player, acknowledged the compliment.

'This is a wonderful welcome party,' Giuseppe said. 'How fortunate for you to have family here, Vincenzo.'

'I never knew my uncle until I came to Australia, but now I know how generous he is. He gives away his money and finds jobs for people who need help. Every Friday he has a party here in his warehouse. You will always be welcome,' said Vincenzo.

Antonio nudged Giuseppe. 'You could ask for a job.'

Giuseppe glanced at Giovanni, who was pouring glasses of red wine from a long-necked dark green bottle. He felt too shy to ask Giovanni about work while he was his guest.

'I'll wait a little while.'

'No, let's talk to him now,' said Antonio.

So Giuseppe and Antonio wandered over to where Giovanni was sitting. He greeted them effusively, as though he had not seen them for ages.

'Sit. Eat, eat – or Sando will be offended. Tell me, why have you come to Australia? What are your plans? Where are you going? You have family here?'

'My cousin and my uncle are in north Queensland, a place called Innisfail,' said Antonio. 'Cane cutting.'

'Ah, cutting sugar cane. Seasonal work, very hard work,' said Giovanni. 'But makes big muscles. I know some good boxers who used to cut cane. You are going to be a cane cutter?'

Antonio shrugged. 'It's a start. Maybe I'll look for something else.'

'What will you do in Australia, Giuseppe? What did you do in the old country?'

'I am a fisherman.'

Giovanni nodded. 'You will like Sydney. The harbour is full of seafood. There is so much that you can take oysters right off the rocks and from the pylons of the wharves. Sando cooks marinara all the time.'

'At home I hunt for big fish, the *tonno*.'

'Do you have family here in Australia?'

Giuseppe shook his head. 'No, I am alone. Can you tell me where is the best place to go for fishing?'

'Right here. All you need is a boat!' roared Giovanni.

'I cannot afford a boat. But I can work for someone.'

Giovanni dropped his cheerful tone and grew serious. 'Are you a *good* fisherman?'

Giuseppe nodded vehemently. 'Very good. I don't know the waters here but I can learn quickly. The sea is in my blood,' he said earnestly.

Giovanni leaned back in his chair. 'Have some more wine, Giuseppe. I will ask around for you. Come back in a few days, okay? Where are you two going to stay?'

Giuseppe looked at Giovanni and suddenly realised that he had just landed in a strange country with only a couple of pounds in his pocket.

'We haven't found a place yet.' He looked hopefully at Antonio.

Giovanni swallowed a mouthful of red wine. 'I suggest you both go to Signora Pagano's. She has a boarding house in a place called The Rocks. You can easily walk to it from here. Tell her I sent you. I'll see you in a few days, Giuseppe, unless you find some work before then.' He smiled at both young men.

'You are very kind. Thank you, thank you,' said Giuseppe.

'Giuseppe, and you too, Antonio, I must give you a word of warning. It is hard to come to a new country and start a new life. In Australia things are done very differently from the way things are done in Italy, so be careful not to get into any trouble. You will learn.'

'I will never forget my welcome to Australia, Signor Bruscioli,' said Giuseppe, thinking how lucky he was to meet such a good man. He hoped Signor Bruscioli would prove to be as good as his word about finding a job for him.

*

Leaving Vincenzo with his uncle, Giuseppe and Antonio set out for The Rocks to find Signora Pagano's boarding house. The streets were winding lanes, crowded with narrow-fronted houses, some small shops and a few hotels.

'I see why this place is called The Rocks,' said Antonio, looking up at the sandstone cliff that rose above a row of small brick and sandstone houses standing hard against it. They knocked on the door of one of these houses.

The woman who opened the door was short and stoutly built, with grey strands in her dark knot of hair. She threw up her hands and shook her head. 'I have no room. I suppose you got off the *Ricconigi* this morning and have come here looking for a bed? Did someone send you?'

'Signora, Signor Bruscioli sent us. This is my friend Antonio. Soon he will be travelling north. Maybe I will go with him. I am Giuseppe.' He gave her his best smile. 'We would like a room for a short time, please.'

'Well, if that is the case, I have one room. You will have to share,' she said as she ushered them into the tiny two-storey terrace. 'You're Sicilian, eh?' she asked Giuseppe.

'Yes. I'm a fisherman. But I will do any work,' said Giuseppe quickly.

The house was small and dark and Giuseppe could see that the long passageway led to a tiny backyard where a clothesline, propped up by a tall sapling cut with a fork in its top, was strung with washing. Appetising aromas wafted from the kitchen and the house was clean. Their bedroom was compact with two small beds, a nightstand beside each, a trunk at the foot of each bed and a small wardrobe.

Signora Pagano handed them a sheet of paper on which was printed the weekly board, as well as some optional extras such as meals, laundry and ironing. 'If you want to take the room, I'll need a week's rent in advance,' she told them.

When Giuseppe and Antonio handed her their money, Signora Pagano's demeanour became more warm and welcoming.

'I'll get Luciano for you. He might be useful and help you settle in. He is from Naples,' she said.

'We've both been to Naples!' exclaimed Giuseppe.

'Then you will have something to talk about.'

She went to the narrow stairs and shouted. Luciano, a powerfully built Italian about their age, descended the stairs, and greeted Giuseppe and Antonio like cousins.

'Hello! You have just arrived? You have found the best home away from home. Signora is our mother. Also our father and nonna. She is the Big Boss.' He laughed. 'Do you have any plans?'

'Antonio is planning to join his relatives in Queensland, in the cane fields. I may go with him if I don't find any work in Sydney.'

'What sort of work are you looking for?' asked Luciano.

'On a fishing boat. Do you know anyone?' asked Giuseppe.

'Maybe. The Greeks run the fishing boats around here.' He paused. 'How did you find out about this place?'

'Our friend's uncle, Signor Bruscioli, told us to come here,' replied Antonio.

'You have important friends then. Perhaps you would like to come with me for a beer and we can talk some more,' suggested Luciano.

Giuseppe thought about his lack of funds, and decided that if Luciano could help him find work, the investment of a few pennies would be worthwhile. So the three of them set off for the nearest hotel.

'Where are these Greeks who fish?' asked Giuseppe as they walked.

'Around the harbour and over at Manly. Out at Bondi the fishermen sell their catch up on the beach in front of the shops, no one seems to mind. It's a good place, Bondi. You can take a tram right to the beach. There's a couple of boatsheds up at Ben Buckler. The Greeks clean the fish and sell them straight to the housewives. Signora Pagano gets me to buy fish at Bondi most Fridays.'

'Maybe I could exchange fish for board,' said Giuseppe, laughing. 'I am a good fisherman!'

'The Greeks might give you a try. But the Australians won't. They treat Italians like dirt because they think we're here to take their jobs.'

Giuseppe remembered the immigration official in Fremantle. He felt disappointed that according to Luciano this attitude was not exceptional and it showed on his face.

'Not all Australians think like that,' said Luciano when he saw Giuseppe's expression. 'Some of them are good people. You just have to find them.'

*

The corner hotel was dark and quiet. Several men stood at the bar wearing rough clothes, braces showing and with their sleeves rolled up, but they all seemed to have a jacket and hat within easy reach for the homeward trip. Two older men sat rolling cigarettes at a corner table, schooners of dark beer in front of them.

Giuseppe stopped in surprise when he saw a woman behind the bar. She was older than his sisters, and she wore her hair cut short and bright red lipstick. She stopped wiping the wet cloth along the counter and gave Luciano a smile.

'Hey there, Lucky. You've brought a couple of mates along. What's it to be, fellas?'

Giuseppe and Antonio exchanged looks as Luciano leaned on the counter. 'Give them the best beer you got on tap, Myrtle. This is Giuseppe from Sicily and Antonio from Sardinia.'

'Dagoes, I thought as much. Do you good-looking boys speaka da lingo?'

Giuseppe looked at Luciano in bewilderment. He didn't understand a word she was saying, let alone the fact she was there at all.

'She's asking if you want a beer,' said Luciano.

'Yes, thank you vēry much, I would like a beer, please.' Giuseppe ran the words of the sentence together, which made her chuckle.

'What're your plans?' she asked Antonio.

Antonio, who had virtually no English, had to wait for Luciano to translate. 'Please tell her that I'm going north, to Queensland.'

When the barmaid had been given the answer, she commented to Luciano, 'He doesn't look much like a cane cutter to me.' She glanced at Giuseppe. 'And what's your line?' she shouted, as she pushed three glasses with thick creamy collars across the counter, as though by raising her voice he would understand what she was asking. 'Who's buying?'

Luciano put some coins onto the counter. 'Me. It's a welcome to Australia drink.'

'They staying with the signora? Must be getting a bit crowded down there.'

Myrtle wrung out the beery cloth into the slops bucket under the bar as she studied Giuseppe. He gave her a smile and a cheeky wink. She laughed and said, 'He'll do all right. What kind of work you after?'

Giuseppe took a moment to understand she was asking him about work. 'I am a fisherman. I want to work on a fishing boat.'

'Lot of fish in the sea here,' Myrtle replied and yelled across to one of the old men in the corner. 'Hey, Wally, this young fellow wants to work on a fishing boat. Know anybody?'

The old man took a long drag on his cigarette. 'Might. S'long as he pulls his weight. Uses his muscles and not his mouth.'

Giuseppe put his beer down and went over and extended his hand. 'I am Giuseppe d'Aquino. I fish with my father, we catch the big tuna.'

Wally seemed a bit taken aback by his claim. 'You want to work on a boat? Hard yakka, mate.'

'Hard yakka? What is that?' Giuseppe asked.

'Bloody hard work,' was the answer.

'I work plenty hard,' Giuseppe replied.

Wally's companion shrugged. 'Could send him down to Con. He's always whingeing about his crew slacking off.'

Wally signalled to Luciano. 'Hey Lucky, get your mate to go down to Con's at Balmain. He's got a couple of fishing boats. Could be something there.'

Giuseppe didn't quite follow all of this, but he nodded enthusiastically and turned to Luciano. 'Where do I go?'

'I'll draw you a map, luv,' called Myrtle. 'I know the area.'

Giuseppe tried to thank the two men, but they had turned back to their drinks. He swallowed his beer and drew a breath. 'This *birra*, is strong, eh?' he said to Myrtle. 'You have vino?'

'Wine? This is a pub, luv, only alkies drink that sort of stuff, usually out of a brown paper bag,' Myrtle said.

When Luciano had explained what Myrtle had said, Giuseppe looked around at the empty bar and commented, 'No wonder nobody is here to drink.'

Luciano smiled. 'You wait till five. Then Myrtle gets really busy.'

She grimaced. 'Runs me off me feet, the bloody six o'clock swill. Place is like a pigsty. Get your mates outta here before then,' she advised.

'What is this six o'clock swill?' asked Giuseppe.

'Pubs all shut at six,' replied Luciano. 'It's the law. So when everyone finishes work they hit the pub, line up as many beers as possible and drink them as fast as they can.'

'That is crazy,' Giuseppe told Myrtle.

'You got that right,' agreed Myrtle. 'Drink fast and go home sozzled. Give their families hell. Here. This is the address and directions to Balmain.' She gave Giuseppe a dirty piece of paper with a map scrawled on it. 'And,' she added, 'can you give this to Signora Pagano, too?'

To the young men's shock she put her hand down her blouse, pulled out an envelope and handed it to Luciano.

'These are her winnings from the fourth last Saturday. Don't lose them!'

Confused, embarrassed and having no idea what Myrtle was talking about, Antonio and Giuseppe backed out of the bar.

'Her boss is the local SP bookie,' said Luciano. He explained that people were only allowed to bet on the horses at the race track, so the publican took bets for his customers who couldn't get there.

'Of course,' he admitted, 'it's illegal to do this, but lots of people do it, in pubs, barber shops, tobacconists. The police mostly turn a blind eye.'

'Myrtle is a kind lady,' said Giuseppe.

'Barmaids are not ladies,' said Luciano. 'It's not something we would like our mothers and sisters doing.'

'So you don't see proper ladies in there?' jumped in Antonio.

'Not really,' said Luciano lightly. 'When women come into a pub they have a special room to drink in.'

'Well, I thought Myrtle was nice,' said Giuseppe. 'But maybe I should try Bondi first. I'll find Con later if I need to. Do you want to come too, Antonio?'

'No, I think I'll go and find Vincenzo. I'll meet you for dinner tonight.'

Luciano told Giuseppe where to get the tram for Bondi and how much he would need to pay so Giuseppe had little trouble in finding the beach.

His first sight of Bondi Beach as the tram turned down Bondi Road took his breath away. He'd seen some beautiful bays and beaches in his homeland, but this huge expanse of golden sand flanked by rocky headlands caught him by surprise.

No wonder it was crowded with people enjoying themselves. There were motor vehicles parked along the foreshore. People were strolling along the promenade and children were building castles in the sand. There were places to eat and drink, tea rooms and hotels and a great many shops. The colours were so bright and the whole place had a holiday atmosphere. Yet it was still so close to the city.

Giuseppe saw a tea room called Ravesi's, and walked over to it. He asked the Italian waiter working there where he could buy fresh fish.

'There's a Greek fish shop down the road, but you can also buy directly from the fishermen down on the beach or over by the rocks. They sell right from their boat. They should still be about,' he told Giuseppe.

Giuseppe found a small boatshed and a clutter of boats, nets, ropes, baskets and boxes piled on the beach.

There were men sitting around talking and smoking as they cleaned up from the night's catch and morning's fish sale. They all seemed to be Greek.

Giuseppe crouched down and poked through the last box of fish, which had been passed over by customers. 'These for bait?' he asked.

'Help yourself,' said a large man. 'You want to fish? Or to eat?'

'I like to do both,' said Giuseppe in careful English. 'I'm looking for work.'

'You an Italian boy? Just arrived, hey?'

'*Si*. Giuseppe d'Aquino. From Sicily. My father is a fisherman.'

To Giuseppe's surprise the large Greek answered him in Italian. 'I am Kostas. I have worked with Italian men in Australia. They show us all the tricks and places. You worked on a trawler?'

'No. My father and brother have a *barca* . . . but we catch some big tuna. I am the capo,' said Giuseppe proudly. 'I work hard. What fish do you go after here?'

'You'd be surprised what's out there. The harbour is good, and there's plenty of shellfish around the rocks. Rock fish. Outside the harbour, in places close to shore, we chase the big schools when they come by. My cousin has a trawler. Fantastic boat. But the sea out there,' he lifted his chin towards the ocean, 'she can be cruel.'

Giuseppe listened, nodding with interest. He knew that in these foreign waters there would be many species of fish he was unfamiliar with but he had no doubt he could work as hard as anyone else to catch them.

'I want very much to work, to learn. I am happy on the water.'

Kostas laughed and turned to the other men and spoke to them in Greek. Then he said to Giuseppe, 'Why should I hire you, a new kid who knows nothing of these waters? I know a dozen kids, family and friends of friends, I could hire.'

'They don't love the sea as I do! I learn fast, I can find fish and I work hard. I am strong. I can do many things. I will clean the fish, wash the boat, fix nets and ropes. Clean the bottom of the boat . . . anything you ask.'

Kostas held up his hand. 'After you clean the fish, can you sell the fish? Tell the housewives how to cook this fish?' He raised his dark bushy eyebrows.

Giuseppe wasn't sure if he was making a joke or if that was part of the job. 'I prefer to catch them and then eat them after they are cooked by a beautiful woman.'

Kostas roared with laughter. 'I don't think you'd have much trouble selling fish or anything else. But I want to see you catch them. Come here tonight ready to go fishing. We go for snapper and flathead.' He held out his hand. 'Come out on a trial run with us. We'll see how you go.'

'Thank you, thank you.' Giuseppe eyed the small scrappy fish left in the box. 'How much for some for my dinner?'

Kostas scooped up a handful of the little fish and rolled them in newspaper. 'Here, take them.'

Giuseppe thanked him and sprinted back to the tram.

At the boarding house he handed the fish to Signora Pagano. 'For supper. And if I get a job fishing with Kostas, we will eat many, many fish!' he exclaimed proudly.

'I will make zuppa di pesce for dinner tonight.' She smiled at Giuseppe. 'I hope you get the job with the Greeks.'

*

It was a calm night and turned out to be a lucky one. They went out from Ben Buckler and lined the boat up with part of the headland. Kostas used live bait from the tin bucket and he showed Giuseppe the best lure and lead to use.

'Better to let the bait swim so the lead drags along the bottom. Give him a jig up and down every so often to get the flathead's attention. He might make a couple of runs before he takes the bait, but he comes up easy if he swallows it. But if he comes to the boat, don't pull his head out of the water, he'll panic and shake his head and chew through the line. Wait to net him. You understand?' explained Kostas.

It wasn't long before Giuseppe caught his first flathead.

'It's not so big,' he said, feeling disappointed.

'It's all right. Plate size tastes better than the big ones. Look out for the spike here on the head,' said Kostas, quickly piercing the flat skull of the dark speckled fish.

The evening sped by. Giuseppe was happy to be back on the water and catching fish. They moved around to a few favoured spots, landing some silvery pink, bump-headed snapper and some flounder. He was amazed by the different species they caught and quickly realised how the seabed varied from reef to sandy weed and deeper holes. Giuseppe asked Kostas lots of questions and learned rapidly. The other three crew kept to themselves, though they seemed friendly and encouraging enough. In the early hours Kostas headed back to shore.

Giuseppe looked at the waves crashing on the rocks around the headland. 'This is a good place for shellfish?'

Kostas nodded. 'But dangerous. People get washed away. You have to know the tides and be careful of rogue waves.'

Giuseppe nodded and resolved he would have to study this coastline and learn as much as he could. He hoped that Kostas would hire him and then he could save money and invest in his own fishing gear.

Once they had brought their catch to shore, Kostas told Giuseppe to clean the fish. The men worked fast, so that by the time the sun came up all was ready for the first buyers. They mainly came from the local restaurants and fish shops around the eastern suburbs but also from the city. Kostas did all the selling.

When all the fish had been sold, Kostas handed Giuseppe some money.

'You did okay. I saved a small snapper for you so you know how it tastes. If you want, come back tonight,' he said.

Giuseppe broke into a wide smile. 'I have a job fishing with you?'

'For the time being,' said Kostas.

Within a week Giuseppe had become one of Kostas's permanent crew.

*

The following Friday afternoon, Giuseppe decided to visit Giovanni Bruscioli and share the good news that he was working as a fisherman.

Long before he reached Giovanni's warehouse at the wharves, he could hear music and smell delicious food. Giovanni greeted him like a long-lost relative, poured him a glass of wine and sat him down to ask him what he'd been doing.

Giuseppe thanked Giovanni for the introduction to Signora Pagano and then handed him a parcel of fresh fish and told him about the job with Kostas.

'The Greeks are good fishermen. But so are the Italians. You should go south one day and see where they have made their mark in Wollongong and further down the coast.'

'Are these places far away? Because I have no money to travel. And I would rather find my way around this huge harbour. There are waterways that seem to go to the moon!' exclaimed Giuseppe. 'Kostas showed me his map.'

'Yes, but it is not just Sydney Harbour that is magnificent! North is the Hawkesbury River and Pittwater in from West Head, the northern beaches – they all are incredible.' He shouted across the table. 'Stefano, where's your brother's boat? We want to take Giuseppe for a trip!'

*

On the next Sunday Giuseppe, Antonio and Luciano found themselves walking along the pier at Rose Bay, wondering if they were at the right place. They had imagined that they would be going out on a smelly fishing boat, with garlicky picnic food and no shelter from the sun or rain, in the company of other migrant fishermen. But here was a very different world. This place was full of sleek yachts and elegant motor boats.

They were stunned when they boarded Stefano's brother's boat. It was a converted ferry, trimmed with teak and brass fittings; it had comfortable tables and chairs on the deck and bunks below. Food and drinks were already spread out and, although it was not his boat, Giovanni held centre stage. He kept calling Giuseppe and Antonio to come close and then he introduced them to people who all smiled at the handsome new arrivals. Everyone was talking in voluble Italian.

One dark-eyed woman was dressed in a white silk dress with a wide lace hem, a stylish hat and carried a Chinese parasol. She lazily smoked a cigarette as she cast her eye over Giuseppe.

'Who are you?' she asked.

'I am Giuseppe.' Tentatively he shook her hand.

She turned to Giovanni. 'Where have you been hiding this sweet boy?'

Giovanni made a small gesture and replied, 'He is fresh from Sicily, still learning the ropes as you say. Don't frighten him away, Sophia. He is a fisherman.'

She turned her large eyes, outlined in black, to Giuseppe. 'I love fresh fish. Where do you sell your fish, Giuseppe?' She rolled his name off her tongue and another woman in a pleated skirt gave a throaty laugh.

'I work for Kostas the Greek. He sells seafood from the beach at Bondi.'

'Giuseppe, you need your own boat. He must start his own business, Giovanni. Why don't you help him?'

'Oh. No! It will be a long time before I have my own boat,' exclaimed Giuseppe. 'I am still learning where the fish are here.'

'I bet you're a fast learner,' said Sophia, with a smile. She and her friend laughed again, but Giuseppe felt uncomfortable and excused himself. He was quite shocked by the way these women dressed, showing bare arms and wearing brightly coloured lipstick. In comparison the men were conservatively dressed but even Giuseppe knew that their clothes were expensive and most carried gold watches.

Their boat motored slowly around the reaches and bays of the harbour, and Giuseppe lost interest in his fellow passengers, preferring to pay close attention to where they were going and mentally mapping the inlets and coves in his head.

'I wish I did have a boat. I bet there is good fishing in places like these,' he said to Antonio.

'Look at the houses, they are so big. Some even have their own jetties,' said Antonio.

'Maybe that's where the people on this boat live,' said Giuseppe.

'It wouldn't surprise me. I heard them talking about racehorses and betting. I think one of them is a bookmaker. Like the SP bookie at Myrtle's hotel,' said Antonio.

'Whatever they're doing, they are making money,' said Giuseppe, sighing. 'Kostas is kind, but I would like to make more money. I need a second job.'

'When are you going to do that?' said Luciano. 'You're out fishing with the Greeks nearly every night.'

'If I had my own boat, just a small one, I could row around places like this and catch my own fish and sell them before I go to Kostas in the evening.'

'Where would you sell them?' asked Giovanni, appearing behind them.

'I would take my fish to these rich houses and sell them, fresh,' he said with sudden enthusiasm.

Giovanni smiled. 'I'm sure you would do very well.'

By the time they docked later that evening, the long lunch had become an extended dinner. The women pleaded with Giuseppe and Antonio to stay, but both were anxious to go back to Signora Pagano's where supper would be waiting.

Sophia held Giuseppe's hand for a long time as he said his farewells. 'I know we will meet again. Come and see me, I'm sure I can help you get that boat.' She gave a smile. 'Ciao, baby.'

Over their supper that night Antonio entertained the signora and the other boarders with stories about their day out on the rich man's boat, telling them all what a success Giuseppe had been with one woman in particular.

While everyone chuckled with amusement, Signora Pagano snorted.

'She does not sound to me the sort of woman that your poor mamma would think suitable for you,' she said sternly.

Giuseppe ate his fish and said nothing.

He laughed when the other boarders teased him, but Giuseppe started to think deeply about the idea of catching and selling fish himself.

During his time alone, he began to walk around the harbour foreshores. When he was familiar with the eastern side, he talked Antonio and Luciano into taking the ferry across to Manly, on the other side of Sydney Harbour.

They walked from the wharf to Sydney Road and, as they passed the Britannia De-Luxe picture theatre, Luciano said, 'Why don't we go in? Everyone says that *The Mask of Zorro* is a wonderful movie. Do you want to give it a try?'

Giuseppe was not going to tell either of his friends that he had never been to see a moving picture so he agreed. He could scarcely contain his anticipation as they joined the queue to buy a ticket. Inside, Giuseppe stared in awe at the ornate ceiling and the elaborate red curtain. He roared with laughter at the antics of the very stupid Keystone Cops, but when *The Mask of Zorro* started he could hardly believe what he was seeing. The screen was so big that the actors seemed to be in the theatre with them. He watched in amazement as Douglas Fairbanks, playing Zorro, escaped trap after trap, fighting his way out of trouble with amazing swordsmanship. How he wished he was like that, so dashing and so brave. While all the action was going on, the Grand Symphony Orchestra played, enhancing the mood of excitement of the silent movie. Although the captions that flashed onto the screen were in English, they were short enough for him to be able to understand. In his whole life he had never been so enthralled. Afterwards the three of them joined the crowd and strolled along the Corso. The beautifully curved beach was popular with swimmers and families picnicked on the grass beneath the young pine trees. As the young men walked around the rocks to Shelly Beach, Giuseppe mentally made a note of the spots that would be good for fishing. But his dream of fishing the coves and bays of the harbour was firmly lodged in his mind. The more he thought about it, the more he realised that the only person who could help his ambitions was Giovanni.

When Giuseppe told him what he wanted, Giovanni said, 'Show me what you have in mind.'

Giuseppe enthusiastically produced a map he had borrowed from Kostas. 'These are the places I want to fish. I'm after flathead and snapper, maybe flounder, and whiting in the sand beds. I have walked around Balmain and Birchgrove and other harbour places where there are a lot of houses and I think I could sell my fish from the wharf or visit the houses along the waterfront and dockyard area. Perhaps ask a shopkeeper or two if they want to take my fish.'

'And what about fishing gear? If you are going into competition with Kostas will he loan you crab pots and nets as well as lines?'

Giuseppe nodded. 'I explained to him what I want to do. He says that as long as I still work for him, he doesn't mind and he will lend me some lines.'

'I will see what I can do.'

*

A few days later Giuseppe received a note at the boarding house from Giovanni, telling him to come to his warehouse. There he showed Giuseppe an old wooden skiff tied up at the wharf.

'Let me see you row,' Giovanni said.

Giuseppe was delighted to see the old boat. He quickly climbed down the wharf steps, clambered into the little boat and, after placing the oars into the rowlocks, started to row out into the harbour.

'Good, good,' called Giovanni. 'You can bring her back now.'

Giuseppe picked up the painter and prepared to tie the boat up but before he could Giovanni grasped the rope and threw it to Giuseppe.

'Take it. Keep it round at Balmain. Use one of the boatsheds. This skiff is on loan until you can buy your own boat, so don't take it out in bad weather, and don't go out through the heads.'

Giovanni's generosity astonished Giuseppe. He stammered, 'How do I thank you, Giovanni? I will bring you fish every week. I promise.'

'You are a bright boy, a nice boy, Giuseppe. I like you. I want to see you get ahead but there is no easy way to make money except by hard work.'

'I understand,' he answered. 'And I will work hard.'

*

Several mornings later Kostas left Giuseppe on the beach to sell the last of their catch to any latecomers. Kostas was going to look at a trawler that had come up for sale so that he could start netting the prawn grounds.

Most of the shopkeepers, restaurant buyers and local women shoppers had long gone, but it was pleasant sitting in the sun watching the seagulls jostle for scraps or pounce on the tiny crabs that appeared on the wet sand as the tide ran out.

He slid Kostas's cotton Greek fishing cap over his eyes and started to doze.

'Giuseppe? Yes, it is Giuseppe. Ooh, sorry, did I disturb you?'

The voice was faintly amused and familiar. Giuseppe jerked awake, and took off the cap. 'Sophia! This is a surprise!'

She was wearing a light crêpe de Chine dress that blew around her legs, and a shady hat that gave her a casual air. Her fingernails and lips were a startling red. She was so different from the women and girls Giuseppe knew at home. She was older than he was and so independent and forthright. He found her company exhilarating.

'How is the fish-selling business today?'

'You should have come earlier. There is nothing left,' exclaimed Giuseppe, but she shook her head.

'That is all right. I don't feel like eating fish today. I came for a walk by the sea and thought I might take a small cool drink at Ravesi's. Will you join me?'

'Sophia, I am not dressed to go with you,' said Giuseppe, feeling embarrassed at his old clothes. 'I have been working. I smell of fish!'

'*Phhft*, jump in the ocean then!' she laughed. 'Go on. I will watch you. Can you swim?'

'Of course. I have swum all my life.'

Giuseppe felt she was challenging him so he tore off his shirt and sprinted across the beach into the water and dived into a wave, then he surfaced and swam the way he'd learned as a boy in the deep still waters around his island. Feeling refreshed and pleased with himself he shook the water from his dark hair and made his way back to Sophia, but before he reached her, he was confronted by a large man in a suit.

'You can't do this,' the man said.

Giuseppe looked around in bewilderment. He had no idea what the man meant. Perhaps it was because he still didn't understand English very well. '*Scusi?*'

'You can't go around dressed indecently like this,' roared the man. 'You have to be dressed properly on the beach. I'll have to fine you.'

Giuseppe still had no idea what the man was talking about but before he asked a question, Sophia joined them. She said something quickly to the man, giving him her most gracious smile. The man, however, was not placated.

'What is it, Sophia? What have I done to upset this man?'

'He is a beach inspector and when you swim at Bondi, you have to keep a top on. You didn't, so I'm afraid that he is going to fine you.'

'But I have no money. How can he fine me? I cannot pay.'

'Tell your friend that if he doesn't pay the fine, he'll go to gaol,' said the inspector.

Giuseppe understood enough of what he was saying to be completely horrified. 'Sophia, the only money I have belongs to Kostas. I cannot use that and if I go to gaol, I will lose my job with him and will not be able to buy the boat from Giovanni. This is a catastrophe.'

Sophia smiled at the inspector. 'Please understand, sir, my friend has just arrived in Australia and he did not understand how he was meant to behave on Bondi Beach. Could you let him off this time? I would not like to have to write to his old mother and tell her what has become of her boy. It would break her heart.'

The beach inspector looked at Sophia's entreating face as she pleaded with him. 'Just because he didn't know is no excuse, miss, but I suppose I could let him off with a warning, especially as there aren't many people around.' Then he turned to Giuseppe and said very slowly, 'You come to Australia, you obey Australian laws. If I ever catch you again in such a shocking display, I'll throw the book at you.'

Giuseppe wasn't sure what book he was talking about and didn't like to ask. When the beach inspector walked away, Giuseppe realised that Sophia had managed to talk the man around and that he would not be going to gaol.

'How can I thank you, Sophia? I thought that I would be sent to gaol for doing something that I have always done at home. This is a very difficult country to understand.'

'These things happen. Don't worry about it,' she said lightly. 'How about that drink?'

'Why not? I've finished selling Kostas's fish. It will take me a few moments to dry off.'

'Joe, by the time we walk to Ravesi's you'll be dry.'
She stood up as he ran his fingers through his hair to try
and smooth it before pulling on his cap.

'Joe? What is Joe? Why do you call me Joe?'

'That's your name in Australia. Giuseppe in Italy, Joe
in Australia. It's a good strong name. Let's go.'

She walked beside him as if it was the most natural
thing in the world, but suddenly Giuseppe stopped.

'My money! I have only Kostas's fish money!'

Sophia touched his arm. 'I invited you. So I pay. It is
the modern way.'

Sophia seemed to be no hurry and ordered some small
dishes of food to eat with their drinks. Giuseppe learned
a little more about her. She told him she had no children
but he wasn't sure if she had ever been married. Perhaps
she was a divorced woman. Giuseppe had never met a
divorced woman before.

'I have never felt the need to marry and conform and be
a good wife. I am sure that would shock your mother, Joe.'

She was right. His mother would not approve of a
woman like Sophia, but he thought she had a good heart
and she was generous and she seemed to like him, which
flattered him. Just the same, he wondered why she had
allowed him to take his shirt off on Bondi Beach when
she knew that it was against the law. It was a puzzle he
couldn't solve.

'Tell me, Joe, what have you been up to? What are
your plans?'

Eagerly he told her how Giovanni had loaned him a
small boat to start fishing for himself when he was not
working for Kostas.

Sophia nodded. 'This is good. You need to find places to
fish where you know you will always have a good supply.'

'Yes, I am doing that. Every day I am not working
for Kostas I find good fishing spots. Sometimes I dive

overboard and swim around to see what is below, so I know where reefs and ledges and sandy weed beds are.'

'Joe, that can be dangerous. In Australia, the sharks, they eat you! Where are you going to sell the fish after you catch them?' She leaned across the table, looking into his eyes.

'I will sell them on the wharf, or go from house to house. This is what Giovanni and I have decided.'

'Sell direct to customers. What a splendid idea. Your street is the water! Think of all the houses around the city where there are wharves, public and private. If you took the fish direct from the sea to people's homes, how fresh would that be?' She patted his hand. 'And I will be your first customer.'

That evening his plans were discussed around the supper table in the kitchen of Signora Pagano's boarding house.

'You need to work out a route and let people know when you will be there at the wharf, and you must be regular and reliable,' said Signora Pagano.

'How will you keep the fish cool and fresh? Drag them in a sack in the water behind you?' said Luciano.

'If you do that, the sharks will follow you and you'll have a sack full of holes,' said Signora Pagano.

'I will do what Kostas does. Put them in boxes with smashed-up blocks of ice and cover them with hessian bags. I will talk to the iceman who comes here and offer him some fish in exchange for a discount on the ice.'

'Giuseppe, that's a good idea,' said Antonio.

'My Australian friends call me Joe,' said Giuseppe.

'Yes, I am called Lucky,' said Luciano.

'Then I will be Tony,' said Antonio, and the three men raised their glasses to salute their new names.

*

Giuseppe spent days getting used to the little boat and the conditions around the Balmain area. The foreshores were dotted with grand homes as well as the more modest houses that had been built for the men working at Mort's dockyard. Giuseppe planned to sell his catch from the ferry wharf or go door to door asking housewives if they might be interested in buying fresh fish from him.

Sophia took a keen interest in his idea and often called by Kostas at the beach to offer suggestions about how Giuseppe should present himself and what he should say. Finally she suggested he come and visit her house on the waterfront at Balmain so she could introduce him to her neighbours.

Giuseppe rowed to Sophia's jetty and walked up the flagstone steps to her sandstone house with its sweeping views across the harbour. Sophia came to meet him in bare feet and without her usual bright lipstick. With the breeze ruffling her hair, she looked surprisingly young.

'Hello, Joe! Are you ready for a cold drink?'

She brought out a tray with biscuits and a jug of cordial, which she placed on an outdoor table.

'You look hot from all that rowing. Perhaps you should change into your fish-selling uniform.' Giuseppe looked puzzled and Sophia smiled. 'I have a small present for you and your business.'

She disappeared indoors and quickly returned with some folded clothes. 'Try these on.' She held up a heavy cotton apron that had the words 'Joe's Fresh Fish, Straight from the Sea', printed across it. 'I also have this.' She held up a crisp white shirt. 'If you leave your uniform here each week I can launder it for you. Then you won't look like you've just rowed for miles and miles. When it comes to food, women like a salesman to look clean. Hot and sweaty is for the bedroom,' she laughed.

Giuseppe was flustered and didn't know what to say. 'Sophia, this is too much. You are so kind . . .'

She blew him a kiss. 'Go and change and walk with me around the neighbourhood. I'll introduce you to a few people I know well. Then you are on your own.'

The people to whom Sophia introduced Giuseppe seemed delighted to meet him although a couple made teasing remarks about her handsome friend, Joe the fisherman. After these initial introductions, she sent him on alone.

'You'll be fine by yourself,' she reassured him. 'Meet me back at my house when you're finished and tell me how you went.'

He was feeling very positive when he met Sophia back at her house and took off his shirt and apron, folded them carefully and gave them to her.

'Keep the apron, Joe, but this shirt will stay here. I will wash it for you and that way you always have to visit me,' she said.

'And when I do, I will give you my very best snapper fillets,' he said.

'Thank you, Joe. I hope you are always so confident about catching fish. Have you told Kostas of your plan?'

'Yes. As long as it doesn't stop me working on his boat he is okay with me fishing alone with a hand line. I won't show him the apron, though,' he added. 'I am also going after lobster. One woman in a big house said she would be interested if I caught some.'

'I knew you had a good head on your shoulders,' she exclaimed. 'You will do well.'

'Thanks to you, Sophia,' began Giuseppe, 'I don't know how to thank you. You, Giovanni, Signora Pagano, Kostas, so many people have been kind to me.'

She patted his arm. 'You have a good soul, a nice boy. People like you, but try to be careful. You can't trust everyone, you know.'

'No, no,' replied Giuseppe. 'I know. And I am still learning here. Let me see if I am any good.'

*

Giuseppe spent two weeks working out his route around the harbourside suburbs of Balmain and Birchgrove and further away to Woolwich, Greenwich and Hunter's Hill. He still worked for Kostas but he also fished for a few hours on the afternoons he had off. Slowly he learned about the harbour; where to drift, where to enter the quiet coves, where to anchor and where to fish the rocky shelves. He set several lines at a time and occasionally went over the shallow sandbars to net whiting and mullet. Sometimes he caught a fat squid that he would take back to Signora Pagano, who would slice and fry it with garlic. Australians, Kostas had already told him, didn't eat squid.

Finally, when the mid-sized snapper were plentiful he started to make his rounds. Dressed in his clean white shirt and apron, he had no trouble selling his snapper fillets, sweet whiting and flathead. But he did have trouble selling the leatherjackets for, although they were plentiful – indeed they were often in plague proportions around his lines, people didn't like their tough skins, even when Giuseppe explained that if the skin was stripped away, the delicate flesh was light and tasty.

Giuseppe always priced his fish competitively and it didn't take long for the women of Balmain to start buying from the handsome young fishmonger who obligingly filleted and cleaned the fish the way they liked.

*

Sitting beneath the pergola at Sophia's after he had completed his rounds, Giuseppe raised his glass of wine.

'Thank you, Sophia, for all your help. You have been so kind.'

'Joe, you work hard. You deserve to do well.' She leaned over and smoothed his hair.

The gentle caress suddenly made Giuseppe feel light-headed. He closed his eyes and touched Sophia's hand. Gently she pulled his head towards her and kissed him lightly on the lips. The blood rushed to Giuseppe's head and, what with the wine, the perfume of the flowers and Sophia's soft presence, he returned her kiss with feeling. Then, gathering his courage, he wrapped his arms around Sophia and drew her close. But it was Sophia who took control and, still holding each other, she led him inside to her cool white bedroom.

At first Giuseppe was shy, but he couldn't contain the passion Sophia had aroused in him. She gently guided him, smiling at his eagerness, until she could resist no longer, and, moaning softly, allowed Giuseppe to discover for the first time the pleasures of a woman's body.

Later, as they lay together naked, Giuseppe felt truly a man. His shyness had melted and he felt free to touch and explore Sophia's shapely body and kiss her creamy smooth skin. The knowledge that he could give pleasure and make a woman yearn for him gave him a heady sensation.

But soon enough Sophia sat up and nudged him from the bed.

'It is time you returned home. You will be all right, rowing home this late?'

Giuseppe lifted his arms. 'I am full of strength! And now the moon is up. I will row home and sing love songs at the top of my voice!'

'No, you will not. What will the neighbours think?' she admonished him with a smile. 'Go quietly. There is no need to let the world know you have been here so late. Believe me, it is best,' she said firmly.

'Yes, Sophia,' he said meekly. 'Can I come again?'

She smiled and tilted her head coquettishly. 'Maybe.'

'I have left my best snapper fillets for you in the kitchen. I hope you will enjoy them.'

*

On his days off from working with Kostas, Giuseppe would bring his finest fish for Sophia and she would take him to her bed where they would make love.

When he returned to the boarding house one evening, Antonio asked him where he had been. Giuseppe told him about Sophia, in part to let his friend know that he had moved on after his experiences with Bridie.

'I hope you know what you are doing,' said Antonio. 'She's not married, is she?'

'No, of course not.'

'And she lives in a big house. How does she manage to afford such a place?' Antonio asked. 'How old is she?'

Giuseppe was uncomfortable with such direct questions from his friend. 'She looks and seems young. Maybe a little older than me,' he added.

'I've seen Sophia. An attractive woman like her is bound to have rich men friends. Men who would not like you, Joe,' said Antonio. 'You could get into trouble if one of her boyfriends finds out about you. Maybe you should stop seeing her, but you won't, will you. Just be careful, okay, Joe?'

*

But the first threats to Giuseppe came from a very different direction. One morning, before Kostas and the crew started out for the day, the Greek pulled Giuseppe aside.

'I have had a visit from my friend Con. He has sold fish in Balmain for a long time and he knows how you are going around, knocking on doors, and selling your fish in his territory. He told me to tell you to get out of his area.'

'What did you say?' asked Giuseppe. 'I think that if women want to buy fish from me, that is their decision, not his.'

'I told him I would speak to you. I think that maybe you should listen to this advice. Con has some friends who could make things dangerous for you if you continue to enter his territory. I told him that you will stop selling fish in Balmain. I think it's for the best, Joe,' Kostas said.

Giuseppe realised that the Greek was giving him a gentle warning, but he wondered how he would now be able to make money to buy the skiff.

*

Although he no longer sold fish in Balmain, Giuseppe continued to visit Sophia and make love to her. One evening as they lay in bed, Giuseppe asked her why they couldn't do something else as well.

'Why can't we go out somewhere, just to walk or to sit by the ocean?' he asked.

She ruffled his hair. 'Joe, don't you like our time together? Why should we go out?'

'I thought I would save my money to take you to dinner.'

'Don't waste your money on me. I like staying here.'

'You don't want people to see you with me,' he blurted. 'You are ashamed of this poor Italian boy!'

'Don't be silly.' She curled herself around him on the bed. 'I just want to keep you all to myself.'

She pulled his head towards her and started kissing him passionately, as if to prove her point. But suddenly she jerked away from him and jumped off the bed. 'Listen. There's a car outside. Didn't you hear its door slam? Quickly, take your clothes, you must go.'

'Can't you send them away?' asked Giuseppe.

'No, no. Quickly. Go out the back way and get into your boat. But be very quiet. Wait a while before you start rowing.' She pulled on a silk kimono and pushed the naked Giuseppe through the doors and out onto the terrace, throwing his clothes after him. He heard muffled voices coming from the hallway, so he hurried through the garden, pulling up his pants as he went, and went down the stone steps to his boat. He was about to get into it when he discovered he had left his shoes behind. He didn't want to leave them behind as they were his only pair, so he decided to wait till the visitors drove away.

It could not have been more than half an hour before he heard the car leave, so Giuseppe tip-toed back up to the house. The lights were out so he called Sophia's name softly. She didn't answer and Giuseppe realised that she must have gone with whoever it was who had come in the car.

He checked the doors to try to get in to retrieve his shoes but they were all locked. A slight noise made him spin around and, in the light from the rising moon, he saw Sophia's beloved fat cat eating its dinner. He was about to leave when he saw what was in the cat's dish. It was eating snapper fillet.

Angrily he pushed the cat away and snatched up the last remaining piece.

'She feeds the cat the fine fish I bring for her!' he shouted. In a flash he knew that Sophia had never eaten any of his fish. She had fed it to her spoiled cat.

*

Two days later, as he was selling Kostas's fish on Bondi Beach, Sophia turned up and walked over to Giuseppe.

'Joe, I'm sorry about the other night. You left these behind.' She held out a brown paper bag with his shoes inside. 'When one of my friends saw them, they caused me

93

some trouble. My fault of course, but my friend didn't like the idea that I was seeing someone else. It would be safest if you didn't come around for a while.'

'Is he your boyfriend?' asked Giuseppe.

'Just one of my friends, but they all like to think they own me. They don't, but if they find out who you are, they will cause you trouble. They are dangerous men.'

'If they are dangerous, why are they your friends? I don't understand.' Then in a rush of hurt feelings he demanded, 'How could you give my fish to your cat?'

'Poor Joe, I don't really like fish and I didn't want to waste it after all the trouble you took to bring it to me.'

'Those men. I could protect you,' said Giuseppe.

'No, you couldn't. They are ruthless. I am sorry that I put you in danger, but the best thing I can do for you right now is to tell you to stay away from me. Maybe get away from Sydney for a while. It's a pity that this is the way it turned out, Giuseppe, but there it is.' With a small smile, Sophia put a finger to her lips and then placed it on Giuseppe's. Then she turned and walked up the beach.

As he watched her walk away, Kostas came over and gave him a shrewd look. 'You had a tiff with your lady friend?'

'She isn't my friend anymore. I cannot see her again. Her boyfriends don't like me.'

Kostas shrugged. 'Women like that have rich ugly boyfriends. Keep away.'

'She told me to leave Sydney because it could be dangerous for me, but her friends don't know me.'

'They have ways of finding out. I bet the neighbours have seen you and your boat hanging about.'

Giuseppe didn't like the sound of this at all, so he decided that he would find Giovanni and ask him for advice.

*

Giovanni listened to Giuseppe's story about Sophia and nodded.

'I saw she had picked you out on the boat that day, like a ripe peach.' He smiled. 'I can't blame you for liking her, she is a vibrant woman, but she moves in a circle that's not for you, Joe. Your Greek friend is right. Sophia is a lovely lady, but she mixes with some bad people. If they find out who you are, you could be in trouble. I think you should leave Sydney for a while. In a few months you can return, I'm sure.'

'But where can I go? I only know about fishing.'

'And you are a good, hard-working fisherman. Remember the Italian fishing community I told you about just a little south of here, in Wollongong? They are friends of mine and they will help you.'

'That sounds like a good idea. Maybe after I have stayed there for a while, I can go to Queensland and cut sugar cane to make money.'

'When you get to Wollongong, find the Riviera family, they will look after you. I'll send them a message so they will be expecting you.'

'You know people everywhere,' said Giuseppe. 'How can I thank you for the loan of your boat? I am frustrated I can't keep fishing and selling door to door.'

'We Italians have to stick together. Get started in Wollongong and then come back here or go to Queensland, but make sure you have money in your pocket.'

'Why am I always doing the wrong thing? Now I am running away. Or being chased away,' said Giuseppe, sighing.

'You are in a new country, with different customs, different ways of doing things. But you'll find this is a good country with opportunities if you work hard and keep your nose clean – as they say here.'

Giuseppe was sad about leaving Signora Pagano's boarding house and the friends he'd made there. But when he told everyone at dinner that night what had happened at Sophia's place as well as the threats he'd received from Con, and raised the idea of going south, they all agreed that it was a wise idea.

'You take the train, Joe,' said Signora Pagano. 'Then look up these Italian fishing people. If they are friends of Signor Bruscioli, they will give you a job, without a doubt.'

The next morning, Antonio and Luciano went with Giuseppe to Central Railway Station with its grand sandstone entrance and large clock tower. They found the right platform and waited with Giuseppe until it was time to board the train.

The three friends embraced.

'Good luck, Tony, my friend. I hope Queensland works out for you and you don't have to cut cane for too long!'

'When the season is over I will come to the ocean and stay with you and we can fish together!' said Antonio, laughing.

'Good luck, Joe,' said Luciano. 'And look out for the ladies!'

On board Giuseppe stowed his suitcase and pushed open the window to wave to his two friends as the steam engine gathered speed and rolled smoothly away from the station.

The trip passed quickly. Giuseppe enjoyed the spectacular scenery as the train track twisted and turned down steep grades and through tunnels before arriving in Wollongong. The town was situated on a sheltered section of coast beside the blue Pacific Ocean in the shadow of the huge sandstone Illawarra escarpment, which towered above it.

Following Giovanni's instructions, Giuseppe found the house he was looking for at Brighton Beach, right on the harbour. He could hear voices out the back, so he walked around the side of the large house and found a group of Italians sitting in the back garden. Shyly he asked the men which of them was Franco Riviera.

A weather-beaten Italian dressed in old trousers and shirt but with an assured manner came over to greet him.

'So you are Joe? My good friend Giovanni has sent you to stay and work here?'

'Yes, Signor Riviera.'

'Call me Franco. Giovanni tells me that you are a good fisherman. Tell me about yourself.'

Giuseppe enthusiastically nodded and told him about fishing with his father for the *tonno* and working with Kostas the Greek in Sydney; he told him how Giovanni had loaned him a skiff to fish for himself. 'But selling my fish door to door was not liked by the local Greek fisherman and the fish shop owners, so I had to stop.' He did not mention Sophia.

Franco chuckled. 'Yes, I can believe that. People have to protect their interests, though the housewives would have welcomed you on their doorstep. You like to fish? You like to be on the water? Or is it just a means to make a living?' Although he asked the question casually, Franco gave Giuseppe an unflinching look, waiting for his answer.

Giuseppe rushed in. 'How could I look on fishing any other way? Being at sea, understanding the boat, the hunt for the fish and the contest between the fish and me – that is what makes me feel alive!'

Franco nodded. 'You come from a fishing family, unlike me. I come from Piedmont and I taught myself to fish only when I came to Australia. So you have knowledge passed to you from your father, your grand-father, yes?'

'Yes, yes. Of course. My brothers, they fish too. But for me . . . it is different.' He paused, not sure how to explain himself. 'I sometimes feel I can think like a fish. I know their habits and where they go and when they eat and what they like to eat. And then when I find a fish, it becomes a small war, a battle between the creature in the sea and me. And sometimes if the fish has put up a good fight, a clever fight, then I let him go to fight another day, even though my father says this is bad for business.' Giuseppe shrugged. 'I like to use poles and lines, rather than nets, and take on a fish, one on one, but I will do as you tell me.'

Franco cheerfully slapped Giuseppe on the back. 'You are a fisherman indeed. Giovanni was right to send you to me. Come, let's join the others.'

The other men clustered around Giuseppe. Amid much laughter and tales of fishing and dramas at sea, they filled him in on life in Wollongong and its prospects for a rosy future.

'It's such a great place, people come here from Sydney for their holidays,' said one enthusiastic Italian.

'The fishing is truly wonderful,' said another. 'Just you wait and see.'

'Welcome to our club. Welcome to Wollongong!' they all exclaimed, clapping him on the back.

Giuseppe was overwhelmed by their cheerful welcome and generosity. A woman appeared from the kitchen and announced that the food was ready. For several hours they all lingered over wine and an array of dishes that followed each other, course by course, with plenty of talking and laughter. The women stayed in the background, pleased to see their food being appreciated. Eventually they joined the men and sat around the table to eat the sweet dishes and a platter of fruit. Later, over cups of dark Italian coffee, someone brought out an accordion and they sang the old songs from home.

Night fell and Giuseppe wondered where he could stay for the night. It seemed late to be looking for a room. Perhaps he could sleep on the beach.

Then, as though reading his mind, Franco stood up and said, 'Joe, you've had a long day and I know you are wondering where you will sleep. Come with me and I will take you to a boarding house where other men who work for me also live. I think you'll find it comfortable.'

Giuseppe collected his suitcase and, after saying goodnight to everyone, followed his new employer out of the yard, fully expecting a long walk to the guesthouse. But Franco stopped beside a car that was parked in front of the house.

'Hop in. I'll drive you there and introduce you to the landlady.'

Giuseppe could not believe that Franco was rich enough to own his own car, and that he had invited Giuseppe to ride in it. It was the first time that he had ever ridden in a private motor car.

'What sort of car is this?' he asked when they were under way.

'A Model-T Ford. The most common car around. One day I hope to have enough money to buy a better one, but this will do for the time being.'

Giuseppe thought the Model-T was a wonderful machine; it seemed to fly along the road.

'This seems pretty good to me,' he said, trying to sound as though he frequently rode in cars.

But Franco was not fooled. 'This the first time you've been in a car? But you're right, my Tin Lizzie is good. Easy to drive and easy to fix if it breaks down. Maybe you'll own one someday, if you work hard and save your money.'

Giuseppe could not imagine such a time.

It took only a few minutes to reach the boarding house and Franco introduced Giuseppe to Signora Casalegno.

Giuseppe thanked Franco for his kindness and promised that he would be at the harbour bright and early, ready to start work.

The signora showed him to a pleasant room and, as he fell groggily to sleep after so much good food and too much grappa, he wished he could tell Antonio and Luciano about all that had happened. He felt hopeful about the future, but this time he would be more cautious about his actions. But after his evening with the Rivieras he felt enveloped in the warmth and comfort of familiar customs and habits, generosity and hospitality. It was as if the distance across the sea to his homeland was not so great. He felt as though he belonged.

*

Giuseppe worked the long line fishing with Franco and his crew. Once he was confident Giuseppe knew the sea conditions and after he'd seen how capable he was in the snapper boat, Franco allowed him to go out on his own with just one of his boys.

There were three other Italians living in the guest-house, all of whom worked for Franco, and they quickly became friends. The guesthouse was owned by the Casalegnos, but it was the signora who made the decisions. She was businesslike and didn't take a personal interest in her boarders like Signora Pagano had. Signor Casalegno had set up a small bakery and was at work by two each morning. He slept in the afternoon after the bakery closed. The signora made a huge fuss if any of her guests disturbed him, so it was easier to stay away from the house until evening. The three Italian boys showed Giuseppe the best places to visit around Wollongong, going to the beaches or the movies. But there was little that they could teach Giuseppe about fishing and after a few days out in Franco's boat it was obvious to everyone that Giuseppe was a born fisherman. They knew that his father had taught him well and he had listened to what Kostas had to say about fishing in Australia.

Giuseppe loved what he was doing and enjoyed everything about Wollongong. As the weeks turned to months, he thought less and less about returning to Sydney.

Franco was very sociable and he invited all his employees to the parties he usually threw once a month on a Sunday. As time passed and he came to know Giuseppe better, Franco began to ask him home on the other Sundays to discuss fishing. Giuseppe, spruced up and dressed in his best shirt and jacket, would join the family for Sunday lunch after they'd all been to church. He enjoyed being part of a family again and it was over lunch that Giuseppe learned all about his boss and his successful fishing venture.

Franco had arrived in Australia from Piedmont and, despite coming from the alpine slopes near Turin, his love of the sea and his love of eating fish developed into a passion. He was determined to make a new life in a very different world – that of fishing. He told Giuseppe that when he had arrived in Melbourne he had been mentored by an old Italian fisherman who took him into his business and taught him all he knew. When the old man died with no family in Australia or Italy, he'd left his fishing boat and a ramshackle boathouse to Franco.

'But there was a lot of competition around Melbourne and I heard that the fishing was good along the coast here, so I brought the boat to Wollongong.' He smiled. 'It was the right time. I got in first. Other men are starting to come here to fish, too, but I want to keep ahead of them. To do that I need good people. I think you could help me and if you stay with me, I'll do the right thing by you.'

'I am very grateful to you for the opportunity you have given me,' said Giuseppe sincerely.

'My son Silvio is not like you. He is not fond of fishing,' Franco told Giuseppe. 'But he is a very good salesman and he makes a lot of money with his contacts and his hard work. He always gets the very best prices for my fish.'

Giuseppe knew that Franco also had two daughters – Maria, who was still at school, and Evalina, who was nineteen and had finished school and now worked at home with her mother.

Evalina was a shy, sweet girl, who spoke English well and did the shopping for her mother. Every Saturday Evalina bought bread from Signor Casalegno's bakery, which was near the Casalegnos' boarding house and, if Giuseppe wasn't working, he often saw her there and walked with her back to the Rivieras' place.

One Saturday afternoon after Giuseppe had walked Evalina home and carried her shopping back in to her house, Franco called him to come out into the backyard.

'I'm sorting old lines and nets and tidying my workshed,' he explained as they walked across the large yard filled with several nets, boxes and fishing parapher-nalia. He indicated an upturned crate for Giuseppe to sit on, next to a bottle of grappa and two glasses. He poured Giuseppe a glass and handed it to him. '*Salute*. Thank you, Joe, for being such a help to me and my family.'

'I am pleased to be able to help you all. You and your family are good people,' said Giuseppe.

'I have been thinking,' said Franco as he lifted his glass. 'I came to Wollongong before anyone else did to start the fishing business. Now I think there are other opportunities further down the coast. I have purchased another boat and I plan to expand south of here.'

'You would move from here?' asked Giuseppe, surprised that Franco would choose to move from Wollongong.

Franco shook his head. 'Not me. You. What do you think of moving to Whitby Point? It's not many hours from here and the fishing is excellent. It is further away from the Sydney markets but Silvio is sure that we will be able to compete successfully.'

'I don't understand . . . I will go there if there is work you need me to do there. But I know nothing about starting a business.'

'Of course not. I will help you get started, just as I started here. You will need a couple of good men. If you agree, we can go down and see about getting you set up.'

'I do not know what to say. It would be a . . . dream,' began Giuseppe. 'What will Silvio say about bringing a stranger into the family to run part of the business?'

Franco dismissed this with a wave of his hand. 'I have another proposition. I want to make you part of my family. How do you feel about marrying Evalina? She has feelings for you and would be agreeable to such an arrangement.'

Giuseppe stared at Franco while he searched for words. 'She is a very nice girl. A sweet girl. I admire her very much.'

'Then it is settled. She will be a perfect wife for you. It would make me – all the family, in fact – very happy.'

'You have welcomed me into your home, given me a good job, and now you offer to make me part of your family's business and want me to marry your daughter. She is the kind of girl my parents would want me to marry; a good Italian girl. They will be very pleased.'

'Evalina is happy to marry you and to help you start my business down there. I will help you both set up a home as well as the business. You won't do any better, Giuseppe.'

Giuseppe was not sure if Franco was referring to the business offer or to his daughter, or both, so he nodded in agreement. 'I am honoured by your offer. And it is something I would like to do very much. I have always dreamed of running my own – well – of being in charge of a fishing business. Of course I would like to speak with Evalina.'

'Indeed. There is no rush, you must court her properly.'

Giuseppe wondered what his friend Antonio in north Queensland would think, but he knew his friend would tell him he'd be mad to pass up such a proposition. He could hear Antonio saying that, even if the girl was ugly, it was an offer too good to refuse.

And Evalina wasn't ugly. She looked like many of the pretty girls in his village. She had light brown hair, dark eyes, a curvaceous figure, pleasant features and a kind smile. She was a good cook and she knew how to run a household. She would be a good wife. She was not from his village, but he knew that even Nonna Celestina would approve of his choice.

So it was all agreed.

4

South coast, New South Wales, 2011

IT WAS NOT A day to fall in love with Whitby Point.

The sea thrashed angrily onto the empty beach, flinging waves up against the rocky cliffs, and gnawed hungrily at the sloping dunes that protected the small lagoon lying behind the beach. Sea birds huddled at the edge of the lagoon, taking refuge from the howling winter wind.

A lone figure, bent against the wind, fists pushed deep into the pockets of her jacket, walked along the path that skirted the deserted caravan park and camping ground. A change in wind direction blew back the hood of her jacket and her curling hair burst from the restraint of its hair clip.

The woman lifted her head to the smarting sting of sea spray, and changed her mind about walking past the cliff into the small township and harbour. She turned and made her way back around the bend to Pelican Cove, where three isolated cabins were hidden. Despite being spoiled for choice at this time of year, she'd chosen to rent one of these older cabins from a real estate agent in the town because of its seclusion.

The cabins on either side of hers were empty, and their small porches were carpeted with decaying vegetation – feathery needles and leaves from the trees. Their drawn blinds gave them an air of hunched defensiveness; the setting looked nothing like a sunny summer holiday escape. Cassandra Holloway had arrived in Whitby Point a few days ago and, while she could visualise how this place would look in the height of summer, its wintry setting suited her bleak mood.

As she approached the cabins, she saw a car parked by the side of the small dirt road that ran beside her cabin. A man, probably in his sixties, well built and fit and wearing overalls, got out of it as she approached.

'Mrs Holloway? I'm Geoff Spring, the repairman. The real estate agent sent me. A problem with the kitchen, is it?'

'Yes, the stove isn't working. I thought the gas bottle was empty but it's not, so I have no idea what's wrong.'

'No stove makes cooking tricky. These places are getting old. Built in the eighties and haven't been touched since, except for a lick of paint.' He grabbed his toolbox and followed her as she unlocked the front door.

'If it wasn't for the weather I'd use the barbecue. I'm getting a bit tired of meals in a frypan. But I can still boil the kettle. Tea or coffee?'

'You don't have to do that. But if you're making tea . . . Where's the gas bottle? I'll just check that first.'

Finding that it was indeed full he turned his attention to the stove. He fiddled with the knobs, peered into the oven and jiggled the gas line at the back of it. Fifteen minutes later, with the stove fixed, Cassie poured the tea into their cups as they sat at the kitchen table.

'Nice view out there across the lagoon to the ocean between the dunes. Summertime this place is jam-packed. A lot of families have been coming here forever. Book the same spot in the caravan park year after year. It's a bit off the beaten track but for those in the know, it's paradise. This is an odd time of year to come here.' Geoff gave Cassie an enquiring look.

'I wanted a break and the peace and quiet suits me.'

'I don't suppose you're staying long, but if anything else goes wrong, all you have to do is tell the office and I'll be right back out.'

'Thanks, but I'm hoping there won't be any other faults.'

'Righto. If you want to know anything the office can always help you out, or you can give me a ring. I've been here a good number of years now, I know what's what and who's who. Anyway, you probably won't need help because this town is so small, you'll know every inch of it in a day!'

'How long have you been here?' asked Cassie.

'About twenty years. Usual story – my wife and I came on holidays and fell in love with the place. Quit a boring job in Newcastle and started doing handyman work and gardening. I like working outdoors. We lived in a caravan before I built our house. You should come back when it starts to warm up.'

'I don't know. I've only been here a few days but I'm enjoying the cool weather and solitude.'

'You warm enough? Have you got enough wood for the pot-bellied stove and the barbecue? I know the office supplies some, but it's rubbish. I can bring you round some better stuff. I've got a big stash of seasoned wood and a bundle of old fence posts.'

'That's kind of you. I'd like that very much. Could you bring it by tonight so I can have a nice fire in the pot-bellied stove?' asked Cassie, getting up and putting the milk away in the old refrigerator.

Geoff drained his cup. 'No worries. You sure you're okay out here on your own with no phone or TV? 'Course you could rent a telly, there's a connection they put in last year. But you'll have problems with mobile phone coverage out here.'

'Yes, so I discovered. But I found that if I walk out to the edge of the lagoon there's a spot where it works. I don't think I want a TV. For the moment I'm enjoying re-discovering the radio and the joys of a good book. But thanks for asking.'

Geoff nodded and took his cup to the sink, rinsed it and pulled a card from his pocket and left it on the bench before he walked out of the little cabin and closed the door behind him.

Cassie watched him get into his car, touched that he was concerned about her being there on her own. She hadn't felt lonely or at all nervous staying among the whispering she-oaks. Right now she preferred not having people around. And she liked the idea of some good fire-wood. The little cabin would be cosier with a fire burning in the pot-bellied stove.

How very different it all was from the apartment she'd just left behind in Sydney. The slick, modern building that was only a short walk from the law firm where she and her husband had worked, seemed to be on a different planet from where she stood now.

Over the last few days she had tried not to think too much about the disaster that had happened in her marriage, but, now she'd opened that door, there was no closing it as the trickle of memories and emotions swiftly became a flood. She took a deep breath, picked up her pashmina, wound it around her shoulders, walked out onto the little porch, sank into the unravelling wicker chair and stared at the lagoon where the wind was whipping up small foaming waves.

She saw now that the apartment had symbolised her relationship with Hal. It was always about him and what he wanted. She'd argued with him about their first home. She hadn't wanted to live right in the city, she would rather have gone somewhere like Manly, where she'd grown up in a rambling cliff-top house overlooking the ocean.

'I don't want an apartment in the city. The city is cold. Canyons of city blocks, like beehives with tinted windows and little worker bees slaving away inside them.'

Hal Holloway had merely laughed. 'That's us, babe. Worker bees. If you want to get ahead in a law firm, you have to be prepared to work long hours, so you won't want a long commute at the end of the day.'

And he'd been right. They could walk to their office in Phillip Street. But Cassie missed having a garden like the wild sprawling one that her mother tended, as it battled the salt air. Although, as Hal pointed out, she didn't have far to walk to beautiful Hyde Park to enjoy one of the best green spaces in Sydney, even if she had to share it with hundreds of others.

'If you're so keen to have a garden why don't you grow herbs in a pot or something?' he suggested.

So Cassie, who loved to cook, made plans to grow herbs and even tomatoes and salad vegetables on their balcony, but she never seemed to find the time. Indeed, both of them were so busy that they usually ate dinner in one of the restaurants they passed on their way home.

Even on the weekends they didn't just hang out at home. Most Friday nights they went to a bar after work with colleagues, though occasionally Cassie met up with girlfriends when the macho shop talk and egocentric company of the men at her law firm became too irritating. Hal always worked on Saturdays, and often she would also use the weekend to try and stay on top of her very big workload too. Sunday morning was set aside for breakfast with friends, usually from their law firm, and afterwards Hal routinely popped back into the office to sort out what needed to be done in the coming week.

'Hal, I wish we could socialise with people we don't work with. Most of the men in the office drive me nuts, they are so aggressive. Can't we spend time with people who are less ambitious?'

'Cassie, you know that male lawyers are always in fight mode. Other lawyers have wives who aren't involved in law and they don't get it, which is why I'm glad you're part of my world.'

When Cassie first met Hal, she was convinced they were right for each other, that they shared the same goals and dreams. Cassie was a bright girl at school and, because there was an expectation that clever girls went on to do either law or medicine at university, she chose to study law. She met Hal almost straight away as he was in the same year as she was and their paths crossed in class. He was hard to miss – exceedingly handsome, an athlete, articulate and ambitious. He was from a well-to-do family from the leafy, expensive suburb of St Ives. His father was the CEO of a finance corporation. Initially Hal had assumed that Cassie's family business was little more than a fish and chip shop, but when he learned from other students that it was, in fact, the well-known Seven Seas restaurant in Manly, he dropped in with some of his friends and surprised her when she was working there one Sunday. He soon became a regular and he also sought out her company at the university and then they began going out together. A year later they moved in together.

Cassie was impressed by Hal's plans. He told her that the law was the bedrock of a civil society and that although he would initially work his way into a top-level position in an important legal firm, what he really wanted to do was to become a judge. As a judge, he told her, he could make justice really effective.

After university they had both got jobs at the same law firm. Cassie remembered how excited she was when she thought that they would be working together, but it didn't turn out that way. Hal was successful as a criminal defence lawyer and had become more senior while Cassie continued to work in the litigation department. He put in longer and longer hours at work, spending a lot of time with his team. Sometimes, if he was involved with a particularly stressful and tiring case, he'd come home slightly drunk after unwinding with his work mates. At first Cassie commented on his behaviour, but after he snapped and told her that she should know what tremendous pressure he was under, she began to sense that they were moving in different directions.

When Cassie reminded him about his ambition to become a judge, Hal dismissed the idea.

'Don't be silly, Cassie,' he told her. 'Being a judge is too isolating, and it doesn't pay well enough. I can make much more as a partner in a top law firm.'

Now when Cassie spoke of truth and justice, human rights, legal aid, minorities or social issues, subjects about which they had once both been passionate, he became scathing.

'That stuff won't pay the bills or maintain our lifestyle,' Hal sneered.

Then Cassie began to have her own issues to deal with at the firm.

She was shocked when Bronwyn, one of the few senior female lawyers and her supervisor, called her into her office and told her that before she'd hand back Cassie's most recent report, Cassie would have to give her a neck massage. At first Cassie thought Bronwyn was joking, but then she realised the woman was serious. She was actually going to withhold Cassie's work until her neck had been massaged. Cassie started to comply but realised that massaging her supervisor's neck was not right so she stopped and excused herself. Ever since, relations between Cassie and Bronwyn had been very strained. When Cassie asked Hal whether she should say anything to the HR officer, he'd scoffed at her.

'And who are they going to back? A senior lawyer or junior you? Get real, Cassie.'

Other instances that occurred in the office really annoyed Cassie because they smacked of double standards. It seemed that whenever a female lawyer wanted to sit down and discuss something with her boss, she was seen as flirtatious or sycophantic, whereas when one of the men in the office did the same thing, he was admired for being ambitious.

Hal laughed at her observations and told her she was being oversensitive. It was the way it was in all big law firms. Women needed to either go along with it or opt out.

'That's ridiculous,' argued Cassie. 'Why should women go along with it? Why do big law firms maintain an outdated and, frankly, outrageous system that only functions at the behest of male participation? If a woman can see a different and better way of doing things, it's not even considered. Why should we be expected to operate within the parameters of the established ways of doing things if those ways are inefficient and sexist?'

'If you can't stand the heat . . .' Hal shrugged.

'Hal, women do get out of the kitchen,' said Cassie. 'They start their own firms, or work in smaller firms where they're really valued and are much happier and more successful.'

'Your choice, babe. No one is stopping you. But you might find it tougher than you think. Are you going to work your bum off and take a pay cut just to make a point? Is that what you want?'

Cassie never seemed able to win an argument with Hal, but she did find one sympathetic ear at the firm: Marjorie Oldham, who'd worked as PA to a senior partner for years. She listened to Cassie's comments and nodded, agreeing with her that the old-style law firms were having trouble adjusting to new attitudes and work programs, and the need to be more flexible regarding their employees. But, as she said gently to Cassie, 'The majority of women who work in large law firms like this are extremely ambitious, just like the men. The last thing they want is a sign on their backs announcing, "I'm a working mum". So they'll work harder, put in longer hours, work for less, just to prove that they are as capable as their male counterparts. Cassie, if your ambition is different, if you aren't prepared to give up everything else to get ahead, then my advice is get another life. Take your pay packet and walk out the door.'

'Easier said than done,' said Cassie. 'As Hal has pointed out to me on many occasions, where else would I be able to get such good pay? Jobs paying what mine does are not easy to come by.'

'But are you saving anything? What's your and Hal's long-term plan? Time can escape, you know.'

'That's true. We vaguely talk about starting a family. I'd like to have children. But there's no actual plan,' said Cassie.

'How long have you been married?' asked Marjorie.

'Five years,' admitted Cassie. 'I married Hal when I was twenty-seven.'

113

'Then make plans. If you don't, he won't. That's all I can suggest.'

Cassie thanked Marjorie and started to think about her and Hal's life. For one thing, she decided, they had to be a bit more practical about money. They both earned really good salaries but they also spent money without thinking. They ate out nearly every night because it was convenient. Hal only ever bought the best, whether it was a car or a coffee maker. They travelled. On long weekends they flew to lavish resorts on the Great Barrier Reef or to the snowfields. They went to Europe every two years for two or three weeks and stayed at the very best hotels. Hal's suits and shirts were bespoke and he spent a small fortune on trendy casual gear. He was always generous to Cassie and gave her expensive jewellery each Christmas and birthday. They had their own bank accounts and never asked each other what they'd spent. But Cassie knew that if her account was anything to go by, most of his salary would have been frittered away like hers.

Now, looking back over all that had happened, Cassie wondered at what point Hal had lost interest in her. If she was honest, their sex life had become infrequent and mundane. They were both always tired to the point of exhaustion.

Hal had begun to spend even more time with his work colleagues, nearly every weeknight and also weekends. He always had an excuse for not being around. Cassie had thought that maybe Marjorie was right. Maybe she and Hal should have started a family. She had tried to imagine Hal being a father. What sort of an example would he set? Would he give up working late at night and on weekends for his family? She had doubted it.

The more deeply she had considered her future the more she found herself withdrawing. She did her work, although she had to admit that her passion for the law was waning. Hal was absorbed in his cases, the details of which he no longer shared with her, and their conversation shrank to the trivia of daily life.

Then Hal started being nice to her. It was only small things but because it was so unusual for him to give her a smile or a compliment, she assumed that, like her, he was reassessing their future. Perhaps it was the right time to start discussing a baby after all.

How naive she'd been.

One of the worst parts of finding out about Hal and Kellie was the realisation that others in the office were beginning to avoid her or were giving her odd glances. She'd noticed smirks and conversations stopped when she approached. One morning she got to work to find a yellow post-it note stuck to her computer with a scrawled message: 'Watch your husband and a certain someone.'

Suddenly everything made sense. A swift kaleidoscope of images flashed through her mind. She knew instantly who the woman was: Kellie Leslie, an elegant and sassy newcomer from a rival law firm. She was so blatantly ambitious that Cassie had commented to Hal about it. But Hal had seen things differently. 'Well, whatever it takes. Got to give her credit for being up-front. She's bright and good company. She's probably been targeted by jealous women all her life.'

Cassie had rolled her eyes.

One Friday evening when they were having drinks after work, Cassie had watched with distaste as Kellie traded dirty jokes with her male colleagues and revealed office confidences. When she told Hal that she thought Kellie's behaviour was unprofessional, she was surprised when he told her not to be so stuffy. He thought Kellie was a breath of fresh air.

After she found the post-it note, Cassie confronted Hal. Of course he denied that he was having an affair.

But when Cassie told Marjorie Oldham her suspicions, Marjorie said, 'Leave it with me and I'll make a few enquiries.'

'It's like a TV soapie. I just can't believe it.' Cassie was in shock.

From that moment there had been an inevitable unravelling.

When Marjorie confirmed the rumours, Cassie confronted Hal again and he made a reluctant admission and promised that the affair was over. He even agreed to counselling. But Cassie wondered if she really wanted her marriage to continue. She wasn't sure that she really cared to stay on in the law firm either. It would be too humiliating to go on working there after all that had happened. Cassie was in turmoil, so she rang her mother.

'Of course you can come and stay with me. Stay as long as you like. I'll enjoy the company,' her mother Jenny had answered when Cassie told her that she was planning on leaving the law firm and moving out of the apartment while she thought things over. 'But are you sure that you want to walk away from your job? After all, you've done nothing wrong. Surely Hal should be the one leaving.'

'As if, Mum. Hal is the golden-haired boy of the firm. All this has made me realise that Hal is not who I thought he was at all. It's not just this affair either. We are moving in such different directions. I'm not sure that I want to stay married to him anymore. I suppose I should fight for the marriage, but at the moment I can't. I need space and time away from him.'

'But Cassie, if that's the way you feel, why don't you at least stay in the apartment and ask Hal to leave?'

'I suppose I could, but honestly, I've never liked the place. It's always felt more like a hotel room than home. Your place feels like home to me.'

So Cassie had moved over to Manly, taking only a few possessions.

'Why so few?' asked her mother.

'I suppose I could have taken more. Hal wouldn't have put up much opposition but when I looked around the place, I realised that most of the things in it had been chosen by Hal, and I don't really like them that much. Hal liked to buy things that he could show off to guests. I like more sentimental things, photos, old books, pretty vases. You know my taste.'

'I certainly do,' replied her mother. 'There are boxes of your taste packed in the garage.'

'I know. Hal hated my stuff. Said it didn't suit the ambience of our place. Well, when I get a place of my own I'll unpack my things and enjoy them.'

'Any plans in that direction?'

'Mum, if you can put up with me, I wouldn't mind staying here for a little bit while I get used to the idea of being single again.'

Cassie stayed with her mother and continued to see the counsellor until she was absolutely sure that the marriage was over. Hal seemed to be indifferent. But Cassie was not sure what to do about her own future. The law now held little appeal, but she didn't know what else she could do. Her mother suggested that they take a holiday together and, while Cassie thought a break was a good idea, she decided that she wanted time on her own to think through her future.

'Where would you go?' her mother asked. 'The snow?'

'Oh, Mum, I'm not in the mood for après ski. I don't know. Maybe somewhere not too far away, but quiet. I couldn't cope with lots of people.'

'Your father always said that the south coast was lovely at this time of year. A bit wild, but beautiful in its own way. He told me that he went to Whitby Point as a boy and always promised to take me, but we never seemed to find the time. The restaurant business was pretty full on. Anyway, you could give it a go. It's only a few hours drive, and it's the off season, so accommodation won't cost much. When you get back, you might have a better idea of what it is you want to do. I never saw you and a high-powered law firm as a happy fit.'

'Mum, I have no regrets about slogging away to get a law degree. I did like the job when I started but I want to rethink where I'm going and I need a blank canvas, to clear the decks and clear my mind.'

'I understand,' said her mother.

*

When a ray of watery sunshine broke through the clouds Cassie got up from the old chair and shook her head to clear it. Enough, she told herself. Let it go. It's over.

She was finding that her feelings for Hal were evaporating along with the hurt and the humiliation. She knew they had not been on the same wave length for ages and she wondered how they'd lasted as long as they had. Suddenly she had a sense of freedom, of being able to take deep breaths and move at her own pace in her own space away from the hothouse world of the law firm.

The weather looked fine enough for her to walk into the little town. Now the rain was clearing she had time to get there and back before evening closed in. She took a light backpack so that she could buy some milk, a newspaper and something fresh to eat.

Whitby Point was a small town with just a main street and several side streets, some of which led up the hill to small apartment complexes, old-style holiday houses and a few newer cottages, all of which seemed to be holiday rentals awaiting summer visitors. Some of the little shops and cafés were closed for the winter.

As she strolled around Cassie felt very much at home. How nice it was to have time on her hands and no commitments. She browsed in the newsagency and bought a magazine as well as a paper.

'Could you keep a paper for me each day, please?' she asked the newsagent.

'Sure, what's your name?'

'Cassie Holloway.'

'How long do you want it for, Cassie?'

'I'm not sure. Let's say two weeks.'

'You on holidays here? Sorry the weather's not the best.'

'It's okay. I'm enjoying it.'

'We deliver around town. Where are you staying?'

'Out at Pelican Cove. If that's too far for deliveries, not to worry. The walk into town does me good.'

'You on your own?' The newsagent looked concerned and Cassie hoped there hadn't been some criminal on the loose in the area.

'No, I have plenty of company,' she said with a laugh, thinking of her books, magazines and music.

'Good-o, then. See you tomorrow.'

She continued down towards the harbour front, noticing the small library tucked beside a coffee shop advertising its abbreviated winter opening hours. She hadn't spotted a bookstore so she was glad there was a library. The street nearest the seafront contained some lovely old homes. The harbour had been updated recently by the look of things and Cassie wondered if that was for the benefit of the tourists. The fish co-op at the main jetty was a smart building with a gift shop and an attached restaurant shrouded in plastic blinds.

She went into the fish shop and cast an eye over the beds of shaved ice holding that day's catch.

A friendly woman with a big smile greeted her. 'What are you after, luv?'

'What's fresh and local?' asked Cassie.

'Ummn. Not a lot. Weather's been so bad. Leather-jackets, some small bream. Calamari. The prawns aren't local, they're frozen, from Thailand.'

'I'd rather not buy imported stuff,' said Cassie quickly.

'We prefer to buy and sell Australian seafood, but we can't always keep up with the demand, especially in the summer. Anyway, the boss has found one prawn farm in Thailand that is very, very clean and ecologically sustainable. He went over and checked it out before we agreed to buy their prawns.'

'I see,' said Cassie. 'Well, I'll take the squid. Quick and easy to cook.' Cassie handed over her money and stowed the small parcel of squid in her backpack.

'Enjoy.'

'I will. Thanks.'

She walked beside the sea wall and a little park and past an old boatshed where the main jetty had been extended to be part of a small marina. A few trawlers were moored there as well as some leisure boats. The park had a children's playground at one end beside a small stretch of sandy beach. At the other end of the harbour, up against the cliff, she could see an old-fashioned rock pool cut into the flat rocks, with wooden benches running along one side and a little change shed. The high tide was washing across the pool, and beyond the headland she could hear the roar of the ocean swell. She turned and walked back towards her cabin.

Despite being alone she took pleasure in rugging up in her jacket and walking for an hour or more along the deserted blustery beach. She enjoyed listening to music with a glass of wine, or reading, or just dozing, curled on the old, roomy, cushioned lounge. Simple pleasures indeed, she told her mother when she had reception on her mobile phone.

'You're not lonely, are you?' Jenny asked. 'How long are you staying down there? You can't stay there forever.'

'I'm not thinking about anything for the moment, Mum. This is R and R, remember.'

'Of course. I'm glad you're liking it. Have you met any nice people?' asked Jenny.

'A lovely man, Geoff Spring. In his sixties, the local handyman. He's bringing me some firewood,' said Cassie.

'Oh, I see. Not the jetset then?' said Jenny.

'I'm sure there are a few locals at the pub on Friday night but I'm not about to go to find out. I'm fine, Mum, really I am.'

'If you're sure. Well, since you're fine, I've decided to go off for a holiday to climb Mount Kinabalu in Borneo,' Jenny told her daughter.

'Some holiday! And you're worried about me,' said Cassie, laughing. 'Who are you going with?'

'That group of experienced walkers I've travelled with before. I've told you about them. I'll be fine and I won't be gone long,' replied Jenny.

'Take care, enjoy yourself and try to phone me when you can. Love you, Mum.'

*

Late that afternoon Geoff appeared with a load of wood, which he stacked on the side of the little porch. He presented Cassie with a plastic plate covered in aluminium foil. Cassie peeled back the foil and smiled.

'Whiting. What lovely fat ones too. Thank you. Did you catch them?'

121

'Certainly did. Just off the beach. Thought as I was coming this way with the wood, I'd bring the rod for a bit of a fish, seeing as there's a break in the weather.' He glanced skywards. 'Not going to last though, so batten down the hatches. I've only cleaned the fish. Do you want me to fillet them?'

'I can do that, thanks, Geoff. I really appreciate this. How often do you fish?' Cassie asked.

'As often as I can, without the tourists around. The weather might be cold but the fishing is great. Have you ever been fishing?'

'Sure have, Geoff. I know a lot about fish. As a matter of fact, I practically grew up around the Sydney fish markets. I loved going there with my dad.' She smiled. 'My parents owned a fish restaurant. Dad started a little fish and chip shop and it grew into a seafood restaurant. It was really popular.'

'Whereabouts in Sydney was your parents' place? I might have been there.'

'Manly. Right on the Corso. It was called the Seven Seas.'

Geoff looked at Cassie in surprise. 'I know it! Anyone who's been to Manly knows it. Lovely place. Great food! Well, imagine that.' He looked impressed. 'I reckon you could teach me a thing or two about cooking fish.'

'I wouldn't say that. The only time I worked in the restaurant I was a waitress. Dad died some time back and Mum eventually sold the Seven Seas. But Whitby Point seems to be the place to fish.' Cassie was genuinely enthused.

'You bet. This place was once a really important part of the fishing industry. Started by the Italians. Some of them are still around but the place is nothing like it used to be. No, in its heyday, Whitby Point was a thriving fishing town. I remember one time a big bluefin tuna fetched sixty thousand dollars. Sent to Japan of course.'

'What happened to the fishing industry?' asked Cassie.

'Lots of things. Overfishing, too many cheap imports, ocean temperature's changed, government regulations, you name it, but it's hurt a lot of local people, which is why we rely so much on tourism now.'

'That's such a pity,' said Cassie. 'Geoff, would you like a drink? I have red wine or white wine. No beer, I'm afraid. I can always put the kettle on if you'd prefer a cuppa. I'll just put these fish away.'

'Well, a glass of red wine never goes astray.' He sat on the top step of the porch as Cassie went inside and returned with two glasses of wine.

'Cheers. You settling in all right?'

'Feel like I've lived here for ages. Bit cold for swimming, though.'

'The water's always a bit cool here on the south coast, but I like the ocean a bit crisp on a hot day. There're a couple of old fellas here who swim in the rock pool all year round.'

Cassie laughed. 'To each his own. Tell me, I've been meaning to ask someone, how come this is named Whitby Point? Who was Mr Whitby?'

'Can't say who the original bloke was, but Captain Cook named the place when he sailed up the east coast. This little inlet must have reminded him of the fishing town of Whitby in Yorkshire where he learned his seamanship.'

'Interesting. I suppose you never forget the place you come from,' mused Cassie. 'What about you, Geoff? Where was home originally?'

'Not that far from here, the other side of Wollongong, Stanwell Park. Lovely spot, but my family moved up to Newcastle when I was pretty little, though we always went back in the holidays to camp there. You from Sydney? A lot of city people come down here over the summer holidays. Not many around at present. Can I ask why you chose this time of year? Not that there's anything wrong with that.'

Suddenly Cassie wanted to tell someone about her problems and Geoff seemed such a kind man. 'I'm trying to deal with my marriage. Well, actually I'm over it. I'm more adjusting to what to do with myself after I get the divorce. I've also just quit my corporate job and now I'm wondering what I'm going to do next. I always thought I knew what career I wanted, and now I've found that what I was doing was wrong for me. So I'm down here by myself, so that I can have some space to think.'

Geoff nodded. 'It's a bit of a lost art, just thinking and taking it slow and easy. I think people get fearful about all kinds of things and feel that the minute they stop whatever it is that they're doing, their lives are no longer meaningful, productive or fulfilling, when, in fact, it's a great challenge to go slow.' He pointed at Cassie's wristwatch. 'What appointments do you have down here?'

Cassie thought a moment, took off her watch and pushed it into her pocket. 'You're right,' she said, laughing.

'Savour time, don't rush. Fishing makes a clock stop.'

'That's so true. I'd forgotten.'

'By the way, how're you going to cook the fish? In batter with some chips?'

'No way,' said Cassie, laughing. 'I'm just going to toss the fillets in a bit of flour and fry them lightly in butter, put some fresh parsley and a squeeze of lemon juice on top and serve them with a green salad.'

'Makes me hungry. I'd better be off and help the wife rustle up dinner.'

'Sounds good, Geoff,' said Cassie. 'And I'll take your advice. You said that there were Italians in Whitby Point; is there a good Italian restaurant here? I might eat out one night, for a change.'

'Not these days, but the Indian restaurant is really good. I can recommend that.' He glanced at the sky again. 'Cassie, latch things down tonight, I reckon a southerly is going to blow up.' He pointed to a thin layer of clouds accumulating over the hill. 'Thanks for the drink.'

As he left, Cassie suddenly called out to him. 'I know this might sound out of left field, but I was wondering if next time you go fishing, I could come along, too? It'd be great to fish again. I can pick up a line or a rod in town.'

His face lit up. 'A girl who wants to fish! Well that's a treat. I've got plenty of spares. I'll give you a shout next time it's looking good.'

*

Cassie felt happy after her casual chat with the gentle Geoff. He had listened to her, made no demands and held no expectations, and he had given her some very good advice. Her time was now indeed her own.

Simple as her meal was, Cassie enjoyed the time she spent preparing it. She set a place at the table for herself with care. In the gathering gloom she foraged in the scrub behind the cabin for some gum leaves and flowering wattle, and used a glass as a vase. She lit the pot-bellied stove, savoured another glass of red wine and, as the day dimmed, she didn't turn on the radio or her iPod but lingered over her food. She'd decided to leave the squid for another day and eat Geoff's fish, and she was pleased that she had for she hadn't tasted such good fish for a long time. Not since her mother had sold the restaurant. She wasn't sure if it was because the fish was so fresh, or because it was a gift from Geoff Spring who radiated kindness, or because she had cooked it with care and pleasure, or whether it was a combination of all these factors. For the first time in a long while she felt at peace, with herself and with the world. She couldn't quite analyse how or why she felt the way she did, but Cassie sensed that she had reached some kind of milestone.

Geoff was right. That evening a windstorm and rain battered the windows and threatened to lift the roof off the little cabin. Or so it seemed to Cassie as she went to bed by candlelight since the power had gone off.

She was awakened by a crack and a crash and she realised that a tree branch had come down near the cabin. She heard a thump on the little porch, the window rattled and there was a distant flash of lightning. Cassie listened carefully as the noise on the porch continued. She had a vision of a strange man stumbling around outside. She put her head under the doona and for the first time a small knot of fright tightened in her chest.

Nevertheless, eventually she slept and when she opened her eyes she discovered a grey dawn outside. The rain and wind had gone but it was cold. She poked the remains of the fire and put some twigs on the glowing embers, watching with satisfaction as they caught alight.

She boiled some water for a cup of tea and then, holding her mug, with the doona trailing over her shoulders, she opened the door to see what the wild weather had done.

The porch was sodden, scattered with leaves and twigs. As she took a step there was a bang and the old chair tipped up, making her jump with shock. At the far end of the little porch stood a shivering, skinny dog. Cassie moved forward and it lay down, cowering in fright, its chin on its paws. She put her mug down and walked slowly forward holding out her hands for the dog to sniff. The dog squirmed forward on its belly to smell her outstretched hands and then it licked them.

'Oh you poor, pathetic creature,' she murmured. She stroked its head and slowly ran her hand along its flanks. Its ribs were clearly visible through its matted hair. It looked to be a young dog, a black and tan kelpie crossed with something with long hair. It had a kelpie's face and intelligent brown eyes, and a kelpie's body shape but the fur was thicker with black markings against the brown. When Cassie stood up the dog shrank away from her once more.

It took a little while to cajole the dog to come indoors but, bribed with soft words and a bit of toast, he slunk inside. Cassie put a bowl of water down for him and looked for something more to feed him. He quickly devoured a bowl of cereal and milk.

She dressed and cleaned up inside the cabin and swept the porch while the exhausted dog slept in front of the fire. It wore no collar and seemed in such poor condition that she thought it must be a stray. Cassie wondered if it had accidentally fallen from a ute or a truck, or whether it had been deliberately dumped.

When the sun came out Cassie decided to walk into town for the paper and debated whether she should leave the dog indoors as it was still soundly asleep. Instead she pulled out an old beach towel and coaxed him onto the wicker chair on the porch where she left him munching some Anzac biscuits.

As she reached the road the lady from the fish co-op drove past and gave her a big wave. Then the boy who worked in the garage where she'd got her petrol drove past and gave her a grin and a thumbs up. Cassie was impressed by the friendliness of the locals, but when another car passed her and signalled at something behind her, Cassie looked around. Trotting after her was the dog. He stopped when she stopped.

'Oh, no. You were supposed to stay at home!'

The dog cocked his head and gave a tentative shake of his feathery tail. Then he sat and waited.

Cassie turned away and started to walk briskly. When she looked over her shoulder, the dog was keeping pace, maintaining the same distance between them. She stopped;

it stopped. Finally she said to it, 'Listen, if you're going to walk with me, you don't have to be ten metres behind. Come here, and keep up.'

She snapped her fingers and the dog eagerly leapt forward. As she set off again it trotted just behind her right heel. 'So you do know a thing or two. I wonder where your owners are. What am I going to do with you?' she said, glancing down at the dog, who gave her a happy look.

At the newsagency she told the dog to sit and wait and it promptly sat at the entrance and didn't move, but watched her intently as she went to the counter for her paper.

'You got yourself a dog, Cassie?' said the newsagent, peering at the doorway. 'Had it on a diet, eh? Skinny little thing.'

'It arrived on my porch during the storm last night. And you're right, it is skinny. No collar and no idea who it belongs to. What do you suggest I do with it?'

'It sure looks like a stray. I've never seen it round here. Maybe it's got a microchip. You could take it to the vet and get it checked out. He might have a missing dog sheet for the area.'

'That's a good idea. Where's the vet?'

*

'Phew, getting a workout this morning,' said Cassie as she caught her breath at the top of the hill and looked for the address of the veterinary practice that the newsagent had given her. The dog wagged his tail. He didn't look at all out of breath.

The vet's practice was in an old-fashioned rambling bungalow with a wrap-around verandah and spectacular views. Spread out below was the harbour. Cassie could see the main wharf with the fish co-op, the boatshed and an old trawler in the slips as well as the breakwater with its bar opening to the ocean. Beneath the headland was the rock pool. In the other direction, she could see rolling green paddocks. If she walked around to the side of the house, Cassie thought she'd probably see unbroken miles of the southern beach.

She went in the door marked 'Reception', the dog following obediently. Once inside, however, his tail drooped and he looked nervously around at the other waiting people; a woman with a hissing cat in a carry box and another, more elderly woman, holding a very tiny terrier.

The girl at the desk took her details and nodded as Cassie explained that the dog wasn't hers but she wondered if it had a microchip implant that would give its owner's details so she could return it.

As they waited their turn, the dog sat by her chair pressed against her leg, intently watching the comings and goings.

'Dr Phillips will see you now.' The receptionist smiled and pointed to the examination room. Cassie stood up and walked over to it, and the dog followed.

Dr Phillips looked to be in his late thirties with tousled dark brown hair, friendly eyes, an easygoing manner and a two-day growth on his chin. Cassie couldn't help smiling at the smock he wore. It certainly wasn't the businesslike plain cotton jacket usually favoured by dentists, hospital staff and vets. This vet's top was made from a cheerful blue print covered in prancing pink flamingoes.

'Hi, I'm Michael Phillips.'

'Cassie Holloway. I do like your top.' She couldn't let it pass unmentioned.

'Ah, yes. A gift from a local high school student who came here to do some work experience. Now, who's this?' He squatted down so that he was eye to eye with the dog who was cowering close to Cassie.

'That's just it, I have no idea. It's a stray who wandered in last night during the storm.'

Gently the vet held out his hand and let the dog sniff it. He stroked the dog and ran his hands around the dog's head and the back of his neck. 'No collar and very under-nourished. C'mon, matey, let's have a good look at you.' Before the dog could react, he scooped it up, put it on top of the examining table and ran his hands expertly over its body and legs.

The dog never took his eyes off Cassie, as though looking for reassurance.

Cassie patted his head. 'It's all right, old boy. Dr Phillips is a friend.'

'He's decided you're a friend, that's for sure,' said the vet. 'He seems in pretty good condition except he's so thin, and there's a bit of a bump on his hip. I think he's either taken a fall or been hit by something. It doesn't seem too serious, so I don't think it's worth the expense of an X-ray. Let's see if he's got a microchip. No, I can't feel one.'

'I was hoping there'd be one. I hate to think of someone pining for him. I wonder if he fell off the back of a ute or a truck and he's trying to walk home to his family in Melbourne or somewhere,' said Cassie.

The vet chuckled. 'I don't think so. His paws aren't worn as though he's spent a lot of time walking. But he's not a dog I recognise. Young dog, about two years old, I'd say. A kelpie cross, good working dog. Not microchipped.'

'He seems to know a few things. Or he's just smart,' said Cassie. 'I'd look after him for a bit. But . . .'

'I know. You don't want to get attached if the owner turns up,' said the vet. 'I'd keep him here, but it wouldn't be any fun for him.' He rubbed the dog's ear and the dog relaxed.

'I'm down at the cabins by the lagoon. I don't know if they allow dogs but as I'm the only one there so I guess I could look after him . . .'

'Yes, Pelican Cove. How long are you staying?'

Cassie paused. 'I'm not sure. I'm taking a sort of break here.'

Michael Phillips stroked the dog's back. 'You chose a good place, good time of year. The winter here is a well-kept secret.'

Cassie nodded. 'It's lovely. So he seems healthy enough?'

'I'll give you some worm tablets. Buy him some tucker and give him a decent brush. Take him for a run on the beach, he'll be as happy as Larry, I'd say. Perhaps you could put an ad in the local paper to try to find the owner. Call me if you have any problems. Just play it day by day.'

'Just the way I'm living my life,' said Cassie breezily.

'Nothing wrong with that. And this is the right place to do it.' He lifted the dog down, opened the door and walked with her to the front desk.

'You have a great view from up here,' said Cassie.

'Yes. When I was a kid, I used to love watching the fishing fleet heading out to sea at night. Most of the boats are gone now.'

'You're a local then?' said Cassie.

'This was my grandfather's home. Okay, no charge for today,' he said to the receptionist. 'Leave your number with my receptionist and if anyone comes looking for a dog of this description, we'll give you a call,' he told Cassie.

'Thank you,' said Cassie.

'I think he'd better thank you,' said Michael Phillips as he patted the dog. Then he smiled at Cassie, nodded goodbye and picked up the file for the next client.

'Well, I guess you passed,' said Cassie to the dog, who followed her outside with his tail arched, pointing skywards.

*

Cassie put an ad in the local paper, thinking that if it brought no response she'd put up some handwritten posters around town, though she figured in such a small place anyone missing a dog would look in the paper or call the vet anyway. She had no idea what she would do with a dog, so she was determined not to become attached to him.

She told him firmly, 'I'll look after you while you're here. But I'm not going to bond with you and have you take off one day when your owner turns up on the doorstep. Of course, they must have been pretty sloppy people to lose you in the first place. Or did you run away? Are you on the lam, kid? What mischief did you get up to, eh?' As she spoke to the dog, she was pleased to hear her own voice in the small cabin.

The dog listened attentively, head cocked to one side, giving an occasional encouraging shake of his tail. At the word 'mischief', he lay on the floor, looking contrite.

Cassie couldn't help laughing. 'What an actor you are!'

She'd given him some food, including a bone, which he chewed on the porch. He gave it his full attention, equal to that of a school examination paper. At sunset they went to the lagoon and she threw sticks for him to retrieve. Then they went for a brisk walk along the beach before returning to the cabin as darkness fell. She put his dinner on the porch next to his water dish while she lit the fire and started cooking her meal. It felt good to have someone else to do things for and to share the evening with.

'No more lounging around and reading all day. I expect you'll want to get up and get going in the morning,' she said cheerfully, as the satiated dog licked and cleaned his paws before settling down in front of the fire, scraping the old beach towel into a sort of nest for himself.

'I suppose you think that's your place,' said Cassie.

She ate her dinner. Then read more of her book, had another glass of wine and then, feeling drowsy, took the dog for a quick walk before bed.

After brushing her teeth she put another log on the fire. The dog, curled on the old towel, took no notice.

Cassie snuggled into bed feeling more contented than she had in a long time. She felt relaxed. The disturbed and emotional nights of the past year were over. She felt she was doing the right thing, ending her marriage, quitting her job, and changing her life. The emotions of those long, dark nights when she'd cried herself to sleep were still a little painful to recall, but they were behind her now. For the first time in a long time she had utterly no commitments, except for this dog.

Cassie slept soundly, undisturbed by the high winds and intermittent rain. She did vaguely register a sudden thump on the bed as the dog jumped up and wiggled his way up beside her. Half asleep, she reached out and patted his head. It was comforting to know the dog was there. He made her feel safe and not alone anymore. With a sigh, the dog curled up on the doona and slept.

Still dozy in the morning, she leaned over and stroked the dog, who began to nuzzle her hand. Cassie jumped out of bed.

'Don't you try and con me. Outside, Mr Dog. Do what you have to do. The day has begun.'

As the dog sniffed the wet grass, Cassie looked at the brilliant sunrise and felt invigorated.

'I'm so glad I'm here. I wish I could stay. I have a whole life ahead of me. But what am I going to do with myself?'

The dog took no notice so she went inside and made herself a pot of tea and toast. All the while her mind was churning. After feeling that her life was going nowhere, Cassie felt as if a switch had been turned on. She was full of energy and enthusiasm. She couldn't remember feeling

133

this happy in a long, long time. She wanted to make plans. She felt ready to get going. She needed a project.

The dog scratched at the screen door to come inside.

She laughed and opened it. 'I guess you're my project for the moment. Come in, you smart thing.'

He sat neatly, feet together, tail curled, and watched her chew every mouthful of toast.

Cassie shifted in her seat so she couldn't see his pleading eyes.

While it would be months or even longer before the divorce was final, and the apartment would have to be sold and money divided, Cassie knew she was now in a better place than she had been. She had regrets but she knew that the years with Hal, and working in the law firm, had not all been wasted.

She carried her plate to the sink and the dog's eyes followed her. She picked up the last tiny bit of toast crust and stood in front of him. He didn't move though his nose twitched.

'C'mon. Sit up.'

He cocked his head and looked a bit confused, but quickly he understood what she wanted. Sitting on his haunches he lifted his front paws. Cassie held the toast tantalisingly close to his snout.

'Take it gently, mister. Slowly, like a gentleman.'

The dog delicately took the morsel.

Cassie clapped her hands. 'Excellent. Good dog.'

The dog now bounced exuberantly, happy he'd pleased her, and looked around for more toast.

'No more. I'm getting dressed and I think we'll go for a drive and explore the district. I have a good feeling about today.'

The dog wagged his tail, happy to go along with whatever she planned.

5

THE DOG WAS NOT sure about getting into the car until Cassie sat on the back seat and encouraged him to join her. She spread the old beach towel onto the seat and got him to hop in beside her, but as soon as she got out of the car, he leapt up to follow her.

'Listen, mate. Obviously you don't know about cars. Trips in cars are fun. You go to nice places. Behave yourself and you get to come along. Are you more used to the back of a ute or didn't you get any outings?' Cassie asked the puzzled animal.

Finally she got him settled, but as soon as she sat behind the wheel the dog wriggled into the front seat. She pushed him back and held up a finger. 'Stay. Sit and stay.'

This time the dog did as he was told and, looking miserable, he watched her every move. After a while, as the car headed out to the main road, he lifted his head and sniffed the wind blowing in through the top of the window. Cassie turned on the radio and sang along to an old David Bowie song.

Leaving the sea behind her, she headed towards the green hills of the hinterland and began driving past lush paddocks of fat cattle. English-looking cottages, smoke spiralling from their solid chimneys, stood surrounded by country gardens and deciduous trees. Occasionally, on some properties, there were moss-covered dry-stone walls instead of fences. Cassie felt she'd moved into a different country in just a few kilometres.

When she had walked into Whitby Point that morning, the newsagent, who now introduced himself as Ron, had told her about the historic estate of Coolangatta. It was the first European settlement in the district. According to Ron, Alexander Berry and his partner Edward Wollstonecraft had taken up ten thousand acres on the south coast in the 1820s and developed the land into a thriving business.

'Berry was Australia's first millionaire and he founded the dairy industry. The village he established has been restored. It's definitely worth a visit,' Ron assured her. 'Very popular place with tourists and foodies from Sydney. It's got a restaurant, function centres for conferences and it does weddings. We occasionally go there for Sunday lunch. My wife loves the place. They get booked out year round, you know.'

'I might go for a drive. Maybe I could check it out.'

'If you don't want to go there, you could always go on to Berry. It's a gorgeous little town. It's not far. Bit more than an hour,' said Ron.

So Cassie headed up the highway and through the traffic of Nowra. After the low-key, unhurried pace of Whitby Point, this busy city near the naval base made her realise just how peaceful Whitby Point was, certainly at this time of year. She saw the turnoff for Coolangatta, but decided to continue driving on to the township of Berry. Just before she got there, Cassie spotted an elaborate sign pointing to a winery and suddenly decided to visit it.

The winery driveway was lined with rosebushes, all pruned and awaiting spring. A tourist coach was parked at the cellar door, so Cassie stopped at the far end of the parking lot. The dog seemed relieved to get out of the car.

'We'll have to christen the lead I bought you this morning. Now stick with me and we'll just take a bit of a stroll through the garden area at the back. We'll keep a low profile, in case dogs aren't allowed to roam here,' Cassie told the dog.

The vineyards were situated in a pretty spot at the foothills of a mountain range. From the buildings and gardens it looked to be a newly established estate. The tour group from the coach had left the tasting room and were now settled in the restaurant so Cassie tied the dog to a convenient post outside the cellar door and walked in. She picked up a brochure and a wine list from the counter as a young man cleared away the used tasting glasses.

'Want to try anything in particular?' he asked.

'I'm driving, so I can only try a mouthful. I like sauvignon blanc. What is your speciality here?'

'Crisp whites. We grow some grapes for reds but don't blend them here, we send them to one of the bigger estates. But we do have an excellent range of whites, which we make ourselves: pinot grigio, verdelho and sav blanc.' He took a bottle from the fridge and poured a small amount into a glass for Cassie to try. 'Good light colour, hint of green, nice herbaceous touch. Crisp and dry. We also have a semillon–sauvignon blanc blend.'

'This is delicious,' said Cassie, after she had taken a small sip. 'Could I try a little of the verdelho as well?'

He poured. She sipped. 'That's really nice too. I'll have two bottles of each.'

Cassie knew that she sounded as though she was in a rush, but she didn't want to leave the dog for too long. Just as she was about to go, she saw a brochure advertising the Coolangatta Estate. 'I saw the signs pointing to that place. It's big,' she exclaimed as she opened out the brochure. The map in the brochure showed different accommodation buildings, function rooms, a restaurant, a space for garden dining, croquet and tennis courts, a pool and a golf course surrounding the heritage buildings. 'It looks like a whole little township!'

'Yes, even in the early part of the nineteenth century, it had a mill, workshops, blacksmiths and a lot of convict labourers. The estate had a huge business exporting thoroughbred horses to India, red cedar to Europe and cattle, tobacco, cheese and wheat to Sydney. Was quite the showpiece. Then it began to be run down and by the 1940s it was neglected and falling into ruin.'

'Who restored it? What a great thing to do,' said Cassie.

'Yeah, a farmer's dairy cows used to wander through the dilapidated estate and he got the idea of restoring it all. He started in the early seventies. Saved all those old convict buildings. Restored the whole lot. Now it's a popular place. Here's the menu for the restaurant, if you fancy stopping there for a meal. People go to eat or stay over. We get a lot of their guests coming in here.'

Cassie ran her eye over the menu. 'This menu sounds pretty impressive. I'm surprised that a place serving food like this does well on the south coast.'

'That's the point. People like to get away for the food, the wine and beautiful countryside. We run wine and food appreciation evenings here and you'd be surprised at how quickly they sell out.'

'Very interesting,' said Cassie thoughtfully. 'I'll have to bring my mum down here.' She paid for the wine, bought a bottle of water for the dog, untied him and headed back to the car. She poured the water into a bowl, which she'd borrowed from the cabin, and watched him drink before she settled him down again on the back seat and drove out.

'I think it's getting a bit late if I'm going to take you for a run on the beach,' Cassie told the dog. So as soon as she could, she turned off the highway, skirted around Nowra and meandered back towards Whitby Point along a scenic route that twisted its way back towards the coast. When they came to a stretch of open land she pulled over and let the dog run about as she sat on a boulder and looked at the hills, wondering if she could hike up one of them. None of them looked as big as the unusually shaped Pigeon House Mountain, which rose inland of Whitby Point and was named, she'd been told by Ron the newsagent, by Captain Cook because he thought it looked like a pigeon house. 'Perhaps I'll take the Pigeon House challenge,' she told the panting dog, now resting by her feet.

When she got back to Whitby Point in the late afternoon she took the dog to the beach and let him leap into the surf to retrieve sticks in a stretch of relatively calm, shallow water. They were both quite exhausted as they trudged back over the dunes and through a patch of she-oaks following the track back into town.

Cassie hoped that the small supermarket was still open as she needed some dog food. Then she decided to buy a small chicken for herself to roast and make stock from the carcass, which she would use for soup for the next few days. As she stood at the pet food section, she heard a voice behind her.

'Hi, Cassie. Planning dinner for your pal?'

She turned around to see Michael Phillips holding a shopping basket. 'Yes. But I don't know about this processed dog food. It doesn't seem healthy to me. What do you think?'

'I'm sure that young bloke would eat whatever you put in front of him. But as I can see you're a discerning gourmet, you could get fresh meat and beef bones. Don't know how you feel about 'roo meat, but it's lean and good for dogs. Cook it or give it to him raw. I have some excellent dry food back at the surgery. Bit pricey, but worth it. I see you have a chicken there, raw necks are good. You know never to give a dog cooked bones, don't you? They can splinter and pierce the intestine. Not nice.'

'Yes, I know that. But thanks for the advice. I'll get some of that dry food from you,' said Cassie.

Michael hesitated as if wanting to say more, then smiled and headed towards the deli section.

*

The next day, Cassie did little except cook for the dog and take him for a long walk on the beach south of Whitby Point, which they had to themselves. Later in the afternoon, as she was sitting on the front porch reading a book, the dog stood up and gave a low growl. She heard a car door slam and someone walking beside the cabin. The dog bounded down the steps barking with his hackles raised but then stopped barking and began wagging his tail as Michael Phillips came around the corner carrying a plastic bag.

'He's changed his mind about you,' said Cassie, smiling, surprised to see the vet. 'Maybe it was that flamingo top.'

'Dogs know that the smell of the surgery isn't a happy sign,' he said cheerfully as Cassie came back out onto the porch. 'How are you getting on with your new mate?'

'Just fine. We've had a lot of fun, haven't we, boy?'

140

The dog looked at her and cocked his head.

'That's actually why I've come,' said Michael. 'I know who owned him.'

'You do!' Cassie was suddenly frozen to the spot, shocked at the impact his remark had on her.

'Yes. I'll tell you the story.'

Cassie pulled up a yellow painted bentwood chair from inside for Michael and settled herself back into the wicker chair. Michael placed the plastic bag at his side and looked at the dog lying comfortably across the step.

'He's Tom Woodward's dog. Tom lived on a property some way out of town all his life. Ran some cattle and kept a few milkers. Last few years he took to growing roses. Used to bring them into town to the florist till she got married and took off. Anyway, Tom hadn't been seen for a bit, so his nephew went over to check on him. He found that poor old Tom had died in his sleep. Easy way to go, I guess. Animals were in a bit of a state. And the dog was missing.' He smiled at the dozing black and tan dog. 'Tom always had smart dogs, he taught them well. The nephew thinks the dog had gone looking for food. He came to see me to see if anyone had brought a stray in. I realised straight away your dog was Tom's dog. I told the nephew you were dog sitting and he was pleased.'

'When is he coming for the dog?' asked Cassie.

'Well, he says he has enough dogs already, he doesn't need another one, and he wondered if you could take this one on full time?'

Cassie leaned forward and clicked her fingers. The dog instantly woke and came to her side.

'Could you have a dog in Sydney? How is your husband going to feel about it?' asked the vet, glancing at Cassie's wedding ring.

'Frankly, I don't care what he thinks. He loathes dogs and cats. And we own an immaculate modern apartment in the heart of the city, which is not pet friendly.' She took a breath and gave a broad smile. 'But the good news is, we're getting a divorce, and at the moment I'm based at my mother's in a house with a great garden.'

Michael grinned. 'Well, that's good news. I mean for the dog. Sorry you're going through the mess of a breakup. Been there, done that,' he added with a shrug.

'Oh. I see. Would you like a coffee?' Cassie hurried inside feeling a bit flustered. She hadn't expected to feel so strongly about the dog. When Michael had said he'd found the owner, she realised that no matter how hard she'd tried to remain detached, she'd become fond of the kelpie cross.

She carried out their coffees and some milk on a tray and put them on the table.

'And here's the dried food I promised,' said Michael, pointing at the plastic bag on the porch.

'Thank you very much. What do I owe you?'

'They're samples, so nothing. I'm pleased he's found such a good home. Old Tom was good with animals, so he'd started training this chap, but he didn't go in for newfangled things like microchips – or vets, if it comes to that. You'll have to bring him in if you want to microchip him. You might think about desexing him, too.'

'I guess so. What normally goes onto the microchip?'

Michael picked up his mug of coffee and poured in some milk. 'Dog's name, owner's name, address, mobile phone number. All or any of the above.'

'Well, I don't have an address and the dog doesn't have a name.'

'No address? You said you were living with your mother.'

'I am, but it's not permanent. I'm just waiting for the apartment to sell. Then it looks as though I'll have to find a place to live that will allow dogs, and a job to pay for it.'

'What do you do?'

'I'm a lawyer. But, as with my marriage, I found myself locked into something I didn't like and now I want to get out. I guess you make a bad choice and you live with it until something big happens. In my case my husband had an office affair. We worked at the same law firm. It not only shocked me that he was having an affair, but it humiliated me that everyone at work knew.' Cassie couldn't believe she'd just blurted out these details, but she suddenly realised that she didn't care what anyone else thought. She didn't feel embarrassed or afraid of being pitied anymore. It was a good feeling. 'What about you?'

'Oh, the same story, but it was more than a casual affair. My wife ran off with my best friend. Took a bit of getting used to, being cheated on by the two people I was closest to. Wrecked my social life,' he added with a slight smile. 'I used to be uncomfortable admitting what had happened, but time has moved me on.'

'Ouch, that must have been very hard. But, you know, I think the best thing that happened for me was that it gave me the motivation to quit my job. What I'm going to do next I have no idea. My biggest mission in life at the moment is to name this dog!'

Cassie opened her arms, for the first time not holding back on showing her affection for the kelpie cross. The dog put his front paws on her lap and licked her hands. She couldn't help smiling at the vet.

'Any ideas, Michael?'

'Tom's nephew thought that his name was Will, or Bill. He couldn't remember.'

'Bill. He's Bill,' said Cassie firmly. 'That's settled. Do you hear that? You're Bill. Okay, Bill?'

Michael chuckled as the dog pricked up his ears. 'He certainly recognises it. Well, bring him up to the surgery when you're ready.'

'When I can fit it into my crowded calendar,' said Cassie, laughing. 'Geoff Spring is taking me fishing, and I'm thinking of hiking up to the summit of Pigeon House Mountain, and I'm going to drive down to Batemans Bay, not to mention hanging out here and reading a big fat book.'

'Excellent. Maybe you could spare some time and let me take you to lunch on Sunday to a pub I know. The pub's nothing fancy, it's seen better days, but the food is truly amazing. Bill can come along too.'

'Thanks, I'd like that. There are some interesting places around here. Yesterday I called into a winery that seemed pretty good. I brought back some bottles to try. Would you like to try a glass of sauvignon blanc?' she said.

'I think you could twist my arm to celebrate Bill's official arrival in your life,' said Michael. As the evening cooled, they chatted comfortably on the porch over a glass of wine. Michael was pleasant company, Cassie thought. She was glad that she and Bill had met him.

*

The following morning Cassie set off to visit some of the other towns nearby. She called in to Milton and immediately fell in love with the artsy-crafty vibe there and bought Bill a bandanna, which she tied jauntily around his neck. He walked proudly beside her, his tail up, looking pleased with himself. When she stopped at Lake Conjola she could tell by the number of cabins and caravans that this would be a popular place for summer holidays. Further north, near Sussex Inlet, she pulled over to look at the vast expanse of St Georges Basin.

'That's a lot of water,' she said to Bill. 'I wonder if it's used for waterskiing. I don't think I want to go any further. That's enough driving for one day, don't you think? How about we head home?'

The return journey took less time than she thought it would, so, on a whim, she decided to continue south. She'd driven less than ten kilometres past Whitby Point when she saw a sign to a place quaintly named Blue Crane Lake. She was entranced and took the turnoff.

The lake, which narrowed into a river flowing towards the sea, was crossed by a pretty wooden bridge. Scattered around the shoreline of the lake were some old holiday cottages, several boatsheds, a boat hire place, and a small shopping centre that contained a general store with a petrol pump and a sub-post-office agency, a takeaway café and a bait shop selling fishing gear. There was a little park, so Cassie decided to get a takeaway coffee and sit by the water.

Bill was excited to see seagulls landing close by, and he bounced around giving short enthusiastic barks. Cassie sat in the sun on a bench at the lake's edge, sipping her coffee and watching as a pair of pelicans swooped in and landed in the water in an ungainly fashion.

A few small dinghies were pulled up along the grassy banks. Not far away was a jetty where some bigger boats and several houseboats were moored. Across the lake all Cassie could see was a green blanket of trees and the unmistakable shape of Pigeon House Mountain. She realised that the holiday houses strung along the lakeside would have wonderful views. A solitary fisherman was trying his luck from the bridge. On the far side of the lake there was a long two-storey building surrounded by landscaped gardens, which gave the area a holiday resort feel. Bill, meanwhile, had discovered a school of tiny fish darting through the shallows, and he pranced and pounced in the water, snapping mouthfuls of the lake in an attempt to catch the silvery fish.

Cassie was charmed by the peaceful setting. Blue Crane Lake felt like a secret location, tucked away from the coast and the highway. It was different from Whitby Point. More secluded, but she could see that money had been spent on homes and she had the sense the area could become very upmarket if development were handled sensitively. She had noticed several very interesting houses, which were probably architect designed as they blended in well with their natural setting.

She and Bill walked a little further around the lake and she saw a boatshed sporting an open deck which looked as though it had been turned into some sort of accommodation. 'That's a nice idea,' she commented to Bill. 'Throw a line in off the deck and catch dinner.'

She took a closer look – there were a few dead pot plants and the boatshed had dusty windows. Must be a summer holiday place, she thought. As she walked around to the street entrance, she saw a sign beside the front door saying that the place was for lease or for sale.

Cassie stood and stared at the old blue boatshed with its fading and peeling facade. The way the windows and door were designed, the entrance looked like a face. But a sleeping face. From where she stood, the upper storey looked as though it was quite spacious.

'Too bad we don't have a boat,' she said to Bill as they headed back to the car.

*

The next couple of days passed pleasantly. Her mother still hadn't returned from her trek up Mount Kinabalu, so the news of Bill would have to wait.

On Sunday, Michael picked her up for lunch in his well-worn four-wheel drive. Earlier that morning Cassie had felt quite nervous about going out with him, and had begun to have second thoughts. He was the first man that she had been out with since the breakdown of her marriage. She wasn't sure she was ready to date again.

But as soon as she saw his friendly face, she felt pleased that she had accepted his invitation. He apologised for the condition of his car as he put Bill onto the back seat.

'I'm sorry about the state of the vehicle. It's my work-horse. It has to carry all sorts of gear, drive into properties up in the hill country, get into paddocks, cross creeks, you name it. It's not had a very glamorous life.'

'No worries. Bill feels right at home.'

Bill was sitting happily in the back seat with a 'Where are we going today?' expression on his intelligent face.

Suddenly Cassie had a vision of Hal and his hundred-thousand-dollar sports car and almost laughed aloud at the idea of going anywhere in it with Bill.

She had a lot she wanted to ask Michael about the local area, and she wanted to tell him about her trips around the countryside. Once they started talking, the hour-long drive to the pub sped by. Michael turned off the main road, and took a smaller road up to the head-land where there was a strange old building clinging to the edge of the cliff top.

'It looks a bit precarious,' said Cassie as they got out of the car and she saw the crumbling hillside. Signs of slippage and erosion were evident. Not only that, but the entire hotel looked as though it should be condemned. She clipped the lead onto Bill's collar. 'So it's the food that's the attraction?'

Michael chuckled. 'Don't be misled by appearances – hard as that may be. I promised you a special lunch. We'll sit outside, then Bill can be with us. But don't worry. This place is quite safe.'

Michael led the way, followed by Cassie with Bill at her heels.

Cassie was not impressed as they walked past the old reception desk on their way to the beer garden. It was piled with cartons, the carpet was threadbare,

147

and she could see a gloomy staircase leading upstairs. In the dark wood-panelled hallway was a handwritten sign pointing to the bar, the restaurant and the toilets. Despite the abandoned entry she could hear the clatter of dishes and the sound of voices competing with the loud music.

When they entered the beer garden the first thing Cassie noticed was the dramatic view. Part of the lawn area had obviously fallen away over the years, shortening the expanse of grass that was bordered by straggly shrubs. Beyond the shrubs was a wire mesh fence to discourage people from going too close to the edge of the cliff. When Cassie looked down, she glimpsed a beach and she could hear the waves crashing on rocks below. Looking into the long windows of the restaurant, she could see that its décor was circa 1970. Adding to the atmosphere were a bank of poker machines and a row of television sets showing the horse races, which were being studiously watched by a group of punters. There seemed to be a lot of tables and chairs outside, some with umbrellas and most of them full. Michael chose one that was out of the wind, and Bill lay down under the table.

'I'll go and get us a drink and a water bowl for Bill and bring back a menu. There's not a lot of choice, the chef does a limited menu. But it's always good.'

Cassie was amazed by this fusty old place. It was so dilapidated she struggled to imagine it had ever been smart or had pretensions. But it was almost full. It seemed to be a popular spot for Sunday lunch.

Michael returned with a bowl of water for Bill, and was followed by a smiling waitress carrying a tray with two tall glasses containing a pale liquid garnished with a tuft of celery and sliver of pineapple.

'It's the house cocktail. Green apple juice, a shot of vodka, a bit of this and that. It's not too lethal.'

Cassie sipped her tall drink. It was tangy, with a slight kick of fruitiness. 'It's lovely. I suppose the vodka creeps up on you.'

'They have an excellent local white wine here. I thought we could have a glass with the meal if that's okay with you? See if it measures up to that wine you bought the other day, which was great.'

'I'm amazed there are so many people here. It seems so out of the way. And people certainly haven't come for the décor and ambience, although the view is spectacular.'

'Here, have a look at this – it might explain why so many people come here,' said Michael as he handed her a menu.

Cassie opened the plastic folder. The menu listed a few entrees, and some tempting mains with options of salad, vegetables or duchesse potatoes. Desserts were simple: fresh fruit compote, panna cotta, homemade ice-cream or mandarin syrup tart. 'This looks fresh and interesting,' she said with some surprise.

'Would you like an entree? I'm tempted to go for a big meal then I don't have to worry about dinner,' said Michael. 'I know the lamb shanks are delicious. But I'm a seafood man, so I think I'll go for the snapper fillets.'

'It is winter so I'll have the fish pie with potatoes and steamed Asian greens.'

After Michael ordered the wine for their meal Cassie said, 'I suppose you treat a lot of big animals at your practice? I've seen a lot of dairy cows on my drives. It looks like there is still a lot of traditional farming around this area.'

'There are a lot of hobby farmers around here, too – executives who quit the corporate rat race to farm or start a small vineyard or grow some specialty product. Hobby's the word – I doubt they make a living from it. It's a lifestyle choice until they get jack of it and hire someone else to do the nitty gritty for them,' said Michael.

'Yes, I've known several lawyers in Sydney who had weekend hobby farms. They thought it would be a fun retirement project. Usually didn't last. They came back to their harbourside houses, yachts and the golf club.'

'But the old farming families stick it out, though times are unpredictable and it's not a given that their children will follow them onto the land,' Michael told her.

'It's not like the big outback stations around here, is it,' said Cassie. 'Where pioneers settled and families built up those vast properties over generations.'

'Actually, you'd be surprised at the number of people in agriculture, and other industries like fishing, whose families have been here for generations. My family have been fishing these waters ever since my great-grandfather came here in the 1920s,' said Michael. 'But these days farmers and fishermen are facing too many difficulties. So a lot of the farms have been carved up, or farmers have to look at value adding, hence the small sidelines like additional produce, B&Bs, tourism. The fishing industry has been most affected. Whitby Point was once a huge fishing centre, over a hundred fishing boats. There was even talk of a cannery at one stage. Big tuna was big business. They used to export it straight to Japan as well as supplying the Sydney fish markets.'

'So your family was in the fishing industry? Geoff was telling me about its downturn. Sounds a bit complicated, hard to know who's to blame.'

Before they could continue the conversation, the entrees they had ordered arrived.

'This looks marvellous!' Cassie exclaimed.

'Steve's French onion soup is a winner. I have it a lot,' said Michael.

'Steve is the chef here?'

'Yes. A nice bloke,' said Michael.

'The menu and this presentation show a lot of experience. Where'd he train, I wonder?' mused Cassie. 'How'd he end up here?'

'He's from Sydney. I think he got fed up with the city pressure, and he's a surfie. He's a bit younger than me and he likes to stay close to a beach and the coast, and around here is an affordable place for him to live.'

'Any ambitions to move on?' wondered Cassie. 'I know what you mean about the pressure, it's not easy being a chef. My parents owned a restaurant for years, so I know how it is. There was a young chef working in our family's restaurant, he seemed good, but the pressure in the kitchen got to him and he started drinking, and after work he hit the party drugs pretty hard. When he was on top of things he cooked brilliantly, other days he was totally out of it. My mother had to fire him in the end.'

'You know a lot about restaurants.'

'I suppose I do. I'm not a chef, but I do know the business side of running a restaurant. I understood how it all works. I enjoyed helping Mum and Dad. But Dad died and Mum sold the business. She's taken to travelling. She's climbing Mount Kinabalu at the moment.'

Michael laughed. 'How great. My parents aren't quite so exciting. They left Whitby Point when they retired and moved to the Blue Mountains, which surprised me. They said they wanted a change of climate. They certainly got that, but they like it in the mountains – it's quite different from living by the sea.'

'Do you like living here?' asked Cassie.

'Yes, I love this area. It's where my sisters and I grew up. It's special and relatively unspoiled. I've been around a bit. Did a stint as a vet out in Moree and I've done my city slicker scene with an upwardly mobile wife, as well as a six-month locum in beautiful but wet Wales. The climate there was really hard to take and I was glad to get back home. After my divorce I headed back to Whitby Point to lick my wounds. Then my grandfather's old home came on the market and it seemed like fate, so I bought it and set up my practice in it.'

'Hmm, I can understand that,' said Cassie thoughtfully. 'I love my parents' home but I don't plan on living there. It's a great location, and I enjoy being with my mum, but I'll move on.'

'But you do like being there?'

'Yes, in a way. Mum's house is near the beach and I love that, but Manly's always crowded. Not like down here. I'm beginning to think I could get used to the south-coast lifestyle.'

After the waitress brought them their main course, Cassie looked at Michael and shook her head. 'This is amazing. I never for one moment imagined food like this in such a tumbledown place like this pub. Sensational.'

Michael looked pleased. 'I knew you'd like it. It is good. Look, even Bill is impressed.'

Bill had moved from under the table to sit expectantly at Cassie's knee, his nose quivering in the direction of the inviting smells of their lunch.

'Later, mate. We'll take you for a run before we get home. Okay?' said Michael.

'I'm trying not to feed him tidbits when I eat,' said Cassie. 'But it's hard, he always looks so pathetic. And with just the two of us, I'm treating him like my best mate. I'm so glad you found out his story, so I can officially adopt him. For better or worse.'

'His loyalty to you will be absolute,' said Michael. 'You've got a new best friend.' He lifted his glass. 'To you and Bill.'

They finished the meal and then, at Michael's suggestion, they shared a dessert.

152

'I need the walk on the beach now, not just Bill,' she exclaimed. 'Thank you so much, Michael. This meal has been an unexpected revelation.'

'I'll take us back via a different route, there's a spot where we can let Bill run to his heart's content.'

Before they reached Whitby Point, Michael parked near some trees on a wide stretch of grassy verge to let Bill take off across the unfenced land. In the distance they saw a tin roof glinting in the sunlight. It was open land of rich grass, which had once been part of a dairy farm. Bill streaked ahead, nose to the ground, sniffing out rabbits. Cassie and Michael wandered down to the bottom of the slope, where there was a narrow dirt road.

'This track winds around the corner and back up the hill so we can do a circuit back to the car,' said Michael.

'I suppose you get to know all these back roads when you treat animals out here?'

'Yes, I do come out here occasionally,' said Michael. 'There's a small vet practice a bit further south of Whitby Point but the vet's only part time. The next big practice is nearer Bateman's Bay, but I help out if I'm needed.'

As they rounded a bend Cassie called Bill, who took no notice until Michael gave a piercing whistle, which brought him running to their side. He was panting and excited.

'If a dog could smile, Bill would come pretty close,' said Cassie, laughing and giving him a pat. 'Walk nicely now. Heel.'

'He's smart,' said Michael as Bill obediently trotted at Cassie's heel.

'There's a small farm down the bottom of this dip, then the road curves up to where we parked,' said Michael.

'I think I've walked off my lunch, but I won't bother with dinner,' said Cassie as she spotted a handwritten sign tacked to a wooden fence bordering a farm. 'Vine-ripened tomatoes. I bet those are good. Can we pop in and see?'

'Of course,' said Michael and they turned down the rutted dirt driveway.

Cassie spied a large shed, a tractor and a couple of large glasshouses. 'This all looks very neat and tidy,' she said. 'I suppose the tomatoes are grown in the glass houses. I wonder what else they're growing?'

'There's the shed, I bet that's where we'll find the tomatoes. You plan on taking some home?'

'You bet. Can't beat fresh, just-picked tomatoes.'

A grey-snouted dachshund waddled to the entrance of the shed and gave a perfunctory bark. Bill returned with a low growl but stopped when Cassie said, 'It's okay, Bill, we're on his territory.'

Inside the shed, which was filled with farming equipment, several tables were set up, one covered with bags and baskets of tomatoes in various stages of ripeness. Two men were seated at a separate table enjoying a glass of red wine and playing cards. One of them, who was wearing navy shorts and a T-shirt, got up to greet them. He was rotund, balding and short, and spoke with a thick accent.

'Come in. The dogs they are good. My dog, she is very old.'

Bill and the dachshund circled each other, sniffing at tails.

'Hello. I saw your sign about the tomatoes,' said Cassie.

'Help yourself. These green, good for chutney; these soon ripe, good now; and these very ripe, good for passata – tomato sauce.'

'*Da quanto tempo sei stato qui*?' asked Michael. '*Siete una famiglia locale?*'

Cassie stared in surprise at Michael, as the farmer answered Michael, also in Italian.

Michael grinned at Cassie. 'He tells me that his family wanted to start a vineyard but it didn't work out, so now they grow vegetables.'

'You speak Italian very well. At least it sounds as though you do,' said Cassie in admiration.

'Thank you. Actually I learned Italian only recently. Thought I could get closer to my Italian heritage if I did.'

Cassie sniffed the ripe tomatoes. 'Wow, these smell so rich and full of flavour. Two dollars a bag, I'll take three bags, please. I'll find some use for them.'

Michael strolled over to the table where the farmer and his friend had been playing cards. A loaf of bread, torn into chunks, lay on a plate beside a bowl of olive oil. He picked up the dark green bottle of oil, took off the lid and inhaled. 'This smells really good.'

'You're not wrong,' said the farmer's friend with a strong Australian accent. 'Never thought I'd be telling someone bread and oil are a good feed. But my mate has got me hooked on the stuff. He cooks a mean risotto, too. It's our Sunday lunch thing, y'know.'

'Charlie brings some of his lamb and I cook the stew,' said the farmer.

'You should open a restaurant,' said Michael. 'Where's this oil from? It smells great.' He peered at the label.

'It's made by my friend in Victoria. He brings to me when he comes and I sell it to my friends. Like the tomatoes.'

'Can I try some of the oil?' asked Cassie.

'Sure, sure, take some bread and dip.'

Cassie and Michael tore off small pieces of the thick bread and dipped them into the green olive oil.

Cassie raised her eyebrows and looked at Michael. 'This tastes great.'

'I have plenty bottle. You want some? I sell for my friend. Fifteen dollar flagon.'

'I'll take one. Twenty-one dollars for the oil and the tomatoes – what a bargain. What a fabulous foodie day!' She smiled at Michael.

'You're easily pleased. You'll like it around here. There are a lot of local organic farms and people are starting up all sorts of gourmet enterprises around the coast. One of my clients has started growing truffles, and she has trained her pig to find them.'

They thanked the farmer and headed back up the hill to the car with Cassie's purchases.

It was late in the afternoon when Michael dropped Cassie back at her cabin. She offered him a drink but he shook his head.

'No thanks, I have some animals to check on now and an early start in the morning, but enjoy your week.'

'I can't thank you enough. I'll save you some of my tomato sauce.'

It had been a long day. Cassie and Bill stretched out on the porch to watch the sunset through the trees. The temperature began to drop as the sun sank. Cassie wished she could contact her mother as she wanted to share the day with her. She wanted to tell her what a lovely person Michael was and about the ramshackle old pub where she'd had lunch. The more she thought about the food they'd eaten the more impressed she was with it. She'd definitely go back, especially if her mother came to visit. Suddenly she realised how much she'd love her mother to come and experience this place. It would be fun. Bill stretched and came and sat in front of her.

'What? What?' teased Cassie.

Bill cocked his head, looking hopeful, and gently put a paw on her lap.

She laughed. 'Okay. Just because I can't eat a thing doesn't mean you want to skip dinner too, does it? You were very good today. Let's see what we can rustle up.'

She fed Bill and went to check that her car was locked before settling down for the night. There was a note under her windscreen.

Trixie and I are going fishing about 7 tomorrow morning just before high tide if you want to join us. We'll be across from the lagoon on the beach. I have some gear for you. Cheers, Geoff.

'Sounds like a plan, don't you think, Bill?'

*

The sun was obscured behind some cloud, but there was no wind and they had the beach to themselves. Trixie, Geoff's wife, was a tiny ball of energy and Cassie liked her immediately. She'd already caught a tub of long sandworms by dragging a smelly bait tied in a stocking along the sand and then grabbing the head of each sand-worm as it appeared in the wash of the receding waves, then pulling it out.

Geoff was using a big surf rod, walking along the beach and trawling his line as the surf was still not up. The tide was rising and Cassie thought that it looked nice and 'fishy'.

'Cast your line out into the gutter where it's deeper. You can tell where the gutter is by the colour of the water,' said Trixie. 'Or am I teaching my grandmother how to suck eggs? You seem to know what you're doing.'

Cassie dipped her hand into the bait bucket, pulled out a strip of sandy worm and attached it to the hook. She had added an extra sinker to her line to anchor her bait in a hole in the seabed or the gutter. 'A flattie or a jewfish would be nice,' she said.

'I'm after tailor. The cat loves 'em and they're good for bait for bigger fish. If you bleed them straight away they're okay to eat. Does your dog eat fish?' asked Geoff.

'Haven't tried him. I'd have to pick out the bones. Sounds like a bit of a hassle.' She glanced back at Bill. 'Keep away from the bait,' she told the dog as it bounded away to chase seagulls.

157

Although the three of them were separated along the beach looking for the best spots, they were united in their pleasure of wading into the edge of the surf to cast their lines, or walking along the beach with their lines dragging behind, then winding in and landing a fish.

After three hours the sun finally appeared from behind the clouds. They'd each caught several fish, lost several others, and were wet and pleased with their morning's effort.

'Have you had breakfast?' asked Cassie.

'A cup of tea or coffee wouldn't go astray,' said Geoff. 'I'll clean your flathead in exchange.'

'It's a deal,' said Cassie. 'It's only ten-thirty. What a great way to start the day.'

After they'd washed the fish and the saltwater and sand off themselves, Cassie carried mugs of coffee out to the porch. Trixie was carrying a plate from their car.

'I made a cheesecake if you'd like some.'

'Wow, that looks good! How nice of you.'

'Trixie's the dessert queen around here,' said Geoff proudly.

As Trixie cut slices of the perfect-looking cheesecake, Cassie said, 'I took a drive out of town to Blue Crane Lake. It's a beautiful spot. What's the fishing like down there?'

'You need a boat to get to the good spots in the lake. But the place gets plenty of people in the summer. Did you see the glamorous condo complex that's just been built there? Very upmarket, but low-key, if you know what I mean.'

'Some famous architect designed it,' added Trixie. 'It certainly blends in with the surroundings.'

'I love the old boatsheds. I think I'll go back and browse around.'

'You'll know this area pretty well before too long,' said Geoff.

'Does this taste as good as it looks?' Cassie asked as Trixie handed her a slice of cheesecake. Her eyes widened as she took a bite.

Geoff laughed and Trixie looked pleased.

'Told you,' said Geoff.

'It's heavenly. Thank you, Trixie,' said Cassie. 'I can't believe how good the food is around here. I had lunch at the old Cliff Top pub yesterday. Shocking building, but great view and stunning food!'

'Oh, that's Steve Baxter,' said Trixie. 'He's turned into quite a chef. He did some catering for a while, but needed full-time work. I'm glad he's found a niche.'

'I imagine people go to that pub mainly for the food,' said Cassie. 'Is he a local?'

'Don't know much about him, except that he used to live in Sydney and he loves to surf,' said Geoff.

'He's no self-taught cook. Properly trained,' added Trixie.

'I'd say, from what I sampled, that he could work in any big city restaurant, but obviously that's not his style,' said Cassie. 'And Trixie, your cheesecake is up to any multi-star restaurant.'

'Thanks, Cassie. I love to cook. We must be going. It's been a great morning. Enjoy your flathead.' She gathered up the container she'd brought the cheesecake in and nudged Geoff.

'We'll have to get together for a bit of a barbie. Glad you and the dog are a permanent item,' said Geoff.

'Me too. It's been a lovely start to the day. So different from my last life!'

'Why don't you stay around here?'

'Don't be silly, Geoff. Cassie said she's a lawyer. And she's young, not retired like us.'

'So what? Young people live here, too. Better place to live and work than the city if you ask me. Course I'm prejudiced,' said Geoff.

'I don't want to be a lawyer anymore. I don't plan to go back to it. This place has spoiled me. I'm having a very good break.'

'You deserve it, I'd say. Anytime you want to go fishing or come round for a cuppa and one of Trixie's creations, just give us a hoy,' said Geoff kindly.

'I will. Thank you both,' said Cassie, feeling very touched.

'See you. Enjoy the fish, and keep the rest of the cheesecake,' said Trixie.

*

'You're late,' said Ron, glancing at his watch as Cassie arrived to collect her morning paper.

'Went for a morning fish with Geoff and Trixie Spring. Got a few too.'

'Good one. What else you been up to?' He rang up the newspaper.

'Cruising round the countryside. I like Blue Crane Lake.'

'That's the hidden gem of this area. But not cheap. Lot of Canberra and Sydney people own places there. You thinking of buying?'

The question caught Cassie by surprise and she found herself answering Ron before she'd thought about it. 'Kind of, but not a posh place. There's a boatshed for lease there that looked comfy. I could try it on for size maybe. See if I like it. Use it as a weekender perhaps.' She was thinking aloud. 'It's just a thought. I'm going to have another look at it this morning.'

And, with Bill at her heels, she walked back to the cabin, muttering to herself and the dog, 'What on earth am I thinking?'

But once she returned to Blue Crane Lake she felt again that the place was special.

'What have I got to lose by just looking?' she said to Bill. 'It mightn't be any good after all.' And with these words in mind, she entered the real estate office and asked to see inside the blue boatshed.

Karen the agent was busy and friendly. 'Here's the key,' she said. 'You go down and look around. I'll meet you there in twenty minutes if you don't mind. I just have to meet someone to get a contract signed and then I'll join you.'

Cassie stood on the broad footpath, which she supposed was originally a space for a boat, in front of the street entrance to the boatshed. The double doors of the boatshed had been converted to large windows and between them was a bright red door with a brass handle and ship's bell on the side to use as a doorbell. She unlocked the door and Bill raced inside.

The building was bigger than she'd realised. There was a narrow wooden staircase leading to a loft area. To her surprise the downstairs living area contained a stack of tables and chairs. This living area flowed towards two bi-fold doors. When she opened them, sunlight and fresh air blew in. Bill bounded onto the deck in delight, then lay down under the railing with his paws hanging over the edge, watching small mullet darting in the water below. There was an old boat ramp but the best part, Cassie thought, was the small wooden jetty, which, although in bad condition, had two fat pylons at its end, each holding a contemplative pelican.

Bill spotted them at the same time as she did.

'Don't you dare. Leave them be,' warned Cassie. 'Let's look upstairs.'

The loft was surprisingly spacious with a bed by the window, a comfortable chair and a tiny bathroom and toilet. Bill leapt on the bed and peered out the window.

'It's a nice view of the lake, eh?' said Cassie, imagining lying here at night with the smells and sounds of the lake and the rumble of the ocean in the distance. 'But off the bed, Bill. Not our place.'

'Hello, anyone home?' the estate agent called out.

'This is very cute,' said Cassie, coming downstairs. 'Does the furniture stay?'

'If you want. There's heaps of it.'

'Yes, what are all the tables and chairs doing here?'

'The guy who lived here before used to run a café here. Served coffee and hamburgers. It was a bit of a mates' hideaway and he only charged mates' rates, so the place went broke and he walked out when he couldn't pay the rent.'

'Is there a laundry?' asked Cassie.

'Yes, there is a laundry. Small but functional. Do you want to look?'

'I like the kitchen,' said Cassie, looking at the cooking area, which was separated from the main living space by a counter.

'There's a barbecue tucked away somewhere. It was sometimes used out on the deck. Those awnings wind out over it. Good for shade and they keep the rain off, too. The place has been empty for some time. And you have to be careful on the jetty. There are a few planks rotted away. Do you have a boat?'

'No,' said Cassie with a laugh. 'But it'd be fun to get a tinnie.'

'There used to be a small boat, I think, but it doesn't look as though it's here anymore.'

'That's not important. How long is the lease?' asked Cassie. 'And is my dog allowed?'

'Six months or a year, with an option to extend. The dog's not a problem.' Karen looked at Cassie and Bill. 'What do you think? It gets busy here in the summer. Not quiet like now.'

'I like the peace and quiet,' said Cassie. 'How noisy does it get?'

162

'Jet skis have been banned from the lake, thank goodness, but there are a lot more people around. Bit different from Whitby Point. Holidaymakers come here for the fishing, the park and the lake, but this place is less about families and more about relaxing.'

'What's the rent?' asked Cassie.

Karen told her.

'I just love it here. Okay, how do I apply for it? How soon will I know if I've got it?' Cassie could hardly believe herself. On a practical level it was daft to take on the lease of the boatshed, but on another level it was an opportunity too good to let slip through her fingers. The place was captivating. She could afford six months rent and, she told herself, she deserved a bit of peace and quiet and a place to relax while she made decisions and plans for her future. Yes, it was definitely the right decision.

'I'll talk to the owners but they're keen to lease it. I've got the forms with me. If you put your application in today, I reckon they'd approve it pretty quick. When would you want to move in?' asked Karen.

'As soon as possible,' said Cassie. 'I can't wait.'

6

CASSIE ENJOYED THE EASY routine of her mornings: the sound of the sea; the salty tang in the air; the rustle of the wind in the casuarinas; Bill's amiable yawns and stretches before he licked her hand to hasten her move from bed; and later the smiling faces who greeted her on the walk to the newsagency to collect her newspaper, where Bill had become something of a celebrity.

'This is a beautiful new world,' she murmured to the dog as she buttered their shared piece of morning toast. Her life here was so different from the hectic pace and stress of living in a city, working under pressure in a law firm, not to mention the unsatisfactory nature of her marriage to Hal. Only now, as she felt so calm and relaxed, did she realise the extent of the daily tension she'd been living with before she had fled to her south-coast hideaway.

'Well, Bill, now I've made this mad decision to move into a boatshed, we're going to have to live with it, but it won't be stressful, I can guarantee you that,' she told the attentive dog.

That morning, she and Bill walked into town as she wanted to share her news about the boatshed with someone and as her mother was still not contactable, she headed up the hill to the lovely old house where Michael had his veterinary practice.

Tara, who doubled as veterinary nurse and receptionist smiled at Cassie and Bill. 'It's lovely that you decided to adopt Tom Woodward's dog. What's his name?'

'Bill. I've come to make an appointment to have him microchipped.'

'Hello there, Cassie. Hiya, Bill.' Michael came out of the examination room and greeted them both cheerfully.

Bill, who had been sitting quietly, leapt up at the sight of a friend.

'I'm just making an appointment to have Bill microchipped.'

'I think I have a small window before the next appointment. Come on in.'

Michael lifted Bill up onto the examination table and Cassie held him. The chip was put in so quickly that Bill barely noticed a thing.

'Do you just want your mobile phone number on the database? No address?' asked Michael.

'I have an address but it might be only temporary.'

'Oh? You're moving back to Sydney? We can always change your details.'

Cassie shook her head. 'No, I'm not going back to Sydney. You're the first person to know. I've signed a lease on a boatshed at Blue Crane Lake . . . Am I nuts?' she asked with a smile.

Michael burst out laughing. 'That sounds terrific. The lake is a gorgeous place. Is the boatshed habitable?'

'It's totally liveable, though it needs a few bits and pieces done. The previous tenant used the front part as a small café, but that doesn't matter. I love the whole set-up. I've leased it for six months. I'd love you to take a look at it.'

'I can do that. I know I've got no late appointments, so if nothing else comes up we can run over and you can show me later this afternoon. If there is an emergency, Tara, the vet nurse here, can ring me and I can get back here pretty quickly. Is it furnished?'

'Yes, the furniture is not too great but it will do, so I can move in soon. I'd love your opinion.'

'Okay, I'll ring you as soon as I'm free, stay in mobile range.'

*

They picked up the key from the real estate office. While Cassie opened up, Michael walked around the boatshed. Bill went straight to the doors leading onto the deck, waiting for them to be opened. Michael picked his way along the jetty, startling two blue herons sitting on the pylons. At first Bill lay on the deck looking for fish, but the tide was too low and the fish had disappeared from the ankle-deep shallows. Scrambling off the deck, he followed Michael to the end of the jetty.

Cassie was investigating the kitchen as Michael and Bill came in.

'There are a few broken planks on the jetty – nothing that can't be fixed. Now let's see this interior. You could always live out on that deck. It's very pleasant. There's a nice breeze, even though it's a bit cool, and there's no mud so you won't be plagued by mozzies or midges.' Michael gazed around at the dining and sitting area, the counter and the kitchen and the front entrance where tables and chairs were stacked. 'This is interesting. Planning on a lot of parties?'

'The furniture's left over from the café.' Cassie opened what she thought was a cupboard but it turned out to be a small pantry. Looking up she could see that above the existing kitchen cupboards was extra storage that went right up to the high ceiling. 'Wow, this is more compact than a ship's galley, but it's been well designed,' she exclaimed. 'I'll take you upstairs and show you that, if you like.'

'This is great,' said Michael, looking around the loft. 'It's very cleverly thought out, and I love the view. I think you and Bill will be very comfortable here.' He paused. 'Have you made any other plans?'

'Like a job?' she replied. 'I'm thinking about it.'

'Actually, I meant social plans. Would you like to come over for dinner tomorrow night to celebrate your boathouse? Bring Bill of course.'

'Thank you, Michael. That'd be lovely.' They smiled at each other.

*

The following evening, Cassie found she was looking forward to going to Michael's for dinner that night. She took her time dressing, paying attention to her hair, clothes and makeup.

'Not that it's a real date,' she said to Bill. 'He's just so easy to be with.'

She checked herself in the bathroom mirror. She'd put on her best jeans and teamed them with a cashmere jumper. Wishing that she was tall and willowy rather than petite, she added a pair of black high-heeled boots. She bundled her dark auburn curls into a knot on top of her head, leaving some tendrils falling around her face. Finally, she added a little mascara to highlight her green eyes.

Then she tied Bill's bandanna around his neck and drove up the hill to Michael's house.

The sun had well and truly set as Cassie and Bill walked to the front entrance. Bill seemed relieved they had bypassed the surgery.

'Hello, you two,' said Michael as he opened the front door. Bill darted inside and instantly the dog screeched to a halt as a large tabby cat marched down the hall towards him.

'Don't worry, Cassie, the cat is used to dogs. He hangs around the surgery. Bill, this is Toledo the tabby.'

Cassie watched Bill lower his tail and ears and start to tiptoe around the large cat, which ignored him. But as Bill crept past with apparent relief, the cat took a swift swipe with his paw and struck a lightning blow on Bill's tail. The dog took off down the hall while the cat casually strolled away.

Cassie giggled. 'Cats! They rule the world.'

'You look very nice,' commented Michael as he led her down the hall.

'Thank you. I brought some wine. I hope you like it,' she said in a rush to cover up the pleasure she felt at the compliment.

'You didn't have to do that, but thank you. I have a nice champagne chilled. Would you like a glass of that first?'

Cassie nodded as she cast a curious glance around Michael's living room at the eclectic mix of furniture, paintings, books and antique rugs. Through the plate glass windows she could see out into the pitch-black night.

'I bet this has a great view to the beach in the daytime,' she said.

'It certainly does, although it can get a bit breezy out on the verandah at times. But it is relaxing. Your new abode has a great outlook over the lake. And you can throw a line in and catch dinner.'

'Do you like to fish?'

'I haven't fished for a while. Too many years slogging away on my great-uncle Ricardo's fishing boats when I was young, I'm afraid. I'm over cleaning fish for pocket money.'

'I know you told me that your parents had moved to the Blue Mountains, but are there other members of your family still here? Do they still fish?'

'Absolutely,' said Michael. 'In our family, it is expected that you follow your father and your grandfather. Respect your elders and wait your turn, that's the Italian way. My great-uncle Ricardo is nearly ninety, but he still runs the family fishing fleet, although it's a lot smaller than it used to be. It's his son and grandson who do all the fishing now. Cousin Frank is a great at selling the fish, too.'

'It's good they're keeping up the family tradition,' said Cassie. 'You say your family's Italian, Phillips isn't a very Italian name.'

'My mother is from the Italian side. She was an Aquino. But my father was the local accountant and worked for my grandfather before he married my mother. Whitby Point is a small community.'

Michael picked up the ice bucket with the champagne bottle in it. 'Do you mind coming into the kitchen while I throw the last bits together? Bring your glass.'

Cassie sat on a stool at the long kitchen counter. 'Can I help?'

'No, thanks. Everything is under control.'

'It smells fantastic. What are we eating?'

Michael lifted the lid of the large casserole dish on the stove. 'Sicilian fish stew. Old family recipe from my great grandmother, one of the nonnas.'

'It must be wonderful to belong to a big extended family. It's just Mum and me in my family now that Hal and his relations are history. It must be nice to have a heritage and a family like yours.'

Michael laughed. 'I suppose so. A lot of the old ways persist but now everyone considers themselves true-blue Aussies. If you throw in that parsley, we're ready.'

Michael served up the stew in the kitchen and took the plates out to the dining table.

'Do you like cooking?' he asked Cassie as she ate.

'I do. But I didn't do a lot in Sydney. Too busy. My father was the chef in the family. Michael, this stew is delicious.'

'Are you going to tell your mother about the boatshed or is it going to be your secret hideaway?' asked Michael.

'She's arriving back from overseas in a day or so and I can't wait for her to come down and see the boatshed. Knowing my mother, she'll think it's a terrific place.'

'What about your girlfriends? I bet you'll be overrun with Sydney mates wanting to come down for weekends on the south coast when they hear about your new place.'

'I don't think so. Either they are having babies, or working crazy hours, or both. Anyway, I worked such mad, long hours over the last few years, I hardly saw them. I feel a bit out of touch.'

'I think that even if you move back to Sydney, you should keep the boatshed as your idyllic retreat.'

'It does feel a bit like that,' agreed Cassie. 'I can't wait to move in.'

Much later, curled in her bed at the cabin with Bill sleeping solidly alongside her, Cassie thought back over the evening, marvelling at what she had been missing for so long: the easy warmth and company of an interesting man. Michael and she had talked about so many things from music and art to food, travel, friends and books.

She had found herself laughing and feeling relaxed. It was such a good feeling. Bill had slept on the floor by her feet, waking occasionally to cast a wary eye at Toledo who was curled in a ball on a nearby armchair. When she'd left, Michael had opened her car door for her, staying in the driveway until she turned out of it and onto the road. It had been a lovely evening and she hoped it would be repeated.

*

Cassie had just walked out of the newsagency the following morning when her mobile phone rang.

'Hey, Mum! You're back. How was it?'

'Unreal. Stunning. It was a really hard climb, two days, but I made it to the top. Now I want to go back and see more of Borneo. It's so beautiful. How are you? You're still down on the south coast? You must be liking it,' said Jenny enthusiastically.

'Love it. But Mum, I want you to come down. You have to see this place. When do you think you can come?' asked Cassie.

'Really? It's that good? Your father was right about it then. He always said it was lovely,' said Jenny. 'Cassie, I've only been home a day. You're hard to reach on that mobile. There must be a lot of black holes. Are you coming back home soon?'

'I don't feel in any rush. Mum, I really want you to come down here and see if it's just me, or if you think the place is as nice as I do. You could just come overnight if you're busy,' pleaded Cassie.

'I do have a bit of catching up to do. But you've got me curious. I'm having dinner with Donna and Dave to tell them about my climb so I can't stay long, but I can drive down now, spend the night, and come back the tomorrow,' said Jenny.

'That'd be fabulous, Mum. I'll give you directions to my cabin here at Pelican Cove. You won't have any trouble finding it.'

*

Jenny and Bill bonded immediately.

Bill had barked when the strange car pulled up, standing protectively beside Cassie, but when she ran to hug her mother, he too hurried forward, tail wagging, waiting for pats and endearments.

'Mum, this is Bill.'

'Well, you're a fine specimen, young man,' said her mother, scratching behind his ears. 'Does he come with the cabin?'

'He does now. He's mine. I've adopted him.'

Jenny raised her eyebrows. 'So he'll be joining us when you come back to Sydney?'

'I'm not sure. It's a bit of a story. Come on in, and we'll get you settled and then I'll take you on the tour of the area and tell you all about it.'

Cassie drove her mother around Whitby Point to show her the little town, stopping off at one of the local shops to buy some cheeses and olives, and, over coffee in the solitary café that was open, she explained her plan to rent the boatshed for six months.

Her mother stared at her. 'Cassie, this is a lovely spot, but it's a holiday place. Could you live here full time? What would you do? You can't just bury yourself here. You were the gal working fourteen hours a day! What would you do with yourself in a quiet backwater like this?'

'I guess it does seem strange,' said Cassie easily. 'But it's the first time in my life I've had time to take a breath. I went from school to university, then to work and marriage. I've never really done anything on my own, never even considered any life other than in the fast lane.'

172

Jenny nodded. 'I do understand. Maybe you should travel. I'll lend you the money till the apartment sells, if you like.'

'Thanks, Mum. I'll think about travelling but I don't need to borrow money at the moment. I've got weeks of holiday pay left, so I'm fine. Now, I really want you to come and see the boatshed. It's only a ten-minute drive away. The place isn't expensive and I'm only renting it. Mum, I want my own space to call home.'

'Between my place in Sydney and your retreat down here, I suppose this could be a nice arrangement for me, too,' said Jenny. 'Let's go and have a look at it.'

As Cassie drove into the little settlement of Blue Crane Lake, her mother became instantly enthusiastic.

'This is gorgeous,' exclaimed Jenny. 'What a pretty area. Seems different from Pelican Cove. Maybe a bit more upmarket, but in a low-key way. Some of those houses over there look pretty classy. But you can't beat being close to the water. Where's your place?'

Cassie parked outside the blue boatshed and Bill jumped out and raced around the front to the jetty, giving the herons a warning bark.

'What do you think?' asked Cassie as her mother stood thoughtfully, regarding the front entrance.

'How can I tell if you don't open up?'

Cassie unlocked the front door and started to chatter, 'It needs work, but Geoff – you'll meet him – will do it and . . .'

'Cassie, just let me get in the door and wander about!'

Bill rushed straight to the bi-fold doors, anxious to get out onto the deck. To his joy the water was high enough for him to watch the little fish swimming below.

'This is a great deck, and it has an awning. I'd live out here. Perhaps not in winter, but when the weather starts to get warmer, it will be lovely. What an outlook! Where's your bedroom?' said Jenny.

'It's upstairs, Mum. In the loft.'

Cassie sat on the deck while her mother explored. How lovely to know that she could do this any time of the day, and she wasn't even going to feel guilty about it.

'This is the life, eh, Bill?' she remarked to the dog. Bill, his head hanging over the edge of the deck, eyes fixed on the darting fish, took no notice. Cassie closed her eyes in the winter sunshine.

'Well, Cassandra, I'm knocked out by your boatshed.' Her mother sat down in a faded canvas deckchair.

'In a good way?' Cassie asked.

Her mother flung out her arms. 'Cass, look at this place! The view, the location, the set-up! This whole area is really lovely. It makes me wonder why your father never brought us here.'

'Yes, I know. But this is pretty good, huh? Even have my own resident herons sitting on those pylons. It seems that the name Blue Crane Lake is a bit of a misnomer according to Michael, Bill's vet. The birds aren't cranes at all, but herons.'

'Is that right? But, Cassie, this place is a gift. I know what I'd be doing here if it were mine.'

Cassie stared at her mother. 'What did you have in mind? Remember, I'll be living here, not you, though you're welcome any time.'

Her mother shook her head. 'When you said it had been a coffee shop tacked onto a cute water's edge home, I didn't visualise this.'

'What are you suggesting? That I renovate it? I'm only leasing, although of course I have a few ideas to jazz the place up a bit.'

'Cassie, with very little effort and by being a bit more creative than the previous occupants, this place could be a goldmine! It's the perfect location for a restaurant, or perhaps a café or bistro.'

'Mum! It's going to be my home! I just want to live here and relax and enjoy it!'

'Yes, darling, but you wouldn't have to run a big place, or even have long hours. This could be made into a great little local place that tourists would love to visit. And you can live here as well. How perfect.'

'I hear you, Mum, it's what you would do, but I've never run a business before. You've had years in the restaurant trade, and you and Dad were hugely successful at what you did, but I'm no chef like Dad was,' protested Cassie.

'Neither was I, but you're like me. You know how to run a restaurant. I used to watch you, and I know that you have an instinct for it. I was always grateful for the times you helped out. You have absorbed more about the restaurant business than anyone who's graduated from some fancy hospitality school. Hire a chef to do the cooking. You can run the rest. In summer this area must be super popular. I wasn't thinking about your having a place like the Seven Seas that could seat over a hundred. No, a place like this should be casual, intimate and exclusive. And think of the seafood on your doorstep, so to speak!'

'Not just the seafood, Mum, you can't believe the local produce in this area. It's absolutely amazing. So fresh and such great quality,' blurted out Cassie, infected with her mother's enthusiasm. 'The dairy foods, you wait till you try the cheeses I bought today, the organic vegetables, and there is quite an Italian influence . . .' She stopped. 'Well, I just stumbled across some things . . .'

'See, subconsciously you've been doing the research! You just don't see the bleeding obvious under your nose! What else are you going to do with yourself down here?

A break is all very well, but you can't do nothing forever. You'd go nuts in no time.' Jenny looked out across the lake. 'What a view. You could put a few tables out here and customers could choose to eat inside or outside. Perfect.'

'You really think it would work? How much would I need to outlay? Theoretically, I mean, just supposing I went along with your mad idea,' said Cassie.

'The bones are here. The tables and chairs seem fine, but the kitchen and loo definitely need upgrading. Maybe put in a cool room, if you can afford it,' replied Jenny.

'Mum, you know what would be good out here, rather than having a few small tables, I could put in one or two long communal ones. It gives people a chance to meet each other, especially if they are on holidays,' said Cassie thoughtfully, glancing around the deck.

'Great idea! See, you're thinking already about your own style. Of course the big thing is the food. Obviously seafood . . . What else?'

'I haven't had time to think of that yet! Let me get used to the idea first.'

'Sounds to me as though you've had some ideas already, without even knowing it. But first you have to find a chef. Maybe you could ask some of your friends for ideas.'

'I will. Anyway, if I do go along with your crazy idea, I know what I'd call a restaurant here. The Blue Boatshed!'

'Love it! Let's crunch some numbers.'

'I don't know, Mum. I worked out I could pay the rent without any trouble, but starting a business, that's a different kettle of fish – so to speak!'

Her mother laughed. 'Give it a whirl, Cassie. The place just needs zhushing up, and clever planning, cooking, and selling the concept, and half of what you need is here already.

And my offer of financial help still stands. Remember, the basic rules are keep it simple, keep it genuine. You watch, start in a modest way, stick to those rules and the bigshots will soon copy you, like they did with your dad. He started a fish and chip shop and did so well with it that it grew to be the Seven Seas, which was copied by many, but they never did as well as your father because they ignored those two rules.'

Cassie smiled. 'I can't see me being copied and I don't know that this is my life's calling, but after my hellish life as a lawyer, a restaurant sounds like a welcome change. It just might work.'

'Of course it will. Cass, you know enough to know that it's hard work, dealing with staff, suppliers, health regulations, picky customers and all the nitty gritty that comes with a restaurant, but it's nothing you can't handle,' said her mother encouragingly.

'If I do start a restaurant, it won't be big like yours was. There's a big restaurant complex up the coast at a place called Coolangatta, and I have no intention of going in that direction,' said Cassie. 'I see this more as opening my home to friends who are dropping by.'

'Sweetie, actually, you will be opening your home,' responded her mother with a smile.

*

Cassie had asked Michael, Geoff and Trixie to come over that evening to meet her mother. She put out the cheeses and olives she had bought that day along with some water, biscuits and Italian bread sticks. She suspected that Trixie would turn up with something delicious to share and she was right. When Geoff and Trixie arrived, Trixie proffered a plate to Jenny.

'Hello, I'm Trixie. This is my hubby, Geoff. I've brought a little something to eat.'

'I'm Cassie's mum, Jenny Sullivan.' Jenny drew back the cloth from the plate and exclaimed at the still-warm savoury tart. 'This smells wonderful. Tomato tarte tatin?'

'Lovely roasted vine-ripened tomatoes and caramelised onion. Easy to nibble,' said Trixie.

'Trixie, another masterpiece, thank you. I'll see if I can find some little plates and forks. What would you like to drink?'

'Thanks, Cassie, I'll have a beer if you've got any,' said Geoff. 'Trix?'

'I'll have white wine, thanks, Cassie,' said Trixie. 'Your daughter's lovely. We so enjoy her company,' she continued to Jenny.

'And a good fisherman,' added Geoff.

'Yes, she and her dad used to fish and surf together. They had a special bond, perhaps because Cassie was an only child,' said Jenny.

'Cassie told me that your husband has passed away. That's very sad for you. He must have been quite young,' said Trixie.

'Pat died several years ago now. He was a lot older than me, actually. Eighteen years, in fact.'

'You must have been a child bride,' said Trixie.

'Not quite,' said Jenny. 'He had opened a restaurant and I went to work for him as a waitress, to help pay my way through uni, and I fell in love with him. Pat was such a lovely, kind man. There never seemed to be an age gap at all. I never regretted marrying him.' She smiled and changed the subject. 'I can't wait to try that tarte. Cassie said you were a good cook. You'll have to recruit Trixie, Cass,' Jenny told her daughter as Cassie handed out the small plates and forks.

'Shhh, Mum. Give me a chance to tell Geoff and Trixie my news,' said Cassie, but she got no further as Michael arrived and Bill romped through the group to greet him.

Michael shook Jenny's hand.

'I'm Michael. It's good to meet you, Jenny. I hope you enjoyed your mountain-climbing adventure.'

'So you're the vet that Cassie's been telling me about,' said Jenny with a meaningful smile at Cassie.

'What would you like to drink?' Cassie asked Michael, ignoring her mother as she handed him a plate with a slice of the tarte.

'One of your delights, Trixie? A beer would be good, if you have one, thanks, Cassie.'

'Of course,' said Cassie. 'Okay, everyone, now that you're all here, and have met my mum, I have an announcement. I took Mum to Blue Crane Lake and showed her the boatshed I've decided to rent. She loves it.'

'Great, Cassie,' said Geoff. 'I think I know the place. I knew you'd end up one of us.'

'Wait, there's more,' said Cassie laughing. 'My mother has suggested that, as the boatshed was once a café, I should continue the tradition – but do it a little differently.'

'It's been closed for some time,' said Geoff. 'You're going to re-open it? And live there, too?'

'It's a very pretty setting,' said Trixie. 'I don't think they made the most of that café.'

'It'll need a bit of TLC, won't it? I'll help you with anything you want done,' offered Geoff.

Michael had been watching Cassie. 'This is a surprise, going into the hospitality business.'

'I'm not exactly a stranger to it, but I'm open to ideas and suggestions.'

'You must meet my cousin Frank Aquino,' said Michael. 'I told you about him and, if you are going to have seafood on your menu, he's your man.'

'Seafood? Are you going to serve meals and not just coffee and cakes?' asked Geoff.

'We thought that Cassie could create a small but interesting menu to serve to a hopefully discerning clientele,' said Jenny.

'How fabulous. That would really suit Blue Crane Lake,' said Trixie. 'I'd love to help.'

'Trixie, I think that Mum is right. I should hire you to make the desserts and a few specials like this,' said Cassie as she bit into the light flaky pastry.

'Easy, I can do that at home. But I'd love to help out in the kitchen and if you need me for the boring stuff like cleaning, I'm your girl,' offered Trixie.

'The first thing Cassie needs to do is to talk to the real estate agent to find out if it's okay with the owners to re-open the café and for her to make changes. Then she'll need to check with the council regulations to see if it's okay to remodel or renovate, and then get Geoff onto it,' said Jenny. 'I'd love to be part of this but I'm really sorry, I have to go back tomorrow.'

'Mum, that's okay, you'll be back. You won't be able to keep away!' said Cassie.

'Darling, remember I'm driving to Broome in a convoy with a group of friends in a few days. I'll be away for several weeks. It's a long drive. But I'll keep in touch, and give you the benefit of my experience. But enough of food and restaurants. Michael, Cassie tells me your family have lived here quite a while.'

'Four generations. Actually the family and most of the town will be celebrating my great-uncle Ricardo's ninetieth birthday shortly. Cassie, would you like to come? It will be a lot of fun. Geoff and Trixie are coming, aren't you?'

'Yes. We're coming,' said Geoff. 'One of the first jobs I had when I came here was for the old man. He has a bunch of stories to tell, that's for sure.'

'Yes, he does, when he's in the mood and he likes you,' said Michael.

After Trixie and Geoff left, Cassie decided to take Bill for a quick walk.

'Anyone fancy a walk with Bill and me? Do you want to come, Mum?'

'Bit too cold outside for me, Cass. I'll stay nice and warm close to your pot-bellied stove, thank you. I can start cleaning up while you're out.'

'I'll come and keep you and Bill company,' said Michael.

'What do you think of the restaurant idea?' asked Cassie as they headed towards the lagoon.

'It makes sense, if that's what you really want to do?' said Michael carefully.

'It was Mum's idea, but it really feels right to me.'

'Then go for it. If it works you'll be able to pay your way and have a lovely lifestyle, even if you don't make a fortune. Are you going to be the chef too?' Michael asked.

'No. I know the sorts of dishes I'd like to have on the menu but I'm not a cook. You know who I'd like to talk to? That chef Steve at the Cliff Top pub where we went for lunch.'

'You're right. He'd be a great drawcard. So you're going to try and poach him?'

'Entice. I'm hoping he might be ready for a place that's a bit smarter than that awful tired old pub.'

'It would be great if you could get him. You might have to give him a bit of free rein though. Chefs are notoriously temperamental, aren't they?' said Michael.

'They can be, although my father was never like that. He was always quite calm in the kitchen, even when things were frantic. Yes, I'll chew that over before making an approach. But I'll get started on the renovations straight away.'

'I'll tell my cousin Frank that you want him to supply seafood to the restaurant. You'll like him, everyone does.'

'Thanks. Come on, Bill, time to head back. I can hardly see where I'm walking, it's so dark out here,' said Cassie. 'Michael, I'm glad you don't think the idea of a restaurant is totally insane. I know I can make it work.'

'I think it's a wonderful idea,' said Michael, taking her hand as they walked back towards the cabin, 'especially as it will keep you here in Whitby Point.'

*

When Cassie contacted Frank, he sounded very positive about her plans. It was just what the area needed, he told her enthusiastically as they talked on the phone. Her timing, he said, was terrific, and the boatshed was a clever concept. She should definitely specialise in seafood.

'My seafood, of course! Are you going to cook cutting-edge cuisine, traditional, Italiano, or safe?' he asked. 'I know someone who has started an eel farm. His smoked eel is sensational.'

'I don't want to scare customers away too quickly. Does middle-of-the-road sound a bit boring?' said Cassie.

'We'll see. When can you meet me at the fish co-op? I'll give you a seafood lunch to sample that will give you a bit of inspiration. How's that sound?'

'It sounds great. When will it suit?'

'How about Monday, at noon? See you then. Michael said you were a cute little redhead, so I'll look forward to meeting you.'

*

Cassie thought hard about the best way to approach Steve Baxter to offer him the job as the chef in her not-yet-opened restaurant. She didn't want to ask him while he was working so she decided to ask Michael for his ideas over a glass of wine on her porch one evening.

'Yes, that's going to be difficult. You can hardly front up to the Cliff Top,' agreed Michael. 'But I know where he is every Saturday.'

'That's tomorrow. Where?'

'Steve doesn't work the day shift on Saturdays, so he comes down for a surf at Littlemans Beach. When I close up the practice at midday and go down to the beach, he's usually there – especially if the waves are good. Come down to the beach and I'll introduce you. He's got a classic Simon Anderson board, an Energy single fin.'

'I doubt I'll recognise it. It's been quite a while since I've been surfing.'

Michael laughed. 'Do you surf? I could meet you there and we could catch a couple of waves. It's probably the only way to get hold of Steve. He'll stay out there for hours.'

'I haven't been surfing for years.' Cassie was suddenly flooded with memories of lazy Sundays at Manly. 'Dad used to take me out.'

'Did he teach you?' Michael asked. 'You must have had some father. I can't imagine my father ever being on a surfboard.'

'Yes, he was special. We used to sit out the back and talk about all sorts of things, abstract things that had nothing to do with our everyday lives. I thought he was very wise. Maybe because he was so much older than my friends' fathers.'

'Did your father come from Manly?' said Michael.

'I don't really know. When he talked about his life it was usually about the restaurant and how great Mum and I were. He didn't talk about the past, only the present and the future. He always told me to keep an eye towards the future and not look over my shoulder or have regrets. That was a handy piece of advice.'

'He sounds like a great dad. I learned to surf here on the coast with my friends. I thought that I could spend my whole life just surfing, but then I had a reality check and decided that I would rather work with animals.'

'When I was a teenager, I was never fanatical about surfing like some of my friends were, but I was chuffed that I managed to master my board and could tackle a decent surf with confidence and not make a goose of myself.'

'Did your husband surf?' asked Michael.

Cassie laughed. 'I did try to get him out, but he said that he wouldn't be seen dead carrying a surfboard. Not sophisticated enough for Hal, I guess. He preferred the lap pool at the gym.'

'I think swimming laps is so monotonous and boring,' said Michael. 'Are you going to give the surf a go?'

'I'm out of practice, and I didn't bring a swimming costume because it's winter, let alone a wetsuit, and I don't have a board and the weather and the water are freezing,' Cassie replied.

'Is that all? Easy to solve. I'll call a couple of my cousins and I'm sure they can lend you a costume. I can find a wettie that would fit you. I have some stashed away for when friends come down. And I can loan you a board. Or I could double you on my long board.'

Cassie laughed. 'I once rode double on a boy's bike and of course he sped down a hill to show off, and we crashed. I still have the scars on my knees, so I won't be doubling up, thank you.'

'Right then, no doubling. I'll bring a board for you and a wetsuit. I'll get a couple of swimming costumes dropped around to the surgery, which you can pick up and try on. So, no excuses. Meet me down at Littlemans Beach about one tomorrow.'

'Why not? Okay, let's do it,' said Cassie.

*

The next day, the sight of Michael sitting on the sand beside two boards, hugging his knees and intently studying the waves, made Cassie feel shy. She was nervous, wondering if she could still paddle out, pick the right wave, stroke and stand up on a board, but she guessed that it would be like riding a bike. It would all come back to her once she started.

'At least it's not a huge swell,' she said to herself.

Michael jumped to his feet as she approached. 'There's a nice break down to the right. What do you think? You ready?'

She dropped her towel and sunglasses onto the sand and took the board Michael lifted up for her. He was wearing faded board shorts and, when he stripped off his jumper, his body was lithe and well built. It was the first time Cassie had seen him out of long pants and a shirt and she felt disconcerted at how attractive he looked. They wriggled into their wetsuits.

'No Bill?' asked Michael.

'No, I didn't want him to see me make a fool of myself, so I gave him a big bone and a bowl of water and left him back at the cabin to amuse himself. Lead the way. Is Steve out there?' Cassie said.

'Way out the back. We'll paddle out to him when you're ready. Okay?'

Cassie paddled out strongly even though her arms began to ache. It all started to come back to her: the personal challenge of becoming one with the ocean, the time to sit and drift, how to pick exactly the right wave. While she waited, she stared down into the clear water beneath her. Her thoughts drifted and the distractions of daily life dissipated. She had always liked the simplicity of surfing, the skill it needed and the endless challenges it presented. It didn't require gadgets, technology, noise, engagement with others, just herself against the surge of the sea.

After fluffing the first few, Cassie caught a decent wave. She felt a sense of elation, her feet moving on the board as it ripped across the curling wave. She could feel the thrust of power under her and it ignited many sensations. She let out a triumphant yell of joy. When she turned and paddled back out, Michael skimmed past her on a wave and gave her a big thumbs up.

'Fantastic!' he shouted.

Out the back Cassie lay on her board to catch her breath.

Michael paddled over to her. 'Now you're back in the saddle, how do you feel?'

'Incredible. I could do this every day!'

'Do you want to try to run down the chef?'

'Okay.'

It was a long way out to where the larger, less frequent, waves broke. Here, there was time to sit and wait, while watching the horizon for the incoming shadowy lines of the swell that alerted the surfers to an approaching set of waves. Michael paddled slightly ahead of Cassie and approached a stocky man sitting on his surfboard concentrating on the approaching swell.

'Hey, Steve. Catching any?'

'Hiya, Mick. It's not bad. How're things?'

'Good. Can't complain. I've brought a friend to meet you. This is Cassie. She's new to the area.'

'Hi there. Where you from? You made a good move coming here.'

'Hi, Steve. City escapee.'

'On holiday or are you staying?'

'Hopefully staying, but that might depend on you. I asked Michael if he'd arrange this introduction.'

Steve gave her a puzzled look, then, holding a hand up to shade his eyes, checked the horizon for waves.

'Is that so?' he said, turning back to look at Cassie.

'Yes. I ate at the Cliff Top a week or so ago. Very impressive, well, the food was.'

Steve chuckled. 'Yeah, the place is a bit of a dump. What did you want to talk to me about? You having a party or what?'

'No, it's not a function. Something else.'

'Don't say wedding. I don't touch 'em.'

'No. Actually, I'm thinking of opening a small restaurant at Blue Crane Lake. I'd like you to be the chef. Create the menu, work with me, help style the cuisine. Whatever input you'd like.'

'You don't say. Hang on. Here we go!' He crouched and leaned forward and paddled furiously, as did Michael.

'Go for it, Cassie,' shouted Michael.

The wave looked as though it was going to be huge as it ballooned behind them. Cassie put her head down and dug her arms deep into the water, trying with all her strength to gather as much speed as she could. Then she felt the lift as it swelled beneath her and, gripping the board with her toes, she sprang to her feet, knees bent, flinging out her arms for balance. She dared not look behind at the wall of water, but concentrated on watching the tip of her board, adjusting her weight to slide across the wave as it rushed forward, avoiding the nose of the board digging into the wave and tumbling her underwater.

The ride seemed to last forever, she could hear nothing but the rush of the wave and see nothing but the beach skimming towards her. She shot past a paddler and a surfer sitting on his board and suddenly the wave deflated, drowning in upon itself. She rolled off the board, and felt her feet touching the rough sand. Her knees were wobbly as she headed for the beach.

'Wow. What a ride! You had enough? That was some finale,' said Michael, laughing.

'Hey, Mick, you guys getting out?' called Steve. Michael nodded and Steve paddled easily to the shallows, stood up and walked to where Cassie was sitting on the sand.

'I'm pooped. It's been years since I've surfed. I haven't had a ride like that for ages,' she panted.

'Well, you haven't forgotten.' Steve put his board on the sand and then plopped down beside her, flicking his wet hair back from his face.

'Cassie, I reckon you will be down here every day now,' said Michael.

'In between running a restaurant, eh? Where is it?' asked Steve.

'The old boatshed, the blue one. It used to be a coffee and hamburger place, I think. It's small, but I'm after a small but select clientele. Tables on the deck and inside. Concentrate on local produce. Especially seafood . . .'

'You know Frank Aquino?'

'Not yet but I will soon. Are you interested?'

Steve looked at the ocean for a moment. 'Could be. I live closer to Whitby Point than the pub, so I'd get more time to surf.' He thought for a minute more. 'Can I have a look at your set-up?'

'We're not actually set up yet. I have to make a few changes first, but I'm interested in any ideas you might have. Name a time when you want to meet there,' said Cassie.

'What about this arvo?'

Cassie thought quickly. She could get the keys from the real estate agent. 'Sure. How about four?'

'Okay. See you there. See ya, Mick. I'm going back in.'

They watched him head back to the water, his board tucked under his arm like it was part of his body.

'What do you think?' asked Cassie.

'He's interested. The next bit will be up to you and the . . . what are you calling it?'

'The Blue Boatshed.'

'Good call,' said Michael. 'And remember, if you need me to help, just shout.'

'Thanks, Michael,' she said. 'You've already been so helpful. It was great that you could introduce me to Steve. Catch him off guard. A bit unorthodox, but he didn't say no right off.'

Later that afternoon Steve, dressed in jeans and a T-shirt with a surfing logo on it, walked slowly around the little kitchen and then out onto the deck.

'I remember this place. It was pretty shocking but it's got a lot of potential.' He stood on the deck as Bill eyed him curiously. 'Nice space out here. Great view.'

'I was thinking of a couple of long tables out here and a more elegant set-up inside.'

'You could also put three or four small tables out the front, on that big cement area, and you could use that stand-up bar and counter stools as well. Kitchen needs a bit of an upgrade and they'll make you put in another toilet, but I reckon the place could be kinda fun, if you hit the right note.'

'I'm over trends and fashions and fickle bars and joints. I want people to come here for the food. Your cooking teamed with the fabulous local produce. The setting is a plus.'

Steve rubbed his chin. 'Have you checked out the local providores? Cheesemakers? Vegie mob? You know the high school runs a farm and they sell what they grow to the community? Good stuff, too. Some exotic vegies. Seafood is covered. And the local pork is a winner. I don't do bread or sweets unless it's an emergency.'

'I've got that covered. I've heard there's an Italian baker a bit further down the coast who's terrific, but I

189

haven't tested him yet. And Trixie Spring is my dessert queen.'

'Geoff Spring's old lady? I heard she was good. Look, I'm interested but we have to talk bucks and frankly I'd like to be flexible. I don't have cash to invest. At first I thought that you're probably just a city girl with more money than sense but now I think you might have more sense than money. Am I right?'

'Close. What do you mean by flexible?'

'You mentioned having my own input, having a say in things. I've always had a lot of ideas. I'm a good chef, even if I say so myself, but working at the Cliff Top – you can't imagine – it's like pulling teeth to get changes on the menu. If a dish is popular, it stays and stays and there's no room to move away. It kills me having a set menu when suddenly there are pomegranates or something else seasonal, but you can't use them because they're not on the menu.'

Cassie understood his creative frustration. 'Sounds like the law firm where I used to work. No room to move there either. But, here, collaboration is what I'm after. I love the ambience. I love the food that's around here. I love how there's a bit of an Italian backdrop to this area but I don't want to make this an Italian bistro. The seafood is great, but so is a lot of other food from around here. We can talk to Trixie about matching her desserts with what you want to do.'

'I'm over fusion, but what we could do is showcase the great produce available here on the south coast. The people we want to come here will know what they're after. They want healthy, homemade, keeping it real, "love with the grub" food, but with style. Know what I mean?'

'I do. Food with heart. Do you have any specialities?'

'Signature dishes? Nope. Don't want to set myself up and then have to put that special dish on the menu all the time. I like to cook what's fresh on the day so to speak. If I have a favourite cuisine, I suppose it's Italian.'

'Steve, your ideas are exciting. Tell me a bit about yourself. I can't offer you anything to drink, I'm afraid. Place isn't mine till next week.'

'That's okay.' He sat down on the deck and Bill mooched close. Steve held out his hand for inspection and then rubbed Bill's ears. 'That's a nice dog.'

'Yes. Bill found me and that's how I met Michael.'

'You met his family yet? They're part of the fabric of this place. You'll like Frank, he'll like you. He likes the ladies, does Frank, but he's all right.'

'I've been invited to Michael's great-uncle Ricardo's ninetieth birthday. I suppose I'll meet the family there.'

'For sure,' said Steve. 'I was invited too but I'm working. Always working. What sort of hours are you thinking of for this place? You getting some help in the kitchen?'

'Yes. Trixie. She's great, really efficient, no nonsense. She'll be good but I need backup. She'll cook her dishes at home and we can finish them off here. I'm sure we can get a kitchen hand and waiters.'

'Shouldn't be too much trouble. Lot of women around here looking for part-time work.'

Cassie liked the way the conversation was going, as if Steve was already part of the team. They began talking food and the hours that the restaurant should open. She told him about her family's connection to the food industry, and by the time he stood up to leave, she realised he hadn't told her a thing about himself.

'I'll let you know next week, if that's okay. What's your phone number?'

'We haven't discussed money.'

'For me it's about other things. This could suit me better than the Cliff Top. Just got to talk to someone first.

I know a guy who could take my place up at the pub so I wouldn't be leaving them in a hole.'

'I understand. Here's my mobile number. I'll be moving in here soon, but mobile reception at Pelican Cove is dodgy, so you might have to leave a message. I'll call you back.'

*

Franco, 'call me Frank', lived up to the charm and banter of his phone call. He looked far more Italian than Michael. Indeed, Cassie thought Frank had the heart-throb good looks of an Italian movie star. He was tanned with perfect white teeth and, while not very tall, he showed off his muscled physique in a tight T-shirt only partly hidden by a leather jacket.

He spoke loudly, calling out greetings to the men in long plastic aprons sorting through the day's catch at the fish co-op.

'Operation's not as big as it used to be,' he told Cassie. 'Most of those guys are crew, but a couple are boat owners. I've got my own business and my own boats, so I don't do much with the co-op, but I like to look in from time to time to see how things are going.'

'Do you send fish to Sydney?'

'Most of it. Some of the top, top chefs call me when they want something. I send really special stuff to Tetsuya. He's one classy chef.'

'What's always around? Snapper? Flathead? Whiting? What's available fresh? That's what we'll put on our menu.'

'Nothing frozen, eh? Are you going to work like the Mediterranean places – cook what's fresh on the day?'

'That's the plan,' said Cassie. 'I'd like to specialise in as much local produce as possible.'

'You know what you're doing then.'

'I grew up in a fish restaurant. My mum and dad used to run a big one in Sydney.'

'We have a lot in common then. Our family are all fishermen, since my great-grandfather came out here close to a hundred years ago. Of course Michael let the side down, him being a vet. But what a team you and I are gonna make!'

Frank became serious as the two of them inspected the seafood packed into plastic tubs on beds of crushed ice. He gently picked up some crabs and showed Cassie. Then he inspected a fish, lifting it tenderly with two hands.

'Beautiful quality. Seafood is different from meat. It's more delicate and doesn't have the muscle meat has because of its environment so it needs to be kept at the proper holding temperature in storage. The best chef can't fix the quality of seafood if it's been roughly handled before it gets to him.'

'I'm impressed. I think my father would have agreed with you there. He always said that fish had to be respected. Is the catch handled as delicately on the boats?' asked Cassie.

'As best we can. Fishing is a rough business. We still do it the old way with nets and poles. No big mechanised systems like those damn super trawlers. We're small, slick and sustainable. My father used to say his grandfather could talk to the fish, he could think like fish and he just had an instinct for finding them and catching them without any of today's technology.'

'Really? That's amazing,' said Cassie. 'By the way, Michael's asked me to great-uncle Ricardo's ninetieth birthday. I'm looking forward to it.'

'Well, Michael beat me there, I was going to ask you. Yes, my grandfather's big party. He's the family patriarch, so you'll meet all the family! Cast of thousands. Save a dance for me, okay?'

'Dancing! Will you have a band?'

'Of course. It's an Italian family gathering, so there'll be eating, drinking, singing, telling stories, kissing kids and more eating.'

'Wow. I come from a very small family, I'm an only child, so I like the sound of your big party.'

'That's too bad. Who did you play with or fight with when you were growing up?' asked Frank. 'Are you going to have a lot of kids?' He leaned towards her with a big smile.

Cassie changed the subject. 'I still have to get the restaurant set up. I think I have a chef coming on board, but also I need a regular supply of good seafood.'

'Of course you do. I'll look after you. We need a really good eatery around here. Are you going to do Italian?'

'No. We're not going the full Italian route, more local country. But as the chef has a bit of a passion for Italian food, we'll probably include a pasta dish or two.'

'Sounds good. Listen, let's go to the wharf. I've had a lunch prepared for us, one of the old family favourites so you can try out my seafood in situ as it were.'

'You didn't have to do that, but thank you.' Cassie was hungry and flirtatious Frank was good company.

Life was definitely looking up.

7

THERE WAS SUDDENLY A lot to do. Cassie felt at times as though she was surfing. She was on a wave and it was rushing forward and she wasn't sure whether she'd be wiped out or whether she'd ride it into the shallows and land on the beach. She felt exhilarated by the adventure of setting up her restaurant in spite of the risks she was taking. Each morning as soon as she opened her eyes she leapt happily from bed and began planning the day. It was so different from the times she'd had to drag herself, feeling weary and dejected, to face another day at the law firm.

She looked out of the loft window of the boathouse and across the calm lake at the morning mist rising from the water. She'd moved in only a couple of days before, but already it felt like home.

'Bill,' she told the dog. 'Who knew we could have it so good?'

Cassie called Jenny to tell her about her meetings with Steve and Frank. She listened to Jenny's advice on the financial organisation and paperwork involved in setting up a restaurant as well as her ideas for the kitchen.

'I thought the renovations would be more expensive than they are, but Geoff seems to be quite cluey and got me some good deals. Now that Steve has agreed to be chef he's also taking a passionate interest in the kitchen remodelling. The new layout is going to be much more efficient. Steve has made sure he has more room to work. Michael told me about a family estate that's come up for sale so I'm going over there to check it out and see if there's anything I can use. Apparently there's a big collection of cutlery, dishes, platters and vases that have been sitting in cupboards for years and years. Heirloom stuff that no one wants,' said Cassie.

'You won't want it either. You can't put heirloom fine china through an industrial dishwasher in a restaurant!' exclaimed her mother.

'That's what I told Michael but he said that it was all going for peanuts, so there's no harm in looking. At least if there are some decent big vases they could be useful. Anyway, Michael says it's a beautiful old estate and worth seeing. We're getting a preview before the dealers descend.'

'Well, it sounds like a nice day out. You seem to be getting along well with Michael,' said Jenny.

'Yes, he's sweet,' said Cassie, 'but before you say anything more, I'm not rushing it. It's just nice to know he's around.'

'If you say so, dear,' said Jenny. 'I feel guilty that I can't be with you but I'm off tomorrow on this trip to Broome. It's been organised for so long, I just can't pull out at this stage. I'll try to ring you when I can, so I know what you're up to.'

'I'll be fine, Mum,' said Cassie.

*

Saturday afternoon was clear with a nip in the air. Michael drove between the tall gates at the entrance of the estate and along a gravel driveway lined with ageing cypress pines. The formal gardens around the house were neglected, as were the paddocks spreading into the distance. The stone mansion was covered in ivy and a wisteria vine weighed down the front portico. The sandstone steps were covered in leaves and the windows were dusty and shut tight.

'Do you know how long it's been empty, Michael? It looks abandoned but it must have been grand in its heyday,' said Cassie. 'It's very English, even down to the four fancy chimneys.'

'The old lady who owned the place had been in a nursing home for many years. There was a caretaker here looking after the place, I believe. Anyway, the heirs are nephews who live in the UK and they have no desire to come out here. I'll park around the back near the stables. Laurie from the solicitor's office is meeting us here with the key to the back door.'

A young woman was waiting for them. She introduced herself to Cassie. 'Hi, I'm Laurie, from Mr Walker's office. Hi, Michael. How're things? Everyone's looking forward to your uncle Ricardo's birthday. It'll be some bash.'

She led them through the large back door into a vestibule full of cobwebby gumboots. Old raincoats, hats and jackets hung forlornly from pegs.

'It's very dark inside, I'll open a curtain so we can see better, as there's no power. All the china is set out in the dining room. I can't believe how much there is,' said Laurie.

'How many bedrooms are there?' asked Cassie, looking at the broad staircase leading upstairs.

'Six, I think, and a children's nursery above that. There's so much to be sold off. Sad really, isn't it.'

'Can we have a look around later?' asked Cassie. Then she gasped as Laurie pulled aside heavy curtains in the dining room and light flooded in, revealing piles of china and glasses and serving dishes stacked on the long dining table, on the sideboards and along the floor on one side of the room. 'There's enough here to stock a department store! Or three restaurants,' she exclaimed.

'It doesn't look as though it's ever been used.' Michael picked up a dish and turned it over. 'It's called Blue Daze, and it's pretty sturdy.'

Cassie picked up a white plate edged with a blue band that ended in a knot.

'This is rather nautical, but how much of it is there?'

Laurie lifted up a long velvet tablecloth. 'There are cartons of it under here. Boxes of it.'

'Here's another setting with the same pattern – smaller plates, bowls and serving dishes. Why would they have so much of it?'

'I believe there was a plan years back to turn the house into a boutique B&B, but it never happened. There's lots of linen that's never been used, either,' said Laurie.

'They must have been planning weddings and other big events. I just love it. It's good, solid china. Just perfect for what I need. Look, there's a setting in blue. I could mix it with the white,' said Cassie, seeing in her mind's eye the fresh blue and white theme of the restaurant.

'Why not look at the linen too? It's in one of the bedrooms. I'll give you the tour,' said Laurie.

*

'I'm glad we came in your big four-wheel drive,' said Cassie as Michael stacked the last of the cartons of china and glassware and canteens of cutlery in the back while Cassie piled the damask cloths and dark blue napkins onto the back seat between the glass vases and serving platters. 'I would have paid ten times the price they were asking for all this. It's stunning. Just perfect. Laurie, please thank Mr Walker for me,' said Cassie.

'He's only too glad to see the pile go down. A dealer is coming to look at the artwork, but there's all the farm equipment and the tools and the other household items. I believe there are quite a few Sydney dealers interested in seeing what's on offer.'

'Thank you again for coming out and letting me go through this first,' said Cassie.

'When is your restaurant opening? It sounds as though it will be very nice,' said Laurie.

'I'll send you and Mr Walker an invitation to our preview, so you can see for yourself,' promised Cassie.

'I think I'd better store all this at my place, until your remodelling is complete,' suggested Michael.

Cassie gratefully took him up on his offer, although there were some items that she kept to use immediately. When she had first moved into the boatshed she had bought herself some cheap bed sheets. Now she decided to replace them with the bedding she'd bought from the manor. She would luxuriate in fine linen sheets and lace-trimmed pillow cases and snuggle under her goose-feather doona covered in white embroidered damask.

That night she spread Bill's beach towel across the bed. 'That is your spot, okay? No dirty paws on this glorious linen, mate!'

Together they lay awake staring at the stars and listening to the lap of the water, until it sent them to sleep.

*

Several days later Cassie was down on her knees cleaning the long-unseen dregs of her kitchen after Geoff had pulled out the old stove and cupboards and taken them away to the tip. She wore old clothes, had tied a scarf over her head and knew she had dirt on her face where she'd wiped a filthy hand across her perspiring brow. Bill suddenly gave a low, unfriendly growl and went to the front door. Cassie got up and followed him to investigate.

'What's up, mate?' The dog was sniffing at the closed door. Someone rapped on it.

'Sorry, we're closed for renovations.'

'Hey, c'mon, Cassie. It's me.'

She froze and, sensing her dismay, Bill broke into a frenzy of barking. 'Hal? What are you doing here?'

'Let me in for God's sake and I'll tell you. It's good news.'

Cassie grabbed Bill's collar, saying, 'Stay. It's all right. I think.'

She opened the door to see Hal standing there, his Porsche parked out front. He gave a grin and raised an eyebrow. 'Caught you at an inopportune moment?'

Cassie was flabbergasted. He'd caught her off guard. She was annoyed by the intrusion out of the blue and the fact she knew she looked a total mess. 'What are you doing here? How did you find me?'

'I hadn't realised you were in hiding. Can I come in? Or will the mongrel attack?'

Cassie patted Bill and spoke in a soothing voice. 'It's okay, Bill.' But Bill was not convinced and gave another low growl. Cassie turned and walked indoors. 'C'mon through to the deck. As you can see I'm renovating.'

'Good grief. What is this place? Surely you're not living here? I ran into your friend Sarah and she said you'd moved down here, so I thought I'd check in.'

'What do you care, Hal?' Cassie sat on a chair on the deck and waved him to another one. She'd be blowed if she was going to offer him anything to drink.

'Don't be like that, Cass. I do care. Despite everything, I know I did the wrong thing by you, but that doesn't mean I don't care what happens to you. I can't believe you're living here, in a dump like this. Anyway, you'll be happy to know that the apartment has sold, so you can afford to do better than this. What are you doing here?'

'I'm opening a restaurant.'

Hal threw back his head and laughed. 'Good God. You're turning into your mother. Listen, we got twenty grand over the asking price for the apartment, so you don't have to bury yourself in a shed in this backwater. Come back to Sydney. I mean, what are you doing with your life? You can't stay here! You have a law degree!'

Cassie felt herself bristling. Hal had the ability to make whatever she was doing seem trivial. 'We're getting a divorce, so I can do whatever I want. And you know what? I am so glad to be out of Sydney and out of law. I have a life. I surf. I have a dog. I have friends. And I'm going to start a business.'

He shook his head. 'You're throwing your life away, Cass. Come back to Sydney. Can't we be friends?' He leaned forward, giving her the crooked smile and using the cajoling tone that used to win her over. 'You used to work for one of the biggest and best law firms in the country. Opening a restaurant is such a comedown. I'm sure I could get you your old job back.'

Before she could reply, Cassie was saved by a shout at the door. Bill leapt forward and started barking again. Unfazed by the dog, Frank came through the door carrying a box.

'Cassie, look what just came in.' He grinned at her. 'You look cute. Cleaning, huh? Where's Geoff? Isn't he supposed to be helping? Oh, sorry, didn't know you had company.'

Cassie stood up. 'Frank, this is Hal. A friend from Sydney. He just stopped by.'

Hal stood and shook hands with Frank, giving the handsome fisherman the once-over then, turning to Cassie with a bemused expression, he said, 'You have settled in well.'

'What have you brought, Frank?' asked Cassie.

'If you and your friend Hal want lunch, look at these little beauties.'

'Hal can't stay for lunch,' said Cassie briskly as she looked in the box he put on the table.

Frank pulled back a wet layer of sacking. 'Straight off the boat. Sweet fresh lobsters. Be a shame not to have them fresh. But you can freeze them if you want.'

Hal gave a whistle. 'That's sixty bucks a plate for one of those, and the rest!'

'Not in my restaurant. Frank, would you please do me a big favour and drop them up to Michael? I don't have a stove at present. I'll give him a call and maybe we can share them later.'

'Sounds good. We need a feed like these for your opening, eh? Nice to meet you, Hal.' Frank gave Cassie a wink and left.

'Frank, Geoff, Michael? Lobster feasts? Have you settled in with some handsome Mediterranean lotharios? I didn't think brawn and no brains was your style.'

'Oh, it makes a nice change,' she said airily. 'And Hal, everything they say about Latin lovers is true.'

Hal's expression darkened and he pulled out his car keys on the gold Porsche keyring. 'I thought I'd bring you the good news about the apartment. It would be nice to keep some sort of civil relationship going, but if you want to slum it down here with a bunch of fishing thugs, so be it.'

'I intend to,' said Cassie, then she suddenly realised the true purpose of Hal's visit. 'Kellie's dumped you, hasn't she? She's worked out what you're really like and left, and now you're lazy and arrogant enough to think you can pick up with me where you left off. There is no chance, so goodbye, Hal. Say hello to your parents for me. I'd better get back to my cleaning.'

Hal turned and walked away, banging the door shut behind him. Bill watched him go, then, as they heard the Porsche roar to life, he looked at Cassie and wagged his tail. She patted his head. 'You're the man in my life, Bill old boy.'

*

Michael's great-uncle Ricardo's ninetieth birthday celebrations were held in the community hall. Cassie had never been to a party like it. The room was decorated with fishing nets and photos of Ricardo's fishing exploits as well as colourful posters of the Aeolian Islands where his family was from originally. Two barbecues, one seafood, one meat, were sizzling out the back where a bar was set up and, inside the hall, long tables were laden with food. A small band played old Italian favourites. Children were everywhere and everyone was dressed in their best. The mayor was on hand to make a speech. Michael introduced Cassie to members of his family, which was so extensive that she lost track of them all. But everyone was welcoming, happy and obviously enjoying themselves. The initial formalities were not very formal, with guests interrupting and calling out comments in Italian and English.

A group of elderly women sat to one side gossiping in Italian, men gathered round the bar and barbecues to discuss football, younger children ran around, and teenagers danced together and giggled under watchful eyes.

Ricardo sat in a chair by the bar until he was ushered over to sit at the head of the table. Cassie looked at the imposing figure of Ricardo, with his shock of white hair, bright eyes and even teeth, and thought to herself what a handsome family the Aquinos were. Suddenly there were whispers and a ripple of excitement swept around the hall.

'What's going on?' Cassie asked Michael.

He smiled. 'It's a surprise guest. Uncle Pietro, Uncle Ricardo's brother, has come here from the USA for the birthday party. Uncle Ricardo has no idea.'

'That's a big effort. He must be pretty old?'

'He is, but he's younger than Uncle Ricardo. Uncle Pietro is a bit of a Hollywood celebrity.'

'Really? An actor?' Cassie tried to recall the name, but couldn't.

'No, he's not an actor. He's a set designer. Pietro d'Aquino. He's worked on a lot of big movies in Hollywood, and a few in Europe, too. He's won two Oscars.'

'Wow. I can't believe you have someone so talented in the family.'

'I haven't seen him for a while. He came out here maybe about fifteen years ago, but the last time I saw him was when I passed through LA ten years ago. He lives in one of those old mansions in the Hollywood Hills.'

'He certainly chose a different path from the rest of the family,' said Cassie.

Michael nodded. 'I'll take some photos of this. Ricardo will be so surprised. He told the family not to make a big deal of his birthday, to save it till he's one hundred, but who was going to listen? I'll just grab some shots. Back in a few minutes.'

Cassie watched the scramble around the doorway. A cheer went up and an aisle formed as the special guest walked towards Ricardo. Someone tapped Ricardo on the arm and pointed.

Pietro, smiling broadly and brandishing a white hat in greeting, came towards his older brother. The guests broke into applause and shouts of 'Bravo, Pietro!'

As soon as Ricardo saw his brother, tears sprang to his eyes and he held out his arms to embrace him. They hugged, kissed each other on the cheeks and talked all at once while everyone else congratulated themselves on the success of the surprise.

Cassie was moved at the sight of the two brothers greeting each other. Ricardo finally sat down again. A chair was found for Pietro and the family now all came to embrace and welcome him. Cassie was intrigued by the contrast between the flamboyant Pietro in his pale pink linen slacks and navy blazer sitting beside the rugged Ricardo dressed in a sombre dark suit and conservative blue tie.

'This is some surprise, eh? Beautiful, beautiful, isn't it?' said Frank as he put an arm around Cassie's shoulders.

'Hello, Frank. Yes, it's very touching. You have an amazing family.'

'Yes, it's quite something to get everyone together. All the rellies are here from Wollongong as well as from Sydney and even interstate. I'd better go. I have to get the mayor to do his bit. Are you being looked after?'

'Yes, thank you, Frank.'

'Say, have you met Howard and Marie?' He waved over a couple from the other side of the hall. 'These people make the best cheese on the south coast. Well, in Australia, come to that! Meet Cassie. And here comes cousin Michael.'

'We know Michael.' Howard smiled. 'He looks after our best milkers.'

'Howard and Marie have their own herd of Jersey cows and they make their cheeses from their milk. They win prizes at the Royal Easter Show. You'll have to get some for the boatshed, Cassie,' said Michael. 'In fact you should go visit their farm, Sublime Pastures. You'll have to leave Bill at home, though; no dogs allowed. It's all biodynamic.'

'I'll leave you folks to it. See you for the cake cutting,' said Frank.

'I'd be very interested in seeing your farm, Howard. I'm looking for good local produce for the restaurant I'm starting,' said Cassie.

'We supply a few places in Sydney as well as the local supermarket in Whitby. We do a line of gourmet cheeses you might be interested in. Here's our card,' said Howard.

'They make some fantastic Italian cheeses too. Their burrata is my downfall,' said Michael.

'I'll make an appointment,' said Cassie, slipping their card into her handbag. 'Are you also connected to the Aquino family?' she asked Marie. 'I'm wondering why you're specialising in Italian cheeses.'

'Of course! I'm the niece of Ricardo's wife's sister,' said Marie.

Cassie laughed. 'What a family! Did you get some good photos of the surprise arrival?' she asked Michael.

'I did. Thank goodness the surprise *was* a surprise, but there's more to come. There's still the cutting of the birthday cake, as well as dancing and of course yet more food. I hope you're not bored – any time you want to leave, let me know.'

'No, this is fun. Everyone is terrific, not to mention the food!'

'We're about to go and eat. Do come and visit our place, Cassie.' Howard and Marie waved as they headed for the still-groaning tables of food.

'How's life in the boatshed going?' Michael asked.

'Bill and I love it. It's a bit basic, especially without a working kitchen. Bit hard to cook everything in a microwave, but I'm looking at kitchen equipment, ovens and hot plates with Steve. So things are moving on. The best part is the end of the day when everyone has gone. Bill and I sit on that deck by ourselves and admire the lovely view across the lake. Very special.'

'Bit of a change of lifestyle for you. Oh, here's Ray, Ricardo's son, to make a toast. Raimondo is Frank's father.'

Ray made a simple but moving speech saying that the family were not only proud of Ricardo reaching the milestone of ninety but also of his lifetime of achievements not just in the fishing industry but in the Whitby Point community. He then introduced the local mayor, who had been asked to make the formal toast.

The mayor kept his remarks brief, paying tribute to Ricardo and his remarkable family.

'The Aquino family are part of the history of the New South Wales south coast – from Wollongong to Whitby Point and other far-flung locations. Along with the local fishing fraternity they established a significant industry, exporting to Japan and other international markets. From their Italian heritage they have blended the best of the Mediterranean traditions with the finest Australian ways, using a combination of old-world skills to focus on sustainable and environmentally safe fishing practices. The Aquino family have upheld the best of their old country and combined it with the Aussie way of life to be an example of what multiculturalism really means. Ricardo's father Joe, who landed here as a young man and made good, should make every Australian migrant feel proud. Ricardo has followed in his father's footsteps. He is not just a great fisherman but a good citizen whose involvement in his community, always with the highest ethical standards, is a beacon for us all. I now have the honour of proposing a toast to you on the occasion of your ninetieth birthday – *buon compleanno!* To Ricardo!'

Everyone raised a glass, waved, clapped and sang 'Happy Birthday'.

The cake was cut and slices were passed around as the band took to the stage to play once again.

'This is yummy – a kind of Italian–Aussie sponge cake combo,' said Cassie. 'Topped with whipped cream and strawberries like a pavlova!'

'The custard in the middle is special, it's got home-made limoncello in it. Now, come and meet Uncle Pietro. I'll introduce you to Uncle Ricardo as soon as we can get him on his own.'

As they approached Pietro, the elderly man rose to his feet, took Cassie's hand and kissed it. 'Charmed. Michael tells me you are new here. A wonderful addition to a sleepy village!' His accent was American and the combination of European charm and friendly American manners was captivating. Cassie felt flattered.

'Thank you. I don't believe it's as sleepy as all that, although I suppose after Hollywood it might look that way. Are you busy with a film at the moment?'

'I lead a simple life these days. I pick and choose my projects now, though I have agreed to be the set consultant for the remake of *Don Quixote* with Johnny Depp.'

'Johnny Depp, wow!' said Cassie. 'Do you travel to the locations of the films you work on?'

'Not anymore. Travelling tires me. When I came here I flew first class and that helps.'

'It must mean a lot to your brother to have you here,' said Cassie. 'He has quite a family.'

'I can't keep tabs on all of them anymore.'

'Hollywood is a big jump from the fishing industry,' said Cassie.

'I was never cut out for the fishing industry. I get seasick!' said Pietro, laughing. 'I was the creative one so I made the big move.'

'You certainly are creative,' said Cassie. 'I'd love to know more about how you work, but there's so many of the family wanting to chat with you.'

'We can catch up with you again later, Uncle Pietro,' said Michael. As they moved away, Michael said quietly, 'Cassie, some of the family are gathering at Uncle Ricardo's house for a quiet drink when all the formalities here are over. Could you stand to come along? Leave the dancing and drinking to the others?'

'That would be lovely, if you're sure I won't be out of place at such a family gathering. Michael, is d'Aquino your uncle Pietro's professional name?'

'No, it's our original family name. When his father came to Australia, he wanted to fit in, so he dropped the 'd' from d'Aquino and insisted that he be called Joe instead of Giuseppe. The story goes that he also wanted to call his sons Australian names, but my great-grandmother Evalina wouldn't hear of it, so they were all given Italian names. Now, of course, there's a mixture of Australian and Italian names in the family.'

'You certainly are an interesting family. I'm looking forward to meeting more of them.'

Later after the party had ended, Michael and Cassie went to a large brick house built above the wharf some time in the seventies, although the interior looked more like the 1950s. There was family memorabilia throughout most of the rooms.

'It's a bit of a museum. Uncle Ricardo can't bear to throw away anything to do with the family.'

'I think that's nice,' said Cassie as she stopped in front of the fireplace. Above the mantelpiece was a glass-fronted box in which was mounted a large forked spear. 'What's that?'

'That's a *traffena*. They used it to spear the big tuna back in the old country. It belonged to my great-grandfather

Joe. He brought it with him when he left his island home in Italy to come to Australia.'

'That's some family heirloom,' said Cassie.

'Yes, our family has much to thank my father for,' said Ricardo, coming up behind them.

'Uncle, this is Cassie, she's just moved here. She's going to start a restaurant at Blue Crane Lake.'

'Wonderful, wonderful. You have introduced her to Frank, of course.'

'Yes, thank you, he has. I wouldn't buy seafood anywhere else. He brought me some enormous lobsters the other day! I couldn't believe the size of them,' said Cassie.

Ricardo smiled. 'When I was a young boy, my brothers and I used to go diving for them. But Pietro was not so good!' He smiled as Pietro walked over to them. 'He was more interested in sunbaking or going to the pictures.'

Pietro laughed. 'Now every time I eat a lobster tail I think of you, Ricardo.'

'Rubbish. You're too busy with your movie stars to think of us. But I am glad you are here.'

'Come, everyone, we must all drink another toast to my aging brother,' said Pietro, raising his glass.

'You are not so far behind me,' said Ricardo fondly.

Some more people came over to congratulate Ricardo so Michael and Cassie moved away. 'They are very different characters,' said Michael. 'But very close. I'm so glad Uncle Pietro came.'

'Yes. Ricardo said that he had other brothers. Where are they?'

'He meant my grandfather Carlo. He died a long time ago.'

'Oh, that's sad. Did you know him?'

'No. It happened years before I was born.'

'Still, you do seem to be a close-knit family,' said Cassie.

'We are,' said Michael. 'We all tend to do our own thing, even keep a little distance, and I can go some time without seeing any of them. That way we never wear out our welcome. But if I see a cousin or some relative in the street, like Frank, I always stop and chat for a bit. We all know we're here for each other if anyone needs us, blood being thicker than water as they say.'

'This is special, to be in the place where the family started its life in Australia and still has a sense of connection with each other across the generations. Everyone seems very proud of Ricardo's father Joe.'

'There are a lot of stories about him. He was a very strong character and a very successful person who arrived in this country with nothing but with hard work built up a flourishing fishing business, which continues to this day. Cassie, there are my parents. Let me introduce you.'

Cassie shook hands with Michael's parents, Bob and Greta, and asked them how they liked life in the Blue Mountains. Then Michael's sisters Rosemary and Linda, from Melbourne and Sydney respectively, joined them. Chatting to them all, Cassie was impressed by their friendliness and their interest in her restaurant project. A dark Italian-looking woman wandered over to join their little circle.

'Cassie, have you met Angela? This is Frank's wife,' said Michael.

'Nice to meet you,' said Cassie, hiding her surprise, as she had no idea that Frank was married.

'Nice to meet you, too. How are things with you, Michael?' Angela asked.

'Just the same. No, actually, things are good, really good. Hasn't this event been a success? I think Ricardo is really chuffed at all the attention, despite saying he didn't want any fuss.'

'I was a bit worried that he might overdo things, but it's all good. I'd better go and see to the kitchen. There's more food if you'd like some,' she said to Cassie.

'I couldn't! I feel I've done nothing but eat. It's all been delicious. Can I help you?'

Angela shook her head. 'It's okay, we have it organised, but thanks.'

As she walked away Cassie said to Michael in a low voice, 'I didn't realise Frank was married. Does he have kids?'

'Three boys and a girl. Frank likes to flirt so he doesn't talk about his family to attractive young women,' said Michael. 'But he never puts a foot wrong or does anything he shouldn't. He knows Angela would eat him alive.'

Cassie laughed. 'Well, I was glad Frank came by with the lobster when he did. My soon to be ex-husband dropped in unexpectedly and I gave him the idea I'm surrounded by handsome Italian studs down here.'

Michael smiled. 'There's a whole tribe of us. Take your pick! Let us know if your ex visits again!'

'I doubt he'll drop by again. I've made sure of that.'

'Good,' said Michael, smiling. 'Had enough family chitchat? I have another family lunch tomorrow so I'm ready for a break.'

'It's not so late, why not drop me home and stay for a drink on the deck if you like. Bill will be pleased to see you and anxious for his dinner.'

'I'd like that. I'll just let them know we're going.'

'I'll say goodbye to your uncles. They're quite a pair,' said Cassie.

*

Michael lingered, reluctant to leave the deck where they were sitting. The stars were bright, reflecting on the lake's smooth surface. The occasional splash of a jumping fish caused Bill, who was stretched out between them, to lift his head every now and then.

'Probably a mullet. Not worth the effort, Bill. Go back to sleep. Do you want anything to drink, Michael?' asked Cassie.

'No, thanks, I've had enough and I have to drive home. I should be going. It's been a big day, a big week, actually. I'm glad for Ricardo's sake it all came together and that Pietro was able to make the journey.'

The two chatted about the party and Cassie told Michael how nice his parents and siblings were.

'Yes, they are a good bunch. They're probably back at my place now, so I'd better head home. Guess this hasn't been such an exciting day for you, eh Bill? No walk tonight.' He patted the dog.

'I'll make it up to him in the morning. Goodnight, Michael. Thanks for a terrific day.'

He smiled. 'I've noticed that you've stopped wearing your wedding ring.' And with that he reached out and wrapped his arms around her. Instead of pulling away Cassie lifted her face to his and he kissed her. It was a kiss of warmth, hinting at more to come. Finally they separated, both a little breathless.

'I'd better go, right now. Or I won't want to go,' he said softly.

Cassie felt confused. She wasn't entirely sure that she wanted him to go either, but she knew that this was not the right moment for him to stay. So she said nothing but watched him as he turned and walked out into the night.

*

The days blurred in a frenzy of activity as Geoff and his offsider, an energetic young chippie, flung themselves into fixing up the restaurant. Additional talents – a sparky and a plumber – came and went. Geoff ran every decision, large and small, past Cassie and even though she had no expert knowledge, she discovered she could visualise and understand what he was talking about.

'Geoff, I don't know the mechanics of how you can do this, but I can see that by facing this way, with the door opening that way, we could open up that space a bit more, and then we could squeeze another cupboard in.' She waved her arms about and pointed, and, amazingly, Geoff nodded and knew exactly what she meant.

Cassie was physically and mentally exhausted from dealing with the chaos of living with builders and the remodelling, thinking through all the other things that had to be done and hunting down the things she needed. Equipment, menus, staff, marketing, publicity, supplies, produce and deliveries all had to be set up. She spoke to her mother when she had the chance and was grateful that Jenny knew exactly what was going on and could offer practical advice.

'Pay careful attention to the lighting, Cassie. It plays such a big part in the ambience of the place. I'm pleased that you've given up the idea of linen tablecloths for every day. It would cost you a fortune in laundry bills. Save them for special occasions, private functions,' she advised. 'How are you going with wait staff? Got anyone yet? I think it's a really good idea that you're going the local fresh and organic route and using what is in season and available, but it's a lot more trouble than using general wholesalers.'

'I know, Mum. But using as many local ingredients as possible is part of the attraction and the theme of this place. Fresh, wholesome, organic and unusual food. Creative cookery. I want this to be a place where you turn up on the day and eat what's available. Maybe limited choice, but always fresh and fabulous.'

'There you go. Perhaps you could set up a mystery plate each day. Use whatever is abundant, on special, or in oversupply and throw it into a special dish,' she suggested. 'Of course the biggest worry for you is running out of local produce. These speciality farmers aren't into mass production and their crops mightn't be particularly reliable.'

'True, but I figure that the shortages will be mainly in winter and I won't have so many customers then. I may close altogether,' Cassie replied.

She rose early every day, and made it a habit to have a solid breakfast before Geoff and the others arrived as she rarely stopped for lunch and was on the run most of the day. Bill waited patiently for his breakfast and then the two of them went for a quick walk, arriving back to find Geoff hammering and measuring.

She and Steve spent hours going over menu plans and contingencies should the ingredients they wanted not be available. They visited Sublime Pastures and sampled their cheeses.

'I have the tomato man with his mate's olive oil signed up. The organic vegie farm will be our main supplier, which we can top up with seasonal produce from wherever we can source it. I have my eye on that old fig tree in Michael's garden that his grandmother planted. The organic beef farmer has some beautiful cuts. And Angela, Frank's wife, told me about an old chap who makes his own salamis and pressed meats as well as smoking his own hams, and he'll even smoke fish for special orders,' Cassie told Steve.

'Sounds as though he does a lot. I hope he isn't too old for such intensive, hands-on work,' said Steve.

'Angela told me he has a grandson who wants to learn how to do that sort of thing, too, so he's passing on his skills,' said Cassie. 'I think quite a few kids have found a vocation in the food industry these days.'

'It could have something to do with all those cooking shows on TV. Kids want to become chefs,' said Steve. 'But training in a kitchen is hard work, especially when you're at the bottom of the totem pole. I was trained by a great chef, but, boy, did he work me hard. Still, the food industry is a great thing to be part of, if you're prepared to put in the effort. Good on those who want to try.'

'I hope the staff will work out,' added Cassie. 'Sonia and Amy seem enthusiastic and as young mothers they are really keen to job-share the waitressing role.'

'Jobs are a bit hard to come by in this neck of the woods, so I'm sure they'll put in the effort. More importantly, I need a sous chef. Someone willing to do the grunt work for me in the kitchen who can also whip up a side dish.'

'Yes, I know. I'm on the case. How would you feel about someone not so young?'

'As long as they can keep up with the pace. Who do you have in mind?'

'Mollie. A friend of Trixie's. Trixie says she's got energy plus and is looking for work. She was thinking of starting a lawnmowing business!'

'Well, she sounds energetic enough. I'll meet her for a chat. Peeling vegetables and stacking the dishwasher, cleaning up and stirring sauces ain't for everybody!'

Almost every evening, after the tradesmen had left and Steve had gone home, Michael would arrive at the boatshed after he'd shut up the surgery, usually bringing with him some sort of dinner for both of them to share. Cassie was always disappointed when some animal emergency prevented his coming.

'The place looks as though you're getting close to opening!' he said as the restaurant neared completion.

'I've been thinking about the sort of event I want to put on to celebrate our opening.'

'Hope I'm invited.'

'Don't be silly. Of course you are. I couldn't have done it without you,' said Cassie.

'I don't think that's quite true, but I was happy to have input into the wine selection when we visited that winery you found,' he said with a smile. 'What do you want to do for the big opening?'

'I want as many people as possible to come, so I thought I would have a very simple menu. But I'll have to charge people for the meal or I'll go broke on the first night.'

'That's right. You have to be sensible. Why don't you let people know that part of the cost of the meal will go towards a local charity?'

'What a great idea. People will be happy to do that. Did you have any one in mind?' asked Cassie.

'I've always been associated with the Royal Life Saving Society – why not choose them?'

Cassie laughed. 'I reckon Steve will go along with that, too.'

'Are you getting any media?' asked Michael.

'I'll invite the local newspaper and the local radio station said they might send someone if the time suits.'

'When you're up and running smoothly, you could look at getting some metropolitan media coverage.'

'Baby steps, Michael. I don't want to get too ambitious. I just want to stay solvent.'

'You will! It's a great location for people exploring the south coast. You wait. Steve's food and the fact everything you're serving is organic and locally sourced will get you a following. Does the Chamber of Commerce and the local tourist information know about the opening?'

'They're on the invitation list.'

'Good job. You've thought of everything. I can hardly wait.'

Cassie smiled to herself. Michael had been so supportive and she was grateful for his interest, and it was not just because he was a refreshing change from Hal. She realised that her feelings for Michael were deepening.

*

Sooner than she could have imagined, the Blue Boatshed was starting to look pretty slick. Not in a trendy city way, but with a casually elegant beach look. A cheerful striped awning sheltered the tables near the front entrance; there were tubs of bright red geraniums at the doorway; and on the shady cool deck over the water was the long communal table Cassie had originally pictured. It had all come together even better than Cassie had imagined. She'd painted the tables and chairs white and each table was set with the blue and white plates as well as a small vase of white flowers that she'd picked from the massive bush in Michael's front garden. It all looked tasteful and slightly European because she'd bought a roll of red and white cotton gingham and Trixie had run up dozens of colourful serviettes. The clean, freshly painted surfaces; the airy, open-plan seating; the hospitable sitting room area, which served as a bar and place to drink coffee; and the compact and efficient kitchen all looked professional and inviting.

When it came, Cassie couldn't have ordered more perfect weather for the evening of the opening of the Blue Boatshed. The sea and lake were calm and shining, the stars glittered and, even though it was still very cool, there was not a breath of wind. Tall gas heaters at either end of the deck kept things warm, while inside candles and subdued lighting gave the place a cosy ambience. All the things on the 'to do' list had been ticked off and the staff were ready and excited. Steve, though faintly stressed, was on top of everything. Trixie had delivered her desserts and was staying on to help Mollie in the kitchen.

Jenny had arrived earlier in the day with a huge arrangement of flowers.

'Made it back from Broome just in time for the grand opening,' she told Trixie.

Cassie was at the front of house, as hostess. It did feel like a party for friends. After the warmth of Cassie's greeting, all the guests quickly felt the same. Bill was restricted to the front entrance where he was the official welcomer, though his brief barks were hardly heard above the chatter and laughter.

'The starters were divine, no wonder the waitresses were besieged, drinks flowing, people are getting on and enjoying themselves. Everyone is having a ball,' said Jenny quietly to Michael.

'You must be proud of Cassie for pulling this off,' said Michael.

'I'm pleased to see her so happy. This place has given her a new lease on life. I hadn't realised what a rut she was in or how unhappy she was in that marriage or working in that law firm. But out of bad things, good things can come. And you have been incredibly supportive and helpful, too, for which I thank you,' added Jenny. 'As have all your family. In fact the room seems to be packed with Aquinos!'

'Yes, with Uncle Ricardo's ninetieth birthday not long ago and now this, I don't think I've seen so many rellies under one roof for ages.'

'Is your uncle here? Cassie said he was very sprightly for his age.'

'Not so sprightly that he goes out much at night. Jenny, speaking of relatives, this is my cousin Frank. Have you met? He's responsible for supplying the seafood selection tonight.'

Jenny shook hands with Frank who looked resplendent in a striped sweater and lavender silk shirt.

'So you're Cassie's mother? I see where she gets her beauty.' Frank gave her a cheeky smile. 'This place is a very welcome addition to our area, as is Cassie. Will you be a regular visitor, too?'

'I hope so. In between my travels,' said Jenny, enjoying the banter. 'I'm looking forward to your feast of the sea. What do you recommend?'

'The prawns are local, and perfection. And I had a hand in catching the magnificent snapper that is also on the menu. It was swimming only hours ago.'

The official photographer, hired for the evening, stopped and asked to take their picture. Frank put his arm around Jenny's shoulder and flashed a big smile for the camera.

Guests were finally seated and the two waitresses began serving the meal. Now serious attention was given to eating and discussing the food. As the evening wore on and guests were convinced the food was an undoubted hit, the mood mellowed and Cassie circulated among the tables. She could tell that the night was a smashing success. The compliments were universal and genuine, and Steve was finally cajoled into emerging from the kitchen to take a bow.

Cassie made a simple speech, thanking everyone for coming and supporting the Blue Boatshed.

'I can't imagine undertaking a dream like this anywhere else. Everyone has been so supportive of this venture. Thank you all for that. I hope the Blue Boatshed will bring more business and visitors to this very special place. Thank you all, again.'

She moved around the room speaking to people individually.

'Tonight is going to be quite an act to follow,' declared Ron, the newsagent.

'Well that is exactly what we intend to do! Just get better,' said Cassie.

As the last guests left and Trixie and Mollie prepared to go, leaving the kitchen spotless, Steve downed the last of a glass of red wine.

'Congrats, Cassie. We're off to a good start.'

'If there were any hiccups in the kitchen don't tell me now. We'll talk about it tomorrow.'

'Tonight was brilliant,' said Michael. 'You wait, through word of mouth, this place will be packed out in no time. With so many people here, you should have raised quite a bit of money for the Life Saving Society. Speaking of which, will you have any time for a quick surf soon?'

'I might pass for the present. I'm working now and we open for lunch tomorrow.'

'Lovely to see you again, Jenny. Congratulations on your amazing daughter,' Michael said with a glance in Cassie's direction.

'Yes, she is very clever indeed. Of course she had good training from her father and me, but she's certainly put her own stamp on this place. I'll be sending friends down from Sydney! And of course I'll be back soon myself.'

Cassie walked with Michael to the door.

'Where's Bill?'

'He put himself to bed upstairs. I think he got a bit overwhelmed by so many people.'

'He'd better get used to it! It was great. I know how hard you worked,' said Michael.

'And we do it all over again tomorrow. I guess it'll keep me out of mischief.' Cassie stifled a yawn.

Michael kissed her. 'Take care. See you soon.'

'Good night, Michael. And thanks, again.'

Later, after Steve had left, Jenny gave Cassie a huge hug. 'Well done. A restaurant is a lot of work, but it's so rewarding when it works and yours will. You have good support down here. Nice people. Now, are you sure about me taking your bed?'

'Absolutely. Bill is up there but once I'm settled here on the sofa he'll come and join me. Thanks for everything, Mum.'

'You're welcome.'

'Sleep well, Mum,' said Cassie.

*

Cassie sat at the end of her jetty slowly reeling in her line. She didn't always catch something when she fished at sunset on the full tide, but she found it a relaxing way to end the day when they weren't open for dinner. The restaurant was open for lunch six days a week and served dinner only on Friday and Saturday nights. The evenings had initially been slow, but now, as the weather was becoming warmer, and the advertising campaign was taking effect, more people were venturing out to eat. The deck was especially popular, often with people who were dining alone, and several friendships had been stuck at the long table. There had been some initial hiccups in the running of the place but nothing too serious, just needing the smoothing out of routines and systems. The staff rubbed along well together.

She felt the planks in the jetty wobble but didn't turn around. Bill knew who it was and wagged his tail. Michael sat down beside her, his legs dangling above the water. He leaned down, staring into the water where small fish were chasing the burley Cassie had dropped on the surface. Bill nudged him, wanting his ears scratched. Michael cuddled the dog and rubbed its head.

'Shh,' Cassie warned Michael, as she concentrated on the tip of her rod, which was gently bending. 'C'mon, take it and run, you silly fish,' she muttered. There was a sudden tug and the line spun from the reel. She jerked the rod upwards and began winding in the line.

'Could be a decent bream,' she said as she saw the greenish glint of the fish and lifted it from the water, grabbing it to release the hook before she dropped the fish into the bucket behind her.

Unusually Bill took no notice of this action, but leaned against Michael who still held him close.

Cassie glanced at Michael. 'You're quiet.'

'I didn't want to distract you.' He leaned his head on top of Bill's and closed his eyes.

'Michael? Are you all right?'

He bit his lip and straightened, releasing Bill. 'Uncle Ricardo died.'

'No! Oh, Michael. I'm so sorry.' She reached out and put her hand on his shoulder. 'What happened?'

'Well, he was ninety. His heart wasn't very robust. He had a bypass operation some time back, so I suppose it was always on the cards. We were amazed he managed to get this far.'

'He made it to his ninetieth. That was a good thing. Thank goodness your uncle Pietro came out for it. This is so sad. I'm so sorry. Is there anything I can do? How's the family?'

'Sad, a bit in shock. Frank told me that it was peaceful. Uncle Ricardo complained a bit, said he wasn't feeling well and went and lay down for a nap after lunch, and he just didn't wake up.'

Cassie began winding in her line. 'Let's have a drink. A toast to Ricardo. I'll treat you to dinner, too, if you like.'

'Thanks. I want to go up to his house. That's where the rest of the family will be. But yes, a small drink would be nice.'

Cassie quietly poured two glasses of wine as Michael reminisced about Ricardo. 'He worked hard to make a success of the business, just like his father had. Just Pietro left of that generation now. It's very sad.'

'Your uncle Ricardo should have written a memoir. Put things down for the younger generation, so they'd know their family history,' said Cassie.

'How true. I wonder how many families think about writing down the memories of the older generation and then, before anyone does anything, it's all too late.'

Cassie reached out and took his hand and they sat quietly, Bill at their feet looking from one to the other.

'He knows you're upset,' said Cassie.

Michael nodded, drained his glass and stood up. 'I'd better go. Thanks for letting me have a bit of down time.'

'That's what I'm here for. Let me know if there's anything I can do. Anything.'

She walked with him to his car and he hugged her goodbye, holding her tight.

'I'll be thinking of you and your family,' Cassie said softly.

'Thank you,' replied Michael as he got into his car and drove off to join the rest of his family in mourning Ricardo Aquino.

*

The funeral was a big event. Everyone from the district seemed to be there. The mayor, the local member of parliament and even the local television station attended. Cassie sat with Geoff and Trixie at the back of the church for the requiem mass.

'There are so many people here,' whispered Cassie. 'Far more than at his party. They are even standing outside, listening to the funeral over the loudspeaker. I've never seen such a large funeral.'

'Everyone will want to pay their respects. He was a pillar of the community,' Geoff whispered back. 'Like the mayor said at his birthday party, Ricardo was a very important and respected man on the south coast. His death is the passing of an era.'

Cassie looked towards the front of the church where all of the Aquinos were sitting.

Such a large family, she thought. It must be wonderful to have each other for support at such a sad time.

After the funeral there was to be a large get-together at Ricardo's home. Cassie approached Michael outside the church and apologised that she and Trixie couldn't attend the gathering as she had to open the restaurant. Michael nodded and said he would see her later. As she attended the lunch time rush, Cassie's thoughts returned to Michael and the Aquino family. Although she hadn't known them for long, her heart grieved for these wonderful warm people who had helped her settle into Whitby Point where she now felt so at home.

*

A few weeks later when the Blue Boatshed had been running successfully, Cassie thought she would like to go to Sydney to visit her mother.

'Go, Cassie. Take a break,' said Steve. 'If you go after lunch on Sunday and come back Tuesday morning, you won't even be missed.'

It had been some time since she had left for the south coast and when she returned to Sydney, Cassie realised she hadn't missed the city at all. She enjoyed sitting in Jenny's garden and catching up with a couple of her friends the next day, who politely said that they were intrigued by her 'cute little restaurant'. But even in those couple of days Cassie knew that Sydney was no longer for her. The traffic was abominable and the parking was atrocious and that was just the tip of the iceberg about what was wrong with living in Sydney.

How did I cope with this? she asked herself. Life is so much easier at Whitby Point and Blue Crane Lake.

So the best part of her time away was the drive back down the coast to Blue Crane Lake. Cassie sang along with Regina Spektor and made mental notes of things she needed to discuss with Steve about the restaurant. *Her* restaurant. It was hard to believe that not so long ago she had been in the depths of despair and now she had established her own business. How good was that?

And all the time she was away she thought about Michael. She couldn't wait to see him and tell him her thoughts about Sydney . . . Just thinking about him gave her a shiver of anticipation and pleasure, and she was forced to admit to herself that she was falling in love with him. The more she saw of Michael, the more she recognised his wonderful qualities: his kindness and decency, his balanced view of the world and his gentle humour and thoughtful intelligence.

*

That evening, Michael called around to see her. He said he was glad she was back safely and had enjoyed a good time in the big smoke.

'And not anxious to go back any time soon,' she assured him.

'I made a small acquisition while you were away that I thought I might share with you.'

'I'm curious, give me a clue.'

'You'll need a swimsuit and a picnic basket. Bill might need a life jacket,' he said.

'Boating?' asked Cassie.

'Sailing. I bought a Cavalier sail boat. There are a few nice places to sail to around here.'

'How fantastic. What a great idea. I'll bring the picnic,' said Cassie.

'Maybe one Sunday afternoon, after you've closed up. Okay with you?'

'Perfect. I can't wait,' said Cassie.

'Good.' Michael fondled Bill's ears.

'I suppose I'd better be going,' he said reluctantly. He looked at her. 'I missed you while you were in Sydney.'

'Did you?' Cassie smiled back. 'You don't really have to go, do you?'

'Not if you don't want me to,' Michael said, taking a step closer to her.

Cassie lifted her arms. 'No, I don't.'

Without a word, Michael took her in his arms, enfolding her as they kissed. No more needed to be said.

*

It was late in the afternoon. Lunch had been cleared away, the staff had just left and Cassie was updating her ordering records on the computer when Bill gave a short bark, recognising whoever had just come through the door. As Cassie lifted her head Frank stormed inside with Bill following, the dog's tail down, ears back. Neither looked happy.

'Hi Frank, what's the matter?' Cassie came out from behind the counter.

Frank's face was red and furious. 'I'm amazed you can show your face here! How could you? I can't believe you could be so two-faced, so sneaky! You conned him! An old man! What a bitch!'

'Excuse me, Frank, I suggest you back off, calm down and explain yourself. What are you talking about?'

But Frank was so angry he was almost at the point of being out of control.

Cassie stood her ground. Bill moved close beside her, never taking his eyes off Frank.

'You know damn well how you weaseled, how you stole, money from Uncle Ricardo. He was old, he didn't know what he was doing!' Frank was shouting.

'Frank, sit down! *I don't know what you are talking about!*'

'Why do you lie? It's written in black and white. How do you think the family feels at what you've done? And after what our family has done for you?'

Cassie was close to tears. 'I'm calling Michael. I don't understand. Tell me what I have done!' She raised her voice but it trembled. Bill gave a low growl.

Frank narrowed his eyes and hissed at her, 'My grandfather's will. We've been told what's in it. Now why would he leave you a quarter of a million dollars? You! With your family. Your father of all people! Did you come down here just to get in the old man's ear? At least tell us that.'

Cassie simply stared at him. 'I have no idea what you are saying. Ricardo's will? He left money to me in his will? That's impossible. It must be meant for someone else.'

Frank's voice now dropped to a menacing whisper. 'After what your father did. Don't think we won't fight this. It's wrong. You conned us all. You won't get away with it.' He paused and said deliberately, 'And I'll make sure that no one will supply this place with food so no one ever comes here again. I'll see to that.'

'What do you mean about my father? What did he do?' There was a knot in Cassie's belly and tears filled her eyes. 'What's my father got to do with this? I don't know what you are talking about.'

'No? Well, I don't believe you. You have some hide coming to Whitby Point and bringing back all the pain and the bad memories.'

'What happened? Tell me! Tell me.' Cassie thought that at least one of them was mad.

'You're Cassandra Sullivan, aren't you?'

'I was before I got married.'

'And your father was Patrick Sullivan, wasn't he?'

228

'Yes, he was Pat Sullivan, but why do you want to know all this?'

'When anyone is stealing a quarter of a million from my family, I want to know who it is, so I had my solicitor make enquiries.'

'But I still don't see . . .'

'Everyone knows that your father killed Michael's grandfather, Carlo. Don't tell me you don't know that. And now my grandfather leaves you money in his will. How did you work it?'

'Never! No way,' Cassie shouted, shaking her head in disbelief. 'How can you say my father killed someone?'

'A court of law said he did. And he went to gaol for it. He should never have been let out. And now you have the cheek to come down here and try to get in with us using another name. How low can your family go?'

'I just don't understand what you're saying. I never tried to get money from your grandfather. I only spoke to him for five minutes. Michael was there the whole time,' she cried, tears streaming down her face.

'Say what you like. No one here will believe you, especially not Michael when he learns that you're Patrick Sullivan's daughter. And you're not getting your hands on our two hundred and fifty grand. No bloody way. That money belongs to my family.'

He spun on his heels and stormed off, slamming the door behind him.

Cassie stared after him trying to take in the facts of Frank's tirade. Her beloved father, the wise and gentle Patrick, had killed Michael's grandfather? Gone to gaol for it? Impossible. And now Ricardo had left her a quarter of a million dollars. Why on earth would he do that? It was all madness.

Shaking, Cassie picked up the phone to call her mother, hoping that she could give her some answers, but then her heart lurched as if being squeezed. Maybe her mother didn't know anything. Maybe her father had kept it all a secret. Could it possibly be that his walking away from his past as if it never happened was his way of putting some dreadful event behind him? Or maybe her mother knew everything and was keeping it all a secret from her. But would her mother do that? She felt confused and betrayed. She put the phone down. She needed to think. It all had to be a terrible mistake. There had to be a simple explanation. But a quarter of a million from a man she had met for only five minutes needed more than a simple explanation.

Then she thought of Michael. When he found out about the money, he would hate her too.

Cassie crumpled to the floor and flung her arms around Bill. She buried her face in his fur and sobbed.

8

Whitby Point, 1933

JOE STEPPED AWAY FROM his car and wiped his hands on the polishing cloth. He was about to drive up to Wollongong to see his father-in-law and then catch the train to Sydney. He took great pride in owning this car and wanted it to look as new as the day he'd purchased it. He rested his hand on the curve of the maroon mudguard and thought back to his first ride in a car when Franco Riviera, his father-in-law, had driven him in a Model-T Ford to a boarding house in Wollongong. From that day Joe had dreamed of owning a car of his own. And now here he was, a successful fisherman with his own staff of young men, managing part of a network of fishing businesses owned by Franco, as well as being a well-respected citizen of this small coastal town. Australia certainly had proved to be the land of opportunity for Joe Aquino.

'Giuseppe!'

Joe smiled to himself. The rest of the world called him Joe, except for his mother.

'Yes, Mamma. Please get the children. I am ready to say goodbye,' he said in Italian, for his mother had refused to learn any English.

The boys raced to him; their mops of dark brown hair shining in the sun. Ricardo, the oldest at age eleven, reached him first, followed by Pietro and then five-year-old Carlo, the littlest one, who hugged him around his legs.

'I won't be long. I will be back the day after tomorrow,' Joe promised them. 'I am going to see Grandfather Franco and then the next day I have business to do in Sydney. Now you be good for Nonna. Promise?'

'Yes, Papà,' said Pietro.

'We are always good,' said Ricardo impishly.

'I'll miss you,' said little Carlo.

'I'll be back before you know it.'

'Nonna won't speak English,' complained Ricardo.

'Good, so you will learn two languages. You are very lucky that Nonna has come to love you and look after you,' said Joe firmly. 'When I come home, we can do something special.'

'Can we go out on your big boat? *Sea Queen*?' asked Ricardo.

'You are still too young for the trawler.'

'Let's go to the pictures, then,' said Pietro.

'Perhaps we'll all go fishing down at the beach when I come back. But only if you are well behaved.'

'They will be fine,' said Giuseppe's mother, Emilia, gathering them to her side.

'*Grazie*, Mamma.' Joe kissed his mother, grateful as always she had agreed to come to Australia and help raise his sons after the sudden death of his wife Evalina.

Joe's life had turned upside down when Evalina had died giving birth to Carlo. She had devoted herself to running their home and raising the children and took little interest in the fishing business except to fret during the days Joe was away at sea. Indeed, she became happier as the business grew and Joe spent more time on land, only going out occasionally on one of their smaller vessels, but never on the trawler, which stayed out at sea for a week at a time. Joe had always appreciated Evalina and had been saddened by her passing.

After Evalina's death Joe had hired a succession of women to help him look after the boys, but, as far as Joe was concerned, none of them reached the high standard of care and devotion set by their mother. Joe could think of only one solution and so he sent a message to his mother back in Italy, asking her to come and help.

Emilia d'Aquino knew where her duty lay. Although both her husband and mother had died, she had not been lonely. Her numerous children visited her every day, as did her lifelong friends in the village, but Giuseppe now needed her, so she agreed to make the voyage to Australia to raise her grandsons.

Sometimes Joe worried that his sons would not remember their mother, but he made sure that they visited her grave frequently. He also remained close to Franco, Evalina's father, and Silvio, his brother-in-law, not just as business partners, but as good friends, and he visited them every time he went to Wollongong.

*

As Joe's Chevrolet pulled into Franco's driveway in Wollongong, Franco came out to greet him.

'Welcome, welcome!' Franco said as he hugged Joe. Over the years, Franco had changed little, except to put on a some weight. He was still the welcoming, gregarious man he had been when Joe first met him more than ten years ago. 'Are you taking the car all the way to Sydney, or leaving it here and catching the train?'

'I'll leave it here and take the early-morning train. I don't want to deal with the busy streets of Sydney.'

'Good, good. Come inside, have coffee and we can discuss your meeting with the bank tomorrow.'

Although there was a branch of their bank in Wollongong, Franco had always made it a habit to discuss his company's business with the bank's head office. He always said that he didn't waste his time with anyone less important than the man at the top.

'We have to ask for a loan to repair and even replace some of my equipment, especially the engines on the small boats,' said Joe, accepting a cup of coffee. 'And Franco, I also want to raise the matter of a canning factory. If you can preserve vegetables and meat by canning them, then I'm sure you can do the same with fish. This is what we should be doing.'

'You're probably right. There are always better ways of doing things. Look how road transport is taking our fish, packed in ice, up to the Sydney markets the same day it's caught. Ten years ago we would never have been able to do that. In those days the fish we caught in Wollongong were sold in Wollongong. Now we have a much wider market. But Joe, this Depression is making the banks very cautious about lending money. They won't take any chances, so I doubt they'll give you a penny for your canning idea, but you can always ask. Just make sure you get the loan for your engines.'

'Of course.'

'It is good that you are always thinking about ways to improve the business. You like to try new ideas. You know, many Australian fishermen don't try different things. They do what they have always done and so they

234

have not weathered the present hard times as well as we have,' said Franco.

'Remember how I was so worried when I first started out working for you that I would lose my fishing gear because I didn't know the seabed, that I made myself a special line to discover the layout of the seabed!' said Joe, smiling.

'I don't think I've heard that story,' said Silvio, Franco's son and Joe's brother-in-law, as he joined them.

'Pour yourself some coffee,' Franco said to Silvio. 'I'm surprised that you don't know what Joe did, but it was very clever. Go ahead, Joe, tell him.'

One of the nicest things about Franco was his pleasure in reminiscing about the cleverness of his son and his son-in-law. He never tired of their success stories, no matter how often they were told.

'Actually, Silvio, it was quite simple,' said Joe. 'I took some sinker lead and melted it down and poured the lead into an empty tin and stuck a loop of wire into it so I could attach a line to it. I made the lead into a concave shape and let it cool.'

'How did that help you work out what was on the bottom?' asked Silvio.

Before Joe could tell him, Franco answered with obvious delight, 'That was the clever part. He filled the top of the tin with mutton fat and dragged it slowly over the seabed. When he pulled it up, he could see by the markings on the fat if there were traces of sand or seaweed on it, or if it had passed over a rocky area. Then he knew where the best places were to fish. Clever.'

'Yes, indeed,' said Silvio.

'And I learned the sea bottom so well I decided to use the long line like we had back in the old country,' said Joe.

'I did not think that long line would work when you told me about it,' said Franco. 'Actually I did not understand it at all until I saw it in action, and it caught so many fish.'

'But only if the weather conditions were right,' Joe reminded him.

The line Joe had constructed was around two hundred metres long and had about fifty branch lines, each with its own hook. One end of the line was attached to a weighted buoy and as the boat moved away from it, the branch lines were flung out of the boat, to the left and to the right until the last branch line was dropped and then that was attached to another weighted buoy.

'I remember the first time you used it, you took me out with you to show me how it worked and by the time you had finished dropping the last buoy line, it was time to return to the first one and haul it up. Fish after fish were coming up and most of them were big snapper. It was the same for all the lines,' said Franco with relish.

'I remember that,' said Silvio. 'Joe caught so many fish. We sold them to the coalminers and railway workers and the crews from the coal ships. I was so busy dealing with the sales that I could stop going to sea altogether, and we were also able to buy Joe his own fifteen footer.'

'I loved that boat,' said Joe, with a smile. 'It had a sail, so I didn't have to row all the time.' He sighed. 'New ways are good, but some old ways are good, too. My family has a long history as fishermen, so I don't want to discard all their ideas.'

'Your people certainly knew how to fish, and they taught you well,' said Silvio.

'Quite right,' said Franco. 'With your skills, Joe, it is no wonder that the business is doing well, even in these troubled times. Five steamboats at Whitby Point, as well as the trawler. Maybe you will be able to convince the bank that some of the engines should be converted to diesel. But enough of this business talk. It is getting late. Do you know what I have arranged for your dinner, Joe?'

'Steak,' answered both Joe and Silvio together. It was a family joke that Joe the fisherman liked nothing better than a good steak.

'You thought I didn't know that you sneaked off with a snapper to swap for steak at the butcher's shop,' said Franco, laughing. 'But I did, and you earned it.'

'I don't think that I will ever be tired of steak. What a country to be able to get such meat – lamb, mutton, steak. I had very little meat as a boy. I never tire of it now,' said Joe, recalling that although his mother had always managed to put a meal on the table, the occasional chunk of sinewy goats' meat was a great treat.

'Yes, your favourite meal has been prepared for you: steak, eggs and chips.'

'Thank you, Franco. You know, my mother is still amazed that I can eat so much meat at one meal. She thinks that a large family in Sicily could live off what I can put away.'

Joe always enjoyed the company of Franco and Silvio. They were always so optimistic and obviously fond of him and they always made him feel not just part of their business, but part of their family as well. Franco had even suggested from time to time that Joe should remarry to provide a mother for his grandsons. Joe would shrug his shoulders and say maybe one day.

*

Next day on the train, Joe carefully placed his hat on the rack and settled into his seat to think about what he planned to say to the bank manager. Franco was right. They needed to convert the engines of the small vessels into diesel. It would make the operation much more efficient and cut down on their overheads because the boats would need smaller crews, and, more importantly, they would not be tied to a central coal-loading depot. On reflection he also realised that the times were not right for his idea for a canning factory so he would have to wait until things were better before he pursued that plan.

At Central Station Joe pushed through the crowds on the concourse to the exit. He had planned to take a tram to Martin Place in the heart of the city, where the head office of the bank was, but as he was early he decided to walk.

It was a bright spring morning and the leaves of the plane trees in the park were just coming into bud, but the rest of the area near the station was shabby and run-down. Joe became quite distressed by what he saw. The effects of the Depression were far more obvious in this part of the city than they were in Whitby Point.

Men, down at heel, with drawn, worried faces, stood in groups, some sharing a cigarette. Some looked as though they might be farm people hoping to find work in the city. Joe thought about the city people who had turned up in Whitby Point, also looking for jobs. But there was no work anywhere. Not surprising, he thought, when the unemployment rate was twenty-five per cent.

Desperate-looking women clutching children asked for money to buy food. As he walked on, Joe saw a long queue and realised that there must be a soup kitchen nearby. He knew how well-off he must look and his heart twisted in sympathy for the people in the queue. It was not so long ago that he had been poor. But despite the poverty on his island, his family had always had something to eat, even if it was just weeds and nettles collected from the hillside and made into a broth.

Joe trudged on, his head down, avoiding eye contact with anyone. He passed a partially demolished building, which he could see was being used as a shelter by those with nowhere else to go.

He turned to cross the street and from the corner of his eye he saw the figure of a woman hurrying down the road. Head down, she was hunched into her coat, which had definitely seen better days. A knitted beret was squashed onto her hair. She looked like many of the other people he had seen at this end of town, but something about her caused Joe to give her a second glance.

He caught his breath, stopped, then spun around and began to run after her. He knew who she was. No one else had a head of red curls like that. He could barely manage to get out the name that was burned into his heart.

'Bridie?'

She jerked as if slapped, threw a swift glance over her shoulder and quickly hurried on.

In two strides he was beside her, spinning her around to face him.

'Bridie, it's me, Joe, Giuseppe. Is it really you?'

'Giuseppe, is that you? You look very well.' There was little warmth in Bridie's voice. She spoke as though he was no more than an acquaintance.

Well, thought Joe, maybe after all this time, that is all I am.

'Bridie, let me buy you a cup of tea,' he said. 'I want to talk to you, find out what you've been doing.' As he took her arm, he could feel her thinness through the worn fabric of her coat. He knew that things were not good for Bridie.

She pulled her arm away. 'I'm sorry but I can't spare the time.'

'Bridie, a cup of tea for old times' sake, surely, and you can tell me all about yourself.'

Suddenly Bridie's eyes filled with tears.

'Oh, Giuseppe, you were always so kind to me, but I think by the look of you that we have travelled very different paths. You look so, well, prosperous.'

'I've been very lucky, but perhaps you have not.'

Suddenly Bridie looked at Joe in defiance. 'I haven't, and you can't possibly understand, so I think that it's best if we forget this meeting.'

Joe stared at her. 'Forget you? I have never forgotten you for one day since you walked away from me, and I will not let you disappear again. You must tell me what has happened to you. Besides, aren't you interested in what I've been doing?' he added, hoping that Bridie's curiosity would get the better of her.

'That would be unkind of me, wouldn't it?' she said with a faint smile.

They found a small tea shop and Joe ordered a pot of tea for two, even though he didn't usually drink tea, as well as a plate of scones, which he didn't eat, but thought Bridie would enjoy.

They were served quickly and as Bridie began to pour the tea, Joe asked, 'So, you married Ronan?'

With a shudder, Bridie broke down completely and sobbed.

Joe handed her his handkerchief and Bridie wiped her eyes. 'Have something to eat,' Joe suggested. 'And when you can, tell me what happened.'

Bridie sniffed and took a bite of scone. 'These are delicious. I hadn't realised how hungry I was. Yes, I married him. He was a good man, but not a very strong one. He tried lots of jobs, but they never seemed to last. When we had our son Patrick, Ronan tried even harder, but the work was always too hard, too physical. He used to go down to the wharves and queue up to get a day's work, but the foremen knew him and knew that labouring work was beyond him, so they didn't employ him. Gradually, we lost everything. We moved from place to place, avoiding paying our rent if we could. Oh, Giuseppe, I felt like a criminal, but once Patrick came, what else could we do?'

'My poor Bridie. If only I had known, I would have helped you.'

'Giuseppe, I had no idea what had happened to you or where you were, so I couldn't ask.'

Joe glanced at her worn coat. 'Does Ronan have a job at present?' he asked gently.

'He died about two years ago. He got pneumonia and even though the hospital did their best, they couldn't save him.'

'So now you are even worse off?'

'In a funny way I'm not. I get the widows' pension, which isn't much, but it's more than Ronan and I sometimes had and, together with the child endowment, I manage. I've got a room in a house in Surry Hills with a bed and a gas ring so I can cook our meals. Patrick's just started school. We survive.'

'And your family, Bridie? Have you contacted them?'

She nodded. 'I wrote to tell them what had happened, but there is no more money in Ireland than there is in Australia, so they can't help me. I just have to manage as best I can.'

Joe looked at her. 'How brave you are. Just like you always were.'

'Not a lot of choice,' said Bridie bitterly. 'What have you been doing since last I saw you, Giuseppe?'

Joe told her about Franco and their fishing business south of Sydney and how successful it was. 'I even have my own car now,' he said proudly.

'I always knew you would do well. Are you married?'

'I was. My wife Evalina was a wonderful woman. She was a good wife and mother. She always looked after the boys and me and never complained when I was away fishing, although I knew that she worried. I have not one word of complaint about her, except that she left me. She died giving birth to my youngest son, Carlo.

He has just started school, too, so it sounds as though he is about the same age as your son Patrick. I have two other boys – Ricardo, the eldest, and Pietro.'

'Giuseppe, that is such a sad thing to have happened, especially when you seem to have been so happy. Who's looking after your boys while you are in Sydney?'

'My mother came out from Italy to look after us all.'

Joe glanced at his watch. 'I will have to go soon. I have an appointment with my bank in Martin Place.'

Bridie rose out of her seat. 'Please, don't waste any more time with me. I feel so, so . . . embarrassed that you've seen me like this.'

'I'm sorry that times have been so bad for you. But things will change now. Come on, we have to go. I mustn't be late.'

'Thank you. I don't want to hold you up.'

'When does your boy finish school?'

'Three o'clock.'

'Plenty of time then,' said Joe. 'You're coming with me. I'm not letting you out of my sight.'

He took out his wallet, left some money on the table and took Bridie's arm as they walked out of the tea shop and headed towards Martin Place. But when they reached the imposing bank headquarters Bridie shrank back.

'I can't go in there. My clothes are not respectable enough to be seen in there with you. What will people think? I'll wait out here.'

'Nonsense, of course you can come in with me,' said Joe firmly. He sensed her discomfort but he was determined not to lose her a second time.

'Giuseppe . . . Joe, I will embarrass you.'

'Bridie, all these years I have never stopped thinking about you, so now I've found you again, I'm not losing you. Please come inside and wait for me. I won't be long.'

Joe led Bridie to a chair in the reception area outside the office of the loans manager, ignoring the cool look of the secretary.

'Mr Aquino,' she whispered. 'Is your, er, companion seeing Mr Braxton as well?'

'Mrs Sullivan is with me. She is an old friend. Please look after her for me. If she is not here when I come out of Mr Braxton's office, I will hold you responsible,' he said quietly and firmly.

The secretary flushed. 'Yes, Mr Aquino.'

As Joe walked into the manager's office, he heard her say, 'Mrs Sullivan, would you care for a cup of tea?'

But Bridie shook her head. 'No, thank you. But is there a ladies' room I could use, please?'

Joe emerged from Mr Branxton's office about half an hour later, carrying his hat and with his overcoat on his arm. He shook hands with the loans manager, who gave Bridie a quizzical look.

Joe looked fondly at Bridie and said, 'Mr Braxton, this is Mrs Sullivan. An old friend.' Smiling, Joe put his hat on his head, took Bridie's arm again and walked from the office.

'I feel eyes burning a hole in my back,' said Bridie who, nonetheless, held her head erect. 'I think you scared the secretary. I went to the ladies' and I couldn't have been there more than a couple of minutes when she came to find me. What did she think I was going to do, climb out the tiny window?' Bridie laughed and Joe almost shouted with joy to hear it. This was the Bridie he knew, the woman who was not afraid to travel by herself halfway around the world to get married, leaving behind her all that was familiar, ready to take on the challenge of a new life in a new country. Joe had made her feel that she was that woman again, pretty and confident with her self-respect restored.

'Bridie, you said that your son will be home about three? We have enough time to create a surprise for him. Come with me.'

'What are you talking about, Giuseppe?'

'Joe, remember. Only my mother calls me Giuseppe now, and you are certainly not my mother. I'm taking you to Farmers Department Store. You can buy yourself some new clothes, for Patrick as well as yourself. If you want to go to the hairdresser there you could, then we'll pick up Patrick and catch the train to Wollongong where I left my car. From there we drive to Whitby Point, which is where I live. It's a small place but you will like it. And so will Patrick.'

Bridie stopped in the middle of the footpath.

'Joe, this is crazy talk. After all these years you expect me to drop everything and take off with you to become, what, your mistress? It is nice to see you and know how well you are doing, but the rest is just impossible . . .'

'Bridie, you becoming my mistress is the furthest thing from my mind. I want to hold you and kiss you just as I imagined I would all that time ago on the ship. My feelings for you haven't changed. I want to marry you, make you part of my family, bring you into my home, not have you tucked away somewhere. I love you very much. I always have.' He looked intently at Bridie, who stared back at him in astonishment. 'You don't feel the same as I do? I'm sorry, I should not have asked so soon.' His voice lost its confidence.

'Joe, this is all too much of a rush. It's been thirteen years and I have to think about what you are saying.'

'I understand. I am asking a lot of you, but please let me at least buy you and Patrick some new clothes.'

Bridie smiled and looked at her faded coat. 'We could certainly use them, especially Patrick. Thank you for your offer.'

Three hours later Bridie emerged from the department store attired in a simple dress and jacket, carrying gloves and a new handbag, and, for the first time in a very long time, wearing immaculate stockings and new shoes. Her curls had been tamed by the store's hairdresser into neat rows and her face had been treated by a beautician. Now her fine skin glowed, her freckles had been dusted with face powder, her lashes tipped in mascara and her mouth shone with a pale pink lipstick.

'You look wonderful,' said Joe, thrilled to have helped her look more relaxed and happy.

'It's too much. You've spent far too much money on me,' began Bridie, but she couldn't hide her pleasure and delight.

Because it was nearly time for school to finish, and in spite of Bridie's protests, Joe hired a taxi to take them to the place where she and Patrick lived in Surry Hills.

'Joe, you are wasting money. We could easily walk.'

Joe was shocked as they drove past the mean-looking houses of the Surry Hills slums. Sitting cheek by jowl, the houses opened up straight onto the street and dirty children played in the gutters.

'You can't live here,' Joe exclaimed. 'It's so squalid.'

'Well, beggars can't be choosers,' Bridie replied tartly. 'My neighbours are good people. We all help each other. I would find things much harder without their support.'

The taxi pulled up outside one of the cramped houses and Joe followed Bridie inside.

'Oh, you're back. I've got Patrick in here,' a voice called out.

'Thanks, Ruby. Send him in.'

As Bridie opened the door to her room a small boy rushed to her.

'This is my son Patrick.'

'Hello, I'm Joe. How do you do, Patrick?'

'Mr d'Aquino and I knew each other a long time ago. We came to Australia on the same boat,' explained Bridie.

Shyly Patrick shook hands with Joe. 'How do you do?' he asked.

Joe followed Bridie into her room. It was tiny, dominated by a single bed. There was also a little table and one hard wooden chair. The floor was bare except for a small worn rug. Joe knew that the place would be cold in winter and stiflingly hot in summer. He was dismayed by what he saw. His beautiful Bridie should not live like this.

There was a sharp knock on the door and a voice called out, 'Can I come in?'

'Yes, of course. Joe, it's my friend Ruby. She always keeps an eye on Patrick for me, like she did this afternoon.'

Joe found it difficult not to stare too rudely at Ruby. She had brightly peroxided hair, red painted nails and wore a gaudy kimono. She reminded him of someone, and then it struck him that Ruby was a cheap edition of Sophia, his first girlfriend in Sydney.

Ruby stared at Bridie in her new clothes with her styled hair and then looked at Joe in his handsome coat and hat and gave Bridie a knowing look.

'Ruby, this is Joe, a very old friend who has been very kind to both Patrick and me this afternoon.'

'Pleased to meet you, Joe. How do you know Bridie?'

'We came out on the same boat to Australia. Bridie taught me to speak English.'

'She did a good job then. You don't sound too much like an eytie at all. Bridie, luv, can I borrow a bit of sugar? Went to make meself a cuppa and found I was out.'

'Help yourself.'

'How many people are living in this house, Bridie?' Joe asked.

'There are six rooms. Some have single people, like Ruby, others have more in them, like Patrick and me.'

'That's very crowded.'

'Look, Joe,' said Ruby, 'some of us think that having a roof over our heads, even if it comes with bedbugs, is better than sleeping rough.'

'A lot of people think we're lucky,' said Bridie gently. 'Some people have to live in caves and out at La Perouse there's a whole township of huts made out of tin, cardboard and canvas.'

'Yeah, and the governor's wife went out to have a gander and said that some of them were so nice that she wouldn't mind living there at all. Then she went back to her posh Government House,' said Ruby, chuckling disparagingly.

'It was an unfeeling and patronising thing to say,' agreed Joe.

'Well, nice to meet you, Joe. See ya, Bridie,' said Ruby, subtly winking at Bridie.

'No, Ruby, it's not what you think,' whispered Bridie as she closed the door behind her friend.

'You're very quiet, Patrick. How was school?' asked Bridie. 'You should see the things we've bought you today.'

'Mum, Father O'Malley came around to school today and you know what? We all had to line up and he gave everyone in the school an orange. And we were allowed to eat them straight away. Boy, it was good.'

Joe's heart sank. He never thought about what his boys ate. They had plenty of food but here was this little boy, thrilled by an orange.

Patrick became even more excited when Bridie showed him the clothes Joe had bought for him, but all Joe could think was that he had to do something to get them both away from this squalor. Finally he said, 'Bridie, my heart is breaking. You can't raise a fine boy like Patrick in a place like this. Surely he deserves something better. I know I rushed you this morning expecting us to get married. I can see that now. My offer to take you both down to Whitby

Point to live still holds. But this time there are no conditions. It's a great town for Patrick to grow up. Lots of fresh air, places to explore and it's so clean compared with these slums. No bedbug would dare to show itself there. There's an excellent boarding house. If you won't move for your own sake, please think about my offer for the sake of the boy, and if, say, after six months, you want to come back, I'll understand and I won't stand in your way.'

*

They sat side by side on the train, while Patrick looked out of the window, so excited to be on a steam train he could scarcely speak.

Joe talked to Bridie about the fishing business at Whitby Point and his dreams about the future. 'I wanted a loan to start up a fish cannery. My father-in-law thought that the bank wouldn't lend the money on such a speculative venture, and he was right. Mr Braxton told me that it was not a propitious time for new ventures like that. He did, however, agree to a loan that will allow me to replace our boats' coal-fired steam engines with diesel.'

'Is that good?'

'Of course. Diesel is cleaner and I won't be tied to coal bunkers or need to hire a man just to load fuel, so it will keep our overheads down. We have to watch every penny in these times.'

Bridie shook her head. 'Fishing is something I know nothing about. But it sounds interesting.'

'It can be exciting too. You wait. I'll take you and Patrick out with the boys sometime.'

As the train steamed south, Patrick sat silently looking out of the window, seemingly mesmerised by what he could see, the string of Sydney suburbs giving way to a sprawl of bush through which he could see glimpses of a magnificent escarpment.

Joe watched him and noticed that the little boy constantly put his hand into his pocket, as if checking to make sure that something important was safely tucked inside it.

Joe smiled at Patrick. 'What have you got there? A lucky pebble? I always used to keep a shell in my pocket.'

Slowly, a trifle reluctantly, Patrick withdrew his hand from his pocket and showed Joe what he was carrying. Joe stared in amazement. It was the small wooden elephant he'd bought for Bridie in Colombo all those years ago.

'That is very special indeed,' he said softly. 'A lucky elephant. Keep it safe.' He curled Patrick's fingers over it and watched as the little boy placed it carefully back in the pocket of his short pants.

Joe looked at Bridie. 'You kept it, all these years,' he said.

'It was a souvenir of a very happy day. I haven't had a lot of those and now Patrick has something that he can play with. He doesn't have any toys but he loves his little elephant.'

Joe said nothing more, but was filled with joy at the thought that Bridie had kept the little wooden elephant all this time. Surely this was a sign he was more to Bridie than just her English pupil.

Joe watched Bridie as she chatted quietly to Patrick. He looked at her glorious red hair and thought how lucky he was to find her again. He had always been content with Evalina. She had been a placid, dutiful wife and he certainly had no complaints about their relationship, but Joe knew in his heart that he had never felt the passion for Evalina that he'd felt for Bridie, a passion that had not diminished in all the years since he had first seen Bridie in the ship's little recreation room.

As the journey continued, Bridie started to ask him a lot of questions about his family and his sons and about Whitby Point, especially the school.

'I'm sorry, Bridie. I don't know all that much about the school, but the boys all seem to be happy there. They can read and write, at least Ricardo and Pietro can, Carlo only just started, but I've no complaints.'

'Joe, tell me about where Patrick and I are going to live.'

'I propose that you and Patrick move into Mrs Ambrose's guesthouse. I will introduce you as my old friend, now widowed, which is exactly what you are,' he said. 'And we'll go from there. You'll like Mrs Ambrose, she's a kind soul.'

Bridie was silent for a moment then asked, 'How is your family going to take to me?'

'Bridie, you are a lovely person and everyone will love you, wait and see.'

'You make it all sound so simple,' said Bridie, sighing. 'I feel like I'm in a dream. Everything has moved so fast. I just hope I don't wake up.'

'Bridie, it will be simple, trust me.'

But of course, it wasn't.

*

A few days after her arrival, Joe brought Bridie home to meet his mother and his sons. Bridie and Patrick had moved into Mrs Ambrose's guesthouse, where Patrick had a room of his own for the first time in his life, and he was enrolled at the local school. Joe visited Bridie and Patrick, meeting them in the front parlour so that there could be no gossip. Joe found that he and Bridie had no trouble finding things to talk about and they enjoyed each other's company, but little Patrick was harder to get to know.

Joe judged that Patrick Sullivan was a boy who had seen too much hardship, pain and fear in his short life, although he seemed to retain an innocence and sweetness about him as if he believed that the world was a better place than it appeared. He was a quiet boy, with a reserved manner, always well behaved and polite. His mother didn't spoil him, which made a change from his own children, who were, as far as Joe was concerned, overindulged by their grandmother. Indeed, he frequently had to remind his own family that in an Italian household, the father's word was law.

Upon his return from Sydney, Joe had sat his mother down and explained that he was bringing someone home whom he'd met years before, and who was now widowed and had a young boy about Carlo's age. Emilia peered at him.

'Where is she from? Her family? Do we know them?'

Joe had feared that this was going to be a problem. 'Mamma, she is not Italian. She comes from a good family in Ireland. She is kind and good but she has suffered a lot. Her husband died and she has no family in Australia, so it has been difficult for her. She has just moved here to Whitby Point and I thought it might be nice for her boy to meet my boys.'

His mother gave him a shrewd look. 'Why did she not go home to her family?'

'Times are very hard in Ireland, like back in Italy. There's no money for such a trip.'

'Why is she here?'

'Because, Mamma, Whitby Point is a better place to live than where she was living in Sydney.'

'Does she speak Italian?'

'Only a few words. But she taught me to speak English. Perhaps she could teach you English, too.' Joe smiled.

His mother bristled. 'I have no need to speak *Inglese*. Bring her and the child to visit if you must. I hope you know what you are doing.'

'I'm just being a good friend.'

*

Bridie's first visit did not go well. Emilia made little effort to get on with her. The older boys were polite enough to both Bridie and Patrick, but they soon grew bored and fidgeted until all the boys were sent outside to play while the three adults sat down to coffee and Emilia's home-made crostelli.

Bridie courteously asked Emilia how she had made the sweet biscuit, and Joe translated the answer, but it was an unsatisfactory conversation.

Eventually Emilia looked at Joe and asked, 'How long must I sit here pretending to be nice to this girl?'

She may have spoken in Italian but Bridie looked as though she understood the intent of her words.

'Mamma, could you go outside and keep an eye on the boys, please?' suggested Joe, giving her a frown.

'You have never asked me to do that before,' replied his mother, but nevertheless she took the hint and left the room.

'Oh dear, she doesn't approve of me at all,' said Bridie, sighing.

'Nonsense, of course she likes you,' said Joe emphatically.

At that moment there was a yell from Ricardo and Carlo came racing into the house and disappeared into a room, banging the door behind him.

Joe strode outside. 'What's going on?'

'It was Carlo,' cried Ricardo. 'He's locked Patrick in the woodshed. He said he's going to chop his legs off with the axe! But he's just pretending.'

Joe and Bridie went running over to an old shed where Emilia was battling with a rusty bolt.

'Patrick, are you all right?' called out Bridie.

'Yes, Mum. But it's really dark in here. That boy said there's a snake.' Patrick started to cry.

'There's no snake, Patrick. Here, let me.' Joe reached past Emilia and yanked back the bolt. He entered the spidery darkness of the shed and lifted Patrick out.

Bridie hugged him, but Patrick pushed her away and, wiping his eyes with the back of his hand, sniffed, 'I wasn't scared.'

'What happened? Why did Carlo do such a thing to Patrick?' demanded Joe.

'He said, he said . . . he said Patrick was telling lies. Patrick said that you came and visited him and his mother and that you really liked him. That's not true. We're your boys, not him,' said Ricardo.

'Now, now, don't talk like that. Of course you're my boys, but Patrick is new to your school and I was friends with his mother a long time ago, so I want you to be his friend, too. He doesn't know anyone and he doesn't have brothers like you do. I want you to be kind to him, do you understand?' said Joe in his firm voice.

The boys knew it was better not to argue.

'I will go and speak to Carlo. Pietro, take Patrick down to your grandmother's chickens and see if you can find some eggs.'

Patrick glanced at his mother and whispered, 'Carlo doesn't like me. He's mean.'

'He's probably very nice when you get to know him,' said Bridie.

'I didn't do anything,' protested Patrick.

But Pietro took his hand and said, 'I'll show you the chickens.'

That night, after Patrick had gone to sleep, Joe and Bridie sat in Mrs Ambrose's parlour talking quietly.

'I feel terrible. Your mother doesn't like me. Maybe she thinks I'm chasing your money. And the boys aren't very comfortable with us either.'

'Nonsense. If Mamma is suspicious it's because you're not a so-called nice girl from our village. Anyone who doesn't fit that description is going to have trouble with her at first. Things will change when she gets to know you. And the boys will be fine. I know that Carlo was unkind to Patrick but you have to remember, he's the baby of the family so he likes to be the centre of attention. Ricardo and Pietro liked Patrick. I'm sure.'

'I hope so,' replied Bridie.

*

Joe took Bridie and Patrick to his house several more times. Emilia always cooked a wonderful meal, and Bridie always complimented her on her cooking, but the conversation never went any further. However, the two older boys began to take an interest in Patrick, even though, as they pointed out to their father, he was really too young to be bothered with. Nevertheless, they seemed to like playing football with him in the backyard, and they even went as far as praising his tree-climbing skills.

'See,' said Joe, 'the boys are coming around.'

'Only Ricardo and Pietro,' replied Bridie. 'Carlo doesn't seem to have changed his mind at all.'

'He will, he will. Give it time.'

A few weeks later as they sat in Mrs Ambrose's front room, Bridie told Joe how difficult it was for her to fit into the life of Whitby Point. 'It's a very pretty place,' Bridie said, 'but it's so quiet. When Patrick's at school, I go for a walk and I can't find anyone to talk to. Your mother seems to have friends, but they won't speak to me. I'm not Italian.'

'But Bridie, there are a lot of people in Whitby Point who aren't Italian. What about the church? Is there no one there to talk to?'

'I suppose so, but people here are so different from Surry Hills. I know that everyone lived on top of each other there. I know it was a slum. But if you wanted to talk to someone, you just opened your door. Here, it's different. You have to go and find someone in particular.'

'Give it time. Things are bound to be different from the city here, but you'll get used to the place.'

'At least Patrick is happy at his new school. He's made some friends and he's certainly learning. And the school is much nicer. Not so cramped and he loves having that huge playground to run around in.'

'Whitby Point is not all bad then?'

'No, Joe, it isn't.'

That evening before he left the guesthouse Joe had a quiet word with kind Mrs Ambrose and when he visited Bridie again a couple of days later, she told him that Mrs Ambrose had taken her to a Red Cross meeting.

'They do such wonderful work, Joe. On the surface Whitby Point looks so pretty and shows a serene face to the world, but when you go to a Red Cross meeting you realise just how much work is needed to keep food on the table of some of the families around here. I thought that poverty existed mainly in the city, but that's not true. It's bad down here, too.'

'Yes, Whitby Point is not immune to what is happening in the rest of the country,' said Joe. 'But it is good that you want to help.'

'In fact, Mrs Ambrose said that if I really wanted to do more, I should also join the Country Women's Association. They also do a lot of work to relieve the plight of poor country women. Joe, I can see that there is much that should be done, and I want to help. Mrs Ambrose said that they could use all the help they can get, so I told her that I'd join.' Bridie's face lit up as she went on. 'It is so good to be made to feel useful.'

Joe smiled to himself. It was wonderful to see Bridie enthusiastic and interested in what was happening in Whitby Point. She just needs a little more time and she'll come around to the idea of marriage, I'm sure, he thought.

*

On a Saturday afternoon a month later, Joe and Bridie decided to take the boys down to the beach. It was low tide so they could collect pipis. Joe loved the taste of the sweet little shellfish hidden in the sand. They had been very successful in their pipi hunt and Joe carried a bucket of them as he strolled slowly with Bridie towards the headland while the boys raced ahead to explore the rock pools.

Suddenly there was a lot of shouting and one of the boys let out a scream.

Joe dropped the bucket of pipis and both he and Bridie ran towards the rocks.

At first all Joe could see were Pietro and Carlo standing on the rocks. Pietro was shouting and Carlo seemed to be crying. Then, to his horror, he saw that Patrick was floundering in a rock pool that had a fast-running channel heading towards the ocean and that Ricardo was trying to swim over to the little boy. Both of them were being swept towards the open sea.

Joe clambered over the rocks and jumped into the water where the channel met the ocean just as Patrick was swept towards him. At the same moment a wave broke, pushing them both back onto the rocks. Ricardo, who had managed to get himself out of the pool when he saw his father jump in, grasped Patrick's hand and pulled him while Joe pushed him out onto the rock ledge. Then Joe heaved himself out of the pool and lay exhausted on the ledge beside him. All of them had grazed and bleeding arms and legs.

'Are you okay?' Joe asked Ricardo.

'Yes, Papà, I'm fine.'

Joe looked at his son with pride. 'That was a very brave thing you did.'

'I don't think Patrick can swim,' Ricardo added in a matter-of-fact way. 'Might be an idea if we teach him.'

Patrick said nothing. He clung on to Joe, burying his head in Joe's shoulder. Then, just as Bridie reached them, he looked up at Joe and said, 'I love you. You saved me.'

Joe just smiled, but he was touched by Patrick's words.

Bridie wrapped her arms around her son. 'Why on earth did you jump in that rock pool, Patrick? You could have drowned.'

'Where's Carlo?' asked Joe, alarmed, suddenly aware that his youngest child was no longer on the rocks with them.

'He's over there, Papà,' said Pietro.

Carlo had shrunk back towards the cliff face away from the surging water and was watching them.

'Poor boy,' said Bridie. 'He must have got a terrible fright.'

'I think that Carlo did something to Patrick,' said Ricardo. 'That's why Patrick jumped into the water.'

Joe saw that Patrick's hand was tightly grasping a small object.

'What've you got?' he asked Patrick. 'What is it?'

Patrick opened his hand to show Joe his wooden elephant. 'Carlo threw it in the water,' he said.

Leaving the other boys with Bridie, Joe marched over to Carlo.

'That was a really, really stupid thing to do, Carlo,' he shouted at his son. 'Why did you do it?' He gave him a light clip across the ear. 'You could have got us all killed.'

'He's a baby!' Carlo shouted back at his father. 'That's a dumb toy.'

'You took Patrick's favourite toy. You know it is very, very precious to him.'

Grudgingly Carlo nodded.

'That little elephant was all that Patrick ever owned in his life before he came to Whitby Point. And I happen to know that it belonged to his mother and it's very special, but you took it away. You deliberately wanted to hurt Patrick. Why, Carlo? What has he ever done to you?'

Carlo glared in fury at his father. 'You like him better than me, don't you!' he shouted.

'Son,' said Joe, 'that's not true. I love you just the same as I always have. Now I want you to come over and say you're sorry.'

Meekly Carlo went over to Patrick and reluctantly apologised for throwing the elephant into the water and frightening everyone and causing such trouble.

Sighing, Joe ruffled his hair. 'That's a good boy,' he said.

On the walk back from the beach the boys were subdued. Bridie and Joe walked a few paces behind them as they spoke quietly about what had happened.

'Bridie,' said Joe. 'I can't apologise enough for what Carlo did.'

'Joe, it wasn't your fault and I thought you handled things well. Both you and Ricardo were very brave and in the end no one got hurt. But it made me think. If my son can tell you that he loves you, then I can too. If that offer of marriage is still open, I'd like to take you up on it.'

Joe couldn't speak. He took Bridie's hand and squeezed it and held it tightly all the way home.

*

The wedding was held in the little church of St Mary's Star of the Sea. It was a small gathering by Italian standards. The boys and Emilia, who had made a small festive gesture by adding a lace collar to her black dress, sat primly in the front pew. The boys wore formal white button-down shirts and matching knickerbocker pants. Joe wore a dark suit with a flower in his buttonhole and had insisted that Bridie buy an outfit from Sydney.

She had chosen a beige silk three-quarter-length dress cut on the bias and trimmed with a satin bow and draped tulle that hugged her trim figure. A tiny matching hat with a soft feather trim nestled into her auburn hair, and cream netting covered her shining, joyful eyes. She carried a simple bouquet of white roses as she walked down the aisle, escorted by her proud son.

Joe thought she looked like a Hollywood movie star and he couldn't keep his eyes off her or stop smiling. He could hardly believe that after all these years and after everything that had happened to both of them, Bridie was at long last going to be his.

Franco seemed genuinely pleased that Joe had found such happiness. At first Bridie had felt uncomfortable meeting Franco as she knew she was replacing his late daughter. But Franco soon put her at ease, telling her that Joe was indeed a lucky man to have found such a beautiful wife.

'It's not right for a man and those young boys to be on their own without a woman's influence.' He glanced across at Joe's mother. 'Emilia is a good woman, but old-fashioned and set in our Italian ways. I'm sure my daughter would be pleased to know that her sons will have someone with more modern ideas in their lives, so to speak.'

Franco's son Silvio and his wife were also pleased for Joe. Several friends from Wollongong and Whitby Point as well as Joe's fishing crews made up the rest of the group at the church.

There was no time for a honeymoon but, if the truth was told, Joe knew that Bridie would not have wanted to leave Patrick behind anyway. On their wedding night, back at Joe's house, Joe reached into his pocket and held open his hand. Nestled in his palm was the thin gold and garnet ring that his grandmother had given him, the one that Bridie had rescued from the pawn shop.

'It's too delicate to wear, but I'd like you to have it anyway,' said Joe, placing it in her palm.

'You kept your grandmother's ring, after all this time. I'm so glad . . .' said Bridie, her eyes misting as she looked at the worn little ring.

'I kept it tucked away and thanks to you, my darling, it was given to me twice. Once by Nonna Celestina and once by you. And now I will give it back to you. The circle has closed.'

*

Joe and Bridie were very happy. The relationship between Bridie and Emilia evolved into a kind of truce. In the kitchen Emilia remained the boss, but Bridie asserted her domain on the enclosed verandah where she supervised the boys' homework and, over time, had more and more to do with their upbringing. She even learned Italian. Joe taught Bridie to drive the car, which she loved to do. Emilia continued to walk to the waterfront and meet her Italian friends to exchange gossip, while Bridie became more involved with the Red Cross and the Country Women's Association.

Everyone seemed to know their place and was content, except for Carlo. For while Ricardo and Pietro happily accepted Patrick into the family, it was evident to everyone that Carlo disliked his step-brother.

But whenever Bridie raised her concerns about the situation, Joe always said optimistically, 'Give it time. It will all work out.'

Bridie told Joe that she was not so sure but she would not let the situation cast a cloud over the happy life she now had with Joe.

9

Indian Ocean, 1939

JOE DREW ON HIS cigarette before he flipped the butt over the side of the ship and walked back to his cabin. As he opened the door he smiled at Bridie, who was sitting at the mirrored dressing table putting on her favourite earrings. 'It's breezy out there. You might need your wrap,' he said.

'Maybe it will be too cool for a walk around the deck after dinner. My hair will get blown to pieces.'

Joe sat on their bed and watched her. Her figure was as trim as the day they'd met some twenty odd years before. 'You look beautiful. You always do.'

'It's nice to see you all dressed up in a dinner suit. You look so handsome. This trip has been glorious and we're just starting out on our holiday!' said Bridie happily.

Joe leaned down and kissed the top of her head affectionately. 'I just wish we hadn't lost so much time when we could have been together.'

Bridie gave a small smile. 'Just be glad and happy that we're together now.'

'When we first met all those years ago on the *Ricconigi*, did you like me just a little – or a lot?'

'Of course I liked you, we were friends.'

'But at night, alone, did you ever dream of me? Think what if . . . ?' persisted Joe.

'Joe, darling, stop teasing. We've had six glorious years together. And each year is more wonderful than the last,' she said softly. 'And yes, deep down I did think of you, and wonder what might have been had things been different.'

'I never stopped loving you! When I think back to our time on that cargo ship I kick myself that I didn't persist a bit more. Maybe if I had you would have forgotten about Ronan.'

Bridie shook her head. 'Things happen when they're meant to, Joe. And this is our time.'

'It certainly is.' He reached for her hand and kissed it. 'We waited long enough for a honeymoon. I'm looking forward to seeing Italy again but I don't imagine that my home will have changed much.'

'I don't think that things will have changed much in Ireland either, but it will be good to find out.' Then she added, 'We're going to be away such a long time. I do hope the boys are being good for Nonna.'

'Don't worry, darling. Ricardo is quite responsible and the others will be okay. My mother will be quite strict, I'm sure. But let's forget about them for a while and enjoy ourselves. We've planned this trip for such a long time.'

'Yes. You have worked so hard. You deserve this holiday.' She stood up in her shimmering satin gown and held out her fur stole to Joe, who wrapped it around her bare shoulders.

'I believe we're seated at Captain Jorgensen's table tonight. And tomorrow we'll go ashore in Colombo. Do you remember the day we had there?'

'Of course. I wonder if the little shop where you bought my elephant is still there.' Bridie smiled at her husband. 'How different this voyage is from the old *Ricconigi*. Remember that awful food!'

Joe chuckled. 'I'm trying not to. Travelling first class is much, much better. Do you remember my good friend Antonio? I'm sorry that we lost touch when I had to leave Sydney in a hurry, but I like to think that he's as successful and happy as me.'

'I hope so, too.' Bridie looked into Joe's smiling eyes. 'We've both seen some hard times and now we have the good times. I hope that our boys' future will be bright too.' Bridie's smile suddenly faded. 'Oh Joe, you don't think there'll be a war, do you?'

'Hush, Bridie. This is a time for us to escape all our worries.'

As they walked to the dining room, Joe reflected on the last few years. He knew that his mother was disappointed that he had not married an Italian girl and she hadn't always made life easy for Bridie. But to her credit, Bridie had managed to juggle her position as wife and mother, gently melding the family together to become a harmonious unit. He smiled as he thought of coming home from work one night to find his mother quietly darning socks, Bridie bottling fruit, the boys doing their homework and the table set, all waiting for his arrival before they sat down to eat, and he had felt overwhelmed by how lucky he was. Later that night in bed, holding Bridie in his arms, he thanked her for all she did and the happiness she had brought to his life and home.

And so he had insisted they take their long-delayed honeymoon.

Over dinner at the captain's table the talk soon turned to events in Europe.

'Do you think that there will be war in Europe, Captain?' asked Mr Whittaker, an English banker.

'Highly unlikely,' the captain replied. 'Herr Hitler has got what he wants in Europe. He won't ask for anything more. He signed an agreement with Mr Chamberlain in Munich to that effect.'

'Rubbish,' said another Englishman, who had the bearing of a military officer. 'I wouldn't trust that man an inch. He's hoodwinked Chamberlain to give Germany time to increase its forces even more and when he's ready he'll unleash them on all of us. Churchill's right: unless we act soon, Hitler will take all of Europe.'

'But are France and England ready to act?' asked Joe.

'They are building up their military strength but whether that will be enough, I don't know,' replied the officer.

'If there is a war, will Italy join in with Hitler?' the Englishwoman sitting next to Joe asked.

Joe shrugged his shoulders. 'I don't know. From what I read, Mussolini has ideas of grandeur for Italy. He wants to build a new Roman Empire. That was the reason he invaded Abyssinia, wasn't it?'

'That was a shambles,' said Mr Whittaker. 'Sending in machine guns and planes against a bunch of natives. It was shocking how they used mustard gas. Apparently thousands died, and not just the Abyssinian soldiers. The spray from the aircraft poisoned the lakes and rivers, not to mention the ground crops and animals.'

'It just showed that the League of Nations is a toothless tiger,' remarked a Frenchman. 'Nothing it tried to do could stop the invasion. And besides, after that, Italy

265

left the League altogether, so there wasn't anything that could be done for the Abyssinians anyway. It was all dreadful.'

'I thought Mussolini was held in great respect by the Italians,' said the woman next to Joe.

The Frenchman ignored her, then continued, 'The upshot of it all is that Mussolini has aligned himself more closely with Hitler.'

'Mussolini wants total access to the world's oceans,' said a doctor seated at the end of the table.

'Just for starters,' added the British banker pithily. 'The question is, will Italy go to war if Germany does?' he asked Joe.

'I think Mussolini would only do such a thing if he could see some big advantage for Italy. Italians don't like to become involved in wars. I speak from experience. I was a soldier in the last war.'

Seeing Joe shift uncomfortably the captain changed the subject. 'Mr Aquino, how long is it since you were last in your homeland?'

'I left Italy as a young man, and have lived in Australia for nearly twenty years. This is my first trip back. I am taking my wife to visit the island where I was born.'

'It's the first holiday we've ever had together. So far it's been wonderful,' said Bridie brightly, trying to lighten the mood.

The captain smiled at her. 'That's good to hear, Mrs Aquino. Will you be visiting your homeland as well?'

'We certainly hope so. I would like to see the changes in Ireland since independence.'

'The Irish Republican Army is still causing a lot of trouble in the north,' said Mr Whittaker.

The captain signalled the waiter to refill their glasses. 'That's true. We live in challenging times. But for now, let us enjoy ourselves, shall we?' he said.

After dancing to the music of the ship's band, Bridie and Joe strolled, arms linked, along the deck back to their cabin. It was a still evening. The moonlight cast a shimmering trail across the tranquil sea. They paused at the railing and Bridie leaned her head against Joe's shoulder.

'How peaceful. I'm glad I changed my mind about coming out on deck. It's very beautiful here.' She sighed and looked up at him. 'Joe, I hated all that talk of fighting and dictators at dinner,' she said.

'Yes, men and their wars.' Joe put his arm around her and pulled her close. 'But there is truth in their speculation. It's a funny thing, but I don't feel connected to Europe anymore. Australia is my home and my children's home and our future. Do you feel the same?'

Bridie nodded. 'Oh, yes. I hate to admit it, but I don't feel the same way I used to about Ireland either. I have followed such a different path. Maybe this trip is to say goodbye to the past.'

That night they made love and Bridie fell asleep curled beside Joe. But Joe didn't sleep right away. He lay awake, feeling the powerful vibration of the ship's engines far below. As they journeyed closer to Italy, he could feel the pull of his memories and childhood, and he wondered again at the way his life had changed since, as an inexperienced and poor young man, he had set out from his island carrying Alfonso's battered suitcase containing his few clothes, the precious traffena and a swag of dreams. How lucky he'd been! Now he had Bridie as his wife, as well as a family of strong boys. He looked forward to telling his relatives of his good fortune.

*

As he had guessed, on his return to the island with Bridie, Joe found that little had changed there. He was sad his father and grandmother couldn't meet Bridie, but all his brothers, sisters, other relatives and childhood friends gathered at his late parents' little cottage, where his eldest brother now lived, all keen to see and hear how their Giuseppe had become successful in Australia, and interested in meeting his pretty, redheaded wife.

Joe was excited by the reunion and delighted to introduce Bridie to them but found that, after the casual cheerfulness of Whitby Point, the closed and traditional society of the island felt suffocating.

When the two of them walked around the little port, the old women, all dressed in black, studied Bridie with critical eyes as they sat outside their doors and crocheted, or severely swept their steps or gossiped at the market stalls with their meagre array of produce.

'I don't think that things are any better here under Mussolini than they were before. The islanders are still very poor,' Joe confided to Bridie, looking at the posters of the dictator that were stuck on the public buildings.

Hand in hand, they strolled through the small township and its outskirts to the places Joe knew well, and he told Bridie stories of his childhood. He had often spoken to her of Angelica and of the importance of Alfonso in his life. Joe was delighted when his brothers told them that Alfonso was still living alone in his windswept shepherd's cottage in the hills. For Joe the highlight of his trip to the island was visiting his elderly friend.

'You have done well, as I knew you would,' Alfonso told Joe over a glass of grappa in the kitchen, a scene that brought back many memories for them both. He smiled at Bridie. 'And you have a lovely wife, who speaks very good Italian.'

'Thank you,' said Bridie.

'She keeps my mother happy by speaking Italian with her,' said Joe. 'Mamma is very settled in Australia although she clings to the old ways and refuses to learn

English, but she is strong like the olive trees and loves the boys. Now, tell me, Alfonso, what do people really think of Mussolini and his Fascists? I have tried to ask my brothers that question, but they avoid a straight answer.'

'Mussolini's very popular and his popularity increases all the time, especially after the conquest of Abyssinia, but most people on the island have become disillusioned with Fascism. There has been no improvement in their lives, they are still poor, but people don't like to speak out for fear of incurring the attention of the police, who are as corrupt as ever. I fear that things will never change for the better on this little island. But it's good that you have a new life that you love.'

'My home is a small town, but a happy place and there is a future there for my sons. Franco, my first wife's father, allows me to make my own decisions, so I am the boss. Fishing is in my blood, Alfonso, and the fishing is good off Whitby Point.'

'And you, Alfonso, have you never thought of leaving here?' asked Bridie gently.

'Yes, Alfonso,' said Joe quickly. 'You must be lonely here. Why don't you come to Australia? I'll look after you.'

'Thank you, thank you, but I'm an old man now. You are kind and generous, but I am content with my simple life and my books. I did my adventuring in my youth. I am pleased to have seen you again. I always knew you would succeed because your heart is good, Giuseppe.'

Outside they all embraced and there was dampness in Joe's eyes as he took Bridie's hand to go back to the little port. He did not turn around as he followed the familiar track down towards the village, leaving Alfonso, wrapped in his old coat, standing on the hillside watching them go for what they all knew would be the last time.

Bridie listened with interest as Joe spent time sitting on the stone wall of the harbour front or on the deck of a fishing boat talking with the men he'd known as a young boy. That night, Bridie told him that she was amazed by how much the men knew about the sea.

'I have great respect for the knowledge and the skills that these fishermen have passed down from father to son for generations,' said Joe. 'They know the rhythms of the sea and the migrations of the fish; they know every stone on the seashore and the structure of the seabed, the weather patterns and how to handle their boats in any conditions.' Joe rubbed his chin, as though coming to a surprising conclusion. 'But now I realise that they want to continue in the old ways they know.'

'Not everyone embraces new things like you do, Joe,' Bridie said.

Joe smiled. 'They have no inclination to change, to grow, to try something different,' he said. 'When I first came to Australia I thought the fishermen there lacked knowledge because they had no traditions, it meant that everyone had to learn for himself by trial and error.'

'But that's why you have done so well, Joe. You are prepared to experiment, to take a chance,' said Bridie. 'I am very proud of you.'

Several days later it was time to leave the island. As they boarded the little ferry to go to Messina, Bridie asked Joe if he was sad to go.

'No,' replied Joe. 'Maybe one day I'll have the chance to visit again, but I certainly wouldn't want to live here any-more. And now we'll explore the rest of Italy!' he declared.

When they arrived in Naples, Joe told Bridie what he had thought when he'd first arrived in that city almost twenty years ago. 'To me it was the most magnificent place in the world. And I'll never forget how delicious the pizza I ate here was!'

'And I'll never forget the wonderful Neapolitan music,' said Bridie.

So they set off to find a romantic little *trattoria* where they ordered pizza and red wine and were serenaded by a local tenor.

The following morning, Joe left Bridie in their hotel room to dress and went to find a morning newspaper and have a quick coffee before they went to breakfast as Bridie didn't care for the strong Italian coffee. When he returned he looked pale and waved the paper at Bridie.

'Joe! What is it?'

'Germany has invaded Poland and Britain has issued an ultimatum demanding that Germany withdraw. If Germany doesn't, then I suppose it will be war. We will know in a few hours.'

'What will happen to us if war is declared? Will we have to go home?'

'Bridie, I don't know, but it does sound serious.'

She sat on the edge of the bed. 'How horrible. If there is a war, do you think that Italy will join in?'

Joe sat beside her and read through the front pages. 'Mussolini's a Fascist and he could side with Germany, but Italy is poorly equipped industrially, so it may take some time before he decides which way to jump. But, darling, if war is declared, we may have to think twice about carrying on with our journey.'

They had breakfast and took a stroll around the city. They could not ignore the knots of men talking in cafés and women gathered together around doorways, their faces all showing concern. But in other parts of the ancient seaport, life seemed to continue as it always had, with the business of going to sea and looking after the safe arrival of shipping, small and large, under the ever-present shadow of Mount Vesuvius.

They ate a late lunch at a small café. Both toyed with their food. Finally the news came. A man rushed into the café calling to his friend that he had just heard on the radio that Britain was now at war with Germany.

'I expect that will mean that Australia, as part of the British Empire, is at war, too,' said Joe quietly. 'I think we must return home as soon as we can get a ship.'

'Will the voyage home be dangerous?'

'It could be. The sooner we go the better.'

'Joe, I'm so scared. The last war was terrible. It was supposed to be the war that ended all wars, but now it seems that it wasn't. I'm glad our boys are far away from Europe. Yes, I want to go home.' She reached across the table to him and they held hands tightly.

The return journey from Genoa on a much smaller ship was a far cry from the glamorous voyage to Europe, but Joe and Bridie were simply relieved to arrive home safely. As they crossed the Indian Ocean there was talk of submarines, for they had learned that submarines were active in the Atlantic Ocean as soon as war was declared. But all they saw was one American warship, which was neutral, as America was determined to stay out of this European fight. As Bridie told Joe, it was comforting in one way to see it, but worrying in another.

Silvio met them at the dock in Sydney and drove them home to Whitby Point, filling them in on the news and rumours about the war that were now dominating the radio airwaves, newspapers and public gatherings.

'How are the boys? And Nonna?' asked Bridie.

'Everyone's fine. The boys will be pleased to see you.'

'They're probably just looking forward to the presents we've brought them,' said Bridie lightly.

Silvio laughed. 'No, they really missed you,' he answered and then began to tell Joe what was happening with the business.

Walking into Whitby Point for the first time after their return, Joe found that all the talk was about the war. People met in clusters to chat about it and in the pub everyone had an opinion about what the next government announcement from the Prime Minister, Mr Menzies, might be. Veterans who remembered the outbreak of the previous war thought that the country was far better prepared this time around.

'But there hasn't been the mad scramble to enlist,' said one survivor of the Western Front. 'People know what they could be in for this time. The Somme was a hard lesson.'

'I wonder if they'll try to introduce conscription again. Don't want to send too many of the lads, though. Need some men to stay at home to do the essential work. Can't expect women to do it,' said the publican.

For the next few months life pottered along as normal during what people were calling the 'Phoney War'.

But as Bridie said to Joe after dinner one night, 'I can't help feeling I'm waiting for the other shoe to drop!'

Joe nodded. 'I don't like the sound of what's going on over there. Thank goodness our boys are too young to enlist.'

'Ricardo is almost eighteen. Boys his age fought last time, but thank heavens this time they are only taking men who have turned twenty. I just pray it will all be over before Ricardo's old enough to fight,' said Bridie, sighing.

'I hope you're right. I need him here to help me,' said Joe. 'He seems to have a good feel for the fishing industry, unlike Pietro, who takes no interest in it at all. Won't even go out on the boats without a fuss!'

'Joe, dear, Pietro has other interests. He loves the movies and art. He's in the school play, you know. Is it really necessary that he go into the fishing business if he so dislikes it?'

Joe looked at her with some surprise. 'I never considered that. I mean, it's what we Aquinos do. We follow in the family business. He's very lucky to have the opportunity! What will happen if all the men are needed for the war? We will need youngsters like Pietro and Carlo to work on the boats.'

'I wish it would all go away, evaporate,' said Bridie. 'I just want to get on with our lives without this war hanging over everything.'

The boys, however, talked about nothing else over dinner.

'I could pass for twenty-one,' said Ricardo. 'I could join the militia. I'd have to do three months training. Maybe I should try to get into the regular army.'

'Don't be ridiculous,' said Joe. 'You are not yet eighteen and we need you on the boats.'

'I can do what Ricardo does on the boats,' said Carlo. 'Why can't I go fishing? Why do I have to stay at school?'

Joe looked at his youngest son and spoke kindly but firmly. 'You are strong for your age and, yes, you are a good worker. But your education is important. The smarter you are, the more you get ahead. School is the most essential thing for you. For all of you.'

Pietro nudged Carlo. 'If you did your homework sometimes, you wouldn't find school so bad.'

'You only like school because of the art classes. You're a sissy.'

'No, he's not!' said Patrick.

'Shut up, Patrick!' said Carlo, giving Patrick a shove. 'Keep out of it! No one cares what you think.'

'Carlo, that's enough!' roared Joe.

'I've offered to help you with your schoolwork, Carlo,' soothed Bridie. 'And there's nothing wrong with being an artist.'

274

Joe stood up. 'Boys, leave the table now. Ricardo, you stay, I want to speak to you.'

Bridie and Emilia gathered up plates, taking them to the kitchen as the other three boys headed to their rooms.

Joe poured himself another glass of red wine and put a small amount into Ricardo's glass.

'Son, you are almost eighteen years old. I understand how you feel, how you want to get out and experience life. But this is not the moment. We don't know what's in store and I need to know that I can count on you here, working with me.'

Ricardo looked pleased at his father's comments. He lifted his glass of wine. 'I'll always stick with you. We have a good life here. I hope it will always stay this way.'

'War will change things. I have seen how people are living and struggling in Italy. You have no idea how well off we are in Australia. Coming here was the best thing I ever did.'

'So you no longer have strong feelings for Italy?' asked Ricardo.

'I have my memories. But I wouldn't enjoy life back on the island now. I didn't like what I saw of Fascism. I don't want to be told by a dictator what I should think or do. I want to make up my own mind.'

'Maybe this Phoney War will all come to nothing,' said Ricardo hopefully.

Joe rose. 'Somehow, I don't think so. We can just be glad we're far from the action.'

*

Joe was right. In May 1940 Germany invaded the Low Countries and France; the 'Phoney War' ended and the real war began in earnest.

Shortly afterwards, Bridie was sitting at home in Joe's small office sorting through bills and receipts, and thinking how pleasant the office was because it was such a sun trap on a cold winter's day, when Joe appeared at the door.

'This is a nice surprise. What are you doing home at this time?' Then, on seeing Joe's face more closely, she asked, 'What's wrong?'

'It's just been announced on the radio. Mussolini has declared war on the Allies. He's thrown his support behind Hitler.'

'Joe, why would he do that?'

'I think Mussolini saw how swiftly Germany overran France and thought that if he waited much longer the war would be over and he'd miss out on a share of the spoils, so he's joined Hitler. I bet a lot of Italians have no idea what they're fighting for or why,' he added.

'Will this have any effect on the Italian community here?' wondered Bridie.

'Who's to say? I, for one, wouldn't dream of going back to fight for a dictator. I love this country. It has given me so much, including you. And our sons are Australian. Maybe I should join up and fight for this country.'

'Don't be silly, Joe, you're too old to enlist. And you do so much for the community already,' said Bridie, struggling to keep the alarm out of her voice.

'You're right, I am a bit old to be fighting and the war is a long way from here. Let's just keep doing what we do best,' said Joe, giving her a kiss.

Life continued in its normal routine at Whitby Point, but there was a lot of discussion about whether to enlist or not.

'I'm not sure I'll enlist. I have no desire to kill other people's sons,' the baker told Bridie.

'Well, my son's joined up,' said one of his customers. 'He thinks that we should fight for England.'

Patrick, Carlo and Ricardo were all wrapped up in news of the war, listening to the radio, exchanging stories with friends, each reacting in his own way. There was a lot of bravado and talk of bombs and aeroplanes and destroyers, and scorekeeping as to which side had destroyed more than the other. Ricardo put up a map of Europe on his bedroom wall and plotted the German advance using drawing pins. But Pietro told them all that war was stupid and refused to take part in their discussions. He announced that he'd joined the local theatre company, to get away from the incessant talk of war at home, he said.

Bridie encouraged Pietro, although Joe was uncertain that he wanted his son on the stage.

When the theatre company put on a show, Pietro had a part, singing in the chorus. He asked Bridie to help him rehearse his dance steps and he talked his grandmother into making his costume. He persuaded Emilia to add some extra finishing touches to it, including a feather in his beret, saying that he wanted his costume to have panache.

Bridie insisted that all the family go and see Pietro's show. Ricardo and Patrick enjoyed themselves, Carlo made jokes about it, Emilia was scandalised by the amount of makeup Pietro wore on stage and Joe remained entirely non-committal. Pietro told them all that being involved in the theatre, even a small amateur production, was the greatest fun he had ever had, and he could hardly wait until he had another chance to perform.

A few weeks later, Bridie had to travel to Sydney to see the dentist as she was not very happy with the one in Wollongong and she knew that her teeth needed attention. She spoke to Joe and Patrick about her plans one morning.

'After my appointment with the dentist in Sydney next week, there are a few hours to wait before the train back, so I thought I might take Pietro to the Tivoli. There's a show based on a Hans Christian Andersen story and Pietro might like to come with me to the matinee. Patrick, would you like to come too? I doubt Carlo or Ricardo would enjoy it, though.'

'I don't know, Mum. I like the idea of going to the city with you, but I'm not especially interested in going to the theatre to watch singing and dancing. That's definitely something for Pietro.'

'That's fine, Patrick,' said Bridie, giving her son a quick hug. 'Tell you what, next time I go to Sydney, it'll just be the two of us. Maybe we could go to the zoo or something.'

Shortly afterwards, as Joe was walking along the verandah, he heard shouting coming from Patrick's bedroom. 'What is going on?' he called.

'Patrick kicked me,' whined Carlo.

'Is that true?' asked Joe. 'Why did you do that?'

'Carlo said that my mother liked Pietro more than me and that's why she's taking him to Sydney.'

'That's nonsense. How childish. I wish you two boys would stop your fighting. You both go on and on about stupid matters and upset the rest of us. You need to just grow up, both of you.'

Joe marched off and, as he did, he saw from the corner of his eye Carlo scurrying off to tell Emilia about the fight. Joe knew that she would take his side.

I thought they would grow out of this squabbling by now, but I suppose I'll have to wait a little longer, he thought to himself.

The following week, when Bridie and Pietro arrived back from Sydney, Joe asked them how they had enjoyed the show.

'It was wonderful,' replied Pietro. 'I just loved it.'

'I'll say,' said Bridie, with a smile. 'I don't think he moved for the entire time. It was as though he was transfixed.'

'It wasn't just the show, although the dancing and the sets were fantastic. Certainly showed up our poor attempts in Whitby Point. The theatre was wonderful. It had velvet seats, elaborate lights and those carved cupids. The whole thing was magic. I know what I'm going to do now,' enthused Pietro.

'Sing? Dance?' asked Bridie.

'It doesn't matter. Just be a part of it all.'

*

Not long afterwards, Joe returned from his boat to find a white-faced Emilia weeping in the kitchen and a policeman standing awkwardly by the front door arguing with Bridie. Joe didn't recognise the policeman as being one of the local police whom he knew.

'Mr d'Aquino, the government has issued a summons for Italians to be detained in internment camps for the duration of the war if it is thought that they could pose a threat to the security of Australia,' the policeman announced.

'That's ridiculous! He's an Australian now. He's been here for nearly twenty years and he's a valuable member of this community,' said Bridie angrily.

'According to my papers Giuseppe d'Aquino is not an Australian citizen,' said the policeman.

Joe was shocked. It had never occurred to him that anything like this would happen to him. 'This is ridiculous. As if I would do anything against this country.'

'It's the law, Mr d'Aquino. You have to come with me,' said the policeman.

Bridie looked at him and said, 'Joe, you can't just let them take you. You have to fight this. What will the family do without you? This isn't at all fair. You know that you love this country. You have done nothing to deserve being locked up. Can't you stop them?'

'How do I fight the law? Anyway, it would be pointless to argue with the messenger. I am sure that in time the authorities will realise their mistake and all will be well,' Joe said quietly. 'Besides, darling, this is not the place to make a fuss. I don't want to upset my mother more than necessary.'

Bridie nodded, then she asked the policeman sarcastically, 'And where are you sending these Italians who call Australia home, work hard, raise their families and are good citizens?'

The man shrugged and looked uncomfortable. 'It's war time. The government made a law that enemy aliens must be supervised. It's my job to enforce it and to take you to Sydney, to Long Bay Gaol. You'll be interrogated there and if they want to detain you further you'll be sent to an internment camp, maybe at Hay, although there are some camps in other places. If you're considered trustworthy, they might let you out during the day to work on nearby farms.'

Joe knew that it was highly unlikely that the Italian community would resort to sabotage or pose any kind of threat to Australia, but since Italy had allied herself with Germany, the lawmakers in Canberra were shutting down even this remote possibility.

'Maybe there are some Fascist groups making noises and sending goods to Italy for the war effort, but everyone knows they are a minority. They make trouble for everyone,' Joe said to the policeman but, even as he did, he knew it was pointless to argue.

'Where there's smoke . . .' began the policeman.

Just then Emilia appeared and threw a barrage of urgent questions. When Joe explained to her what was happening, she began wailing again and Bridie gently took her back inside.

'She's worried that you'll take her away as well,' Joe explained.

'No, just you. That's my orders. Can you pack a bag? I can give you fifteen minutes,' said the policeman.

Joe was swamped by a wave of despair. How long would he be away? What would happen to his family, his fishing business? Would the authorities understand that he was absolutely no threat at all to Australia's interests and let him go?

When Bridie returned to the verandah, she was very calm. 'Joe, Nonna and I will help you pack. There is nothing this policeman can do for us. As he said, he has his orders. But I can do something. You are well liked and respected in this town and I am going to fight to get you out and I'll make sure that the whole town is behind my efforts. I'll speak to the mayor and other important locals. I'll start up petitions. I'll make such a fuss that they'll have to let you out. Joe, I am sorry that none of the boys are here to say goodbye to you, but I'll explain it all to them and I'll make sure that the business continues to run smoothly while you're away. I promise you won't be away for long. Trust me. I love you and I'm not going to let you just disappear into some camp without a fight.'

Arriving at the internment camp in western New South Wales a week later, Joe was shocked to find himself thrown into a fenced camp containing a barren block of wooden buildings not much better than sheds with bare earth for the floor and only basic facilities. With its turreted watchtower, guards, barbed wire and high walls, Joe felt that this internment camp was no better than a common prison and those in charge treated the inmates with hostility and suspicion. Speaking in Italian was forbidden, the food was atrocious and everyone was bored. The dormitories were overcrowded. The men slept in bunks on sacks stuffed with straw and with only a thin blanket as protection in the cold weather. Tents, housing as many as six men, had to be erected. Newspapers, though severely censored, were permitted – as was sporadic mail.

When Joe was first arrested, he'd been questioned at length in Long Bay Gaol in Sydney about his political beliefs and his life in Italy.

'Why did you travel back to Italy last year?'

'You fought in the Italian army. Are you preparing to fight in it again?'

'Why have you never taken out Australian citizenship?'

'Does your family in Italy support Mussolini? What do you think about the dictator?'

'Are you a Fascist?'

Joe thought that the questions were ridiculous. He tried to explain that his trip to Italy was part of a belated honeymoon and had no political purpose. He was sorry that he had not taken out citizenship, but he had not thought it necessary because he felt part of Australia anyway. No, he was not a Fascist, he believed in democratic government. No, he didn't like Mussolini, and when he fought in the Italian army it was on the side of the Allies.

But his answers failed to impress. He was told that while he might consider himself to be a model citizen, the Australian government could not take his word for it and he would be interred for the duration of the war.

For the first few weeks at the camp, Joe fretted for his family and his business. He had heard nothing from Bridie and he wondered about her efforts to get him out. Depressed about the whole situation he told himself that there was nothing anyone could do for him and that he would just have to learn to make the best of the situation while the war lasted.

One day he heard that several more Italians were coming to their camp from an overcrowded camp in

Queensland. Through the wire fence Joe watched the men file off a dusty bus looking tired and incurious about their new surroundings. Joe was about to turn away, when one of the new internees caught his eye.

'Antonio! Tony!' Joe jumped up and down, trying to catch his old friend's attention.

Tony paused, looking around.

'It's me, Joe! Giuseppe!'

Tony spotted him and gave a wave.

When they found each other they embraced, grinning madly, hardly believing the coincidence of being in the same camp.

'This is the best thing that's happened to me in a while,' said Tony, looking older, but very fit and tanned. 'Do you want a smoke? I guess we have a lot to catch up on.'

When Joe told him about finding Bridie again and marrying her, Tony slapped his friend joyfully on the back.

'That's wonderful news! But it's sad that you lost your first wife. Still, she gave you three good sons, so things have worked out for you.'

Tony told Joe that he had never got as far north as Innisfail, but had instead worked hard in the cane fields around Ayr.

'I was very lucky, too. I married an Australian girl and we saved and bought our own cane farm. I tried to find you at one stage, but it is hard to leave the cane fields, there is always so much to do, and you were a long way away in New South Wales. I figured wherever you were, it wouldn't be too far from the sea. I've produced a lot of sugar and two daughters,' he added proudly. 'Life was good till this mess happened.' His face darkened in anger. 'The police started working their way down the coast from Cairns to Brisbane, rounding up Italians, people like me, even tracking them to the middle of isolated cane fields! But Joe, it's even worse than that. I found out that some disgruntled folk have sold out their mates for money or to settle a grudge with totally groundless accusations. Don't know who to trust these days.'

Joe shook his head. 'Tony, people are in here just because they're Italian. Doesn't matter what their political convictions are – Fascists, Communists, neutral. It almost makes you cry when you think of the poor buggers who left Italy to escape Fascism only to end up here.'

'The guards think we're all just "eyties" but there seems to be a very mixed bunch in here.'

Joe nodded. 'People in here come from all parts of Italy and have all sorts of occupations. There are a couple of doctors, a chemist, various engineers, a real estate agent, at least three accountants, people who have their own businesses. I've met taxi drivers, cooks, carpenters and a blacksmith. I'm the only fisherman,' he added with a slight smile.

'Do you know that I came down here with a man from Piedmont who has a son serving in the Australian army and they still locked him up! Madness!'

'It's hard on everyone's family,' said Joe. 'Bridie is very capable, but it won't be easy trying to run a fishing fleet by herself and my sons should not be raised without a father to guide them.'

'I have the same concern about Marion and the cane farm. It's going to be hard to make up the financial loss after this bloody farce,' said Tony.

Joe had worked long and hard on his fishing boats, believing that his reward for his sweat and honesty would be economic security and political freedom, and this treatment was a hard pill to swallow. All over the camp Joe heard tales about the injustice of the enemy alien internment system from people who wanted to share their stories.

'My son received notification from Italy that he had to turn up to do his national service or be arrested. He didn't answer because as far as he's concerned, Australia is his home. He even went and joined the Australian army. But just before he was due to be shipped overseas, the police arrived demanding to know where he'd been born. When he told them it was Italy he was accused of being a Fascist and interned.'

'I was rounded up at work and not even allowed to go home to say goodbye to my family or collect some clothes, and I told the police that I became a citizen in 1928 and I am now a subject of His Majesty King George the sixth, but they took no notice!' another angry man told Joe.

Others told of being taken into custody on a Sunday when it was known they would be at home. Sometimes, Joe was told, houses were searched and if letters from Italy were found they were deemed to be incriminating evidence. A man related how one of his children's toys was confiscated because it was thought to be a machine for producing Morse code.

Joe had been in the internment camp for several weeks before he finally received a letter from Bridie. It had been censored. The name Whitby Point had been blacked out, which amused Joe. Did the authorities think he would have forgotten where he came from? But there had been little effort made to delete anything else.

My darling Joe,
We all miss you very, very much, but we are coping without you (just). The business is fine. The boys are helping so much. Ricardo is a tower of strength. He knows so much about how the business works and I rely on his advice all the time. You should be very proud of him. Patrick and Carlo have suspended hostilities and come straight from school to the wharf to lend a hand. Even Pietro has pitched in, although he never stops complaining about smelly fish. Still, his heart is in the right place. I don't know how I would manage

without your mother, either. After she got over the shock of your arrest, she completely took over the running of the house. She won't let me lift a finger and does all the house-work and cooking so that I can keep the business going.

Poor Franco and Silvio have both been sent to the internment camp in Cowra. I think their wives are finding it a battle to keep the fleet going in Wollongong because many of the Italians they employed have also been sent to camps. I think they are trying to hire retired Australian fishermen. I hate to have to tell you this, but I'm having to do the same thing as we have lost some of our men as well, not just the Italians who have become internees, but also our Australians as they are joining up. Just the same it is a pleasure to be able to give work to someone who has not had a proper job in years because of the Depression, which I have done on two occasions now. These men have proved to be hard workers and tell me so often how grate-ful they are to be employed that they embarrass me.

Joe, my darling, the whole town was really shocked when you were taken away. I thought that when I started a petition to have you released that I might have trouble finding support, but I was very wrong. Everyone I have asked has been happy to sign. My friends in the CWA have taken the petition out of town to their friends on the farms and when I asked the mayor if he could help he said that it was a disgrace that a good citizen, such as yourself, should be taken away for no good reason and that not only would he be happy to support the petition but he would raise the matter urgently with our local MP.

Please look after yourself and don't get too down. I'm sure that it will only be a matter of time before you're out of there and home to us.

You are in my thoughts, day and night.
All my love,
Bridie

As the days dragged by, Joe began to think that Bridie's efforts had all been for nothing, when suddenly, without any fanfare, he was released. Indeed he was bundled out of the camp so fast that he only had a quick chance to tap Tony on the shoulder to wake him and tell him he was leaving and that he'd make contact with Tony's wife as soon as he could.

Joe was deposited at the nearest railway station and given a train ticket to Sydney and a couple of shillings for food. It was a long and tiring trip. There were not enough seats on the train and he had to stand for much of the way. He wished he'd been able to contact Bridie and arrange to meet her in Sydney and travel back to Whitby Point together, but organising a long-distance phone call, especially with so little money, proved to be impossible. He consoled himself with the thought of how surprised she would be when he got home. How he'd missed her, longed for her, and soon he would be with her again.

From Sydney, he started walking south. Several times he managed to get lifts and a few miles from Whitby Point a milk truck stopped and picked him up, dropping him at the turn-off into the town.

He walked home, relishing the smell of the sea, the fresh air, the greenness of the hills, and the peace of the pretty coastline and town. In a place like Whitby Point, it was hard to believe there was a war being fought, or that good men were being incarcerated unjustly. The morning was filled with sunshine. He realised how hungry he was and he looked forward to his mother's fresh bread and eggs and a tomato from the garden for his breakfast.

A car came to a halt beside him and an elderly man flung open the passenger's door.

'Hey Joe, did you escape?'

'Sure did. How're things, Sam?'

'Fine, just fine. Damned glad to see you. You got sprung from that camp, eh? That petition must have worked. Whole thing was bloody ridiculous. No one in Whitby Point thinks you're an enemy agent. Does the missus know you're coming home?'

'No, I'll just surprise her.'

'You certainly will. Good to have you back, Joe. The whole town will be pleased.'

Sam let Joe out of the car outside his house.

'Appreciate that, Sam,' said Joe as he jumped out. 'See you round.' He turned and raced up the steps of the verandah, calling Bridie's name.

Bridie was at the end of the verandah watering some plants and she dropped the watering-can and raced to Joe, laughing and crying at the same time.

'Joe, I can't believe it's you! I have missed you so much.' She put her arms around his neck and kissed him in a way that proved her point.

Soon there were shouts and cries from the boys and sobs from his mother as the house awakened to Joe's homecoming.

'I haven't eaten good food for ages, and I'm starving,' Joe declared above the rest of the noise.

Quickly the house was filled with the smell of coffee and toast, and the sound of laughter and everyone talking at once carried down to where the boats were rocking at anchor in the little sheltered harbour.

*

After Joe came home, things almost returned to normal. Unfortunately there were conditions attached to his release. He had to report to the police station every day, but this soon became part of his routine. He was also forbidden from going out on the large trawler so, if he went fishing at all, he had to confine himself to the smaller boats, and even for that he had to apply for a permit. In addition he was not allowed to travel more than twenty miles from Whitby Point. Joe was concerned about how things were going for the family in Wollongong and he frequently phoned to discuss and help manage Franco and Silvio's end of the business with their wives.

One day, after such a phone call, he said to Bridie, 'Those women, especially Silvio's wife, are very capable. They know what they are doing. But getting suitable men for their boats is an ongoing problem. So many men are needed for the armed forces, heavy industry is expanding at Port Kembla and the coal around Wollongong can't be mined fast enough. I'm glad I've got Ricardo. He's becoming more and more important to us and I'm glad that the war is so far away that he doesn't feel the need to join up.'

*

Less than a year later, however, the war came a lot closer to Australia with the bombing of Pearl Harbor and the disastrous fall of Singapore. People began to fear a Japanese invasion of Australia.

'Do you really think that the Japanese will attack Australia?' Bridie asked one night over dinner.

'Our coastline is vulnerable. There's no way we can patrol every inch of it,' said Joe. 'I truly hope we're not going to find any foreign subs off our beaches.'

After dinner Joe went to check the boatsheds and make sure all the fuel and gear was safely locked up. All seemed secure enough so he got back into the car and, on a whim, drove a little further along the coast road, stopped and got out to look at the beach. A fence of barbed wire was strung along the length of it, although it appeared to Joe to be a pathetic defence against any attack from the darkening sea. As he stood there a sense of worry swept over him. This vast island continent seemed so vulnerable in its isolation. He had made Australia his home and he loved the place and he didn't want his boys to lose the freedom and the opportunities that he had enjoyed.

He looked out to sea and thought he could see a long black shape, shark-like, moving through the water beneath the surface. He remembered how, as a boy, he'd had a sixth sense about what was beneath the waves. Now he stared at the horizon, trying to see if there was an unusual white wash, the sign of a vessel, but he could make out nothing. He shuddered and hurried back to the car, driving carefully through the blacked-out town to his home.

Bridie looked up from her knitting as he walked in. 'We were getting worried about you. It's just come over the radio that there's been a possible submarine sighting, just north of us, off Nowra.'

Joe shook his head. 'Don't worry. It's probably a false alarm. Anyway, we know our drill and what to do.'

That night he held Bridie in his arms and prayed the war would soon be over. But to his dismay, a couple of days later, Ricardo broke the news that he had joined the navy.

'I know that you need me here to help you, Papà, but I also think that I should help defend my country. I'll be at sea, so I'll be fine.'

Joe stared at his son. He felt very proud. He knew that things in the business would be hard without Ricardo, but he also knew that his son was doing the right thing. 'Have you told Bridie and Nonna, yet?'

'No, they'll make a fuss.'

'Ricardo, they will be like me. Proud of your decision.'

*

After a brief training period, Ricardo joined the destroyer HMAS *Arunta*, which was deployed escorting convoys to New Guinea in the war against the Japanese. A couple of weeks later, the Australian government requisitioned Joe's trawler for the duration of the war so that it, too, could be used in this vital work.

'It's terrible, losing my trawler, but, funnily enough, not having it makes the loss of Ricardo a less difficult hole to fill. Bridie, do you think things will ever go back to the way they were?' said Joe, as they sat on the verandah.

'Joe, I've had an idea that might help alleviate our manpower problem. Why don't you let me drive the fish up to Sydney? You can't go, and it seems a waste to send one of the men when he could be far more use on a boat.'

'Bridie, I can't let you do that.'

'Why not?' replied Bridie promptly. 'You taught me to drive the car. How much harder can our truck be? Joe, lots of women are taking over men's jobs these days. In factories, on farms, everywhere. Look at Franco's and Silvio's wives. You never thought that they could run the business, but you've said yourself that they are doing really well. I'd like to feel that I'm doing my bit for the war effort. I know that my work for the Red Cross and the CWA is important but this is a time when we all have to pull together, so I want to do more. Nonna will feed the boys and look after the house while I'm away. And I don't have to do it all the time. Just when you are really short-staffed.'

'You probably won't be able to go every day because of petrol rationing, but let's see how we go.' Joe gave a deep sigh. 'Nothing seems right, does it? You want to drive a truck and I'm going to let you. The world has turned upside down.'

Bridie enjoyed driving the truck to Sydney a couple of days a week. She liked delivering the fish to the markets where she talked with the traders, finding out how things were in Sydney. The invasion of Sydney Harbour by Japanese midget submarines had brought the city directly into the war. Some people, she was told, had fled the city, looking for safe havens. She also learned that the influx of American soldiers had changed the city. Everyone seemed very hopeful that General MacArthur would be able to bring the war to a speedy conclusion, although everyone acknowledged that beating the Japanese wouldn't be easy.

'Joe, the Americans are turning the tide of the war in the Pacific. It can't go on forever. Things will go back to normal one day, I'm sure,' she told Joe after she returned from Sydney one evening.

'Well, I hope when it is over we can build the business back up. But those men coming home . . . I wonder how Ricardo will be . . .' His voice trailed off.

Bridie sat on the arm of his chair, put her arm around his shoulder and leaned her head on his. 'He will be fine. He's at sea, and when the war is over he'll come back here and work with his father again. You know that's all he's ever wanted.'

'I know. Maybe because he's the eldest but also he's the one most like me when it comes to fishing. I was thinking I might send Carlo up to work with Franco and Silvio for a while once they're back home and Carlo's finished school. Patrick says he's happy, but do you know what he wants to do with his life? Has he said anything to you?'

'I genuinely think he loves it here, the fishing, the sea, the people. It's changed his life, mine too, being here, being with you . . .' Her voice caught, and she hurriedly wiped away a tear. 'I love you so much, Joe.'

'Bridie, it's you who has made the difference. Everyone in the town admires and likes you and my family thinks I am the luckiest man alive. Me too.' He touched her hand. 'You're right. The war will end, Ricardo will come home, Franco and Silvio will be released, and we can all get on with the business and enjoying life again.'

'Yes,' replied Bridie. 'And it can't come soon enough for me.'

Bridie's prediction was right. With the entry of the Americans into the war, the Allies began to gain the upper hand in North Africa and in the Pacific, but the end was slow in coming. Eventually, however, after the invasion of Italy and then the D-Day landing in France, the race to Berlin was well and truly on. Finally, at the beginning of May 1945, the Germans surrendered. While Australians were pleased that the war in Europe was over, their celebrations were muted as everyone was aware that the war against Japan still had a long way to go.

As Joe and Bridie walked back from church, where they had been for an early thanksgiving mass, Bridie voiced what had been on both their minds. 'I know that it's wonderful that the war in Europe is over, but I won't feel really happy until Ricardo is back home. I suppose that's not going to happen until the Japanese are well and truly beaten.'

'Yes, it's hard to be really enthusiastic about peace in Europe when my son is still out there in the Pacific, still fighting, but at least it means that Silvio and Franco will come home now and some of the men who used to work for us will come back to Whitby Point. So let's at least acknowledge the victory by doing something for ourselves.'

'You're right, peace in Europe is worthwhile. I suppose it means I won't be driving up to Sydney as much anymore. I shall miss that, but it will be nice to be at home, looking after all my men. How do you think we should celebrate VE Day?'

'Just look at the weather, it's a beautiful morning, good tides, no wind, slight swell. I thought we'd go fishing. Proper fishing. Up the coast.'

'What? Out to sea?'

'Why not? We've never been out in the boat, just you and me. We've been out with the boys but never just us. It's a bit late to get started and we've missed the best of the morning, and probably the fish as well, but it doesn't matter, we're taking the day off!'

Joe looked so pleased with the idea that Bridie said, 'I don't see how I can refuse such an offer, darling.'

Joe spoke quietly as he got the boat under way. The May morning was still chilly as they chugged through the channel towards the open sea. Bridie, rugged up against the cool wind, sat beside Joe in the shelter of the half cabin and watched him confidently steer the small launch across the harbour he knew as well as his own backyard. The sun was emerging above a puffy layer of clouds and the water gleamed where the bow parted its silky surface. The land gradually grew distant behind them as the little boat travelled towards the horizon.

Joe stared ahead, a slight crease in his forehead as he studied the ocean. Suddenly he pointed ahead and said triumphantly, 'Birds.'

Bridie shaded her eyes against the glare and, finally, she too spotted the distant flicker of diving and soaring sea birds.

'They're after bait fish. A good sign. The big fellows will be in after them, too.' Joe pointed the bow at the ruffled patch of water dotted with feasting birds and increased the speed of the boat.

He circled outside the shrieking birds and cut the engine, quickly jamming a baited fishing rod into the small holder he'd attached at the gunwale on the stern.

'You take this one, I'll get the other one out.'

Bridie shrugged out of her jacket but before she had taken the few steps to the stern, the rod jerked wildly, bowing to the water, the line streaming out.

'Grab it and start winding,' shouted Joe. 'If he runs, let him.' The second line, barely in the water, zinged away from the boat and Joe grabbed that rod, grinning. 'This is what we want.'

Bridie felt the strain in her arms as she inched the line back onto the reel, bracing her knees and thighs against the boat to steady herself.

'Don't fight him, let him take some line, now pull back and up, now lower the rod and wind. Pull up, wind down,' Joe told Bridie encouragingly.

'It's a tug of war,' she panted, but slowly she began to gain line on the fish.

Joe nodded as he wound furiously with his own rod. 'Tuna,' he shouted as he caught his first glimpse of his fish while it flung itself around in a frenzy. He landed the fish, dispatched it swiftly with his knife and went to Bridie's side.

'This is heavy – or is it just me?' Bridie asked.

'No, you're doing fine. He took a lot of line off you. Just keep winding.' He watched her bite her lip as she strained at the bending rod. 'Want me to help?'

She shook her head. 'No, no, I'm gaining. I can feel it. Oh, there it is!'

There was a flash of silver in the water. Joe leaned over the side with his gaff, hooked the fish in the gills and heaved it over the side where it thrashed about at their feet.

Joe lifted the fish to get the hook out of its sharp, pointed mouth and said, 'Be a good ten pounds. Well done, my darling! Mamma can stuff this and we'll roast it over the fire. Let's go again. Here, try some squid this time.'

'My legs and arms ache after that effort. But I don't care. This is so much fun. I can't wait to catch something else. Oh, Joe, this is so exhilarating. I can feel my adrenalin pumping.'

Joe couldn't help but smile at his wife's enthusiasm.

They drifted for five minutes and then Bridie's rod was hit with such force it almost jerked from her hands.

Clearly more confident, Bridie started to reel in the shuddering, fighting fish as Joe let out a shout that his line was struck, too.

They landed three more similar-sized yellow fin tuna and then the excitement stopped. They drifted in silence, scanning the water, rods poised.

'The fish have moved. Bring your line up and we'll move too.'

He started the engine and cruised slowly eastwards. Bridie leaned over the side.

'Don't you just wish you could magically see down there, and see what the fish are doing, where they are,' she said.

'Hmm. You know, as a kid I always felt I could do that,' said Joe. 'I could feel when they were around. I saw a fish in a wave when a storm was coming once. I was with my father and that fish looked at me. It was like it knew me.'

'Was it like a mermaid?'

'No. More like Uncle Salvatore. It had an ugly face with bulging eyes and fat lips.'

'Your uncle wouldn't like to hear you say that!'

'He drowned a long time ago. He was a good man. I used to think that perhaps the men who were lost at sea became fish.' He looked away. 'I had some imagination, eh?' He cut the engine. 'I reckon this is the place.'

Joe deftly re-baited their rods and dropped the lines over the side. They sat in comfortable silence, watching the sea, trying to see through the blue layers to the world beneath. Bridie kept the line across her finger as Joe had shown her, ready to feel the slightest nibble or tug.

'Do you think Patrick understands fishing the way you and your boys do?' she asked suddenly.

'Definitely. Certainly more than Pietro, who isn't interested in the sea at all. Ricardo is really dedicated, I know he will run things when I retire and do it well. And Carlo, he likes the physical work of fishing. Patrick? He's solid. He's a fine boy, Bridie. I'm proud he is part of my family. My son.' He smiled at Bridie.

Suddenly there was a mighty yank on her line and before she'd brought her fish to the surface Joe was hauling at his line. They landed some smaller fish and were kept busy baiting, dropping lines, pulling up more fish, sometimes landing them, sometimes not.

Joe was proud of Bridie, overjoyed that she was enjoying the day out with him. Then the fish suddenly disappeared again. They shared a thermos of hot soup and some sandwiches and hard-boiled eggs, as the boat bobbed quietly up and down while they waited for some more action.

'Fishing is all about patience,' said Joe.

'I know. I wouldn't normally be able to sit still like this, just waiting, with nothing going on around me,' admitted Bridie. 'But for some reason, this doesn't bother me. It's peaceful. I'm glad you suggested this. I can understand why you love the sea and the challenge of it all. Thank you, Joe dearest. I won't forget today.'

Joe, smelling of fish and bait and the salty tang of the sea, leaned over and kissed her. 'Nor will I.'

*

Two days later the weather closed in and the sunny day they'd enjoyed at sea seemed as though it had happened in another time and place. The wind howled and the rain lashed. But, surprisingly, despite the rough conditions, Joe's crew netted a decent haul of fish. Another of his boats found some lobsters under a rock shelf and this, combined with a decent haul of prawns from the Wollongong boys, made a trip to the Sydney markets a worthwhile venture.

'I'll drive it up,' said Joe.

'Joe, I know that it's probably not necessary now to report to the police station every day, but you haven't yet been told officially not to. I wouldn't like you to take the risk of driving to Sydney. If you got caught, it could be awkward. I can go. I know the road really well and it might be my last chance to do it.'

Joe knew she was right. He couldn't afford to have problems with the authorities, even if he was almost sure that all the restrictions he had been placed under over the last few years would shortly be lifted.

'You're right, of course. But, Bridie, you will be very careful driving in this weather, won't you?'

'Don't be silly. I'll be fine.' She kissed Joe lightly, hopped into the truck and drove away.

Patrick and Pietro were in the kitchen that evening, helping Nonna prepare spaghetti, meat sauce and roasted slabs of eggplant topped with tomato and cheese. Joe was about to tell them how good it smelled when there was a knock at the door. He wondered who would be calling at the evening mealtime.

Sergeant Anderson, the local policeman, was standing on the verandah with a stricken look on his face.

'Joe, can you come outside?'

Joe shut the door behind him. 'Is it Ricardo? Has something happened to him?'

The sergeant twisted his cap in his hands and cleared his throat, seeming unwilling to speak.

Joe glanced over his shoulder into the wet evening and knew at once that something terrible had happened to his beautiful Bridie.

'Mrs Aquino . . . there's been an accident.' The sergeant's voice cracked with anguish.

'How bad is it? Where is she?' Joe braced himself against the door.

'It happened on the Bulli Pass. The fog was so thick, the road was slippery. Not her fault, a bus lost control . . .'

'Tell me, tell me, Sergeant, how bad?' Joe seemed unaware that his voice had risen. 'Where is she?'

'There was nothing anyone could do. She died at the scene. Joe, Joe, I am so sorry, I don't know what to say. She's been taken to Wollongong Hospital. I can take you there, but it's late.'

Joe made a wild move towards the police car parked out the front. 'Let's go, take me to Bridie. Quickly.'

The sergeant paused, trying to find the words to say that there was no need to hurry anymore. 'The boys, your mother, do you want me to tell them?'

The door behind Joe opened and Patrick came outside.

'Papà Joe? What is it? We are ready to eat when Mum arrives.'

The sergeant reached out and steadied Joe while he turned to face Bridie's son.

'Patrick. Come here.' Joe's voice said it all.

Suddenly Patrick cried out, 'No, no! My mother. It's my mother, isn't it? What's happened?' He pummelled Joe's chest as he tried to hold him. Joe's tongue stopped in his mouth, so it fell to Sergeant Anderson to tell the young man that his beloved mother was dead.

Patrick disappeared into the darkness at the end of the verandah as Carlo and Pietro came hurrying to see what was going on.

On hearing the news, Pietro tearfully embraced Joe and went back inside. A moment or so later, Emilia's wail shattered the night.

'I'll wait here for you, Joe. You go and see your mother,' said the policeman.

Joe felt as though he had entered a labyrinth of grief. Bridie had been the light of his life. He had loved her as he had never loved another person. He had no idea how he would live without her.

'Mamma,' he asked softly, as he approached his mother, herself shaking with grief. 'What am I going to do? How can I go on without her?'

She looked at her son with dark, pained eyes. 'I will help you, Giuseppe. I am here for you and the family.'

Tears streamed down Joe's face as he went to her, knelt before her and, putting his head in her lap, wept. Slowly she stroked his hair with hands that had cooked and cleaned and sewed, hands that had dug in the earth, soothed babies and buried children. She crooned an old song she remembered from her childhood because there were no words she could say to her son that would ease the terrible pain in his heart. At last Joe rose to his feet.

'Tomorrow I will need to go to Wollongong and see Bridie. I will take Patrick. You can look after the others, yes?'

His mother nodded.

'Thank you, Sergeant,' Joe said to the policeman still waiting patiently on the verandah. 'Could you drive me and Patrick up to Wollongong in the morning? Thank you for all your kindness.'

After Sergeant Anderson had gone Joe found Patrick sitting on an old chair in the backyard in the soggy darkness as fog and sea mist wreathed around him. Joe pulled up another chair and sat beside him.

'It's not fair,' said Patrick, anger, hurt and fear shaking his voice. 'Everything was so good.'

'Yes,' agreed Joe. 'It's not fair.'

They sat in a heavy silence for a moment or two. Then, in a low voice, Patrick said, 'Do you think she felt anything? The bus didn't hurt her, did it?'

'I don't know, son, but I do know that her last thoughts would have been of you.'

'What are we going to do?' It was the cry of a little boy, wrenched from the heart of the strong youth trying to control himself.

'We will go on, as your mother would want.'

There was a long pause.

'I've been thinking. Maybe it's time I left school and moved on. I don't want to be an imposition to you or to Nonna. I'm not really your son.'

'What rubbish,' retorted Joe. 'The day I married your mother, you became my son as much as the other boys. I always wanted you to take my name, Aquino, but your mother wasn't so keen because she said that Ronan Sullivan was a good man and you should always carry his name. But I always thought of you as one of mine. When you have finished school, I would like you to work with me, unless, of course, you have different ideas.'

Patrick shook his head. 'I like fishing and the sea. I have learned a lot from you.'

'You're smart, Patrick, so stay on at school for as long as you can, and remember this is your home and we are your family.' He touched the boy's shoulder. 'I love your mother and I'm going to miss her every single day for the rest of my life. I know you will, too. Whatever you do in the future, just make her proud. Tomorrow morning I'm going up to Wollongong to identify her. Would you come with me? I could use your company.'

Patrick nodded and the two walked slowly back into the house.

*

The funeral was one of the biggest seen in Whitby Point for a long time. Before the requiem mass, which was held in the same church in which Joe and Bridie had been married, Joe and Patrick quietly said their private farewells.

'You really loved her, didn't you Papà Joe?' Patrick said.

'Yes. I loved her kindness, her bravery and her joy of living. She had so much to give. I will never forget seeing her red curls bounce away from me at the wharf when we first came to Australia, thinking that I would never see

301

her again and that my life would be poorer for that. Her presence in my life has been such a blessing – not just for me but for all of us.'

'She said we could never repay you for your kindness.'

'You have no debt to repay. You are family,' said Joe. Then he paused, watching Patrick, and asked, 'What have you got there, son?'

Patrick had taken something from his pocket and was putting it into the coffin. He opened his hand to show Joe. It was the little wooden elephant, bought so far away, so long ago.

'I wanted to give this back to her. I don't need it anymore.'

Joe nodded and put his arm around Patrick's shoulders as the two of them walked away together.

Bridie's mass was attended by family, friends and most of the community. Franco and Silvio, released from their camp, stood sadly with their families. This was not how everyone had imagined their homecoming. Ricardo had been told the sad news, but it was impossible for him to get home for the service.

Pietro, Carlo, Patrick and Silvio, all dressed in dark suits, carried Bridie's coffin from the overflowing church.

Bridie was buried in the cemetery situated on a small hill above the town facing the sea.

Several days later Joe walked up the hill alone, stood by her grave and looked at the wide blue ocean, which seemed to stretch to infinity. This was the sea they'd crossed together from the homes of their birth, leaving behind poverty and family, sailing to they knew not what and with few possessions besides hopes and dreams. And how those dreams had been fulfilled. Their struggles and sacrifices had forged a family and a future together.

Joe stood on the windswept hill and promised Bridie that he would make sure their dreams would go on and that their boys would have a bright future. As he turned and walked slowly back down the hill to the home where he and Bridie had been so happy together, he softly said to himself, 'Ah, Bridie, my love, my life, I miss you very, very much.'

10

Whitby Point, after the Second World War

JOE STIRRED IN HIS sleep and rolled onto his side to reach out for Bridie. The cool, smooth, empty sheet was yet another reminder he was alone.

Time was not the healer he'd been told it would be. Although years had passed, he missed Bridie as painfully as the day she'd died. Everything he did, he still did for her. It was as though she was watching and he couldn't afford to fail at any task. He was grateful for the support he had received from his friends and family, but they could not fulfil the physical longing he felt for Bridie; they could not abate his need to hold her and touch her, to make love to her, to simply see her going about her chores each day, to hear her sweet voice, to exchange a quick word, a touch, a smile.

He sighed. He pushed his pain deep down, into the hole in his heart. Not that anyone really understood the depth of this sorrow, for Joe's natural ebullience always rose to the surface to disguise it, and his cheerful demeanour, ready smile and teasing words hid the grief with which he lived. His bones creaked as he lifted himself out of bed.

And yet, in spite of the sadness he felt for the loss of Bridie, he knew that he had much for which to be thankful. His family and business flourished. Ricardo had survived the war safely and had come home, apparently little the worse for the experience. He had married Rosina, a nice girl of Italian parentage, whom he had met in Wollongong. They now had three children, Raimondo and two younger daughters.

Carlo had also married Gail, a local Australian girl, and they had a daughter, Greta. Neither Patrick nor Pietro, who was now living in Los Angeles, had married, despite Joe's hints that he would like more grandchildren.

Even though two of Joe's nephews from Italy had been captured by the Allies in North Africa and had spent the remainder of the war as prisoners of war, Joe had to admit that, apart from the loss of Bridie, the Australian Aquinos had survived the war relatively unscathed. Franco, who had failed to get his nephews out of Italy before the war started, was told when the war finished that the two brothers had died in the fighting. After the war, he was scornful when he heard that some Italian immigrants in Wollongong wanted to save enough money to be able to return to their villages and set up their own businesses.

'Such a foolish idea,' he had told Joe over a coffee when Joe had visited him in Wollongong. 'There is still so much poverty and hardship back in Italy, why would you bother? We are far better off in Australia.'

'I can see their point,' Joe replied. 'Many Italian fishing families on the south coast lost money in the war when their fishing boats were requisitioned to be used as minesweepers, or as cargo carriers. And if that's not bad enough, I know of Italians who are still regarded with suspicion by their neighbours because they were imprisoned in internment camps. Maybe they have a right to want to leave.'

Nevertheless, many Italians continued to see Australia as the land of opportunity, and in the 1950s there was a huge growth in migration. Some of these new Italian immigrants made their way to the south coast of New South Wales and into the fishing industry.

Joe watched the new arrivals blend into the Australian way of life in their own ways, and to the local Australians they were all just Italians. Joe, however, could see that there was a subtle distinction in the attitudes of those who had arrived in the twenties, those born in Australia to Italian parents and the more recent postwar arrivals. Sometimes he thought that these differences almost led to an 'us and them' mentality, which was creating problems. While the influx of more Italian fishermen helped rebuild the fishing industry in Whitby Point after its decline in the war years, Joe became concerned that the growth was too rapid.

'Most of that new lot are a bunch of amateurs, who call themselves fishermen. They don't know what they're doing. They overfish and they'll bugger it up for everyone,' he fumed to Ricardo one evening after their boats had taken a smaller catch than usual. 'The fisheries people just keep handing out licences like lollies and more and more boats are coming in. They're all after the same population of fish. How will the fish have a chance to breed? Everyone knows that the numbers of flathead we're getting now are much lower than a few years ago and I can't say I'm surprised. There's too much competition.'

'But Papà, if that's true, why doesn't the government do something?' asked Ricardo.

'Politics,' Joe replied. 'Different states have different regulations. Neither the states nor the federal government really want to know about fishing. They put it in the too-hard basket, and no one will accept responsibility for it.'

'What can we do about it? We can't change things,' said Ricardo, trying to soothe his angry father.

'I'm going to try to,' said Joe with determination. 'Take the size of the mesh holes in the nets, for example. If there were bigger holes, smaller fish could get away and have the chance to grow, instead of just being discarded when they are caught because they are too little. It's such a waste. I'm not the only one who thinks that. I've heard that the scientists, the CSIRO, are also concerned about the decline in fish stocks. They have organised for a group of fishing inspectors to come and see what happens if different-sized mesh is used. I've volunteered to take them out and show them. Want to come?'

*

A few weeks later, Joe and Ricardo took three fishing inspectors out on one of their boats to catch fish using nets with different-sized mesh. From the sampling, it was obvious to Joe that the best size mesh to use in order to maintain fish stocks at a reasonable level was one with a gap no smaller than eight centimetres. The fisheries inspectors seemed to agree with him and he received a letter from the CSIRO to thank him for taking part in an 'invaluable experiment'. Joe was elated. He felt that at last something would be done to make the fishing industry more sustainable. He was devastated when he learned that the New South Wales government proposed to make the minimum mesh size only six centimetres.

'Useless, totally useless. That's not going to help fish numbers,' he fumed to Patrick.

'I don't understand how the government could have taken such a decision,' said Patrick. 'Your results were so good. Everyone said so. Why weren't they implemented?'

'The net manufacturers objected. They claimed that it would be too hard and too expensive to make any adjustments. Of course they could do it. But they think that if they complain loudly enough, they won't have to make the changes and so they will maintain their profits.' Joe pulled his fingers through his greying hair in frustration, as though trying to tear it out.

'There's nothing more you can do then?' Patrick said sympathetically.

'Patrick, I think that this is just the first battle. The war is going to be a long one, and I'm going to fight the government and all those cowboys out there who want to get rich quick and don't care if they ruin the industry in the process.'

Finally the New South Wales government did realise that fish stocks, especially flathead, the fish most favoured by consumers, were being depleted at an alarming rate. So it came up with a novel solution. It thought that changing the names of less popular fish would make them sound more palatable, increase the demand for them and take the pressure off flathead. Much to the amusement of the Aquinos, nannygai were now called red fish and leather-jackets became known as butterfish.

'Changing the names of fish isn't going to stop the cowboys. They'll just overfish those as well,' said Joe, shaking his head at the naivety of the government.

The last straw for Joe came when the New South Wales government restricted the legal size limit of flathead that could be caught.

'Sounds like a good idea, I know,' Joe told Ricardo as he poured them both a drink late one afternoon after the day's fishing. 'But now we have to compete unfairly with the Victorians down south because their legal size limit is smaller and they can still send their undersized flathead to the Sydney markets. Everybody – the cowboys, the government – seems to want to ruin us.'

'What are you going to do, Papà? Have you got any ideas?' asked Ricardo.

'I have been thinking about what would be best for us. First, I want to start up a fishing co-operative here at Whitby Point. That way we are less reliant on the Sydney fish markets. Secondly, I think we should look at serious tuna fishing.'

'I think the idea of a co-op is great, but the tuna season is very short. Will it be worthwhile?' asked Ricardo anxiously.

'Yes, I know it only goes from early October till December, but I think we can adapt our larger trawlers to tuna fishing without too much expense. What is really good is that the fish-canning factories, Pecks in Sydney and Greens in Eden, have upped their price for tuna. Now that makes tuna a very viable addition to our usual catch.'

Joe put his plan into action the following spring when the weather was calm and the tuna were on the move north. He used fishing poles imported from Japan and lures made to resemble squid, which he imported from America. A crewman would toss plenty of live squid out of the trawler to attract the tuna to the side of the boat. Two poles were attached to the lines and lure as it would take two men working in tandem to swing one fish aboard. Each man had his pole resting in a harness to help take the weight, so the heavy fish could be flung quickly over the railing of the trawler and onto the deck behind them. When the tuna hit the deck the quick-release hooks allowed the men to catch the next fish as quickly as possible. Joe told everyone that they could expect the work to be fast and furious once they had the tuna swimming next to the boat.

One day as the trawler moved far out from the coast Joe told his sons what his father had told him: to watch the sea ahead and look for signs of the migrating tuna. The clues could be either dolphins, which frequently swam with the big fish, or birds, which would be diving for whatever the tuna were chasing.

Suddenly Patrick shouted that he could see that the surface of the sea in front of them was rippled and he now spotted the diving birds. As they got closer they could make out a huge school of fish, their dorsal fins occasionally jutting from the surface of the water. He pointed to a patch of ocean where small birds seemed to be dancing on the surface of the sea.

'That's where the lead fish will be,' Patrick shouted over the noise of the engine.

'We all know that,' Carlo said scathingly, as the boat drew closer to the mass of fish. 'This school is enormous. I reckon it'd cover an area bigger than a tennis court.'

Joe ignored the bickering and lowered a bucket to take the temperature of the water.

'Sixty-five degrees,' he told everyone. 'Those tuna will be yellowfin. They like the warmer currents. I think we'll try over there.' He pointed ahead to where the water surface was marked by a line of flotsam. 'That line is where the cool front from the Southern Ocean meets the warmer waters of the eastern Australian current. If you look past it towards the deep blue colour, you'll see what we're really after.'

Their eyes turned to where Joe pointed and they saw a bronze patch seething with flashing dark blue bodies that showed glimpses of silver and gold as they swam through the water. Joe told one of the crew to start throwing the live bait to the tuna and everyone took up their poles, ready to start landing the fish.

But no one on the trawler was prepared for the onslaught of the huge fish as the tuna snatched at the bait and grabbed at the lures in a wild mass. Two poles flew overboard and one of the crew lost his balance on the slippery deck, but he resumed his place and continued throwing a lure into the turbulent water filled with ferocious fish.

The men worked quickly, never taking their eyes off the lure. The moment one disappeared into a gaping mouth, they lifted the poles in an effort to hook the fish, bending their knees and pulling the flexible pole upwards, so that the fish was carried into the boat on its own momentum. With what looked like a simple flick, the men were hauling in the fish faster than Joe could count. A tuna of twenty or thirty pounds was literally flying through the air, sometimes overshooting the trawler altogether and going over the other side of the boat and back into the sea to swim away at dizzying speed. Joe thought back to his fishing days in Italy where it was a triumph to catch just a single fish. Here they caught dozens and dozens.

The boat slowly circled the school, its deck alive with drumming tuna. The power of their constantly beating tails, their mouths gasping, forced their gills open so hard they produced a strange squeaking noise. Joe thought that if he strained his ears closer he would understand their cries as they died, their large black eyes watching him.

When they returned to port with their huge catch, everyone was celebrating.

'That was just amazing,' said Ricardo. 'If we could catch fish like that all the time, we would never have any worries.'

But that spring was a hard one. The subsequent catches had been smaller and the weather was frequently so bad that no one could take their trawler out at all. Joe spent hours by the radio listening to weather reports and swapping news with those skippers who had taken their chances and had ventured out further down the coast. Joe also spoke to the spotters.

Most of the fishermen used spotters, pilots who flew their planes over the sea looking for schools of fish, especially tuna in the season. Joe had a particular mate who would notify him at once if he flew over any interesting activity that could indicate schools of fish. Chris was a young pilot, but a good one, who was always excellent company when he visited Whitby Point. So when Joe received a call from Chris early one morning, to tell him that he could see a big school of fish a few miles off a well-known reef, Joe decided to take the trawler out.

'Ricardo, see where Carlo and Patrick are and get a crew together. Chris has radioed in about a big school. He thinks they could be yellowfin.'

'What about this weather? It's not good. What's the forecast?' Ricardo asked.

'Dicey, but my instincts tell me it's clearing.'

'Okay, Papà, I guess you know best,' said Ricardo in a voice which suggested that he was not as confident as his father.

In no time Ricardo had found Patrick and Carlo and rounded up three more crew members. The gear was checked and they quickly set off in the *Egret*, one of Joe's smaller trawlers.

'It would be better to go out in something bigger, but it would take too long to round up more crew and we need to get going quickly,' Ricardo explained.

'This will be fine,' replied Joe. 'The *Egret* is a good vessel. She'll get the job done. Anyway, let's get this show on the road. If we don't clear the harbour right away the harbour master might advise us not to go at all and we'll be stuck in port.'

They passed through the harbour and out to sea, but within twenty minutes conditions had deteriorated as the south-east swell worsened, whipped by a stiffening wind. Joe glanced at the sky and exchanged a look with Ricardo.

'We've got a fair distance to the reef. Hope that the weather doesn't get any worse. Chris gave me pretty specific co-ordinates and said that it was a heavy-sized school. Lots of birds marking the lead fish.'

Everyone was wrapped in their oilskins. Carlo and the other men sheltered in the cockpit as the *Egret* ploughed through the rising wind and waves. Then a rain squall reduced their visibility.

Patrick peered through his binoculars, trying to make out birds or any other clues that might lead them to the school. 'It's near impossible to see anything in this rain,' he said.

Ricardo nodded. 'Needle in a haystack. But we might get lucky.'

'Luck has nothing to do with it,' said Joe cheerfully. Patrick and Ricardo exchanged a smile.

'Nice to know that you're still optimistic,' said Patrick.

'What's that to starboard?' called Joe.

'Sea birds. They're either being buffeted by the wind or they're diving onto something!' shouted Patrick.

'It's not far off the reef marker Chris gave us, they must be travelling fast. Big fish,' said Joe and spun the wheel.

They were alert as the boat changed direction, bracing themselves as the waves hit the *Egret* broadside. Joe brought the wheel around, steering the trawler in a line to meet the travelling school of fish.

'They've come off the reef. Been feeding there,' Joe muttered.

'That patch there, ahead,' shouted Carlo from the bow, his excited voice rising above the sound of the waves.

'Right, let's get into them,' called Joe as the crew jumped to their positions, ready to get the lines out.

The vessel was heaving in the growing swell, yet they managed to land several large tuna before conditions deteriorated even more. They turned back towards the reef to make another run, but the current had become treacherous and waves were now towering over them and breaking across the deck.

'Let's give it one last shot.' Joe could hardly be heard over the wind and rain.

'Papà, are you sure that you want to do this? Maybe we should just try to get back to port,' Ricardo shouted back.

Patrick took out the life jackets and handed them to everyone. Joe hesitated, then he told Patrick to take the wheel briefly while he quickly put his jacket on before sending him back to the *Egret*'s rail with the rest of the crew. They were all knee-deep in rushing water as they gamely threw out the pole lines, even though it was hard to see where the fish were.

Above the sound of the waves they could all hear Joe shouting, 'The buggers are still out there!'

And, almost at once, they hooked a big one. But as the tuna came close to the boat it became clear that the rough seas would make it difficult to lift the large fish on board with the poles. Ricardo leapt to the railing with the gaff ready to strike a blow to kill it. Carlo was ready to lash the fish to the side.

'Ricardo!' shouted Joe as he saw a huge wave roll towards the vessel. 'No! Leave it!'

But his call was too late. The wave hit with great force. From the wheelhouse came the sound of breaking glass and wood. Joe was left desperately clinging to the wheel as the wave swamped the *Egret* in its watery grip. She was a tough old tub and she righted herself even after taking the full force of the rogue wave. But this was too late for Ricardo, who had been swept overboard.

'Get the lifebuoy over,' screamed Patrick to Carlo. But Carlo was already pulling the bright red and white buoy from the wheelhouse wall, and he hurled it into the churning sea where Ricardo had last been seen.

While Joe furiously spun the wheel and then cut the engine back to neutral, the *Egret* almost stood on her stern. Patrick scrambled onto the shattered remains of the wheelhouse roof looking for any sign of Ricardo.

Joe's anguished cry rose above the clamour of the wind and rain. 'Can anyone see Ricardo? We have to find him. I can't leave him here.'

Then, suddenly through the noise of the weather and the sea there was a loud crackle in the damaged cockpit and Joe could hear the voice of Chris the spotter over the radio.

'*Egret,* I see you. Are you in trouble?'

Joe fell onto the microphone and shouted back. 'Chris! Ricardo's gone over the side. He's got a life jacket on but we can't see him. The waves are too bloody high. Can you can see him? Direct me. Over.'

'Roger. On to it. Over.'

Chris's aircraft appeared and descended low over the ocean. It began to circle methodically above them. Everyone on board was frozen in shock. Time had gone into slow motion. Even the roar of the wind and water seemed to fade into the background so that the only sound they could hear was Joe's agonised mantra. 'God, save my son. I don't want him lost at sea. God, save my son.'

Then the radio again exploded into life.

'*Egret,* I can see him. To port, to port . . .'

Joe, his face a picture of agony and concentration, brought the boat about and headed in the direction of the low-circling plane.

Patrick sent up a shout. 'There he is. Throw the other buoy!'

Sliding into view one minute, swallowed by a wave the next, Ricardo could just be seen ahead of them.

Joe positioned the boat as close as he could to his son and Carlo threw the second buoy.

It seemed an endless wait for them all and then the line attached to the buoy went taut.

'He's got it!' Chris's voice over the radio was elated. 'Haul away, boys.'

Joe signalled to Patrick to take the wheel as he rushed to the side of the boat where Carlo and the rest of the crew were hauling in the buoy line as hard as they could. Finally he saw Ricardo, his arm through the buoy, literally hanging on for dear life.

Joe was the first to grasp the sodden figure of his son as he and the others pulled the exhausted man over the side of the boat. Ricardo collapsed onto the deck. Joe pulled off his life jacket and rolled him onto his side.

'Son, son, Ricardo, you'll be fine. Someone get him a blanket,' Joe shouted to no one in particular, tears streaming down his face.

Then Ricardo coughed, throwing up the water he had swallowed. His eyes opened and he gave a weak smile. 'Shit,' he managed to say. 'Did you land the fish?'

Patrick smiled. 'No, we went after you instead, though it was a toss-up.'

'This is no time for jokes. Your brother could have been killed and it would have been my fault,' Joe shouted.

Ricardo looked at his father and managed a weak smile. 'Well, I wasn't. I'm not that easy to get rid of, but if we all sit around talking, we won't get these tuna to market and the whole day will have been a waste.'

The tension was broken. Patrick quietly went back to the wheel, turned the *Egret* around and headed back into port. Joe continued to hug his son, crying unashamedly for the loss that might have been. He had spent his life on the sea and for the most part he had loved it, but now it had almost taken his precious eldest son from him. Joe remembered how his own father had warned him that the sea was a cruel and dangerous place and that to forget that fact was tempting fate. He had been foolhardy in risking the lives of his sons and his crew just to chase tuna. He swore to himself that he would never do such a thing again.

Joe only let Ricardo go when he heard a shout from the radio. 'Well done. Have a drink on me. Catch you soon. Over.'

'Thanks, Chris, for all your help,' said Joe over the radio. 'I owe my son's life to you. Thank you, thank you,' said Joe again.

The men on the deck of the *Egret* waved as the small plane dipped its wing and soared away into the stormy sky.

Wrapped in a blanket and holding a limp cigarette, Ricardo sat quietly beside his father in what remained of the cockpit as they motored slowly homewards.

*

The following year, 1957, Pietro flew home to Australia on a Pan American Strato Clipper for a holiday. He hadn't been home for more than ten years. It wasn't just Joe and the rest of the family who were excited by the visit. The whole town was thrilled and the local papers, even as far as Wollongong, had written extensively about Pietro's achievements. With the stardust of Hollywood success on his shoulders he had become a local celebrity.

On the first Sunday he was home, it was decided that all the family should go for a picnic.

'It might be July,' said Joe, 'but the day is so lovely we don't want to waste it inside. If we wear warm clothes, we'll be right. I want to remind Pietro just how lovely Whitby Point is.'

Emilia, who was not as physically active as she used to be, watched carefully as the picnic food and utensils were packed into clean fish crates, and ice was put in another to keep the seafood cool. There had been some discussion about where to go: the beach at Pelican Point, Blue Crane Lake or the lighthouse. They settled on the strip of grass next to the flat rocks under the lighthouse. When they arrived, Carlo and Ricardo went fishing from the beach, while the women went to look for pipis. The pipis they found were then cooked in a large kerosene tin, blackened from previous fires, while Emilia supervised the cooking of fish over the open fire. In case the morning's fishing was unsuccessful, Joe had brought along some prawns and lobsters that had been caught the day before.

Pietro shook his head. 'I don't think you could get seafood as good as this anywhere else in the world. The fish – sublime!'

'It's nothing fancy, just straight from sea to pan,' said Emilia.

After they had all finished their lunch, Rosina and Gail decided to take the children for a walk along the beach and Emilia sat in a comfortable deckchair to have a nap. The five men sat around the fire with a beer or a glass of wine in their hands and started chatting.

'How long since you went fishing?' Ricardo asked his brother.

'Not since I was forced to help in school holidays,' said Pietro, laughing and stretching out his legs that were encased in a pair of expensive-looking slacks. 'I don't have the Aquino touch.'

'Fishing has served our family well for generations,' said Joe. 'Keeps you honest. You can't cheat the sea. You know who is the boss out there.'

'Pietro, what is it exactly that you do? Our job is pretty straightforward. We're fishermen. But what is an art director?' asked Patrick. 'It doesn't sound as though it has anything to do with acting.'

'When we saw you with the Whitby Point Players, or whatever they were called, you looked pretty happy on stage,' said Ricardo, putting his arm around his brother affectionately.

'I did like acting when that was all I knew about the stage,' said Pietro, 'but when Bridie took me to the theatre all those years ago in Sydney, it was the whole atmosphere I fell in love with. After I joined the Independent Theatre Company in North Sydney, I found that what I loved doing was creating that setting, that atmosphere.'

'How do you do that?' asked Joe.

'For the stage, theatre, you design the sets. You create the atmosphere for the play. I do much the same thing for the movies. It's a bit more complicated, but it's the same idea.'

Joe nodded, but in truth he really didn't understand what Pietro was talking about. He had only seen one stage show and that was Pietro in the silly play Bridie had made him go along to all those years ago.

'I suppose you were so good in your theatre work that you didn't have a lot of trouble getting into the movies,' said Carlo a little peevishly.

'No, little brother. Like so much in life there was a lot of luck involved. How about you pour me another drink?'

The conversation paused while they all got themselves another drink and Joe tiptoed over to Emilia to see that she was all right. When they settled themselves back down again, Pietro continued.

'When I first arrived in Hollywood I knocked on a lot of doors. Eventually I managed to get a job with one of the smaller studios working with the construction manager, making sure that the sets were properly built, when the art director was killed in a car accident. The picture was nearly finished, so they made me the art director – just to get the job done – and I managed to do a satisfactory job, so I was hired for another film. I've worked on several movies over the last few years, working with the set designers, with the construction managers and the people who do the set decoration, props and so on. On some films I have to work with the costume designers as well so that every visual aspect of the film is co-ordinated. And I have to make sure that everything stays within budget. That's the really hard part.'

'It sounds complicated,' said Ricardo.

'It can be, but if you really enjoy doing something, I don't think that matters,' replied Pietro.

'Have you met any famous movie stars?' asked Patrick.

'Dozens.'

'Who do you like the best?' asked Carlo, now very curious about his brother's career.

'I think that the nicest one I know is James Stewart. I wasn't the art director for *Rear Window*, but I did help with the set, so I met him a few times.'

All the Aquinos looked very impressed.

'Did you meet Grace Kelly, too?' asked Carlo.

'I did.'

'Wait till I tell Gail. Grace Kelly is her favourite actress,' Carlo said, unable to keep the excitement out of his voice.

The men continued to quiz Pietro about Hollywood. It seemed incredible that one of the Aquino family should have such an exotic life.

'Son, what you are doing sounds wonderful. I am very proud of you,' said Joe.

'That's nice, Papà,' said Pietro. 'There is one more thing that I want to tell you all, that I think is very exciting. The studio has told me that my work on their latest film is so good that they expect it will be nominated for this year's Academy Awards. Imagine an Aquino with an Oscar!'

'That's wonderful,' said Patrick. 'Do you have to do anything more to win it?'

'No, if the Academy thinks my work's good enough, it will nominate me and then my peers on the Academy will hopefully give me their votes. So for now all I have to do is to keep my nose clean and my fingers crossed.'

'What do you mean, keep your nose clean?' asked his father.

'Papà, the Academy doesn't like to have any scandal associated with the awards, so I have to be a very good boy for the next few months. But I've got so much work coming up, I won't have time for anything else . . . Enough about me! Tell me what you lot have been up to, apart from producing children.' As Pietro said this, he winked at his older brother.

Ricardo explained how the Aquinos had moved into tuna fishing and then added, 'While you're here, we could all go out and chase some big ones. Like the old days. Come with us, Pietro.'

Pietro flung up his arms. 'I don't think so. I have lost the touch. If I ever had it.'

'The gear is much better now,' said Carlo. 'You should see how we work. Or are you too afraid of getting dirty these days?' He smiled but there was a challenge in his words.

'I'll think about it.' Pietro was rescued by the children, who had returned from their walk and now wanted Uncle Pietro to play with them.

*

One of the most important events on the Whitby Point social calendar was the annual mid-winter dance, which was always held at the local School of Arts. Probably more than any other function, this event united the community, regardless of age, background or occupation.

A barbecue was set up under the trees at the rear of the hall, while inside a refreshment table, staffed by women from the Country Women's Association, served soft drinks, punch and snacks. But the main attraction was the music and the dancing. A four-piece band from Wollongong – saxophone, drums, accordion and piano – sawed and thumped away with enthusiasm.

The Aquinos always took a big table. This year, as usual, Joe sat at the head of the table surrounded by his four sons. Ricardo and Rosina had brought their children, and Carlo and Gail had brought Greta. Franco and Silvio and their extended families had come down from Wollongong and would stay the night at Joe's and Ricardo's houses.

Everyone stopped at the Aquino table to chat, drink a beer, try the wine, to sample an oyster or a prawn from the giant platters of seafood, or taste the home-baked bread, pickles, cheeses and Emilia's famous salami. But mostly it was to ask Pietro about the movie stars he knew and what they were really like.

The music catered for everyone. The Italians sang along lustily when Neapolitan songs were played. Most people got up to dance under the swirling lights covered with red and orange cellophane. The dance floor was constantly crowded for the barn dance and the Pride of Erin. The older people showed off their quickstep and foxtrot, while the younger ones wanted to dance the latest craze of rock and roll. When the band did manage to play a fast-paced jive, the teenagers had the floor to themselves for their gymnastics, as Joe called it. And as long as there was music playing, the younger children gyrated and bopped around the fringes of the floor, where nearby adults kept an eye on them.

The watchers were country women with their strong arms, wind-reddened cheeks, cushioned hips and sensible shoes, who were happy to dance a slow waltz, but nothing more. Another group of watchers were the Italian women of the community. Knitting needles clacking, crochet hooks dipping rapidly in and out of lacy concoctions of collars and doilies, chattering in the language of distant Italy, and dressed in their uniform of black modesty, they kept a wary eye on their charges.

The girls had spent weeks preparing their outfits. Laughing late arrivals caught everyone's eye when they entered the hall. They had travelled from their homes out of town standing in the backs of utility trucks so their layers of skirts and stiffened petticoats weren't crushed, their beehive hairdos protected by scarves. Even though Emilia's eyesight was not so good, she had helped put together the party frocks for little Greta and Ricardo's girls, who had all insisted on stiffened petticoats and frilled socks.

Ranged around the dance floor were the over-protected Italian beauties and their brothers, who strode the stage of the dance floor with suave nonchalance, confident in their handsome looks, while the uncomfortably shy Australian boys looked longingly at the Italian girls but felt warned off. The cheerful, pretty Australian girls flirted and teased all the boys.

Joe and Franco had not the slightest interest in dancing and they sat quietly together, talking about the old days. Seeing Patrick wander towards them, Joe asked if he would get them a couple of drinks.

'We might be too old for dancing, but we're not too old for the vino, you understand,' he told Patrick with a smile. As Patrick walked off, the two resumed their conversation.

'Of course I didn't have to spend as much time as you did in that wretched internment camp, Franco, but I can appreciate what you're saying.'

'How I missed my family, Joe. Years without seeing them. And for what? I wasn't a common criminal. There was no justice.'

'You are right. We were not common criminals and yet I felt as though I was because there I was, locked up behind barbed wire. It was as though I had done something to disgrace the name of Aquino, and yet I had done nothing. Sometimes I still think that because of the internment camp I have brought shame to my family. Shame is a hard thing to live with.'

As Patrick leaned over to put the drinks in front of Joe and Franco, he patted Joe's shoulder. 'Papà, you could never bring disgrace to the Aquino name. We are all so proud of you.'

'Thank you, Pat. That is a kind thing to say. The Aquino name is very important to me.'

'Who knows, maybe Pietro will bring it even more prestige if he wins an Academy Award,' Patrick replied.

'Who knew that Pietro would have such a career? He has done well, Joe,' added Franco.

It was getting late. Emilia, Rosina and Gail had taken the children home, but the men insisted that they were not yet ready to go. The teenagers had taken over the dance floor and the crowd had thinned as some of the men had gone outside to talk and drink. Suddenly one of the men hurried back into the hall, looking for Joe.

'Joe, quick. There's a fight outside. It's your sons!'

'What!' Joe jumped to his feet and hurried out, followed by Ricardo.

The fight appeared to be more than threats and a scuffle. Patrick and Carlo were struggling together, panting and cursing, their bodies locked, their free arms punching each other without restraint.

'Hey, you two! Break it up. Who started this?' Joe and Ricardo immediately tried to get between Patrick and Carlo. Eventually they managed to separate the two brothers who stood glaring at each other, fists still raised.

'It started over the footy. They argued about the results of the last game,' said one of the onlookers. 'But it seemed to get out of hand. Those two are certainly hotheads.'

'They're always arguing,' said another. 'Righto, come on, boys, do as your father says, settle down. Enough.' But even as the onlooker spoke, Carlo lunged again at his brother and threw another punch. Patrick lifted his arms to protect his face.

'*Basta!*' bellowed Joe. 'That is enough.'

'You bloody idiots. Stop right now,' said Ricardo. He moved between them and hissed at them. 'You are disgracing our family. Think of Papà. Pat, go and get cleaned up. Carlo, come with me. But first, you two shake hands.'

Patrick held out his hand but Carlo turned on his heel. 'I'm going home.'

'Carlo, don't be stupid. Get back here. You can't let Gail see you like that.'

But Carlo, nursing sore hands and a grazed cheek, slipped away into the darkness.

'Patrick, you look a mess. I hope that eye looks better in the morning,' said Ricardo.

'I can't believe you got into a brawl in public over a football game. I thought you had more sense,' said Joe sadly. 'What will people think of us?'

'I'm sorry, Papà, but sometimes Carlo really gets up my nose. It wasn't the stupid game, it's just that Carlo makes me see red at times and I suppose this was one of those times. But you're right. We are getting a bit old to carry on like this.'

'Yeah. And Carlo should grow up, too. You two have always been competitive since day one. I, for one, am sick of it,' said Ricardo, but he put his arm around Patrick as the three of them walked back into the hall. 'If you ask me I think that life's too short to waste it fighting. Find yourself a nice girl and settle down.'

*

Life resumed its routine. Franco and his family returned to Wollongong and Pietro decided to go to Sydney for a few days to visit friends. When he returned the family had only a few more days of his company before he returned to Los Angeles.

In those last days, Ricardo tried to talk Pietro into joining them all on a fishing expedition. 'The weather is good and there are fish out there. We'll just go out for a few hours. Come on, Pietro, you'll enjoy it. It's not often that we get to fish just for the pleasure of it and it would be fun if you came.'

Pietro laughed. 'I don't think so. But I tell you what, anything you catch, I'll help you eat.'

'If you don't help catch them, why should you get to eat them?' asked Carlo.

Joe shrugged. 'Don't push him, but you boys do what you want. I'm going to Wollongong to see Franco and Silvio. I expect to see a fish feast waiting when I get back this afternoon!'

The day had started out calm and grey, the ocean flat, the air still, as if the world was holding its breath. People went about their business, though the streets were quiet at this early hour. Life in Whitby Point was going on in warm rooms, behind closed doors. As Joe drove past the harbour on his way to Wollongong he could see men working in the brisk air, dressed warmly in heavy jumpers and beanies. The water in the harbour was so still that it looked almost like a lake, the boats hardly rocking. In Wollongong a few hours later, Joe felt a change coming before he'd even looked out of the window.

'I think we're in for some nasty weather,' said Silvio.

Joe glanced at the sky as the clouds began to darken. From Franco's house he could see that the surface of the sea had begun to ruffle and move in slow heaving breaths as if preparing for an outburst. The small boats around the Wollongong harbour and outside the seawall turned back into the curve of the sheltered bay. White caps started to form at the crests of rolling waves. In the distance, lightning zig-zagged behind the gathering clouds.

'Think I might try to get back before the weather gets any worse,' said Joe.

'You can always stay here if you don't want to drive in the wet,' Franco told him.

'No, but thanks anyway. I want to get back to my mother. I don't like to leave her for too long. And Pietro only has a few more nights with us.'

'We understand,' said Silvio. 'Drive carefully.'

Driving back to Whitby Point in the storm reminded Joe of the night that Bridie was killed. Not that he needed reminding.

Such a tragedy for my family, he thought sadly, the old ache for Bridie still burning.

It was late afternoon when Joe drove into Whitby Point. The sea was churning and the wind was flinging itself at the boats, buffeting them at their moorings. Joe was relieved to see the *Celestine*, the boat the boys had taken out, safely tied up to the wharf.

The boys are back. That's one less thing to worry about, he thought.

He let himself into the house. Patrick wasn't there and when he looked into Emilia's room he could see her asleep on her bed. He tiptoed away and went to pour himself a drink, but before he could take it into the study, the front door flew open and Ricardo burst in.

'Papà, where are you?'

'Son, son. I'm in here. What's up? Is something wrong?' Joe was immediately concerned by the sight of Ricardo's dishevelled appearance and stressed face.

'Yes. It's terrible. You have to come . . .' Ricardo took a deep breath and in a rush blurted, 'There was an accident. Carlo has been killed. It is terrible, but it was an accident.'

'Killed!' Joe could hardly speak the word. He felt winded, as though he had been punched. He gasped for breath. 'How? Why? Not on the boat? What happened? My son, what has happened to my son? Oh my Lord, Gail and little Greta . . .'

'Papà, it was an accident. Patrick and Carlo. The boat rolled and Carlo lost his footing and fell onto Patrick who was holding the bait knife, and then it just happened.'

Joe was speechless. He felt numb and helpless. Ricardo's agonised words wrenched at his heart. 'Where is Carlo? Have you told Gail? Did you get a doctor? Did you call the police?'

Ricardo shook his head. 'It's too late for a doctor. As soon as we arrived back at the harbour I went up to see Gail. Her parents are with her now, and then I thought I would come and wait for you here, but you were already back. Patrick went and told the police about the accident. But Papà, there was nothing we could do for Carlo.'

'Gail. How did she take it?'

'She is distraught. She said that she knew that the fishing industry was dangerous, but she never thought that something would happen to Carlo when he was out fishing for fun.'

At that moment, Emilia entered the room. As soon as they told her what had happened, she broke down and began to wail. Carlo had always been her favourite. Joe put his arms around her, but nothing he did could stem her tears and shrieking moans. Joe wondered if she would ever recover from such a blow.

Ricardo was still white-faced when there was a rap on the front door. 'That'll be the police, I guess. I'll have to speak to them and I'd rather do it here than at home in front of my family.'

The police sergeant seemed as shocked as everyone else. He told them that Patrick had described what had happened on the boat and asked Ricardo for his version.

'As I told Papà, it was an accident,' explained Ricardo. 'We'd had a good day. Caught quite a few fish, and then the weather started to pick up, so we turned for home. We weren't far out of the harbour when Patrick said that he'd throw in one last line. He picked up the bait knife and then it happened. The boat suddenly rolled and it threw Carlo off balance and he sort of fell into Patrick and the knife went into him. We came back into port right away but Carlo was dead.'

'Yes,' said the police officer, 'that's what Patrick said, too. A terrible accident.'

Joe became agitated. 'Pietro, where is he? Does he know what has happened?'

'No, he said he was going to the pictures, I think. Something was playing that he wanted to see. Do you want me to go and find him?' asked Ricardo.

'He'll be back soon enough. We can tell him then. No need to hurry now,' said Joe, his voice hoarse and barely audible. He looked across at his mother, who was still sobbing quietly in her favourite chair. 'This family has been through some terrible times. We don't deserve this.'

'Mr Aquino, I don't want to worry you any further. I'm sure it was an accident, but I expect that there will have to be an investigation. It's likely that some officers from Wollongong will have to ask some questions as well, just for the record, that's all. You understand.'

As he was speaking, Patrick walked into the room looking pale.

Joe leapt up and embraced him. 'My poor boy,' he said, 'such an awful thing. Where have you been?'

'After I spoke to the police, I went to see Gail. She's gone with her father to see Carlo's body. I can't believe it. It's a nightmare. I'm so sorry it happened. Honestly, it was an accident, though.'

'Yes. Of course it was, but the police sergeant here says that the Wollongong police will want to ask questions too.'

Patrick silently nodded his head.

Joe shook as he said, 'I must go and see my son. This family. So many terrible things happen to it.'

Later that evening, after Joe and Pietro had returned, the four men sat around the kitchen table trying to work out what to do next.

'We will have to organise yet another funeral,' said Joe, holding his head in his hands.

'Don't you think that Gail and her family will want to do that?' said Pietro quietly. 'But I am sure that they would be pleased if you offered your help, Papà.'

'I don't suppose we'll be able to have one until after an autopsy, anyway,' said Ricardo, rubbing his reddened eyes.

'I don't understand why there's going to be an investigation if the police think that it was an accident,' said Pietro.

'I don't know. But my concern is for you, Papà and Nonna and of course Gail. What a mess,' said Patrick despairingly.

The town was thunderstruck by the tragic news of Carlo's death and although the Aquinos would have preferred a quiet funeral, the whole town turned out to show their sympathy for the family. As soon as it was over Pietro flew back to California, leaving Joe feeling even sadder. His family was disintegrating.

The Wollongong police stayed in the background until Carlo's funeral was over but soon after they began to ask questions. Not just of Patrick and Ricardo, who were unable to tell them more than they had already, reaffirming that the incident had been a tragic accident, but also of a lot of the townspeople as well as Joe's employees.

To Joe's surprise the police let Patrick know that they wanted to interview him again. Joe was concerned and suggested that maybe Patrick should have their solicitor with him.

'I'm not sure that it's necessary, Papà, but if it makes you happy I'll ask Mr Walker to come with me.'

On the day of Patrick's police interview Joe became more agitated as several hours passed and still Patrick had not come home. When there was a knock on the door Joe realised that something was very wrong. Patrick had no need to knock. When he opened the door Rodney Walker, the local solicitor, was standing on the verandah looking extremely worried.

'Joe, they've arrested Patrick,' he said bluntly. 'They've charged him with manslaughter. The whole thing is rubbish, but that's what's happened.'

Joe just stared at him. At first he could think of nothing to say, and just waved the solicitor into the house. Then he blurted out, 'Why would they think that?'

'They don't believe either Ricardo's or Patrick's story. They have asked a lot of questions around town and found out that Carlo and Pat did not get on, never got on. Then they found out about the fight at the dance and they are convinced that Pat and Carlo had a fight on the boat that led to Carlo's death and that Ricardo is covering up for Pat by saying the whole thing was an accident.'

Joe looked at the solicitor. 'If my sons say that it was an accident, then that is what it was.'

'I agree. I don't think that the police have much of a case at all, but they seem to think that they have enough to go ahead and charge him.'

'What happens now?' Joe asked.

'For the moment I've got Pat out on bail. There wasn't any problem with that and he's gone around to see Ricardo to tell him what's going on. He's going to have to go to a committal hearing, Joe.'

'Will he be committed?'

'No, the committal hearing will listen to the police evidence against him and determine if there is enough to warrant continuing with the case. I'm not sure that there will be enough evidence, but I think it would be a good idea if we hired a barrister for Patrick, just to make sure.'

'If you think that's best then we must get one straight away. Can you recommend anyone?'

'I'll see if Mr Giles Bartholomew can take the case. He's a QC, very expensive, but he's one of the best.'

'I don't care about the expense. I just want Patrick cleared,' exclaimed Joe vehemently. 'But if your Mr Bartholomew is not successful, what will happen then?'

'Then the case will have to go to trial in the district court in Wollongong.'

'It will never get that far,' said Joe, sounding a lot calmer than he felt. 'The magistrate will know straight away that Pat, of all people, could not possibly kill his brother other than in a terrible accident. But if by chance the magistrate cannot work it out for himself, Mr Bartholomew will have to convince him.'

*

Joe and Ricardo went with Patrick to the local court for the committal hearing. Joe was confident that this would be the end of the matter, but the police prosecution was able to produce a string of witnesses, all of whom testified that Patrick and Carlo didn't get on and that the arguments between the two of them were not a secret. This was enough to convince the magistrate that Patrick did have a case to answer over the death of his step-brother. Now there would have to be a jury trial in the Wollongong district court.

Although Patrick seemed to accept the magistrate's ruling, Joe was distraught.

'I don't understand, Rodney. Why didn't you question those witnesses?' he asked the solicitor.

'Papà, how could he? What they said was true enough. Carlo and I often fought.'

'Don't worry, Joe. Manslaughter is a serious charge. The magistrate doesn't necessarily think that the police case will win, but he thinks that they do have a one, so that is why he has sent the matter to trial. Mr Bartholomew will continue to represent Patrick and he is sure that the charges will be dismissed.'

*

It was several months before the case came up before the district court and in the meantime the Aquinos tried to get on with their lives. Patrick remained out on bail and continued to work on the fishing boats with Ricardo. Even when they were not at work they spent a lot of time together. Joe missed Carlo and was frequently around at Gail's helping her as much as he could and playing with little Greta. He worried about Patrick and the outcome of the court case. Some days he was even relieved that Bridie wasn't there to know what had happened. Emilia found the whole tragedy very difficult to cope with. She looked after Joe and Patrick as well as she always had, but she seemed to have very little to say to either to them or to anyone else.

On the first day of the trial, the two brothers and Joe drove up to Wollongong together. Gail was driving up to the court with her family and Emilia refused to come at all. She would, after all, understand very little of the proceedings.

As they neared Wollongong, Joe spoke, 'No matter what, I know that Carlo died because of an accident, because that is what you two boys have told me. I hold no one accountable. God is the judge here and so we must allow fate to run its course.'

When they arrived at the court, they were met by Mr Walker and Mr Bartholomew, who spoke quietly to Patrick.

'Now, Patrick,' said Mr Bartholomew, 'as I have told you before, the police have only a lot of circumstantial evidence, which, when produced in court, might make for uncomfortable listening, but cannot of itself in any way induce a guilty verdict from the jury. Our trump card will be your brother. Ricardo's testimony will free you. No matter what the prosecution throws at him, I am sure that he will not waver in his story.'

Joe excused himself and went to the bathroom. On his way back he caught Ricardo and Patrick in the hallway in what looked to him like an argument.

'What are you two on about? I don't think this is the time or the place for this sort of thing. We need to be united.'

'Sorry, Papà,' said Ricardo. 'It was nothing. We're both nervous, I suppose.'

'Come on then. Let's go into the courtroom. Get it over with,' said Joe.

'Joe, you and Ricardo will have to stay out here, out of the courtroom, since you'll be called as witnesses,' Mr Walker explained. 'I'll keep you both filled in on proceedings and you'll be able to talk to Pat when court is adjourned. He's still out on bail.'

Joe and Ricardo sat glumly on one of the benches outside the courtroom.

'I think this is going to be a very long day,' said Ricardo.

Mr Walker was as good as his word and came out to tell them about the proceedings whenever he got the chance. 'The coroner gave his testimony – much the same as what he said at the committal hearing. Bit of a nuisance about the bruising, though. When he was asked about Carlo's bruising he said that it was probably caused by being tossed around by the boat but then the police prosecutor got him to modify that testimony, questioned him so he said that it could also have been caused by a fight. Mr Bartholomew got him to retract that when he cross-examined him. Still it won't take the idea of a fight out of the minds of the jury. Pity that. But early days. Ricardo will set the record straight when he testifies.'

That evening, after court was adjourned for the day, they all went back to Franco's house. Patrick was very quiet and when Joe asked him how things were going, he just shrugged. Later that night Joe again saw Patrick and Ricardo in an intense discussion.

The next day, Joe and Ricardo had barely taken their seats in the hallway when both Mr Walker and Mr Bartholomew came storming out of the courtroom.

'What's happening?' Joe asked Rodney Walker.

'Terrible, just terrible. As soon as the judge arrived, Patrick said that he wanted to change his plea to guilty.'

'Change his plea – how can he do that? Why would he do that?' Joe stared at him, not understanding.

'Joe, Mr Bartholomew advised him not to do such a reckless thing, but Patrick said that he couldn't go on lying and he didn't want Ricardo to perjure himself by backing his lie. He said that he had fought with Carlo but that he never meant to harm him, he was acting in self-defence.'

Joe could not believe what he was hearing. Patrick and Ricardo had both lied to cover up what had really happened on the boat. 'Did Patrick say what the fight was about?'

'No, but he should if he wants any sympathy from the judge.'

'Can I see Patrick?' Joe asked, his distress clearly visible on his face.

'I'm sorry, Joe,' said Mr Walker. 'He's already been taken down.'

At the sentencing hearing Patrick would only say that there had been an argument. Carlo had come at him and he had defended himself with the bait knife. The judge was unimpressed by the explanation, pointing out that Patrick might initially have been trying to defend himself, but he was, nevertheless, using a knife against an unarmed man. Consequently, he sentenced Patrick to nine years with a non-parole period of seven years.

Joe could not believe the severity of the sentence. He asked Mr Walker where they could go from here. Mr Walker said that usually there would be an appeal, but that Patrick had absolutely refused this option.

'Patrick told me that as far as he is concerned he will serve out his sentence and that will be the end of the matter. He has no intention of appealing. I'm so sorry, Joe, the whole thing is such a terrible tragedy for your family.'

*

The Aquino family withdrew from the social life of Whitby Point, concentrating on their fishing business and supporting each other. Joe tried to visit Patrick as often as he could, but both of them were uncomfortable during Joe's visits to Long Bay Gaol in Sydney. Patrick did not seem to want to talk about the family so, after a brief summary of what was happening to the Aquinos, Joe would turn the conversation to the business of fishing.

Proudly he told Patrick about how he was using the new echo sounders on the trawlers, which enabled him to better chart the depth and elevations of the seabed and map the reefs. 'A lot of the other vessels can't work out where we go now. Their equipment isn't up to it. Tell you what, we had a bit of fun the other night.' Joe paused, and Patrick nodded for him to continue. 'We found a really good patch of ground to the south-east. Brought in some good catches, which had certain people really curious.' Joe grinned. 'So next time we went out in the dark, really early, before there were any other boats about. We were heading south for about an hour when your brother looked back and saw a flicker of red light. He realised that it was the reflection in a window of someone lighting a cigarette! Buggers were following us – without their lights on!'

Patrick raised an eyebrow and Joe went on. 'It was still dark and we kept leading them on but knew we were heading towards the reef. When dawn came we set about pretending we were preparing to shoot the net and we changed direction. While the boat behind us was also setting up their nets, we took off in a hurry, like we were trawling, and when he tried to follow us he found he was jammed on the reef. So we set off for our real fishing ground and left him there.'

'What happened when he got back?' asked Patrick.

'He was pretty cranky with us. We heard he ordered a sounder quick smart.'

'But, Papà, if everyone gets a sounder, the fish won't have a chance,' said Patrick.

Joe nodded. 'That's what I've been saying for years. Do you miss it, Pat? The fishing? Bloody hard locked up in here,' said Joe, looking around the harsh surroundings and thinking of the fresh air and wide open sea. He knew he wouldn't manage being deprived of being out in the freedom of the sea and the sky.

Patrick held up his hand, ending the conversation. 'I'm doing all right, Papà. I'm pleased you're doing well.'

*

As the first Christmas without Carlo and Patrick approached, the rest of the town came together to celebrate the blessing of the fleet. All the fishing families had spent weeks preparing their costumes, decorating floats for the grand parade and making food for picnics. The Aquino family decided it was time to join in the town festivities again so they prepared a traditional Sicilian luncheon and invited a few of their friends. While every Italian province had their own patron saint, it was St Peter, the patron saint of fishermen, who always led the procession. A priest came down from Wollongong to help the parish priest deliver the blessing at the wharf where all the beautifully decorated fishing boats were moored. The day was filled with celebrations and in the evening the eating and the entertainment continued.

As Joe listened to a singing competition between two local tenors, he was filled with sadness that so many of the people he loved were not there to enjoy this day with him.

Ricardo was becoming restless as more and more Italians moved into the area to fish between Wollongong and Eden. The competition was becoming even more intense.

'Papà, I think we should deal with the Sydney fish markets again, especially when we get really good tuna. The tuna-canning factories that have set up in South Australia have brought the price of tuna down, but I know that the Japanese are starting to pay big prices for the whole fish. What if we start to take tuna to Sydney to sell there for the Japanese market? We can drive up, like we used to years ago.'

'Maybe you're right. But we can still keep the local co-op going for the rest of our catch.'

'And Papà, I was also thinking that I could fish out of Sydney. Just for a while. There are too many boats here now and not enough fish. Sydney might be better.'

'Would you take your whole family?'

'Yes, of course. I'll fish out of Blackwattle Bay, and we'll rent some place around Balmain.'

Joe sighed. He had a lot of memories of Balmain. He realised that he couldn't deny Ricardo his plan, but now he was losing even more of his family. Thank heavens for little Greta. Gail was frequently around at Joe's with Carlo's daughter and the three of them had become very close.

Ricardo and his family enjoyed being in Sydney. The city was certainly livelier than Whitby Point. Joe often came up for the weekend. Once he was sure of the route to Ricardo's house, he was happy to drive all the way, instead of driving only as far as Wollongong before taking the train.

On these visits, Joe usually went out to Long Bay Gaol to see Patrick but when he suggested Ricardo go with him, Ricardo shook his head.

'No, I'll go out another day. That way Patrick will have twice as many visits.'

For Joe, the Sydney of the 1960s was a very different place from the Sydney he had first known all those years ago. Sometimes he and Ricardo would wander around Blackwattle Bay where ageing tramp steamers, old fishing boats, ferries, family boats and work boats were jumbled together in a graveyard of dying vessels. Joe told Ricardo how proud he'd been of his first boat.

'Now I have them custom built. But that first little boat I had in Whitby Point – I could not believe that I had a boat of my own. Of course half of it belonged to your grandfather, Franco, but I was still my own boss.'

'I always think of boats as having their own personalities,' said Ricardo. 'Strong and courageous, seeing us safely through turbulent seas and risky ventures, but each one has her own special quirk, her own peculiar trait.'

Joe laughed. 'I think that's why we call boats "she". They want to do their thing, their way.'

One day as they wandered down to the foreshore at Balmain, Joe told Ricardo the story of Sophia. 'I was very naive. I didn't realise that she belonged to a local gangster, but it all worked out for the best. I had to leave Sydney, and that's how I met Franco and married his lovely daughter Evalina, who gave me three wonderful sons.' Then, as if remembering again that he now had only two of those sons, his eyes filled with tears.

Ricardo put his arm around his father and said, 'Papà, we love you so much. You have been a great father and you have achieved so much in the fishing industry by your determination and innovations. You came to this country with nothing and look where you are today. A pillar of your community and well respected within your industry.'

Joe nodded and they walked on.

*

A few months later, Joe visited Patrick with sad news. Franco had died.

'I suppose that feels like the end of an era for you, Papà.'

'Everything feels like the end of an era. Fishing is now so competitive and our overheads are so high – I wonder where we'll be in ten years time. Ricardo feels the same. I don't think he's very happy with the fishing around Sydney. We're not much better off than we were in Whitby Point. But I had to let him have a go and find this out for himself.'

'Papà, I've been doing a lot of reading about the fishing industry in South Australia. Getting the information hasn't been easy, but I wrote to the CSIRO and because I'm your step-son, they have been very kind to me and sent me a lot of material. You know what I think? If you want the business to expand, maybe you should go over to Port Lincoln and fish for bluefin tuna there. The Japanese pay big dollars for sashimi-quality tuna and, with the canning side of things as well, the South Australian fishermen are doing very nicely.'

'That would be a big move. I'm too old for such a change,' said Joe, shaking his head.

'Papà, you're still in your sixties and you're very fit. Of course you could make the change,' said Patrick.

Joe smiled. 'Thanks for that, but I don't want to leave Whitby Point. Too much of my life is bound up in that place. But I will talk your idea over with Ricardo.'

Next time Joe visited Patrick he told him that he and Ricardo had talked about Patrick's idea.

'Ricardo thinks you're right. Fishing in the Spencer Gulf is the way forward. He's prepared to go over for two or three years and get the business up and running. I'll stay in Whitby Point. Now the only question that remains is where you'll go when you're out of here. Whitby Point or South Australia?' said Joe enthusiastically.

Patrick looked away. 'Papà, I don't think that my heart is in fishing anymore. It's in the Aquino blood, but I'm not sure that it's still in mine.'

'What is this nonsense? Of course you'll love fishing again, as soon as you go back out on one of the boats. It's what we Aquinos do.' He reached across the little table that lay between them and took Patrick's hand.

'Papà, I'm not an Aquino.'

'You are to me,' said Joe simply.

'Thank you, Papà. Thank you for everything. You have been the best father to me.' His words were said with such feeling that Joe couldn't answer for a moment. Then the prison guard signalled that visiting time was done and Patrick got up, smiled at Joe and walked away. It was the last time Joe ever saw Patrick.

Two weeks later Patrick was released. He never returned to Whitby Point or wrote to Joe to tell him where he was.

Joe was devastated.

'Why would he do that?' he asked Ricardo. 'Why would he not tell me he was getting out of gaol? It doesn't make sense to me.'

'Perhaps he just wanted to make a new start. Maybe he wanted to go somewhere where no one knew what had happened. Staying with us would mean that there would always be whispers and gossip,' said Ricardo.

Joe nodded. 'But it is sad if he feels that way,' he told Ricardo.

*

Years later, Joe sat on his favourite chair in the mellow afternoon sun on the verandah, staring at the ocean. His gnarled hands rested on his walking stick. He thought back over all that had happened in his life with pride and regret. He now knew that Patrick's release from prison had been more the closing of a chapter than a new beginning. Every time he thought about Patrick it was with sadness that Bridie's son had disappeared from their lives. He hoped that wherever he was, he was happy.

His son Carlo was another huge loss. How does one ever get over the death of a beloved son? But even that now seemed such a long time ago. Carlo would have been pleased with the way Greta had turned out. Such a lovely girl and now married and expecting a baby of her own. Life goes on, Joe thought to himself.

Ricardo, Joe thought with unabashed pride, had done very well for himself and the Aquinos. After three years away in South Australia, where he had established a successful tuna business, Ricardo had returned to Whitby Point to continue raising his family. They, in turn, were now also becoming involved in the business. Joe thought that Raimondo, whom everyone called Ray, was becoming as dependable as his father.

Pietro had remained in Hollywood, winning many awards for his work as an art director, including two Oscars. Pietro had, over the years, frequently asked his father to visit him, but Joe had no interest in going to Los Angeles. In desperation at his father's continual refusals, Pietro had suggested that they both go to Italy for a holiday. Joe had agreed to this, but only because it gave him the chance to comply with Emilia's request that her ashes be returned to her island.

He thought finally about his two wives. Evalina, good and dutiful, the mother of his sons, the daughter of his partner Franco. He had to admit that marrying her had set him up for life, but he knew that in his heart of hearts his feelings for her could never compare with his love for Bridie. He had so adored Bridie, and the greatest miracle was that she had loved him back. Perhaps God had planned it for a reason, two wonderful women, with whom he'd shared two different lives. But he chided his God for taking Bridie too soon.

And sometimes, when he least expected it, he could still see her red curls bouncing ahead of him into the distance. Joe closed his eyes and a small smile softened his features and he heard, from across the space of time and memory, the lilting voice of Bridie as they'd journeyed across the sea to the place where they'd found their greatest happiness.

11

Whitby Point, 2011

THE REMAINING TEARS BEGAN to dry on Cassie's cheeks. She'd wept into Bill's fur, pouring out her pain and frustration over the shock of hearing that her beloved father had killed Carlo Aquino, Michael's grandfather. The patient dog's coat was sticky and damp with her tears. Cassie had had no idea that her father had even known the Aquinos and now Ricardo Aquino had left her a lot of money in his will. None of it made any sense and it was all simply too hard to take in.

When she had no more tears to shed, she went and washed her face, made herself a cup of strong coffee and dialled her mother's mobile. There was no answer. Then Cassie realised that it was one of the days Jenny played bridge, so her phone would be switched off. She wouldn't be able to reach her till early evening.

As she slowly drank her coffee, she began to think that Jenny probably didn't know anything about her father's connection with the Aquinos either. Whitby Point would be the last place her mother would have encouraged her to visit and settle down in had she known about her husband's history here. And Jenny, like Cassie, had been enthusiastic about the town as soon as she saw it. No, Cassie was sure that her mother was as ignorant of her father's relationship with the Aquinos as she had been. Now she was going to have to tell her mother that the man they both loved, the sweet-natured, patient, gentle Patrick, had been to gaol for killing the grandfather of the man with whom she had fallen in love.

Cassie took her coffee over to the computer and googled her father's name. A lot of Patrick Sullivans came up. She began to scroll through them but after a few minutes of searching, she could tell that none of them referred to her father. She tried some more search options but found nothing useful. Frustrated, she went outside and began to pace up and down the old jetty. She had to find out what had happened between her father and the Aquinos.

Frank was obviously as shocked as she was about the money Ricardo had bequeathed her. For both of them the reason for this gesture was a total mystery, but while Frank was so furious and aggressive, it was unlikely she'd get any answers from him, if indeed he had any. And Michael. How would Michael react to this revelation? Frank's angry words rang in her head: *Your father killed Michael's grandfather Carlo.*

Perhaps it was some awful, silly mistake. Maybe there was another Patrick Sullivan. But then Frank had said that it was Cassandra Sullivan who'd been named in Ricardo's will. Maybe that was another Cassandra Sullivan, too. Her mind was spinning. It was crazy. She tried to get her head around the fact that, according to

Frank, her father had been in prison. That didn't make sense. She had always thought people who had been to gaol as being hard and brutal, but her father was a lovely man, whom everybody adored and respected. There had to be a sensible explanation somewhere. She would simply have to find it. Of course the person she must speak to was Michael, but she dreaded having to do so. She couldn't bear it if what Frank had told her was to come between them. She took a deep breath and tried to put herself in Michael's shoes. How would he feel? Would he want to have anything more to do with her? Would he think that she had only used him as a way of contacting Ricardo? Surely he wouldn't think that she was a gold-digger?

Cassie walked down the jetty and then went up onto the deck. Bill was stretched out, his head on his paws, watching her with concerned eyes. He seemed to know she was distressed but he was unsure of how to help her. When she slumped into a chair he padded over to her and laid his head in her lap. Cassie sat there, scratching the dog's neck until he lifted his head, his ears alert.

She heard a car door slam and her name being called.

'I'm on the deck!' she called out.

'Hey, Cassie.' Trixie and Geoff came around the side, smiling as Bill went to welcome them.

'Hi, fella, you're looking fit and happy,' said Geoff, rubbing Bill's ears. 'Hi, Cass. Hope you don't mind us dropping in. We know you're closed tonight. Trixie made a new concoction for you to try.'

'Hi, Geoff. Hi, Trixie. This is a lovely surprise. Do you want a tea, coffee?'

'Never say no to a cuppa,' grinned Geoff. Then he asked, 'Hey, is something wrong? You look a bit down in the mouth.'

'You might say that.' Suddenly tears streamed down Cassie's face again.

Trixie rushed to her and put her arms around her. 'Cassie dear, can we help? What's up?' When Cassie didn't answer, giving her friend a stricken look instead, Trixie said, 'Geoff, go and put the kettle on. You look as though you could do with a cuppa, too, Cassie luv?'

Cassie nodded and straightened up, wiping her eyes with the back of her hand. 'Sorry. I just heard some really shocking news. I'm trying to take it in.'

'Can we help? Do you want to tell us? I mean if it's personal, we'll understand. But I hate to see you so upset.' Trixie pulled up a deckchair.

Cassie drew a deep breath. 'It's something to do with my family, something I've just found out, and it's so hard to believe . . . I'm just . . .'

'Is something wrong? Is your mum okay?'

'She is at the moment. I'm not sure how she'll feel when I tell her what I've just discovered.'

Geoff reappeared. Trixie let Cassie regain her composure and then said, 'Geoff, Cassie's had some news that's upset her.'

Geoff was immediately concerned. 'Anything we can do?'

Cassie shook her head. 'I feel so terrible. It concerns me and Mum and also Michael. I've just had a visit from Frank Aquino.'

'And he said something that upset you?' asked Trixie with concern.

'It all sounds so bizarre, so unbelievable . . .' said Cassie and told Trixie and Geoff what had happened. 'I didn't even know that my father knew the Aquinos, let alone that he was sent to prison. He would never kill someone. He was not that sort of person,' she added vehemently.

347

The older couple stared at Cassie in astonishment, then they exchanged a glance.

'We've heard the story about one of the Aquino brothers being killed,' said Geoff slowly.

'What? What was the story?' asked Cassie quickly.

'It all happened long before we came to Whitby Point. But yes, we heard that there had been a fishing expedition and that there had been a fight and that one of the Aquino brothers had been stabbed. Evidently the man who did it confessed and went to gaol. I can't remember his name. What was your father's name?' asked Geoff.

'Patrick Sullivan,' whispered Cassie.

'Patrick, yes, Patrick Sullivan. That rings a bell. Yes, that could have been the name. What do you think, Geoff?' asked Trixie. Her husband nodded in agreement and Trixie continued. 'So, have I got this straight? You never knew anything about any of this until Frank told you?'

'I knew nothing. Dad mentioned to Mum that he'd spent time down here at Whitby Point and said that it was a lovely place, and that was all. He never talked much more about it and never brought us here. And he certainly never mentioned the Aquinos.' Cassie was suddenly thoughtful. 'Not that Dad ever talked much about his past. I don't know what I'm going to say to Mum. I can't get my head around it. Dad was the last person who would do anything violent.'

'What a shock for you, Cassie. When will you be able to talk to your mother? Maybe she will know something, and be able to clear the matter up,' said Trixie comfortingly.

Cassie shook her head. 'Mum's playing bridge and has her phone turned off. I'll wait till she gets home. Trixie, I just don't know what to say to Michael.' She looked at them, distraught. 'I can't stay here! If this is true . . .'

'Nonsense, Cassie. We won't let you go. Everyone in Whitby Point loves you!' said Geoff firmly.

'Maybe not when they know my father was Patrick Sullivan.'

'You don't know that,' soothed Trixie.

'Talk to your mum,' said Geoff. 'She might be able to tell you more. Then you can talk to Michael.'

'I don't know what I'm going to say to him. Surely the family would have told him by now about the will. What if he won't have anything to do with me once he knows?' said Cassie fearfully.

'Don't underestimate that man,' said Trixie. 'He's an independent sort of person. Remember, he trained as a vet instead of going into the fishing industry with the rest of the Aquinos. Of course it was his grandfather who was killed, but it was all so long ago. I can't believe he would blame you for that. He'll do the right thing, you wait and see.'

'But what about all that money that his uncle Ricardo left me? What's he going to say about that? I've got no explanation for it,' exclaimed Cassie.

'Can I ask how much we're talking about?' said Geoff.

'A quarter of a million dollars.'

Both Trixie and Geoff stared at her again.

'That is a lot of money,' said Geoff. 'And you have no idea why?'

'None at all,' said Cassie miserably.

'That certainly is a conundrum then, isn't it?' agreed Trixie.

'That's the kettle whistling. Am I making tea or coffee?' asked Geoff as he got up.

'I'll help you,' said Cassie.

'Me too. I'll cut this cake I brought,' added Trixie.

Over their tea they tried to chat about less serious matters, mainly the restaurant, but Cassie remained distracted.

'Will you be all right? Do you want us to stay? Come and stay at our place, if you like. Anything to help, Cassie,' said Geoff sympathetically.

'Thanks, you're both so kind. I'll take Bill for a walk and call Mum.' Cassie gave a wobbly smile. 'I'm glad the restaurant doesn't open tonight.'

When Cassie finally reached her mother that evening, Jenny was on a high. She'd had excellent cards and, what was more, she had played them well. But her chatter quickly slowed and she said, 'Cassie, you don't seem very thrilled for me! In fact you sound quite down, is something wrong?'

'Mum, I have to tell you something and you're not going to like it at all. One of the Aquinos, Frank – you might remember him, he supplies the fish for the restaurant – came to see me today. He was pretty wild and had an outrageous story, which involves us. It doesn't seem possible, but it's about Dad. Did you know that he knew the Aquinos? Is there anything you've never told me about him?'

'Like what, for heaven's sake? He never mentioned the Aquinos to me. Such a small world. Your father told me that he went to Whitby Point when he was young. I assumed it was for holidays. Maybe he met the Aquinos then.' Jenny sounded faintly amused. 'Don't tell me there's childhood gossip surfacing. How odd.'

Cassie could tell from her mother's voice that Jenny had never heard about Patrick's dark past.

'Mum, this is pretty serious. I know why he never brought us here for a holiday, even though he said that he liked the place. He didn't want to come back.'

'You're making this all sound such a big deal, how serious is the gossip you've heard? And does it really matter anyway? It would have been such a long time ago.'

'I know, Mum,' said Cassie miserably, 'but it's not that simple.'

'Darling, what is it? Are you all right? Who's upset you?' asked Jenny, sounding concerned.

'Frank stormed into the restaurant this afternoon. It was after lunch so there was no one else around, thank goodness. He told me that his uncle Ricardo had left me something in his will.'

'Good heavens, no wonder you're surprised. Is that the lovely old fellow who died recently?'

'Yes. I went to his ninetieth birthday party. But Mum, that was the only time I ever met him. Michael introduced us and we had a bit of a chat. And now Frank said that he's left me a quarter of a million dollars in his will. Why would he do that?'

'What! Cassie, that must have been some chat, what did you say to him?'

'Mum! Listen, that's not all.' Cassie heard her mother start to exclaim, but she pressed on. 'Frank was very angry, not just because of the money but because I was Patrick Sullivan's daughter.'

Jenny caught her breath. 'So what?' she asked.

Cassie started to cry. Between sobs she blurted out what Frank had said to her and the story Trixie and Geoff had heard.

'*No!*' shouted Jenny. 'No way! That's not true! There is no way that Pat did any such thing. Good Lord, what a cesspool of lies everyone is swimming in down there! Never. Never ever. You know what sort of a man your father was. They must have the wrong Patrick Sullivan.'

'Mum, Mum, I know. That's how I feel too. Dad was so special, but . . . what if . . . what if there is something to it? When he was young? I mean, I don't know all that much about his past, do you?'

'Well, no,' agreed Jenny. 'He was not a man for looking over his shoulder at the past. He always told us to look to the light ahead. I never had any interest in his past because he didn't. Maybe that's one of the things I liked about him, he didn't come with any of that family baggage that can drag you down. He always said it was just the three of us against the world . . .' She started to cry.

'I agree with you, Mum. It's just too unbelievable . . .'

'What does your Michael say?'

'I haven't spoken to him. I texted him to call me but I haven't heard from him yet. I feel so awful. I don't know how he's going to take all of this. I mean, my father . . . his grandfather, it's such a terrible coincidence. I can't get my head around it all. No matter how I try to sort it out, I can't make any sense of it.'

'One thing's for certain, we need to find out more. I have to come down. Patrick was my husband. I need to know what happened,' said Jenny, her voice sounding firmer. 'I'll be there as soon as I can.'

'Okay then,' said Cassie. 'Mum, before you go, do you have any old letters from Dad tucked away that could give us a clue as to what this is all about?'

'No, no old letters. You know how your father hated to keep junk. He always said how much simpler life is without accumulating anything that isn't necessary. I have nothing of his past at all.'

'I remember.'

'As far as your father was concerned, if it didn't involve either of us, it was irrelevant to him. He was so devoted to you and me, Cassie,' said Jenny.

'I know, Mum. He was a fabulous father. He was always there for me. That's why I can't believe what Frank told me.'

'All I really know about your father's background is that his parents came from Ireland and his mother died in a traffic accident and as soon as he could he went out into the world on his own. He never mentioned anything else about his family so I assumed he had none.'

'Mum, I can only think that all of this is a horrible mistake and the mess will sort itself out.'

'You might be right, Cass. Why don't you try to contact the solicitor who drew up Ricardo's will? Maybe he can explain everything.'

'Good idea, Mum. I'll have to find out who it is though. Anyway, I'll let you go. See you soon.'

For a few minutes Cassie felt buoyed by her mother's suggestion, but then she thought of Michael and spent a restless night wondering what she could say to him. Surely by now he would have heard about the will. Probably the Aquinos were already planning to contest it.

In the morning sunshine, watching Bill chase the seagulls dive-bombing around his morning toast, Cassie began to think about the big picture. Why had she been left so much money in Ricardo's will? She thought back over the five-minute conversation she'd had with him after his party. It had been completely inconsequential. She was pretty sure Michael had introduced her only by her first name. He had never mentioned the name Holloway, let alone Sullivan. Would Ricardo have known from that brief meeting that she was Patrick Sullivan's daughter? It seemed unlikely. To him, she had been just another guest.

She finished breakfast and pulled out the phone book and started to make a list of the local solicitors. One of them must have drawn up Ricardo's will.

'How's it going, boss? Anything special you had in mind for today?' Steve appeared with a notepad, ready for their discussion of the menu.

'Not really. Are you heading to Frank's for seafood?' asked Cassie.

'Yeah. Thought I might check the wharf, too. See if anyone has come in with something they want to sell on the QT. Been a few casual fishing boats passing through.'

'Well, if you do that, keep your head down. We don't want to upset Frank, our main supplier, by buying from someone else,' said Cassie.

'No worries. There seem to be a lot of mussels around at present. Always popular.'

'How well do they freeze? Is it worth stocking up?' asked Cassie.

'Why would we want to do that? We pride ourselves on food fresh from the sea.'

'You're right. My mistake. Take no notice. I'm a bit out of sorts today. Give me a call if you have any questions. See you when you get back.'

'Righto. It's not like you not to be on top of every detail,' he said, giving her a puzzled look as he walked towards the door.

Cassie gave him a weak smile as he left and poured herself another cup of coffee as her mobile jangled on the table next to her. She stared at the caller's ID. Michael.

She took a deep breath. 'Hi.'

'Hi to you.' There was a pause. 'Cassie, the whole family knows about Ricardo's will. Can I see you?'

'Oh God, Michael . . . I knew nothing about any of this, I swear. I'm just so shocked . . . I can't believe it. I don't know why Ricardo left me all that money. I had no idea that my father was connected with your family. You have to believe that he was a good man.' Cassie could hear herself babbling but she couldn't stop.

Eventually Michael said, 'Yes. You've told me that many times. Can I come over?'

'Yes. Yes, please.'

Cassie hung up, and started replaying the conversation in her head. Was he going to take Frank's side and think that she had done something to extort the money from Ricardo, or was he going to believe her when she said that she had no idea what was going on? Michael had sounded calm, but maybe he was too calm. Perhaps he was being detached.

She rushed upstairs, threw off her old T-shirt and put on a clean blue silk shirt over her jeans. She smoothed her hair and added a touch of lipstick and mascara and the jasmine perfume Michael liked. She didn't want to look too contrived, especially first thing in the morning, but neither did she want to appear as wretched as she felt.

Michael rapped at the door rather than wandering around the side to the deck as he normally did. The formality alarmed Cassie but she tried to sound casual and normal.

'Hi, the door's open. We're around the back.'

She was throwing stale bread over the railing of the deck, and watching the small mullet leap for the crumbs as Bill splashed about in the shallows, attempting to catch the fish or at least a chunk of bread.

'Hi.' Michael gave her a smile and then there was a momentary hesitancy on both their parts. Cassie stepped forward and kissed him on the cheek.

'I'm so glad you came. Coffee?'

'Sure.' He leaned down and called to Bill. 'Mate, there's bread over there, forget the fish!'

But Bill was over the whole exercise. He sploshed rapidly from the water and dashed around to the deck to greet Michael, who fussed over him.

Cassie brought two mugs of coffee, handed one to Michael and then sat in the deckchair beside him.

Michael sipped his coffee and eyed Cassie over the rim of his mug. 'How are you feeling?'

'I feel terrible! I can't work out what's going on, and I'm scared you're going to hate me for what's happened.'

She knew her voice was rising but she was close to tears.

Michael leapt to his feet and went over and wrapped his arms around her. 'This is a nightmare, isn't it? My poor darling. Of course I'm not going to hate you. My grandfather died more than fifty years ago, long before I was born. Neither of us can be held responsible for something that happened so long ago. It had nothing to do with us. I should have come over straight away last night, but I was dealing with a cow in labour and I couldn't leave it. I was very surprised when I learned that Frank'd told all the other members of the family, including my mother and my sisters that you must have said something sinister to Uncle Ricardo on the night of his party to make him leave you all that money. I was with you all the time you were talking to Uncle Ricardo. It was a nothing conversation. You didn't say anything to him of significance, unless you were talking in some obscure code. I've let all my family know that.'

Cassie smiled at Michael, relieved that she had his support. Trixie was right, he was the sort of man who would make up his own mind and not be persuaded by the opinions of others. She put her arms around his neck and kissed him.

'Michael, I'm so glad that you're okay with this,' she said. 'Can you tell me, does anyone in your family know the connection between your family and my father? Did he work for them? He never mentioned their name to either my mother or me, but there has to be something – otherwise why would Uncle Ricardo leave me so much money?'

'My mother has no idea. She was way too young to remember the death of her father and later on no one in the family ever wanted to talk about it. She thinks that was because no one wanted to upset my great-grandfather Joe, who was devastated by what had happened.'

'Michael, what am I going to do? I can't just accept the money if I don't know why he wanted me to have it. I feel as though I'm stealing from your family.'

'Cassie, that's nonsense, but we need to find out why you were left the bequest. Don't you agree?'

'I do. I desperately want to find out, too. I don't want it to come between us.' She looked at him with tears welling in her eyes.

'It won't come between us, Cassie. Are you sure your mother knows nothing about this?'

'Positive. Mum and I have racked our brains. Dad never talked about his childhood, his past. Now I guess we know why. We have to find the answer through your family.'

'And for the moment none of them are saying anything. That's not surprising, I suppose. They're as stunned by Uncle Ricardo's will as you are. But Uncle Ricardo must have had a good reason for leaving you all that money. We just have to find out what it was. Sweetheart, I can't stay here any longer. I have a surgery to open and you have a restaurant to run. I'll see you as soon as I close up. But I was thinking, Uncle Ricardo's solicitor is Bruce Walker. He's worked for Uncle Ricardo for years. He might have an idea why you were left the money.'

'Thanks, Michael. I'll give him a ring and set up a meeting. I'm sure he'll tell me I'm the wrong Cassandra Sullivan and that all this is someone else's nightmare.'

'Chin up, Cass. We'll work it all out eventually. And remember, I'm on your side,' he said as he tenderly kissed her goodbye.

Michael was right, she did have a business to look after, and, as if to prove it, her mobile phone rang almost as soon as he had driven off.

'Hey, Cassie, it's Steve. We have a problem.'

'That's not great. What is it?'

'No seafood. For some reason, Frank Aquino has struck us off his customer list. I'm hunting around other places for fish, but suddenly I feel like a bad smell. No one wants to sell anything to me. Have you got any outstanding bills or something like that?'

'No way. Listen, Steve this isn't unexpected though I'd hoped it wouldn't actually happen. There's a bit of a family feud blowing up with the Aquinos and I'm the focus of it. Can you source fish anywhere else?'

'I could phone a mate of mine to see what he's got. Bit of a drive, halfway to Nowra, to get it but that might be what we have to do.'

Cassie dragged her hand through her hair. 'Ring and see what he has. But you won't have time to go and get it. I'll ask Geoff. Is the rest of the menu sorted?'

'Other than the seafood, yes, it's all taken care of.'

As soon as Steve hung up, Cassie rang Bruce Walker's office and asked to speak with the solicitor. The woman on the other end said that Mr Walker was presently engaged with another client, but she would let him know, and she was sure that he would ring back at his first opportunity.

After the lunch service had finished, Steve unbuttoned his white jacket and leaned back in a chair. 'Just as well we didn't have a lot of people in. Seafood was a bit stretched. We ran out of mussels.'

'Look, Steve, there's this family issue that I think I should fill you in on before the gossip starts.'

Steve held up his hands. 'Don't worry, Cass, I'm not going to listen to the gossip. Hearsay multiplies into untruths, I always think.'

'I'd like to tell you anyway. I think I need to tell you, with this seafood situation. Frank Aquino told me yesterday afternoon that his grandfather Ricardo left me a quarter of a million dollars in his will.'

Steve stared at her and gave a long whistle. 'I see.'

'No, you don't see.' Cassie went on to explain what Frank had told her. 'And now it sounds like he's made good on his threat to tell everyone.'

Steve nodded slowly. 'So Frank's doing payback. And your relationship with Michael? I suppose that's now considered a bit suss too?'

'No, Michael believes me and is as confused as I am about this whole business.'

'This sounds like a TV script,' said Steve.

'Sure does. Steve, I won't be happy until I get to the bottom of it all. Either I find out why Uncle Ricardo left me all that money, or I prove that I'm not the Cassie Sullivan named in the will.' She spoke with more determination in her voice than she actually felt and suddenly added, 'You don't think the restaurant was so quiet today because of what Frank's been saying, do you?'

'Don't be paranoid, Cassie,' said Steve. 'Let's wait and see how things pan out. This Aquino thing could all be just a flash in the pan. They'll settle down.'

'I'm not so sure,' said Cassie, thinking of the money in the will. 'Do you think I should confront Frank about this?'

'Not for the time being. The customers won't starve. I'll be able to source whatever we need.'

'Thanks, Steve,' she said, trying to muster a smile.

Just then the phone rang and when Cassie picked it up the voice on the other end introduced himself as Bruce Walker.

'I'm the solicitor handling Ricardo Aquino's estate,' he explained. 'I'm sorry that it has taken so long to get back to you, but I've had to deal with some other priorities.'

'I'm pleased to hear from you,' said Cassie. 'I do hope you can clear up this confusion over Ricardo Aquino's will.'

'There is no confusion as far as I am aware, but we can confirm.'

'Mr Walker, this has all come as a terrible shock to me. Ricardo Aquino could not possibly have left me a quarter of a million dollars. There has to be some mistake.'

'I don't think that is likely, but I can see you whenever you want to make an appointment.'

'Is now too soon?' asked Cassie.

'If that suits you. Say in half an hour?'

Bruce Walker's office was modest since, as his receptionist explained, his main office was in Nowra and he only used this one twice a week. He was a tall man in his late fifties with a clipped beard and plump pink cheeks. He held out his hand.

'Hello, it's Mrs Holloway, isn't it?'

'Yes,' replied Cassie. 'Soon to be ex-Mrs Holloway.'

'I'm sorry, I didn't realise. Please take a seat. It is my job to inform you, Cassandra Holloway, née Sullivan, that you are a beneficiary in the late Ricardo Aquino's will to the amount of two hundred and fifty thousand dollars,' he said with a smile on his face.

'Mr Walker, I don't understand why I am. Are you sure that I'm the right Cassandra Sullivan in the will?'

'Please call me Bruce and yes I'm quite sure. But to confirm, can you tell me your parents' names, old address in Manly and your most recent address in Sydney?'

Cassie told him and Bruce Walker nodded. 'That's what we have on our records, which confirms that you are the same Cassandra Sullivan who is named in Ricardo Aquino's will,' he said.

'But it's ridiculous. I only met the man for five minutes on his ninetieth birthday. Have you any idea why he would leave me such a large sum of money in his will?'

'None at all. My job was only to draw up the document and then determine that you are the right Cassandra

Sullivan and, in doing so, fulfil the terms of Ricardo Aquino's will,' Bruce replied. 'And I can assure you that you are the right person.'

'Can I ask when the will was first drawn up? Was it recently?'

'No, not at all recently. Mr Aquino's will was drawn up years ago and he never changed it. But why you are included among the beneficiaries, I can't say.'

Puzzled, Cassie looked at the solicitor across his desk. None of this made any sense, but at least she could no longer be accused of evil intentions at Uncle Ricardo's birthday party.

'Bruce,' said Cassie, deciding to take the bull by the horns and ask the question whose answer she dreaded. 'I had no idea that there was any connection between my father and the Aquinos, but Frank Aquino tells me that my father went to prison for killing Carlo Aquino, Michael Phillips's grandfather. Neither my mother nor I knew anything about such an event. Can you tell me if it's true?'

The lawyer leaned back in his swivel chair. 'Yes, it's true,' he said.

Cassie felt tears welling up. 'Can you tell me what happened?' she whispered.

'Knowing Frank, he would not have broken that news to you gently. And if you have always been ignorant of it, it must have come as a terrible shock.' Bruce Walker gave her a sympathetic smile. 'It all happened in the late fifties. I believe my father was the solicitor acting for Patrick Sullivan. He was the only solicitor in Whitby Point.'

'Is your father still alive? I'd love to ask him questions,' said Cassie eagerly.

Bruce Walker shook his head. 'No, Dad's been dead for years.'

'Do you know how my father was connected to the Aquinos? I hope you don't mind all these questions, but

I am so confused. I've just found out that I don't know much about my father at all,' said Cassie.

'No, I'm sorry. I don't. I suppose that he was a fisherman working for them. I can't think of another explanation,' Bruce Walker replied. 'I'm afraid all my father's files were destroyed in a fire a long time ago.'

Cassie frowned. 'I've got one final question, if you don't mind,' she said. 'I'm not sure that I have a right to ask this, but here goes. Do you think that the Aquinos will contest the will?'

'That's not for me to say. They are perfectly entitled to do so, but what I would say is that I think they would perhaps not have a strong case. The rest of the family has been well provided for and you are not a late addition to the will, so it is clear to me that Ricardo Aquino was quite sure that he wanted to leave you this money. They would need a lot of compelling evidence to suggest otherwise.'

'Thank you, Bruce. You have been very kind,' said Cassie, grateful that the lawyer had been so friendly.

*

The following morning, Michael called Cassie early. 'Cass? It's me. I've been thinking . . .'

'Hi, Michael, me too.' She sighed.

'No, not about this whole mystery of the will and your father . . . I've been thinking about us.'

Cassie caught her breath. 'And?'

'I think we need a bit of time out together. I was thinking of taking my new boat for a sail – really christen her, I've only made a couple of trial runs. I'd love you to come. Can Trixie hold the fort?'

'Yes, I think she can. It sounds a wonderful thing to do,' said Cassie, laughing and feeling ridiculously happy, even relieved.

'Probably best to leave Bill on shore. Later we'll take him out and let him get his sea legs.'

'What can I bring?'

'The usual – warm jacket, sunnies, sunblock, hat. I have food and cold drinks, but if there are any leftovers of Trixie's desserts, I wouldn't say no.'

'Gotcha. Where will I meet you?'

'I'm moored down at the port where the trawlers are. I'll pick you up at the wharf in about, say, an hour?'

'Great. I'll ask Geoff and Trixie if they'd mind Bill-sitting.'

Sitting on the end of the old wharf, Cassie's heart leapt as she saw Michael rowing towards her from the yacht, the muscles across his shoulders taut under his white T-shirt.

He helped her into the small dinghy and in a few minutes they were beside the yacht as it bobbed gently at its mooring. Michael clambered onto the small but sleek sailboat, secured the dinghy and helped Cassie aboard.

'This is lovely! Compact but comfortable. I love the timber decks,' she exclaimed. Stepping below, she said, 'Two bunks, a kitchen on one side and a dinette on the other, how civilised. Great design!'

'Small gas stove. Everything is stowed and very streamlined. It's got a good engine as a backup, should we need it. The head, that's the toilet to you landlubbers, is in there. We could stay out overnight if the fishing is good, or if we just feel like getting away from everything and everyone.'

'It'll be fabulous in the summer. Find an inlet and moor the boat and swim, picnic, fish, or just explore. Do you know the waterways around here well?'

'I had a little sailing boat as a kid. I've also sailed in Sydney Harbour, although that can be pretty crowded at times. Not like here. Have you sailed much?'

'No, not really. Not what you'd call proper sailing. Junkets around Sydney Harbour on ostentatious gin palaces.'

'With Hal and his cronies?'

'Yes. Usually business related. I couldn't stand the people and the superficiality of it all. They might as well have stayed at the wharf and partied.'

'This'll be nothing like that at all. For one thing, I didn't bring any gin. We'll just head out of the harbour – it's calm enough to hit the ocean and the forecast says it's going to stay that way. We'll sail north and then duck into one of the inlets I know.'

Cassie quickly got the hang of sitting on the edge of the gunwale and holding the jib line as the Cavalier skimmed along. The stiff wind and spray in her face was exhilarating, and she and Michael kept exchanging looks and laughing with the joy of the moment.

'The coastline looks different from the sea, doesn't it,' she shouted to Michael.

They tacked and headed into a channel, passing some tangled wetlands and marshy foreshores. Further along this narrow passage they came to a series of linked lakes. Here the breeze was gentler and they slid effortlessly, silently, across an empty lake. In the distance Cassie could see a flock of pelicans floating serenely. Rolling hills edged the lake and Cassie felt quite moved, not only by the peaceful scene, but being there with Michael.

He smiled at her and Cassie realised that he was possibly feeling the same.

'There's a bit of a cove over there, we can anchor and have something to eat. Are you hungry?' he asked.

'Yes. Must be the sea air.'

The sail flapped like a wet sheet as Michael manoeuvred the yacht into position.

'We'll take down the sails and drop anchor. We'll bring the food on deck. We can use the hatch cover as a table.'

They shared a meal of baguettes filled with salmon, salad and cheese with pickled cucumbers, cherry tomatoes, olives, and a tossed green salad on the side, and a refreshing iced tea. As they finished it all off with one of Trixie's divine desserts, Cassie smiled.

'It doesn't get much better than this. This was a lovely idea. Thank you.'

Michael looked serious. 'I felt it was important for us to get away somewhere quiet. I know you've been a bit battered by this whole series of events over Uncle Ricardo's will.' He drew a breath and before Cassie could think of something to say, he went on. 'I know it must be a shock to you – and your mum. It was for me too. But for better or worse, you and I are now linked and I don't want this situation to come between us.'

Cassie nodded. 'Me too, absolutely. I have to say I felt relieved when Bruce Walker told me that I had been named in Uncle Ricardo's will a long time ago. What I hated was that your family thought I had come down here to extort money from him.'

'As if. Cassie, that's not what I wanted to bring you here to talk about, although I have to say it is a complication. What I want to tell you is that, from the moment I first saw you bring Bill into my surgery, I think I fell in love with you. Then I realised that you were working through a few problems. It's not easy to end a marriage – I know from my own experience . . .' He stopped talking for a moment and studied her face. 'Initially, I just wanted to take things slowly, Cass, for both our sakes. But now, with all of this upheaval, my biggest fear is that these recent events could come between us. I don't know how you feel . . . but I had to say this.'

Cassie couldn't speak. It felt as if an emotional floodgate was opening. The rush of thoughts and feelings about her past and her future, and especially Michael, threatened to overwhelm her. Michael seemed to understand because he reached for her hand and held it gently.

Finally Cassie managed to say, 'I've been feeling the same. In spite of the shock about my father, the money, and everything else that's been going on, the thing that most frightened me was losing you. I love you so much.' She managed a rueful smile. 'So where to next?'

Michael leaned over and took her gently in his arms and kissed her. 'Steady as she goes, skipper. As long as we both feel the same about each other, we'll get through this.'

As they sailed out of the lake back towards the open sea, Michael, clearly happy, began to sing, surprising Cassie not just with his decent singing voice but his song.

'My father used to sing that,' Cassie exclaimed. 'He said it was the only Italian song he knew. I used to climb into bed with him and Mum on a Sunday morning and he'd sing it to me. I have no idea how he knew it. Where did you learn it, Michael?'

'From my mother. She'd learned it from her grandfather, Joe, who used to sing it to her as a little girl.'

'Isn't that amazing? We have something else in common now.' And together they sang the chorus.

Sailing back into the harbour at Whitby Point, Cassie leaned against Michael while he held the tiller of the sturdy yacht. 'I thought you were a bit keen when you came around with those food samples for Bill.'

Michael laughed. 'He deserved some treats. After all, he's what brought us together.' He kissed the top of her head affectionately.

Things are definitely looking up, Cassie thought happily.

But the good feeling didn't last. The next day she realised that people who'd previously passed the time of day with her in chatty exchanges were beginning to avoid her. She was particularly hurt when Ron the newsagent suddenly became preoccupied and busy when she went into his shop.

Then Steve told her that his fishing mate near Nowra had suddenly said that he didn't have enough fish to supply the Blue Boatshed any longer.

'It's rubbish,' said Steve angrily. 'I bet Frank's put the hard word on him. I've tried two other places but we're running out of options. I don't want to have to go up to Sydney every few days for seafood, especially when there's better stuff right here.'

'I'm sorry, Steve. I know it's making your job difficult. But we can't not serve seafood!' exclaimed Cassie in frustration.

'I have a couple of other options. Freelancers not on a contract to sell. Just means a bit more of a drive.'

'I'm sure if you can set it up, Geoff can go and get it. I know he won't mind and I'm damned if I'm going to let Frank defeat me,' said Cassie.

'I'm with you there,' Steve replied.

But the day didn't improve.

Cassie received a text message from Mollie, Trixie's friend who had been working in the restaurant since it opened, to say she couldn't work there any longer.

Cassie rang Trixie. 'Mollie has sent me a message to say that she's leaving. Have you any idea why?'

'Good grief, that's terrible. Perhaps it's because Mollie's husband works on one of Ray Aquino's trawlers. Maybe she heard the gossip and thought that if she goes on working for you, he could lose his job. I'll talk to her but in the meantime I'll come over and help you.'

'Trixie, I hate to impose on you like this but it would be a great help. You're such a good friend.'

'I feel bad about Mollie letting you down, Cassie. Things will turn out for the best eventually, you'll see. Hang in there. I'll be over there in an hour.'

Cassie was glad to see Trixie. The restaurant was fairly quiet, so she had time to tell her about her visit to the solicitor.

'You know, Trixie, after seeing Bruce Walker the other day I am still none the wiser. I wonder if there is still someone around who remembers what happened. Mind you, they would have to be pretty old. Maybe there would be something in newspaper files. How long has the local rag been around?'

'The paper's been around forever. You're right. You might learn something there,' said Trixie.

'Okay, that's my next step,' said Cassie, excitement in her voice.

But before Cassie had a chance to go into town to look in the newspaper office, she had a visitor. Just before they closed the lunch service, Hal walked into the restaurant with a smarmy smile and asked for a table. Cassie nearly dropped the plates she was carrying when she saw him.

'Now what? Why are you here, Hal?'

'Passing through. Just thought I'd see what the Blue Boatshed was like. I saw it mentioned in the Sunday paper. I have to say it looks a bit quiet to me. But I hear that things are going much better for you in another department.' He raised an eyebrow.

'Just what's that supposed to mean?' asked Cassie.

'Rumours abound about your not-so-little inheritance. Seems you have struck it lucky down here with those Latin lovers. I didn't know there was so much money in fishing!'

Cassie was livid. She lowered her voice so that the few other guests couldn't hear her and said angrily, 'Hal, whatever your network has told you, it's none of your damn business or theirs either, for that matter. Now I'm busy, so order a meal or leave my restaurant.'

'Cassie, Cassie, calm down. I also heard that there was a little bit of animosity over your windfall, so I came down to offer you my assistance. You know I'm a bloody good lawyer.'

'Just keep out of this, Hal. It's disgusting how you can smell money.' She turned and walked away.

'Oh well, I guess I'll grab a hamburger in town.' He walked out, surreptitiously watched by everyone else in the restaurant.

Hal's visit rattled Cassie. Whatever his motives were, he was trouble and she wanted him out of her life. She certainly didn't want him rocking her relationship with Michael. She hoped he would take the hint and go straight back to Sydney but later that afternoon she heard the sound of his Porsche outside the restaurant.

'Oh, no, it's Hal again,' she groaned to Steve.

'Do you want me to stay?' he asked.

'No, thanks, Steve. I know you have things to do. He's a pain but I can handle him.'

'If you're sure. I'm heading down south tonight. Hoping I can pick up some fish from a guy I know on a trawler that's coming in.'

'Really? Are we having trouble with any of our other suppliers yet?'

Steve grimaced. 'I'm afraid so. I didn't want to worry you, but someone's put out a story that you don't pay your bills.'

'What? How dare they! Damn Frank Aquino. He's making life so difficult. I suppose we'll have to start paying for our supplies in cash, and that is going to create a huge cash-flow problem. I'm sorry, Steve, thanks for doing your best.'

'No worries. Hey, if you close down, I'm out of a job! See ya,' he said cheerily. He headed out the door as Bill gave a growl.

'Hal, why are you back?' asked Cassie in a tired voice.

'Well, Cassie, you might have told me the full story about this messy inheritance thing. Jesus!' He shook his head.

'Hal, I told you nothing because it has nothing to do with you. I don't need your help, interference or opinions, thanks.'

'How come you never told me your father was a gaolbird? My family will be thrilled to know the girl I married had a father who'd been to prison. I'm beginning to wonder just what sort of a double life you led while we were together. Just what sort of things did you learn from your father?'

'That's a horrible thing to say. My father was a wonderful man and he wouldn't have taught me to do anything that was wrong. If you had known about my father, does that mean you wouldn't have married me?'

'The best I can say is that it would have given me pause for thought,' Hal said smugly.

'Hal, go away.'

'First, I've got a couple more questions. What's the deal with this money? Why did this old fellow leave it to you? Why have you kept it a secret? Didn't want it to come out in the divorce settlement, perhaps?'

'Don't be ridiculous, Hal. I didn't know anything about it until a few days ago. You really think this is all about cheating you? Talk about ego. You are not the centre of the universe.'

'I came down here to help you.'

'Rubbish. You came to see if you could get your hands on Ricardo's money. Listen, Hal, I want you to leave. I am trying to handle this nightmare as best I can and I don't have to explain anything to you anymore.' Cassie stood up and rubbed her eyes, feeling close to tears. 'I have to phone my mother.' Before she'd finished the sentence she thought, Why did I say that?

'Grow up, Cassie! Holy cow, you and your mother. No wonder I never got a look in.'

'Hal, I'm not going to argue with you. I would just prefer it if you got on with your life without me and I'll do the same.'

'Good luck with that money. From what I've heard around town, you stand a snowball's chance in hell of making this restaurant work.' Hal gave her a malicious smile and walked out.

Cassie watched him saunter away and resisted the temptation to throw something at his retreating back. She wondered whom he'd been talking to in town. Damn him. She flopped into a chair.

Bill sensed her mood and came over and dropped his head onto her lap and gave her a comforting look before he lovingly licked her hand.

*

'Oh, that man is a jerk,' exclaimed Jenny as Cassie related Hal's visit. 'I'm sorry I couldn't get away sooner but I'm leaving first thing in the morning. How's everything going? Is Michael okay still?'

'Michael's being brilliant. He's spoken to his mother and sisters and they understand that I didn't influence Ricardo to make him include me in his will. Now they are as puzzled as I am as to why he did.'

'I'm glad about Michael. It's hard for him, too.'

'I'm thinking of marching up to Frank and giving him an earful. Asking him to stop this vendetta against me. It's so wrong,' said Cassie angrily.

'I'd sleep on that idea. Or better still, ask Michael what he thinks.'

'You're probably right,' said Cassie. 'I'm planning on going through the newspaper files from that period and seeing if I can find anything that might help us solve this mystery.'

'Good idea.' Then the brightness seeped from Jenny's voice. 'There's sure to be reports about the trial, I suppose.' They both paused a minute. 'Cass, I still just find it so unbelievable . . .'

'I know, Mum. So do I.'

Cassie felt much better when her mother arrived. Jenny stepped from her car and wrapped her arms around Cassie in a comforting hug. Then she swept into the restaurant, ran a professional eye over things and sat down with Cassie and Steve, who told her of the issues with food suppliers.

'The seafood aside, we used to have a standing deal with the woman who ran the organic markets for our fruit and veg. We'd give her our order and she'd drop it by. Now she says she has too many other commitments to continue doing that.'

Steve rolled his eyes to indicate how feeble he thought the excuse was.

'This whole thing stinks,' said Jenny. 'Cassie had nothing to do with any of this family mystery.'

'You must know how it is in a small town. Everyone seems to think that where there's smoke, there's fire. It's a lot of money that old Ricardo Aquino left Cassie.'

'Is that what you really think, Steve?' asked Jenny brusquely.

Steve leaned back and held up his arms in mock surrender. 'Hey, I'm not saying that. I'm just telling you what other people are saying. All I know is that Cassie has worked hard to get this restaurant up and running, and as far as I'm concerned this place is our number one priority. But we can't get away from the fact that Ricardo's will is causing us a lot of problems.'

'I know. Sorry. I didn't mean to sound so aggressive. I just feel I have to question everyone and everything.'

'Must be frustrating for you both.' He looked at Jenny. 'Cassie told me about your husband. I tried to imagine how it would be if someone I knew and loved suddenly was shown to be the total opposite of what I always believed. Hard one.'

'Yes.' Jenny took a breath. 'It's upset me terribly. And I just don't believe it. We were married for years and years. I loved Pat so much. I know my husband and none of this makes sense to me.' She paused and her voice shook. 'I really want to know the truth. Can you think of anyone I can talk to? Surely one of the Aquinos knows something.'

Steve passed her a box of tissues. 'I'd have a word with Ray Aquino, Frank's father. He's a reserved man but from all accounts he seems to be a decent bloke. Maybe he could tell you something.'

'Thank you Steve. Hopefully Ray can help me,' said Jenny, dabbing her eyes with a tissue.

'Mum, it's worth a try,' said Cassie, hugging her mother. 'Will you be okay on your own? I've got to take care of the restaurant. I have to deal with these supply shortages. It can't wait.'

'I won't be gone long,' said Jenny, resolutely picking up her keys and heading for the door.

A couple of hours later Jenny came back. 'Cassie, is there any way you can leave the restaurant for an hour or so? I think I have a lead on where to find some answers.'

'No worries. It's still a while before we open. I've sorted out the supplies. Trixie's due any minute,' Cassie replied. 'How did you go with Ray Aquino?'

'I'll tell you while we drive.'

Cassie didn't say anything else until they were both sitting in her car.

'Okay, Mum. Where to?'

'The cemetery.'

'I don't understand.'

'I'm not sure I do either, but I think we will when we get there.' Jenny could hardly keep the excitement out of her voice.

'Are you going to tell me how things went with Ray?' said Cassie, bewildered by her mother's cheerfulness.

'Ray was just lovely. He's probably a couple of years younger than me and he plays bridge.'

'Mum, you make bridge sound like a secret society,' said Cassie impatiently.

'It means that we have something in common. I explained to him that I was married to Patrick and that I had no idea about his past. Ray was very kind to me. He told me that the family had been shocked when they found out that Ricardo had left such a large sum of money to someone they considered to be inappropriate. I could see his point.'

'Me too,' said Cassie. 'Did you say that to him?'

'Yes, I did. We had a calm and sensible discussion. We both laid our cards on the table, so to speak, and if you interrupt me again you're never going to find out what he said.'

'Sorry, Mum.'

'I said that your suppliers weren't supplying and that Mollie had resigned, probably because she thought that her husband might be sacked. Ray said he'd speak to the husband and assure him that no such thing would happen if Mollie came back to work for us. He also said that he would speak to Frank and tell him that a personal vendetta would not solve anything. He did say that Frank was pretty headstrong and would probably continue to speak out against you, and that some people in town would continue to take his side. Still, it's a start.'

'Mum, you're a genius. Surely not everyone will be against me. Some people will want to start supplying me again, especially the out-of-towners,' said Cassie, feeling happier than she had in days.

'I'll ignore that interruption and go on with what Ray told me,' said Jenny with mock severity. 'I asked him if he had any idea why his father had left you all that money and, like everyone else, he didn't have a clue. Then I asked him if he remembered the incident and the trial. He told me that he'd been about eight or so at the time and remembered nothing specific except there was some family upheaval and the children were kept out of it. He said there had never been any mention of Patrick Sullivan in the Aquino household after that. It was as though he'd been airbrushed from their history. That's similar to what you learned from Michael's mother, isn't it?'

'I don't suppose that it's all that surprising. Mum, does Ray remember Dad at all?' asked Cassie as she turned the car into the road that led up the hill towards the cemetery.

'Not much. He remembers that he liked him and that your father played with him when he was little. I asked him to explain how Patrick was connected to the Aquino family. He told me he couldn't remember but suggested that we go and look at the headstones in the cemetery. He thinks we might find some answers there. And here we are,' said Jenny as Cassie stopped her car outside the cemetery gates.

'Where will we start?' asked Cassie.

'The Catholic section, I guess. Let's find the Aquinos,' replied her mother.

The two women started to wander around the cemetery. For the most part it was a tidily kept place; the grass was clipped and there were very few weeds. Some of the graves had vases of flowers sitting on them. The plots had plenty of room between each other.

Probably that's because there's so much space up here. No need to squash everyone together, thought Cassie. She moved away from her mother, still not sure what she was looking for.

'There's a beautiful view from up here,' Jenny called to her. 'Nice place to spend eternity. Look what I've found. This area seems to be full of Aquinos.'

Cassie hurried over to join her.

'Look,' said Jenny. 'There's Carlo's grave. And here's a Giuseppe Aquino. Who was he?'

'I think he must have been Michael's great grandfather. Everyone called him Joe. What's on his headstone?'

'Loving husband of Evalina and Bridget. Loved father of Ricardo, Pietro and Carlo. Odd,' said Jenny. 'All very Italian, except where did Bridget come from? That's Irish. Here's Evalina's headstone. Look at the date on it. She died a long time ago. Her sons must have been very young, Carlo just a baby. How sad. I suppose that's why Giuseppe married Bridget.'

'I guess. Keep looking.'

'I've just found it.' Jenny was staring hard at another headstone, set a little apart from the other Aquinos. The inscription on it was faded by the wind and the salt air, but she could still make out what it said. She read it out to her daughter. 'Bridget Aquino, born February 1901, died May 1945. Beloved wife of Giuseppe Aquino. Loving mother to his sons Ricardo, Pietro and Carlo and adored mother of Patrick Sullivan.'

'I'll be blowed.' Tears sprang to Jenny's eyes. 'Cassie, I want you to meet your grandmother.'

Cassie stood looking at the gravestone for quite some time before she said anything. 'Mum, have I got this right? Dad was Bridget's son, and that makes her my grandmother. She married Giuseppe Aquino and she became the step-mother of Ricardo, Pietro and Carlo. Is that how it works?'

'That's my interpretation of what's written there,' Jenny replied in a soft voice, almost too emotional to speak at all.

'So does that also mean that Dad was Giuseppe Aquino's step-son and that the others were his step-brothers?'

Jenny nodded.

'So Dad didn't work for the Aquinos. He was a member of their family. When he killed Carlo, he didn't just kill someone he was working with – he killed his step-brother.'

Jenny looked at Cassie, her eyes still filled with tears. 'I know. But Cassie, if he did such a dreadful thing, why the money? Solve one puzzle and we find more intrigue. Come on, let's get back, Steve will be wondering what's happened to us.'

When Cassie told Michael that it was probable that her father had been the step-brother of the Aquino boys, Michael exclaimed, 'That's incredible. I bet my mother knows nothing about this. How did Uncle Ray know to send you to the cemetery?'

'According to Mum, who is now his new best friend, when Ray was very young, his grandfather used to take him for walks up to the cemetery and linger over Bridget's grave. He used to mutter to himself in Italian, so Ray knew the place was important to him.'

'The plot certainly thickens! What are you going to do now?' asked Michael.

'Mum wants to find out when Bridget married Giuseppe by looking up records at Births, Deaths and

Marriages. I'm going to see if I can find anything in the old local newspapers about Dad.'

*

The *Whitby Point News* had been housed in a small office in the main street of the town since 1925. It was still essentially a two-person band. The editor was Alison Chambers, the granddaughter of the original proprietor, and she worked with a keen young assistant, James Holden.

'Good morning, Mrs Chambers. I'm Cassandra Holloway. We spoke briefly over the phone about my looking through some of the old files.'

'Oh yes. I've made a space for you in our back room. Unfortunately not all our papers have been saved in the new digital format. Some are on microfilm, and some are in the historical society's museum. I've pulled out the papers from around the mid fifties.'

'Do you remember anything about the incident . . . when Carlo Aquino . . . ? Do you remember Patrick Sullivan?'

'No, sorry. I can't help you there. I wasn't born at the time,' Alison replied. She opened the latched half door at the end of the counter and ushered Cassie through. 'The papers are old paste-up jobs, so they are in books. I've found some from the fifties and put them on the table for you,' Alison explained.

'Thank you.'

'It's a bit of a job to go through them; would you like a coffee? Instant, I'm afraid.'

'Perhaps a bit later, thanks.' Cassie eyed the pile of fat bound books with yellowing pages of newspapers sticking out from them.

She settled herself at the work table and started with a volume labelled '1955'. As she slowly turned the pages of the old newspapers she began to get a sense of the community in which her father had lived.

She read articles about the fishing industry and the fish co-op founded by Joe Aquino. There was a photo of Joe with Ricardo outside the co-op building, both looking very pleased with themselves. There was another of Joe standing beside a state fishing minister who, according to the caption beneath, said that Whitby Point was one of the biggest commercial fishing ports in Australia.

There were photos of the beginning of the construction of a timber jetty and the new refrigeration plant. There were slipways, engineering workshops and ice-making facilities. All this gave Cassie a sense of how vibrant Whitby Point had been. She wondered how many of the tourists who now visited this sleepy holiday town really understood the colourful history of the local fishing industry and the dangers, risks and gambles of those early fishing families.

She worked her way through 1955 and almost to the end of 1956 without finding anything directly about her father. Then, under the front-page headline 'First Blessing of the Fleet', she saw a photo of her father. The date was 28 December 1956. There was a photo of a pretty girl, Josi Greco, the Princess of the Fleet, and below the photograph of Josi was one of her father. She read the caption: 'Patrick Sullivan (pictured) retrieved the cross thrown into the water by Fr Della Torre.'

Cassie smiled to herself. What a handsome man you were, Dad, and very fit. Bet the girls all fancied you.

She was more than halfway through 1957 when she found the glaring headline, 'Death of Leading Family's Son' and read the caption to the accompanying pictures, 'Carlo Aquino was tragically killed by his step-brother Patrick Sullivan in a boating accident.'

Cassie took a deep breath as she stared at the photograph of Patrick that the newspaper had recycled from the previous December, his smiling face at odds with the gravity of the situation.

Slowly she read the newspaper account of what had happened.

Ricardo, Carlo and Patrick had been out fishing when the weather turned nasty so they headed back to port. Patrick was about to throw a last line in and was holding the bait knife when a rough wave threw Carlo onto him and the knife pierced him, killing him instantly.

But if that's what happened it sounds like an accident, Cassie thought to herself.

Whether Mrs Chambers had been watching her or just coincidentally found herself with a free moment Cassie did not know or care. The newspaper editor arrived with a small tray with a mug of coffee, milk, sugar and a biscuit, and said, 'I thought you might be ready for this.'

'Thank you.' Cassie straightened up and rubbed her eyes. 'Strange to see pictures of my father as a young man living down here. It was his other life we never knew about.'

'Is that a fact? Goes to show you can't take people at face value. You never really know what's inside people, or what they're capable of, do you?'

Cassie poured milk in her coffee, preferring not to answer.

'I'll leave you to it then,' said Mrs Chambers.

Now Cassie turned the pages more swiftly, looking for more about her father. She found a photo of Carlo's funeral. She looked at it closely. She could identify her father and Ricardo and Joe from their previous pictures in the paper. There was a little Italian woman in black so obviously distraught that she was almost being held up by someone. Cassie wondered who she was. Then, on one of the inside pages, she saw a small story that immediately caught her interest. It was headed 'Hollywood Notable Flies Home after Family Tragedy'.

Following was a story about Pietro d'Aquino, whose visit home to his family to share stories of his glamorous life in Hollywood as an art director and set designer was now blighted by the tragic death of his brother. The story hinted that Pietro might be nominated for an Oscar that year. Cassie smiled to herself, knowing that Pietro had subsequently won two Oscars.

She pressed on. She found stories about Patrick's committal hearing and some months later she read coverage of the first day of the trial. Then, in the very next issue, the paper led with the headline 'Local Boy Pleads Guilty to Death of Step-brother'.

Cassie gasped and sat up so violently that she knocked the coffee cup off the table. How can he have done such a terrible thing? she thought. How am I going to tell Mum? Maybe her father was not the man she had always thought him to be. She sat staring at the headline for some time before she could turn to the next page.

There were a lot of photographs of the participants, especially Joe and Ricardo Aquino, and locals waiting outside the Wollongong courthouse. The newspaper report conveyed the surprise of Patrick's sudden guilty plea and quoted the judge's comments about Patrick using a knife against an unarmed man, which were as harsh as the prison sentence he handed down. There were also photos of Joe and Ricardo, clearly distressed by the turn of events.

Poor, poor Dad, thought Cassie, very near to tears. I can't believe that you were sent to gaol for such a long time. And we never knew.

Cassie leaned back in her chair. After all this research she was still none the wiser about why Ricardo had left her a substantial bequest. She was not sure where she could go now.

She was about to leave the newspaper office and go back to the restaurant when a thought struck her and she returned to the news item about Pietro. She read it again. It wasn't the substance of the story that caught her attention but the timing of Pietro's visit. Had he been in Whitby Point when Carlo had died, or did he come from Los Angeles just for the funeral?

Cassie quickly flipped back through the old books, looking this time not for articles about her father, but ones about Pietro. She found two, both of which affirmed the excitement that Whitby Point felt for a local who had made good in the glamorous world of film. Cassie checked the dates on the articles. They were both written before Carlo's death. Looks like he was here when Carlo died, thought Cassie. She closed the bulky old cuttings book and sat deep in thought. Then she gathered her things and found Alison Chambers at the front desk.

'I'm done. Some of those old papers are just fascinating. Thank you so much for your help.'

'I haven't done anything. But I'm always happy to help if you need it. I'm just glad we're able to preserve all the old back copies. Were they useful?'

'A little, thank you. I have to say reading about the fifties in Whitby Point is very enlightening. I've learned a lot about life in the town in those days. It certainly was a boom time,' said Cassie.

'Yes. There's more to this place than first appears. Did you find out anything helpful about your father? By the way, my husband and I enjoyed a lovely lunch at the Blue Boatshed a while back.'

Cassie smiled broadly at her. 'That's lovely to know. I do hope you'll come back again. Dinner is more popular now the weather is getting warmer.'

When Cassie got back to the restaurant, Steve was beaming.

'We've got a lot of bookings for lunch, and all my suppliers have come good, including Frank. He wasn't gracious about selling me seafood but his father must have said something because he sold me some lovely stuff,' he told Cassie.

Trixie called out from the dining room. 'Mollie wants to come back, if you'll have her.'

'Of course I will. When can she start?' said Cassie. 'Mum, when lunch is over we need to have a talk.'

'I've got some interesting news to tell you, too,' Jenny said. 'But it can wait till later. We're all too busy to talk about family matters right now.'

Lunch indeed proved to be a very busy time. The restaurant hadn't had such a big crowd since Frank's visit. Just the same, Cassie noted that most of the diners were holidaymakers, there were very few locals. Still, she thought, as long as we can keep our reliable suppliers, the customers will keep coming, even if the locals take a while to come back.

After they had cleaned up and Steve began prepping for the evening meal, Jenny and Cassie made themselves a cup of tea and sat on the deck for a chat.

Cassie told Jenny what she had found in the newspaper records.

'I don't care what the records say. I don't believe your father would hurt anyone,' said Jenny.

'Mum, the papers said he pleaded guilty,' said Cassie gently.

'I don't know what the explanation is. I just know your father. He didn't do it,' said Jenny, shaking her head.

Bill was completely engrossed in the raw bone that Steve had given him on the condition that he eat it on the jetty. Even when Michael arrived Bill barely raised his head in acknowledgement.

'Do you mind if I join you, or is this a girls only get-together?' Michael asked.

Cassie jumped to her feet, hugged and kissed him and said, 'No, don't be silly. We're just comparing notes.' She told him what she had found in the newspaper files.

'I'm sorry. It's one shock after another for you two, isn't it?'

'Yes,' said Jenny. 'I just wish he'd told me. It would have made no difference to our relationship and it might have made things easier for him to have been able to share with me what had happened to him.'

'Another thing I found out, Michael, is that Pietro was here, staying in Whitby Point, when Carlo was killed. Isn't that interesting?' added Cassie.

'I suppose so,' said Jenny. 'Do you think he would be able to tell us anything?'

'I guess not,' said Cassie, 'if he wasn't on the boat.'

'Have you been doing detective work too, Jenny?' asked Michael.

'Actually I have. I managed to find out through Births, Deaths and Marriages that Bridget Sullivan married Giuseppe Aquino in 1933. Patrick would have been about five years old then.'

'And he was still in Whitby Point in 1957? He must have lived nearly all his early life here. So he really would have been part of the Aquino family; it's the only thing that makes sense. But now I'm even more muddled,' said Cassie. 'Why would my father never have mentioned the Aquinos and why don't any of the Aquinos know anything about him? I wish Ricardo was still alive, I have so many things that I want him to explain to me.'

Michael, who had been sitting very quietly while Jenny and Cassie talked, suddenly said, 'Pietro's still alive. Why don't we ask him?'

'I've only met him once. He probably wouldn't want to talk to me either, especially when he finds out that his brother left me all that money. I feel that the money will always come between me and the Aquinos,' said Cassie with a sigh.

'Well, it won't affect you and me,' said Michael. 'But I understand what you mean. It will make it hard for the two of us if the rest of the family don't understand Uncle Ricardo's motives. I think we should give Uncle Pietro a ring and ask him some questions about your father and where he fitted in with my family. Can't do any harm.'

'Who's going to ring? You or me? And what time is it in LA?' Michael was right. Pietro might have the answers.

'About midnight. I think I'll ring in the morning. It will be more civilised then.'

The restaurant was very busy that night as well. Jenny was in her element and clearly loved working in a restaurant again.

'I wouldn't want to make a habit of this,' she told Cassie when most of the clearing away and cleaning up had been done and Steve and Trixie had left. 'But it's nice to be back in the action again. There were certainly no complaints from the customers. They loved everything we served. This place is a credit to all the hard work you've done.'

'Thanks, Mum,' said Cassie. 'I appreciate that, coming from such an experienced restaurateur as you, but I could not have done it without a lot of very good help.'

'True, but even the best helpers in the world need to know that they have a dedicated leader who knows what she's doing. Now I'm off to my comfy bed. You sure you're all right on the sofa?'

The next day Cassie could hardly wait to hear from Michael to see if he had any answers from Pietro, so she was a bit surprised when he actually turned up at the Blue Boatshed.

'What happened? What did he say?' she asked eagerly before Michael even had a chance to come inside.

'Cassie, I spoke to him, but all he said was that it all happened a very long time ago and he thought it better to let sleeping dogs lie.'

Cassie looked at Michael in dismay. 'What now?' she asked.

'I think we should both fly to Los Angeles and confront Uncle Pietro.'

12

IN THE DISTANCE, BEYOND the walls and grounds of the classic French-style Chateau Marmont Hotel, Cassie and Michael were aware of the pulse of traffic on the nearby Strip heading into the heart of Hollywood.

'This place is insane,' whispered Cassie. 'Old Europe with a touch of Middle Eastern souk. A hotel whipped up by Baz Luhrmann! Whitby Point eat your heart out!'

'We're coming to see Pietro, a Hollywood legend in his own right, so why not experience another one? I think we deserve a bit of fun, so I thought I'd show you this place,' said Michael as they walked through the lobby of gothic archways, Tiffany lamps, padded and fringed velvet sofas, and deep plush armchairs with gold-tasselled cushions. A waiter with movie-star looks served a late afternoon tea, while another poured champagne into a crystal flute. Cassie stared at the opulence of the coffee house restaurant with its chandeliers and crisp linen.

'Getting a few ideas for the Blue Boatshed?' asked Michael with a chuckle.

'Don't think the brocade wallpaper would work at the Blue Boatshed somehow. The price of the food in this place must be astronomical! Are we going to eat in here or grab a hamburger down the road?'

'Let's eat here. It'll be fun on the garden terrace, seeing and being seen, like everyone else!'

'You're nuts. But I'm liking it,' said Cassie, laughing. 'Maybe we could bring Pietro here, though he probably has been here a zillion times.'

'Maybe, but he told me at Uncle Ricardo's party he doesn't go out much in the evening. He said he prefers brunch or lunch. I'm not sure whether he meant at the same time or not.'

'You said he didn't sound very enthusiastic about meeting us and talking about the past,' said Cassie anxiously.

'Yes, I think he was taken aback when I told him that we'd hopped on a plane and landed on his doorstep so that we could speak with him.'

'I still can't believe I'm here either. You certainly are a man of action, the way you organised someone to look after your practice so quickly. And, you know, I think Mum is really pleased to be running the restaurant for a few days and looking after Bill.'

'So start enjoying yourself. I know this is an emotional trip, and we mightn't learn anything, but if we don't ask Pietro, we'll never know. When he sees us and realises how troubled you are, I'm sure he'll be pleased to help.'

Cassie didn't answer as they were led out onto the garden terrace. Instead she caught her breath at the sight of the lovely restaurant with its comfortable wicker chairs and tables discreetly set amid the flowering vines and Canary Island date palms. Tiki torches flickered against the last of the sunset sky and the city lights of Los Angeles began to glow, creating a spectacular background.

She took the seat the maître d' offered her and refrained from glancing around, even though she just knew there must be famous people everywhere in the dim corners of the garden. Her attention was quickly taken by the menu as Michael ordered them a good Californian sparkling wine.

'Listen to this, Michael, some nice Californian cuisine touches – fresh peach bellinis, sun-kissed stuffed dates with honey and fig puree and gin negronis.'

'I'm hanging out for the "Damn Good Burger". He lifted his glass of sparkling wine. 'Here's to us, Cassie.' They touched glasses.

'Thank you for bringing me here. This place is certainly OTT and expensive, but so lovely.'

'Our hotel is nice but not as flash as this one, so I thought it'd be worth every cent to be here with you and share the experience,' Michael smiled. 'I haven't had a break in a long, long time. All I seem to do is work and occasionally surf, although I do visit this really classy little eatery called the Blue Boatshed. I like the food and the ambience, and I love its owner more than I can say.'

Cassie smiled but still looked troubled. 'Oh, Michael, that's lovely but I just can't get rid of the uncomfortable feeling I have about Ricardo's bequest. I won't be happy about that money until I find out why he left it to me. It's all too bizarre.'

A shadow crossed Michael's face. 'Cassie, it's yours for whatever reason. Stop worrying.'

She nodded but still looked unhappy. 'Okay,' she said. As the waiter hovered to discuss the menu, she turned to give him her full attention. They ordered, and then she and Michael talked about movies and theatre, museums and travel. After a very enjoyable dinner, they had coffee in the main lounge and watched the trendsetters sashay past, all angling to be noticed.

'Do you want to go on to a club? There's a good blues and jazz place not far from here,' said Michael.

'Do you mind if we don't make it a late night? I'm still jet-lagged and worried about tomorrow,' Cassie replied, frowning again. 'I'm scared Pietro might not tell me anything but then what if he tells me things I don't want to hear? Afterwards I might wish I'd never asked.'

Michael took her hand and they walked to the front entrance, where he asked the doorman to get them a taxi. 'I can understand that you must feel anxious,' he said sympathically.

'Pietro is the only person still alive who knew my father when he was young and I have so many questions I want to ask him,' Cassie said as the taxi drove away from the Chateau Marmont.

'Cassie, Cassie,' said Michael, sighing. 'It will all be fine, you'll see.' He took her in his arms and kissed her. She returned his kiss, lost in his now familiar smell and the taste of his lips. As they drove up to the entrance of their boutique hotel off Sunset Boulevard, the doorman smiled at them as he opened the car door. 'Evening, sir, madam.'

*

The next morning, wrapped in fluffy towelling robes, Cassie and Michael sat on their small balcony enjoying croissants and fresh fruit. Stately old palm trees floated on the distant boulevards through the morning haze.

'It's not quite the blue sky or fresh air of home,' said Michael.

'I'm giving up on this tea. It's a teabag in lukewarm water. Can I have some of your coffee, please?'

'Sure. Or there's fresh OJ.' He smiled at her. 'Are you ready for the next big event?'

'As ready as I'll ever be, I guess. Just got to get dressed and then we'll go,' Cassie replied. 'But I'm still nervous,' she added softly.

Their cab wound into the Hollywood Hills, around steep bends where tall trees screened private homes.

'Isn't this fabulous? You'd think Cary Grant or Ginger Rogers might step out of one of the doors,' exclaimed Cassie.

'All very art deco. Built in the twenties or thirties,' replied Michael.

The driver told them the names of movie stars from years past who'd lived in these secluded streets, and eventually pulled into a circular driveway in front of a modest bungalow.

'What a gorgeous old house,' said Cassie as they got out of the cab and walked across the gravel driveway. The house was sheltered by mature trees that leaned against each other. A climbing rose clung to a lattice on the stucco walls.

'This is just so romantic,' said Cassie.

'It's in better condition than some of its neighbours,' said Michael as he peered through the trees at the surrounding houses. 'They could use a bit of TLC.'

'A few grand dames starting to show their age,' agreed Cassie.

The door was answered by a tall and still attractive elderly man with thick white hair, perfect teeth and tanned skin, immaculately dressed in a powder-blue checked shirt with the cuffs turned back and the collar standing up.

'Hello, Michael,' he said in a soft American accent as he shook Michael's hand.

'How are you, George? You're looking great,' said Michael warmly. 'George, this is Cassie.'

391

George smiled at Cassie and gestured for them to enter. 'Pleased to meet you, Cassie. Come on inside. We don't get family dropping by very often.'

The rooms of the house were surprisingly small and cottage-like, and decorated in chintzy shabby chic. Silver-framed photos were on every surface and the walls were covered in paintings and photographs. A series of framed prints of set designs caught Cassie's eye.

George ushered them into a sunny sitting room that opened onto a small terrace with a view towards the city. Pietro, who was seated in a white wicker chair, rose stiffly to greet them.

'Don't get up, Uncle Pietro, please.' Michael went to embrace his great-uncle.

Pietro smiled and held out a hand to Cassie. 'Hello, pretty lady. I remember you. Ricardo's birthday. I'm pleased to see you two are still together. Is this leading somewhere serious?'

'Pietro, don't pry,' interjected George.

Pietro chuckled. 'Would you like something to drink? Juice? Coffee? Tea? We have proper tea,' he said.

'I'd love a cup of tea if it's going,' said Cassie.

'Me too, thank you,' added Michael.

'George knows how to make it, but it took me years to teach him how to do it properly. I'll have fresh juice, please, George.' George headed to the kitchen and Pietro said, 'Sit down, you two. What have you been up to?'

Michael answered quickly. 'We had dinner at Chateau Marmont last night. That was quite an experience.'

Pietro rolled his eyes. 'It's a tourist mecca now. In its heyday it was such fun. Lots of naughty behaviour and anyone who was anyone stayed there. George loathes it now so we never go. Mind you, we don't go out a lot these days, but we like to entertain old friends here. Those who are still around,' he added ruefully.

'Cassie, Uncle Pietro and George have been together a long time,' said Michael.

'We met not long after I first started working here. He's younger than me, but not by much,' he said, his eyes twinkling.

'Has George ever been to Australia?' asked Cassie.

'No, George hates flying. If he can't go by car, he won't go. And I don't think he'd find a lot to do in Whitby Point.'

George came in with a tray set with cups, a teapot and a glass of orange juice, which he handed to Pietro. 'I disagree. I've seen photos and it looks charming. Very scenic. I'd love to paint it,' he said as he poured the tea.

'George is a bit of an artist. Those are some of his paintings,' said Pietro, casually pointing to a couple of delicately detailed watercolours of gardens and flowers. Despite his manner, Cassie heard the pride in his voice.

'They're lovely! Do you exhibit and sell your work, George?' asked Cassie.

'A little. I used to be the one who put Pietro's dreams and designs on paper at the studio. When I retired, I started painting in watercolours. There's a gallery in Santa Monica that takes what I give them, but I only paint when I feel like it now.' He handed Cassie and Michael a cup of tea each.

'We were hoping that you'd stay and have lunch with us,' continued Pietro. 'Consuela – you remember her from your last visit, Michael – has made her famous chili and guacamole.'

'Thank you, Uncle. That sounds lovely. Maybe we'll be able to reciprocate sometime during our trip,' said Michael.

George gave both Cassie and Michael a smile. 'Let's play it by ear, shall we? I'm sure we'll be seeing more of you.'

Michael moved the low stool he was sitting on nearer to Pietro. 'Uncle, you know why we're here? I told you about it when I rang.'

Pietro gave a theatrical shrug. 'Oh, lordy, what now? As I told you on the phone, I try to keep out of family dramas. I don't understand what all the fuss is about.'

'Uncle, it's not really about me, it's Cassie. She has so many questions she'd like to ask you.'

Pietro smiled at Cassie. 'Yes, Michael explained to me over the phone your relationship with my family. I expect you're very pleased about the money Ricardo left you.'

Cassie didn't smile back. 'Since I found out about Ricardo's will my life has turned upside down,' she said. 'My mother and I . . . we never knew anything about my father and the Aquinos and now I need to know.'

'Are you sure you want to? It was such a long time ago,' said Pietro.

'Uncle, I brought Cassie here because you are the only person who can tell her about her father Patrick, and I think she has the right to know.'

Pietro was silent for some time before he said, 'Pat was a quiet boy, kind and always a good person. We got on really well. It was a wonderful thing when he and his mother came to live with us. Our mother died when Carlo was born, and Ricardo and I were still very young.'

'So Joe married my grandmother Bridget. Is that right?'

'Bridie, everyone called her Bridie. She changed our lives. We all adored her. As sweet as a bird, she was. She met my father on the ship out to Australia but she was engaged to another man. Papà said that it broke his heart when she left him at the wharf.'

'So she married my grandfather Sullivan, then? Do you know what happened to him?' Cassie asked. She felt excitement welling up inside her as Pietro spoke.

'I think he died during the Depression. The story Bridie used to tell us was that she was struggling to raise Pat by herself when she met Papà again by coincidence one day in Sydney. He persuaded her to come back with him to Whitby Point and a short time later they were married.'

'She must have been special for all of you to have liked her.'

'She was. So lively and fun and she always took an interest in everything that we did. I loved her. If it hadn't been for Bridie, I probably would have ended up in the fishing industry. She encouraged me to take an interest in the stage. When I was involved in a local production, she insisted that all the family come to watch me. It was an awful show, but she made me feel as though it was wonderful and that I was its star. Then she took me to see a professional production in Sydney. That really opened my eyes. When I said I wanted to become involved with plays and the theatre, she didn't laugh, but helped me to find a way to do it.'

'She sounds like a very understanding person,' said Cassie. 'I wish I had known her.'

'She wasn't just understanding. She was brave and very loyal. During the war Papà was interned as an enemy alien. A lot of Italians were locked up.' Pietro turned and looked at Michael. 'I bet you didn't know that, my boy. Papà was always so ashamed that the government thought he wasn't much better than a common criminal. Anyway, Bridie wasn't going to leave him in an internment camp for the duration, so she started a petition to have him released. She got thousands of signatures. She badgered the mayor, the local MP, the priest, even the CWA, until Papà was freed.'

'I didn't know anything about that,' said Michael. 'She sounds remarkable.'

'During the war she drove the fish truck up to Sydney. The business was short on manpower and she decided that the best way she could help was to drive the truck. The road to Sydney was pretty awful in those days and right at the end of the war she was killed in a terrible traffic accident on her way home.' Even after all the intervening years, Pietro's voice was still filled with emotion as he told the story.

'That is so sad,' said Cassie. 'It's strange to hear about a grandmother whom I never knew and yet she was so special to you and your family.'

Suddenly Pietro stood up, as though something important had occurred to him. 'Excuse me a minute, I have something that I'd like to show you.' Pietro walked out of the room and the other three sat in silence awaiting his return. He was back in less than a minute, holding a little box, which he gave to Cassie.

'Open it,' he told her.

Cassie peered inside the little box and took out a simple ring set with a red stone.

'This ring originally belonged to my father,' said Pietro. 'It was given to him by his grandmother when he left Sicily and she told him to sell it when he needed money. Evidently, when he first came to Australia he pawned the ring, but Bridie went and bought it back and gave it to Papà. Then he gave her the ring on their wedding day.'

'No way!' exclaimed Cassie. 'How beautiful.'

'It's not valuable, you understand, but when Papà died I asked Ricardo if I could keep the ring as a reminder of a beautiful and wonderful person. This ring would mean nothing to anyone else but, as Bridie was your grandmother, I would like you to have it.'

Cassie's eyes filled with tears and her hand shook. 'Thank you so much. I will always treasure it, if you are quite sure that you can part with it.'

'I've got two Oscars because of your grandmother's belief in me. The least I can do is return this ring to her granddaughter.'

'Where are the Oscars? I'd love to see them,' asked Cassie.

'Oh, back there, somewhere.' Pietro waved his hand vaguely. 'I always think that it's tacky to have them on display. I'll show them to you later if you like.'

'Did my father work in the fishing industry?' Cassie asked him. She was starting to realise that, while Pietro was happy to talk about Bridie, he seemed reluctant to say much about her father.

'Pat and Carlo worked for Papà but Ricardo, being the eldest, was destined to take over the business.' He shifted uneasily in his seat. 'George, can you get me some more juice or some water? I need a drink, I've been talking so much.'

'I'll get some water for you,' Michael offered.

'Thank you. That would be nice.'

As Michael headed for the kitchen, Cassie asked, 'Tell me what else you remember about my father. Was he smart at school?'

'He was pretty smart. Bridie encouraged him to stay at school. Actually she and Papà encouraged us all to stay as long as possible, so your father did. As I remember, Carlo left school the minute he could but the rest of us stayed till the end. I don't think Patrick had any real interests outside of fishing and the beach. He loved to body surf. He did like to help Nonna in the kitchen sometimes. Nonna was Papà's mother who came out to Australia to look after us when our mother died. She was a great cook and Patrick used to ask her how to make things. I wasn't above helping Nonna either. I still use some of her recipes, even after all these years.'

Cassie noticed that Pietro, even when asked a direct question about her father, chose to talk about another member of the family.

Michael returned with Pietro's drink as Cassie started to ask another question.

'Did you often go back to Whitby Point after you left for America? I noticed that you were home when . . . the, um, accident happened. I saw your photo in the local paper, and I've been wondering if you know anything more about what happened than what was reported in the paper.'

Pietro shook his head. 'It was a long time ago. I don't remember all the details,' he said, turning his head away.

For whatever reason, it appeared to Cassie that the death of Carlo was off limits.

Then George spoke. He had been sitting quietly in the corner of the room listening to the conversation but now he briefly took centre stage. 'As you say, Pietro, it was a long time ago and I don't think that at this point in time it would do any harm at all to tell this girl the truth about her father. I think that it is the least you owe her. You must tell her what happened out on the boat the day of your brother's death.'

Cassie and Michael stared at George and turned to look at Pietro, who was still looking away from them, staring across the sprawl of the City of Angels. He was silent, but his mouth was working as he chewed his lip.

Michael turned to his great-uncle. 'Please, Uncle Pietro, is there anything you can tell Cassie to help her understand what happened?'

Eventually, after what seemed to be an age, Pietro turned and faced Michael and Cassie.

'George is right. It is time for me to tell you both what really happened on the *Celestine*. You see, I was on that boat.'

Cassie inhaled sharply. Whatever she had expected Pietro to tell her, this was a complete surprise. She didn't know what to say about this revelation, so she said nothing.

Pietro's eyes stared at nothing in particular and, when he spoke again, Cassie realised that the old man had travelled back to that winter's day in Whitby Point in 1957.

*

'Pietro, don't be such a sissy. What's the point coming all the way to Australia if you don't want to share some special time with us? You might never have the chance to do this again. Come on, Pietro, be a sport,' cajoled Ricardo.

'He thinks he's too famous to go on an old fishing boat. Been mixing with the movie stars so he's too good for us now,' said Carlo.

'We won't be out too long, and you can't go fishing with the best fishermen in Australia when you're back in Hollywood,' added Patrick.

Pietro flung up his arms. 'All right, okay! I'll come. I'll just tell Nonna what I'm doing so she doesn't go looking for me.'

'Don't worry about her. I think she's asleep. Come on, everyone, time's a-wasting,' said Ricardo.

They all hurried to the wharf where the *Celestine* was tied up and jumped on board.

'Do you have a spare jacket I can wear?' asked Pietro.

'There's a rain slicker inside the cockpit, but you won't need it. It's a fine day. Let's go. Cast off, Carlo.' Ricardo turned his attention to starting the engine and then pointed the boat towards the open sea.

'I'll help rig you a line, Pietro,' Patrick offered.

After they left the harbour, the sea started to become choppy. Patrick braced himself and began to organise some lines with efficiency born of practice. He laughed as Pietro clung to the side of the boat.

'Look at you, Pietro,' said Patrick. 'You've certainly lost your sea legs.'

'I think you must have been born with sea water in your veins,' Pietro replied grimly.

'I doubt it. Probably my family were potato farmers,' said Patrick.

'Well, if they were you'd never know it from the way you manage at sea.'

'Thanks. I'm not as good as Papà, though. He's still the grand *capo* – the big boss!' said Patrick with a laugh. 'But I do love it out here. The sea, the wind, the hunt. These challenges all make me feel alive.'

'Will you stay here in Whitby Point, Pat, in the business?' Pietro asked.

'I assume so,' replied Patrick. 'I like it here. I like to handle the fish, to talk to buyers, especially the restaurant people. I like to know the different ways they plan to use the fish they've bought.'

'I suppose if you don't go on fishing you could always become a cook, a chef,' teased Pietro.

'I wouldn't think so, but who knows?' said Patrick with a shrug and a smile.

They had been out for less than an hour when the weather started to close in. Rolling dark clouds rumbled from the horizon towards them, causing the old *Celestine* to pitch and roll.

'Should we turn back to port?' called Pietro. 'Do you know what the forecast is, Ricardo?'

'Nothing major, as far as I know. Could get a bit rough, but nothing we can't handle. There's a good reef shelf a little further out. Let's give it a go,' shouted Ricardo.

'Are you okay?' Patrick asked Pietro, who was not looking at all happy.

'A bit queasy. If I'd known that there was going to be such a change in the weather I wouldn't have let you lot talk me into coming. I don't like the look of those clouds.'

'It's just a bit of a squall. Rain won't hurt you,' said Carlo. 'Not unless you really have got used to the soft life in Hollywood.'

'We haven't had a lot of success with the fish. I hope this is worth it,' muttered Pietro to Patrick.

'Don't complain to Ricardo. It's never the skipper's fault!'

After another hour they decided to give up. The deteriorating weather made it too hard to catch fish in the heaving sea.

'Let's pack this in,' suggested Patrick.

'Suits me,' said Pietro with alacrity.

'But we've caught nothing. I told you we should have gone where I said,' grumbled Carlo to Ricardo.

'You want to take over, little brother?' snapped Ricardo.

'Let's just head back,' pleaded Pietro, pulling up his line. 'I think I'm dying.'

Everyone's mood was as bleak as the weather when Ricardo turned the *Celestine* towards the coast. The rain lashed them in spewing gusts; waves washed across the bow and surged along the deck. Pietro huddled against the leeside of the cockpit, hugging a rainjacket around himself. Carlo struggled unsuccessfully to light a cigarette and Patrick started packing the gear away.

'Hey, Pat,' shouted Ricardo from the wheelhouse, 'leave some lines and the gaff out. There's one last spot we can try on the way in. Can't let Pietro go back to the US without catching a decent fish.'

'Don't worry about that, Ricardo, let's just go home,' called Pietro. 'The weather is atrocious.'

'Why are we going to some spot you know when everywhere you've taken us has been no good?' shouted Carlo. 'Go to the spot I told you about. Why don't you ever listen to me, Ricardo?'

'I'm the skipper,' Ricardo reminded him. 'You don't know everything, Carlo.'

'It's too rough, we won't land anything in this weather, no matter where we go,' said Patrick.

'We're not going back without something to show for our time out here. I'm not going to disappoint Pietro. Set some rods, come on, let's trawl,' Ricardo yelled to his brothers.

'If anything hits one of the rods, it's going to be the devil to land it in this sea,' Patrick said to Pietro. 'But he's the boss.'

Ricardo slowed the boat, angling it against the wind, and quickly threw out his favourite lure and jammed the rod into a holder before he went back to the wheel. Patrick and Carlo set their lines. Pietro tried to keep out of the wind, refusing to fish.

Carlo was fishing next to Ricardo's rod. Suddenly, with a high-pitched scream of the line, Ricardo's rod bent in a deep curve, bowing towards the water. Carlo grabbed the rod to lock the spinning, unravelling line.

'Don't touch my rod, I'm coming!' Ricardo yelled, jamming the engine into neutral. Leaping to the side of the boat, he pushed Carlo to one side as he lifted the rod from its holder.

'Fuck off, Ricardo! First hand on the rod gets to play it.'

'Well, I'm here now and I'm playing it.'

Suddenly, before the argument could develop any further, Carlo's rod pinged and his line began to scream off the reel. He reached for the rod, trying to get purchase on the slippery deck as he strained against the weight and speed of the big fish he'd hooked.

'What is it?' Pietro shouted to Patrick, who was reeling in his own line in order to help Ricardo and Carlo.

'Probably a yellowfin.'

Ricardo and Carlo stood beside each other, wildly playing the fish fighting at the ends of their lines.

'We can land only one of these. Let yours go,' panted Ricardo. 'Or I'll cut your line.'

'Back off,' screamed Carlo, fighting to turn the ratchet on his reel a full circle. 'I've got this one and I'm not letting it go just because you say so.'

Patrick picked up the gaff and stood behind both men as they fought to bring in their fish. 'Don't know how you're going to be able to land two big energetic fish side by side. Carlo, you could make room by walking your rod down to the stern.'

'Piss off, Pat. Tell Ricardo to get out of my way.'

'We only need one fish,' shouted Pietro.

With the wheel unattended the boat began to circle, turning broadside into the wind.

'Pietro, grab the wheel, straighten us up,' called Patrick. 'I'll wait here with the gaff and see if I can help land at least one of these fish.'

Ricardo turned to look towards the bow of the *Celestine*, which took his attention away from his rod. In those couple of seconds he misjudged the tension on his line and with a loud bang his line broke, sending him staggering backwards.

As Patrick jumped to grab hold of Ricardo's rod, he dropped the gaff hook overboard. He swore to himself.

Ricardo regained his footing and looked around for Patrick, who handed him back his rod. Patrick then went to where Carlo had moved further along the side of the little vessel. He was struggling against the wind and the sea but gradually, little by little, he began to reel in the fish.

'Ricardo, get that wheel from Pietro and turn the boat. Pat, give me a hand and be ready to strike this bastard when I get him alongside,' shouted Carlo.

'Where's the net?' Patrick looked quickly around for it. Pietro and Carlo let out a whoop as the fish on Carlo's line leapt through the surface of the thrashing sea.

It was a big fish and Carlo was now reefing it in quickly. 'Don't want to lose this one! Help me get it over the side!'

'Pietro, take the wheel again. Just keep it pointed in the same direction. Pat's lost the gaff so I'll go and help land the monster, and then stab it in the brain with this,' said Ricardo as he grabbed the long-bladed bait knife.

In all the confusion Patrick couldn't find the landing net so he braced himself against the gunwale, leaning over the side of the boat, ready to help grasp Carlo's line as the massive fish banged against the hull.

Ricardo pushed himself against the side of the boat to help land the fish, but Carlo elbowed him to one side.

'It's mine!' he screamed. 'Leave it alone. I want to land it myself.'

At that moment the sea and the wind and the momentum of the rolling boat seemed to converge and rock the men together as one. Carlo heaved his rod back into the boat, Patrick grabbed a fin of the tuna in his gloved hand and Ricardo fell against Carlo. They all went down on the deck, the fish pounding and quivering beneath them.

Pietro struggled with the wheel. He had forgotten how hard it was to keep the boat pointing into the wind and he glanced over his shoulder to see if someone was coming to help him. He could see the blood from the fish running down the deck as it continued to thrash about.

Patrick regained his feet first and hauled Ricardo off Carlo. 'Jesus, what happened? That's some fish!'

Ricardo pulled himself up, the bait knife still in his hand, and they both went to help Carlo as the fish slid towards the stern. But as they did so, they realised that the blood sluicing along the deck came not from the fish, but from a wound under Carlo's chest.

'Oh, dear God! Carlo!' Ricardo bent over his brother,

cradling him in his arms and looking from Carlo to Patrick with horror-struck eyes.

'Full throttle, Pietro. Go! Go!' shouted Patrick.

The *Celestine* surged forward, crashing into waves, her hull banging over the rising waves and racing down the troughs, her occupants heedless of the water pouring over them.

Ricardo held his limp brother in his arms, while blood gushed from the deep knife wound beneath Carlo's ribs. 'Carlo, Carlo. Pat, get the first aid kit.'

Patrick was already using a towel to try and stop the flow of blood.

'Carlo, Carlo. It'll be okay, speak to me, Carlo,' cried Ricardo.

Patrick continued to push on the wound. 'He doesn't look good, Ricardo.'

'This was an accident. Mother of God! Hurry up, Pietro!' Ricardo screamed.

'We can't go faster!' called Pietro. 'Can't you stop the bleeding?'

'We're trying.' Patrick looked at Ricardo. They both knew that time was running out for Carlo. The towel was soaked in his blood, his breathing was shallow and he was deathly pale.

'This can't be happening. Oh God, Papà, Papà, Papà, help us.' Ricardo began praying, his words whipped away by the wind.

'There's the coast, we'll get out of the worst of this soon,' said Patrick.

But then Carlo's head lolled to one side. Ricardo sank back on his heels, his face in his hands, his shoulders heaving. 'It's too late,' he said. 'He's gone.' The whole incident had taken just a couple of minutes.

The wind and a wall of water hit the *Celestine*. Pietro struggled at the wheel, glancing back to where Ricardo and Patrick were huddled over Carlo. Pietro felt bile rise in his throat. Then Patrick came into the wheelhouse.

'Should I radio for help, Pat?' cried Pietro. But as he looked at Patrick's face, he put the radio down. Tears streamed down Pietro's face as he handed the wheel to Patrick.

Slipping and staggering from the rough bouncing of the boat and feeling sick to his stomach and almost ready to faint, Pietro reached his brothers. He fell to his knees beside Carlo.

'He's gone,' said Ricardo brokenly. 'It is my fault.'

'It was an accident, Ricardo. Oh my God, Papà . . . this will shatter him,' said Pietro.

'Oh my God! This is a nightmare!' Ricardo was almost hysterical.

For several moments, they both stared helplessly at the lifeless body of their brother, unable to believe what had happened.

There was a brief lull in the wind and over it Ricardo and Pietro could hear Patrick's voice, calm and remarkably in control. 'Ricardo, Pietro,' Patrick called. 'Get the blanket, put it over Carlo. We must talk about this.' He slowed the engine.

Leaving Carlo's body, Ricardo and Pietro huddled beside Patrick as he watched the sea ahead, steering the boat between the waves.

'We will have to think very carefully about what we say,' said Patrick.

'What do you mean?' asked Ricardo. 'It was an accident. The knife was meant for the fish.' His eyes widened. 'Won't people believe us?'

'Yes, it *was* an accident.' Patrick replied firmly. 'But consider the ramifications if we tell the authorities the truth. You will be closely questioned. You have dependants, Ricardo. How will it be if Rosina and the children are dragged into this? And Papà? What will it do to him to learn that one of his sons has killed the other, no matter how accidental? How will he cope?' He looked from one brother to the other. 'Pietro, do you want everyone to know that you were on the boat when the accident occurred? You are flying home shortly and an enquiry will be sure to delay you. And what if those Academy people in Hollywood find out about your involvement in this? Any scandal could ruin your chances of an Oscar.'

'I suppose so,' Pietro replied slowly. 'But what do you propose to do? We can't throw Carlo overboard.'

'No, of course not. I'm going to say that I was the one who was holding the knife. There will have to be an enquiry. Ricardo will back my story and say that it was an accident and that will be the end of it. Even though I am part of this family, my name is not Aquino. If I say I was responsible for Carlo's death the Aquino name will not be disgraced and Papà won't be shamed. Joe Aquino is the only father I know, and I won't let him down. Pietro, you can say that you went to the pictures or something. If we don't tell anyone that you were on the boat, you can't be involved in any scandal.'

'I can't let you take the blame, Pat,' said Ricardo vehemently. 'That's a stupid idea.'

'Think about it, Ricardo. Patrick has a point,' said Pietro. 'Do we really want Papà to have to face the knowledge that no matter how accidental the death of Carlo was, one of his own sons was responsible? No, I think we should spare our father that. As Patrick says, if we get our stories straight nothing will come of it anyway.'

'But I was the one arguing with Carlo. Over that damn fish . . . '

Ricardo's voice cracked and suddenly he rushed to the stern of the boat where the fish lay shuddering, gasping

407

for oxygen. He grabbed the knife, stabbing the fish and shouting incoherently, as Pietro and Patrick watched. Finally he lifted the fish and flung it overboard.

Ricardo leaned down to pick up the knife but Patrick shouted, 'No, no! Don't throw it, Ricardo. No! It will make things look worse!' Patrick gave the wheel to Pietro and made his way to the stern where Ricardo stood with the bloodied knife, crying soundlessly.

Gently, Patrick took the knife from him. 'Ricardo, listen to me. This is what we must do. I will say it was me. We have to do this for Papà, Rosina and your family. But we have to keep this a secret between the three of us for the rest of our lives. Understand? Believe me, it will be for the best.'

'Pat, will this work? Is it the best thing? I am a man. I should stand up and say I was holding the knife.'

'And break your father's heart? You can't do that.'

Ricardo nodded. 'Poor Nonna and Papà. What about Greta? Who will tell them?'

'You must. I will go to the police when we land,' said Patrick. 'The weather's turned so foul there probably won't be anyone around to see us come in, so Pietro can slip ashore quietly. Come on, Ricardo, trust me. This is the best way for everyone. And nothing will come of it. It was an accident, after all.'

*

Pietro's gaze returned from the past but he continued to look out the window as if to avoid the shocked faces of Michael and Cassie.

'Uncle Pietro,' said Michael carefully, 'you're telling us that you and Uncle Ricardo let a man go to gaol for something he didn't do and never gave anyone a word of explanation? To say that I'm appalled is to put it mildly. Cassie, are you all right?'

'Not really. It seems that my father sacrificed a lot, all those wasted years in gaol, starting a new life and never being able to tell his wife or daughter what had really happened. He suffered in silence and we could never share his pain, while the Aquino family prospered.' Cassie almost spat the words out. 'It doesn't seem at all fair to me.'

Michael stared hard at his great-uncle. 'Uncle Pietro, I don't understand why you all let it happen,' he said.

Pietro held up his hands in a gesture of helplessness. 'Neither Ricardo nor I wanted things to work out as they did, but events spiralled out of our control. At first everyone believed that what had happened on the boat was an accident, but then a police sergeant from Wollongong took over the investigation. It became evident that he thought a conviction would be a shortcut to a promotion and he started to ask questions about your father. He found out that Carlo and your father used to argue. It didn't matter that Carlo argued with everyone. Michael, I know that he was your grandfather, but it has to be said that he was aggressive and liked to have his own way and make his own point about everything. Unfortunately, just before the accident on the *Celestine*, Carlo and Pat had a very public fight at a dance and the police used that piece of evidence against Pat to show that there had been long-standing hostility between the two of them.'

'But if the case was going pear-shaped, why didn't you or Ricardo speak out and tell the truth?' asked Michael.

Pietro shook his head sadly. 'Michael, please don't think that didn't occur to us. Ricardo called me after the first day of the trial. He was not at all happy with the way things were going. He told Pat that he was going into court to tell the truth. Pat told him not to be so stupid and that if he did that the jurors would think that he was covering up for Pat and it wouldn't help either of them. According to Ricardo, they had quite a row. Ricardo asked me what he should do. He hated what was happening to Pat and I said that if he really felt that way, he should tell the truth.'

Cassie was about to ask what had stopped Ricardo from telling the truth in court, when she suddenly realised the answer. 'Dad pleaded guilty to prevent Ricardo from saying anything, didn't he?' she whispered. 'He didn't want Ricardo to incriminate himself.'

Pietro nodded. 'Yes, that's what he did. He thought that if Ricardo testified, the issue would become even more complicated. Unfortunately his change of plea had a negative effect on the judge and resulted in a much harsher sentence. I'm so sorry, Cassie. Maybe this is not what you really wanted to hear.'

Cassie looked at Pietro and saw tears silently trickling down his wrinkled cheeks. 'My poor, poor father,' she whispered. 'And he never broke his word. He never told anyone the truth.'

George broke in, 'Well, it's about time that the truth was told. I mean all of the truth, Pietro.'

'What else is there to tell?' asked Michael.

Pietro slowly nodded his head. 'George is right. The story didn't end with Pat going to gaol. Ricardo and I were devastated by what had happened, as you can imagine. Ricardo talked our father into letting him move his family to Sydney to fish, but really it was so that he could be closer to Long Bay Gaol and able to visit Pat more frequently. But the fishing off Sydney was not good and Ricardo couldn't justify staying there. It was Patrick who suggested that Ricardo should start a tuna-fishing business in South Australia. The two of them worked on Papà, who eventually agreed that it would be a sensible move. So Ricardo and his family moved to Port Lincoln for a few years. Pat was right. It did turn out to be a profitable venture for the Aquinos.'

'What happened to my father when he was released from prison?' Cassie said.

'Your father didn't want to go back to Whitby Point because everyone in the town believed he was responsible for Carlo's death. Patrick said there was no future for him there, and he didn't want to have to face Papà anymore. Although Papà still loved him and wanted him to be part of the family, I think your father found that Papà's visits to him in gaol were just too difficult. Maybe it was just too hard for your father to keep the truth from Papà. All the lies, keeping the secret. It was too much for Pat to see the loss and pain in Papà's eyes. Patrick felt that it was easier to just walk away, leave everything behind and start a new life.'

Pietro blinked hard, wiping his face with the back of his hand, before he continued. 'But Ricardo refused to let Patrick just disappear. He told him that he would put up some money to enable Pat to start a business. Patrick accepted his offer on the condition that Ricardo never tell Joe. Patrick decided that he would open a fish and chip shop in Manly because it combined the two things he knew, fish and cooking. Then when your father mentioned to Ricardo that he would like to expand into a seafood restaurant, Ricardo helped him finance that as well. Over the years, Ricardo often met up with your father in Sydney and they would talk about the Seven Seas and Pat would tell Ricardo about you and your mother as well. Ricardo was always so pleased with all of Pat's success.'

'I said you should tell all the truth – that it wasn't just Ricardo who helped set up the Seven Seas restaurant,' said George. 'You did as well.'

'So you two paid my father money for going to gaol instead of Ricardo? Guilt money?' said Cassie acerbically.

'I suppose it was in a way. Money to try and make up for all those lost years. But, Cassie, you also have to remember that Italian families are always there for each other.

My father spent his whole life sending money back home to Italy for his family, so we thought that we were doing much the same thing for Pat. Heavens, we owed him enough.' Pietro looked down and shielded his eyes with his hand. 'But in the end we did it because he was family and we loved him,' he added softly.

'Do you ever regret what happened?' asked Michael. Pietro raised his head and looked straight at Cassie.

'Of course. All of us regretted it. It was a terrible mistake. Looking back, I can see that we panicked. We misjudged what was really important. Patrick thought he was doing the right thing, trying to protect Ricardo, Papà and me. Because he was a Sullivan and not an Aquino he thought he would be protecting the Aquino name. But the truth would not have hurt Papà, he loved all of us,' said Pietro.

Cassie started to cry softly. Michael took her hand as Pietro continued. 'Pat's plan and our decision to go along with it were stupid. What we did created an outcome that no one wanted. It may not have completely ruined Pat's life, but it certainly sent it off course. It broke Papà's heart when Pat disappeared from his life, and Ricardo and I have had to live with our guilt ever since. I was awarded two Oscars but I think that the price paid for them was way too high. I know that people always want to wind back time, but if we could have that time over, with better judgement, things could have been so different.'

Cassie looked at the tired old man. Although what he had told her was horrible and shocking, his words had vindicated her father. 'In a way I can understand what you're saying,' she said through her tears. 'When my mother and I found out that Dad had pleaded guilty, Mum didn't believe for a moment that he was, but I did. I am ashamed that I thought that way. I suppose people can make the wrong choice sometimes.'

'The money that Ricardo left Cassie – was that also part of doing the right thing by Patrick?' asked Michael.

'Yes. Dear Cassie, Ricardo left you a bequest as part of his ongoing debt to your father. The sad thing is that when he met you, he had no idea that you were Pat's daughter. He would have been very pleased to have known you on those terms and to know what a lovely person Cassie Sullivan is.' Pietro gave her a small bow from his chair.

'It was a kind thought of Uncle Ricardo's, but it has brought me problems because none of the Aquinos understand why he left me money. It's created so many difficulties. It makes me think that perhaps I shouldn't accept it,' said Cassie.

George moved in his chair, and turned towards Pietro. 'I am so pleased that you have opened your heart, my dear, and told this lovely young girl the truth, but I think Cassie needs more than just that.'

'What do you mean?' asked Pietro.

'I think we should ask our attorney friend Maurie to take down a statement that Cassie and Michael can take back to your family to explain why Ricardo left Cassie the money.'

'What an excellent idea. It will save me having to field questions from Australia and rehash the whole thing again. So clever. Now I'm feeling very tired and I think I'll lie down. But please, go and share lunch with George. Consuela will be so upset if you don't eat her chili.' Pietro rose unsteadily to his feet and walked to the door. He turned and looked at Cassie. 'Welcome back to the family, my dear.'

Whitby Point, one year later

The last of the guests lingered on the deck of the Blue Boatshed in the balmy night air. The candles had burned low, and the glasses and coffee cups were empty.

'What a fantastic celebration dinner. Congratulations again, Cass,' said Trixie.

'Honestly, the Blue Boatshed wouldn't have won this great foodie award without you all. I can't believe how my life has changed since I first came here.' Cassie smiled at Michael.

'We're putting Blue Crane Lake on the map!' said Steve. 'We had people in yesterday from Canberra who drove here after reading the review in the food section of their Saturday paper.'

'Don't overdo it, luv,' said Geoff. 'Don't want Blue Crane Lake to get overdeveloped.'

'Darling, as I keep telling you, run for council,' said Trixie. 'That way you can have some constructive input into the Lake's expansion.'

'What's next, Cassie?' asked Steve. 'Planning to buy another restaurant?'

'Not at present. It's a nice enough feeling owning one place,' said Cassie. 'And I'm so glad that you and Melinda are living in the loft. It takes a lot of pressure off knowing you're here.'

Steve and his girlfriend Melinda had moved into the boatshed when Cassie and Bill had moved in with Michael in the house on the hill after they arrived back from Los Angeles. Since then, Cassie had awoken each morning to the sound of the ocean and the warmth of Michael beside her. Bill slept at the foot of the bed and initially Toledo the cat had kept his distance, curled up on a chair on the verandah. Over time a truce between the animals had developed and occasionally the dog and cat could be found together in a sunny spot lying side by side.

Taking her mother to one side, Cassie said quietly, 'Mum, I have to keep pinching myself, I'm so happy.'

'I'm glad you put Ricardo's money towards buying this place. You've made such a success of it. Your father would be so proud. And I'm delighted that you and Michael have such a loving relationship.'

'Are you going to stay for the opening of the Ricardo Aquino Marina, Mum?' Cassie asked.

'Would not miss it for the world. Quite a remarkable man, Ricardo Aquino. I'm really pleased that his son, Ray, is carrying on his work to maintain sustainable commercial fishing in the area,' replied Jenny.

'So am I. It seems to me that all the family is pretty remarkable,' said Cassie with a smile.

After the last guests departed, Melinda collected the last of the glasses, blew out the candles and began to close up the doors and windows of the Blue Boatshed.

Cassie and Michael took the last of the bread, walked to the end of the jetty, sat down, legs dangling, and began to crumble the bread and throw it in the water for the fish. Bill nosed his way between them and peered into the glassy dark water.

Michael put his arm around Cassie's shoulders and she leaned against him. 'Happy? You should be. Winning the best new eatery on the south coast is impressive.'

'Probably just a fluke.'

'Don't sell yourself short,' said Michael. He was quiet for a moment, then he said, 'I have a really important question to ask you.'

'What's that?'

'Why don't we get married? Would you marry me, Cassandra Sullivan? Maybe deep down I'm an old-fashioned Italian. I want you to be my wife. I'd like to start a family and spend the rest of my life loving you.'

Cassie was caught by surprise. Her divorce had gone through months before. She and Michael were so happy and compatible together – she hadn't even considered marriage. But now that he'd asked it seemed right and inevitable. And forever.

'Yes. Yes, yes! I love you, Michael Phillips.'

Michael leaned forward to kiss Cassie, but Bill, alert to something in their voices, sat up between them, pushing his head between theirs.

'Love me, love my dog,' Cassie said, laughing.

'And I do,' said Michael, gently pushing Bill down to pull Cassie close.

The dog dropped his head onto his paws and watched the flash of silvery fish attacking the sodden bread. Somewhere a night bird called and, past the dunes, the surf gently thudded onto the beach. Blue Crane Lake was as it had always been . . . a tranquil haven Cassie now called home.

The Road Back

Di Morrissey

Sometimes taking the road back is the start of a journey forward

Journalist Chris Baxter finds himself at a crossroads when his life takes an unexpected turn. Hoping to pick up the pieces, he and his teenage daughter move back to his childhood home in New South Wales to live with his mother, Susan.

But life in the beautiful riverside town of Neverend turns out to be far from idyllic. Chris soon discovers that opportunities for employment are scarce, and it's not long before he finds himself in increasingly dire financial straits.

Then Susan is invited to the reunion of a group of Australians who travelled to Indonesia forty years ago on a graduate programme. The aim was to foster friendship between the two countries but the mission went badly wrong, ending with the death of one of the group. When Chris hears what happened, he smells a story and begins to investigate.

But soon, strange events start to threaten the family and the peace of the small town is shattered. As the intimidation grows, so does Chris's determination to uncover the truth. With his family in peril, he frantically searches for answers – before it's too late.

It's time to relax with your next good book

THEWINDOWSEAT.CO.UK

If you've enjoyed this book, but don't know what to read next, then we can help. The Window Seat is a site that's all about making it easier to discover your next good book. We feature recommendations, behind-the-scenes tales from the world of publishing, creative writing tips, competitions, and, if we're honest, quite a lot of lists based on our favourite reads.

You'll find stories and features by authors including Lucinda Riley, Karen Swan, Diane Chamberlain, Jane Green, Lucy Diamond and many more. We showcase brand-new talent as well as classic favourites, so you'll never be stuck for what to read again.

We'd love to know what you think of the site, our books, and what you'd like us to feature, so do let us know.

 @panmacmillan.com

 facebook.com/panmacmillan

WWW.THEWINDOWSEAT.CO.UK
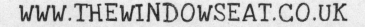

FOR MORE ON

DI MORRISSEY

sign up to receive our

SAGA NEWSLETTER

Packed with **features, competitions, authors'
and readers' letters** and **news of exclusive events,**
it's a must-read for every Di Morrissey fan!

Simply fill in your details below and tick to confirm that you would
like to receive saga-related news and promotions and return to us at
Pan Macmillan, Saga Newsletter, 20 New Wharf Road, London, N1 9RR.

NAME _____

ADDRESS _____

_____ POSTCODE _____

EMAIL _____

☐ *I would like to receive saga-related news and promotions (please tick)*

*You can unsubscribe at any time in writing or through our website where you can also see
our privacy policy which explains how we will store and use your data.*

extracts reading groups
competitions books new events
books discounts extracts extracts discounts reading groups
competitions extracts
books new
events books extracts events
new titles reading groups
interviews
events extracts
discounts books
new books events events interviews new books extracts
events new
discounts extracts discounts
www.panmacmillan.com
extracts events reading groups
competitions books extracts new books